Advance Praise for *Double Vision*

"Great characters and an intriguing premise make for a fascinating look into the realm of higher physics. Welcome to the day after tomorrow. A very solid read."

—T. Davis Bunn, author

"Unique characters and a plot that has more twists and turns than the Cretan Labyrinth makes Randall Ingermanson's *Double Vision* a real page-turner."

—Sylvia Bambola, author of *Refiner's Fire*, *Tears in a Bottle*, *Waters of Marah*

"I can't rave enough about *Double Vision*, Randall Ingermanson's new novel. I don't know when I've read a novel so impossible to put down. Suspenseful action played out with larger-than-life characters makes *Double Vision* truly unforgettable. I predict it will be a book everyone talks about and no one wants to miss experiencing."

—Colleen Coble, author of *Into the Deep*

"*Double Vision* gives readers a delicious insight into the world of cutting-edge technology AND into the personalities such a world attracts. Rich character development, an unpredictable plot, and plausible physics make this novel a thoroughly engaging read."

—Hugh Ross, Ph.D.,
President, Reasons To Believe

"With three unlikely intriguing characters who jump off the page and a maze of tense bio-tech suspense, you'll have blurred eyesight as you try to untangle the twists and turns of Randy Ingermanson's page-turner, *Double Vision*."

—Gail Gaymer Martin, author of *Adam's Promise* and *Loving Care*

Books by
Randall Ingermanson

Transgression

*Oxygen**

*The Fifth Man**

Premonition

Retribution

Double Vision

* with John B. Olson

DOUBLE VISION

RANDALL INGERMANSON

BETHANYHOUSE

MINNEAPOLIS, MINNESOTA

Double Vision
Copyright © 2004
Randall Ingermanson

Cover design by Lookout Design Group, Inc.

Published by Bethany House Publishers
11400 Hampshire Avenue South
Bloomington, Minnesota 55438
www.bethanyhouse.com

Bethany House Publishers is a division of
Baker Publishing Group, Grand Rapids, Michigan.

Printed in the United States of America

Library of Congress Cataloging-in-Publication Data

Ingermanson, Randall Scott.
   Double vision / by Randall Ingermanson.
     p. cm.
   ISBN 0-7642-2733-5 (pbk.)
   1. Scientists—Crimes against—Fiction. 2. Quantum computers—Fiction.
3. Sabotage—Fiction. I. Title.
   PS3609.N46D68   2004
   813'.6—dc22
                                             2004012912

To Eunice and my girls,
Carolyn, Gracie, and Amy.

RANDALL INGERMANSON has won Christy Awards for his novels *Oxygen* (co-authored with John B. Olson) and *Transgression*. He earned his Ph.D. in theoretical physics at the University of California at Berkeley in 1986 and did postdoctoral research in superstring theory at The Ohio State University. He lives in San Diego with his wife and three daughters and has worked at several high-technology companies, including two startups.

He invites you to visit his Web site at

www.rsingermanson.com

ACKNOWLEDGMENTS

I thank:

My many friends at the Coast Vineyard and Kehilat Ariel.

My fellow writers/artists, John Olson, Brandilyn Collins, Kathy Tyers, Mike Carroll, John DeSimone, Rene Gutteridge, Janelle Schneider, Angela Maust, and my many friends in Chi Libris and ACRW. Special thanks to Mindy Clark, Susan Downs, Janelle Schneider, and Meredith Efken for their critiques of the story.

My agent, Chip MacGregor.

My editors at Bethany House past and present, Steve Laube and Karen Schurrer.

My mom and dad.

My three girls, Carolyn, Gracie, and Amy—and our cat, Zephyr.

My Eunice.

PART
ONE

Point of Know Return

"Consequently, the development of a
fully operational quantum computer
would imperil our personal privacy,
destroy electronic commerce and
demolish the concept of national
security. A quantum computer would
jeopardize the stability of the world."

SIMON SINGH
The Code Book, p. 331

CHAPTER
ONE

Keryn

Keryn Wills was in the shower when she figured out how to kill Josh Trenton.

Her best ideas usually came that way, letting the white noise of the pelting spray drown out the outside world. Josh had to die. That was just the way things were. If you were the designated corpse in a Keryn Wills murder mystery, your mission was to die—whether you decided to accept it or not. The only question was how, and now Keryn had the answer.

All that remained was to slam it all down on paper before she lost it, and she had the whole Saturday ahead of her for that. Keryn twisted off the water and shoved back the shower curtain.

Smiley was sitting on the floor watching her, his blue eyes wide and glittery.

"What are you staring at?" Keryn grabbed her towel and began drying off.

Smiley yawned widely.

"You think I'm boring, is that it?" Keryn scowled at him. "Go on, admit it. I won't be hurt."

Smiley meowed and scurried out.

Keryn wrapped the towel around herself and dashed through her bedroom into her office. She grabbed a pen and began scribbling ideas on a white pad. *How Josh Dies. Must look like accident.*

The phone rang.

Keryn looked at the number on the caller ID. *Mom and Dad. Not now. Just let it ring.*

Botulism poisoning.

The phone kept ringing. Keryn reached for her copy of *Deadly Doses: A Writer's Guide to Poisons.*

The answering machine picked up. "Hello, this is Keryn Wills. I'd love to talk to you, but I'm out. Leave a message and I'll call you back as *soon* as I can."

A click, and then her mother's voice. "Hi, honey, it's me. Rusty's still asleep. Long story, but just between you and me and the fence post, he got plastered again last night. Anyway, I just wanted to see how your big date went. Come on and pick up the phone, sweetheart. I know you're there. I want details—big, luscious, foaming details. You *are* home, aren't you? I swear, if you shacked up with that man on the first date, I'm going to call your preacher-creature and tell him you're nothing but a hypocrite, so pick *up* the phone or—"

Keryn snatched up the phone. "Hi, Sunflower."

"Sweetheart, I knew you were there. Now spill. Details. Remind me . . . what's his name again?"

Keryn took a deep, calming breath and exhaled slowly. "Dillon."

"I thought it was Rick or something."

"That's his last name. Richard." Keryn tapped her fingers on the desk, itching to grab *Deadly Doses* and start flipping pages.

"Dillon Richard." Sunflower pronounced it like a disease. "Sounds backwards. What kind of parents would name their boy Dillon Richard?"

Keryn ran her fingers through her wet hair and looked at the picture of her parents on her desk. The picture was five years old, and even back then, Sunflower's hippie ponytail had gone a dull and streaky gray. Rusty's hair wasn't rusty anymore. Mostly it just . . . wasn't. Sunflower and Rusty. Locked in a time warp where the sixties were still groovin' and life was free acid and psychedelic VW buses and Grateful Dead concerts.

"So hit me with some details, girlfriend."

Keryn sighed deeply. *Please, please, please grow up, Mom.* "We went to a play in La Jolla."

"That's it? A play? You didn't eat?"

"We ate. We went to a play. Dillon drove me home."

A moment of horrified silence. "And. . . ?"

"It was a first date."

"And you invited him in? Please tell me you had the sense to invite him in for coffee."

Keryn didn't say anything. It had been late, and Dillon said something about going shooting in the morning. *Shooting.*

"What's wrong with him?" Sunflower's voice had a note of desperate resignation.

"Nothing's wrong with him. He's a perfect gentleman."

"He's *how* old? Thirty-five? Got to be something wrong with him if he's never been married."

"He's shy."

"He asked you out, didn't he?"

Keryn hesitated. "Really shy."

"You're telling me *you* asked him out? Not a good sign, girl friend. Looks bad. Like you know your clock is ticking."

"My clock *is* ticking. It's a biological fact. I'm going to get old and die someday. And so are you. Have you . . . read that book I sent you?"

"I don't read books by preacher-creatures."

"Mom!"

Shocked silence.

Keryn regretted it immediately. That was the only way to shut up Sunflower. Hit her with a chunk of her own maternity. That annoyed her even more than her mortality.

Keryn heard a call-waiting blip on her line. She checked the caller ID. "Hey, um, Sunflower? I've got a call incoming from my boss. Can I call you back later?"

Sunflower slammed the phone down.

Keryn clicked the button on her phone to pick up the incoming call. "Hello, Grant. What's up?"

"Bad news." Grant O'Connell's gravelly voice sounded tired. "I know it's Saturday, but can you come in to work for a couple hours? We need to strategize."

Keryn looked at her scribblings on the paper and tried to remember exactly how Josh was going to die. "Um . . . sure." *I guess.* It had to be bad if Grant wasn't out golfing on a Saturday. "Can I ask what it's about?"

"Not on the phone," Grant said.

Keryn felt her pulse quicken. *Not on the phone?* This was starting to sound like one of her mysteries. Or maybe a John le Carré. "I'm not dressed yet. What time do you need me?"

"Ten-thirty," Grant said. "I've already called the others. Dillon can't get in any earlier."

Keryn wondered why she and Dillon would be invited to the same meeting. He was a Senior Engineer and she was Chief Financial Officer, and that didn't give them a whole lot of common turf. "I'll be there."

"Don't panic," Grant said. "Everything's going to be all right." He hung up.

Keryn stared at the phone in her hand. It hadn't occurred to her to panic until Grant told her not to. She put the phone down and headed back to her bedroom to get dressed.

She could already see that she wasn't going to kill Josh Trenton today.

D i l l o n

Dillon drove carefully into his favorite parking spot. The lot was empty. He stepped out and locked the car, setting the alarm. He walked once around the car and inspected each tire. A knot of anxiety clutched at his stomach. It was highly unusual for Grant to call a meeting on a Saturday. Highly unusual.

Dillon strode across the lot to the bridge. A thin trickle of water ran through the gully. Again, highly unusual. In June the gully should be dry. But this was no ordinary June. It had rained twice already, and it might rain again before the month was over.

"Hey, Dillon!" Clifton Potter leaned out of his SUV and waved at Dillon. "Why'd you park over in the main lot? There's plenty of spots right here by the building."

Dillon did not know how to explain, so he shook his head and shrugged. He had parked in his favorite spot because . . . it was his favorite spot. But Clifton was a Normal, and he could not be expected to understand that.

Clifton shoved his door open and hopped out. He slammed the door and turned to Dillon. "Do you know what's going down?"

"You forgot to lock your door." Dillon pointed at Clifton's SUV.

Clifton shook his head. "Chill it, Dillon! There's nobody here on a Saturday to mess with my car." His long blond ponytail swished back and forth.

Dillon found this unnerving. He did not know why Clifton wore his hair so long. Nor did he know why Clifton used so much slang. Slang made a person hard to understand. After thinking for a moment, Dillon remembered that *chill* had a secondary meaning— something about relaxing. It made no sense to Dillon, but it made sense to Normals, and therefore he made an effort to learn such things. But he would rather that people said what they meant in the first place.

Dillon put a hand on Clifton's SUV. "Last year, 23,378 cars were stolen in San Diego County. The most popular makes among thieves are Toyotas and Hondas. Eighty percent of all cars stolen were left unlocked. You should lock your car."

Clifton studied him and the grin left his face. "Twenty-three thousand?"

"No, 23,378," Dillon said. "That works out to approximately 8.3 stolen cars per thousand residents."

"Dude!" Clifton pulled out his keys and pressed a button. The car beeped and the door locks clicked with a satisfying chorus of *thunks*.

Dillon smiled. You could never be too careful about such things.

"So how was your hot date with our famous author last night?" Clifton said.

Dillon paused for a moment, then remembered that *hot* had a secondary meaning that had nothing to do with temperature. "It went very well. We had dinner and saw *The Tragedy of Hamlet, Prince of Denmark*."

"Spiff!" Clifton said. " 'To be, or not to be,' huh?"

Dillon often felt off-balance when speaking with Clifton.

Clifton used many words that other Normals did not. It made Dillon feel uneasy. Very uneasy. Dillon saw that he could easily change the subject to quantum mechanics, one of his favorite topics. "After the play, we talked about quantum mechanics and multiple universes."

Clifton's face took on an expression Dillon could not parse. "Dude! What's all that have to do with *Hamlet?*"

" 'To be, or not to be,' " Dillon said. "The question Hamlet asks implies that he has a choice, correct? But all choices must be quantum mechanical in nature."

"Um, Dillon, have you been smoking something?"

"Cigarettes are very unhealthful." Dillon could not understand why Clifton kept changing the subject. "I explained to Keryn that all of physics is deterministic, with one exception. When you make a quantum measurement, the result is not determined. The only rational conclusion is that, if we truly have free will, it must be because our thought processes are quantum mechanical. Making a choice is equivalent to performing a measurement on our own brains. A decision defines who and what we are."

"Dude, I bet Keryn thought that was real interesting."

Dillon nodded. Keryn had found it highly interesting. "She had never heard that making a quantum measurement causes the universe to split into several parallel universes. In each of those universes, the result measured is different. Hamlet poses himself a two-state question: 'To be, or not to be.' When he makes his choice, his future splits in two. In one universe, Hamlet chooses to live. In a second universe, he chooses to die."

Clifton was staring at Dillon with his mouth open.

Dillon felt calm again. The multiverse interpretation of quantum mechanics was logical. It was still not as popular among physicists as the old-fashioned Copenhagen interpretation, but the Copenhagen interpretation was not logical. Soon everyone would believe in the multiverse interpretation.

Clifton's cell phone rang. He yanked it out of his pocket and pressed a button. "Yo, hello, this is Clif."

Dillon turned to look at the gully. A mother duck and three ducklings paddled down the thin rivulet.

"Yeah, sure, Kendall's a buddy of mine," Clifton said. "You're the dude who hooked him up with HP? Spiff, man! He had this bogus boss who thought he was God's gift to lasers but didn't know his head from a hole in the wave function. Know what I mean?"

Dillon was beginning to feel uncomfortable again. Clifton's way of speaking grated on him.

"Hold on a sec." Clifton's voice had taken on a peculiar tone.

Dillon turned and saw Clifton walking away from him toward the corner of the building. Clifton looked back at Dillon. Then his head jerked around as if he were embarrassed by something.

Dillon put his hands behind his back and thought about the good time talking with Keryn last night. Keryn Wills was a writer. An intelligent woman. He had enjoyed very much talking with her. She was not a physicist or an engineer, but she had been very interested in how quantum mechanics tied in with *The Tragedy of Hamlet, Prince of Denmark*. She had a quiet way of talking that made Dillon feel comfortable. Also, she dressed neatly. She was a very nice person, and he hoped they could have more interesting conversations.

A horn honked. Grant O'Connell's Lexus appeared at the far end of the building, gleaming in the sunlight. A Lexus was not stolen as frequently as a Toyota, but that was because more people drove a Toyota than a Lexus. Dillon made a mental note to remind Grant to lock his car.

The Lexus pulled up next to Dillon. Grant thumped out, his big ruddy face smiling. He had a bald head with a rim of gray hair around the back of his head. His huge white Santa Claus eyebrows made Dillon a little uneasy, but Grant was a good man and Dillon trusted him. The passenger door opened and a petite young woman sprang out. She had thick frizzy hair of a golden blond color, and she wore a garish pink-and-blue tie-dyed shirt that did not cover her navel. Her faded bell-bottom jeans had a hole in one knee and also did not reach to her navel. Dillon thought that she looked not quite fully dressed, and he felt embarrassed.

Grant came around the car and pounded Dillon on the shoulder. "Dillon, I'd like you to meet our off-site employee, Rachel Meyers. Rachel, this is Dillon Richard. He's the one I was telling you about—the hotshot in C++ and hardware/software interfaces. Dillon, Rachel just got her Ph.D. from Caltech and eats that multiverse thing for lunch. Believe me, you two are gonna have a *lot* to talk about."

Dillon looked at Rachel with interest. "You are a physicist?"

"Biophysicist." She reached out a hand. "Glad to meet you, Dillon. Uncle Grant's told me how smart you are, and I'm *really* looking forward to working with you."

Dillon shook her hand and looked at Grant. "Rachel is your niece?"

Grant bellowed with laughter. "Virtual niece. She's the daughter of the kid brother of my roommate at MIT. I changed Rachel's diapers when she was a baby and watched her grow up, and she's every bit as smart as her daddy, who happens to teach particle physics at Rutgers. Anyway, you're gonna love her, Dillon."

Another horn honked behind them. Dillon looked over Grant's shoulder and saw Keryn's old Honda jouncing over a speed bump. She pulled in next to the Lexus and came scurrying out. "Am I late?"

"Looks like we're all here," Grant said. "Let's get this show on the road. Sorry to make you all come in on a Saturday, especially a great day like today, but let's get it done."

Keryn was looking at Rachel with an odd expression on her face.

"You should lock it," Dillon said.

"What?" Keryn stared at Dillon blankly.

"You should lock your car," Dillon said. "Hondas are one of the two most commonly stolen cars in San Diego County, and Civics are among the most popular models."

CHAPTER TWO

Keryn

Keryn did not like the way the blonde was looking at Dillon. She couldn't be much over twenty-two. Dressed like an airhead. Probably fresh out of college. Grant's daughter? No, he didn't have any kids. Probably a new receptionist or something. But that was crazy. There wasn't money to hire a new receptionist. Whatever. Keryn didn't like the way the airhead's flirty green eyes were drinking in Dillon.

Grant shot Keryn a huge smile. "Keryn, I'd like you to meet our off-site employee, Rachel Meyers. Rachel, this is Keryn Wills. She joined the team part-time back in March to help with the financials. She's our CFO and a really good one. Remember I told you about her? She's our author—written four or five books."

"Three," Keryn corrected him. "Number four is due in August." *And I'm way behind schedule.*

Rachel extended her hand. "Hi, Keryn. I'd love to read one of your books sometime."

Keryn shook her hand. "Um . . . right." She noticed with dissatisfaction that Rachel was not wearing a bra. It was some consolation that she clearly didn't need one. Keryn shifted slightly to her right and smiled at Dillon. "Good morning, Dillon." He was wearing a cream-colored cotton shirt and dark gray wool pants and a muted blue gray tie. Shiny leather shoes. Every other engineer in the company wore blue jeans and wrinkled T-shirts, but Dillon was . . . different. Not weird different. *Different* different.

Grant was striding away toward the corner of the building. "Hey, Clifton? Ready to go inside? We've got a lot to talk about!"

Keryn edged a little closer to Dillon and smiled at Rachel. "So, um, Rachel, what do you do for CypherQuanta? Marketing?"

Rachel gave her a little-girl smile. "Research."

Keryn nodded. *Market research.* Grant was probably paying her chicken feed to call up banks and brokerages to find out what their data encryption needs were. Which was fine, except for one teensy little detail—CypherQuanta didn't *have* chicken feed. Keryn had discussed this nicely with Grant twice in the last month, and she had understood that he agreed. Absolutely no more employees until the next round of funding came through. Cash flow right now was tighter than a Tom Clancy story line, and there was not one extra dime. And now there was some new crisis, which was the reason she had come in to work today instead of killing off Josh Trenton.

Grant came steaming back with Clifton in tow. "Okay, now we're all really here. Rachel, meet Clifton Potter, our Chief Technology Officer. Clifton founded the company with me six years ago, and it's thanks to him we haven't folded yet. Clifton, this is Rachel Meyers, girl genius."

Clifton's eyes widened and he looked Rachel up and down appreciatively. "*Very* glad to meet you, Rachel. What kind of genius are you, exactly?"

"She's a biophysicist from Caltech," Dillon said. "You will like her, Clifton. She knows all about the multiverse."

Keryn blinked twice, feeling very stupid. *A biophysicist? A girl genius?* A very large lump settled in her throat.

"Let's get inside, people." Grant looked around nervously. He leaned close to Clifton. "Rachel's made a breakthrough, Cliffie baby. A grade-A, gold-plated breakthrough that is gonna save our cookies if it pans out."

"Spiff!" Clifton said.

Dillon was beaming at Rachel.

Keryn suddenly felt very ill.

D i l l o n

Dillon sat down at the circular glass table in Grant's office. He laid out a clean white pad of paper and a black Uni-ball pen. Keryn sat on Dillon's left. Grant and Rachel sat across from him. Clifton took a seat on his right. The configuration felt asymmetric to Dillon. Better to have Rachel on his right and Clifton across from him. Then it would be—

"Let's get started." Grant's voice sounded like a wheelbarrow crunching over gravel.

Dillon wondered if Grant had been getting enough sleep.

Grant began clicking a ball-point pen in his hand. *Click-click. Click-click.* "Lost Angels met yesterday, and I gave them a presentation."

Rachel's eyebrows went up. "Lost Angels?"

"Our angel investors," Keryn said. "A Los Angeles high-tech investment club. They funded us for another year last December. Right now they own forty-two percent of CypherQuanta."

"Correction," Grant said. "They funded us in two tranches, contingent on meeting sales milestones."

"What's a tranche?" Rachel said.

"A pile of money." Grant clicked on his pen. "In our case, not a very big pile."

Dillon did not like the Lost Angels group. They were abrasive and rude, and they had taken unfair advantage in the negotiations last December. For a week, Dillon had been afraid Grant might have a heart attack.

"We're ahead of our sales mark," Keryn said. "We needed to place ten units in Q1 and Q2, and we placed thirteen."

Grant's face twisted as if he had just drunk a glassful of vinegar. "Bank of America is returning four units."

A hiss ran around the table.

Dillon felt as if he had been slapped. He had worked overtime to customize the software on those machines. Speed had been a major issue on that contract, and he had found a clever algorithm to get an extra factor of 2.1 in throughput.

Grant *click-click*ed the pen again. "According to them, the units, quote—do not meet our requirements—unquote."

"And that means . . ." Keryn sounded like she was being strangled.

Grant slammed his open palm on the table. "Lost Angels is cutting their losses. They're canceling the second tranche and putting the word out that CypherQuanta is a lost cause."

Clifton swore loudly.

Dillon felt his stomach tighten. It was a terrible blow to have Lost Angels pull out now. Even so, that did not justify taking the Lord's name in vain, especially when there were ladies present. Clifton Potter was a nice enough person, but he ought not to curse in front of ladies.

Keryn was clenching her pen so tightly Dillon could see the whites of her knuckles. "Um, Grant, how are we going to make payroll at the end of the month?"

"That's . . ." Grant cleared his throat and looked around the table. "That's why I called this meeting. We're not getting that second tranche, and we're also not going to get paid on the invoice from B of A. Plus, we're out the cost of parts for those four units."

Clifton leaned back in his chair. "Man, that is so bogus! We met the acceptance criteria on that contract!"

"There was a clause that it had to meet spec for ninety days," Grant said. "They claim its performance has degraded."

"Bunch of wallies," Clifton said. "Let's send Dillon over there. He'll get it working."

Keryn drummed her fingers on the table. "Right, let's send Dillon."

Grant shook his head. "It won't do any good. I've heard something, very back-channel, but I think it's accurate. Somebody on the Lost Angels board has it in for us and is chummy with someone at Bank of America. We're doornails."

Dillon did not see how they could possibly be doornails. It must be a metaphor. He did not like metaphors, because they asserted things that were not true. There was often an interesting explanation for a metaphor, but today he did not have time to ask for an explanation. He must focus on solving this problem. This disaster could bankrupt Grant, and that was not acceptable. Grant had spent a fortune of his own money to start the company. Had it not been for the recession, they would have gone public by now and Grant would have earned back his investment. Dillon could find a job somewhere else, but Grant was almost ready to retire, and his only marketable skill was that he knew how to take risks and make money. Now he had taken an enormous risk and might lose all his money.

Keryn sucked in her breath. "Listen, I know this is going to sound harsh, but . . . I think we need to take steps to maintain the financial integrity of the company. Right away."

"Meaning layoffs," Clifton said in a glum tone.

"No," Grant said. "I've earned the team's loyalty, and I'm gonna be loyal to them. No layoffs."

Keryn sighed deeply. "Grant, I really think we have to worry about keeping our nose above water."

Dillon remembered that Keryn used this metaphor when she meant that they must stay financially solvent. A nose had nothing to do with money, but it was Keryn's way of talking.

Grant looked steadily around the table, and there was an odd gleam in his eyes. He smiled. "There may be a way out. I'm pretty sure there's a way out. Keryn, how long could we stay afloat if we didn't write paychecks?"

Keryn's eyes went very wide.

It struck Dillon that her eyes were almost the color of champagne.

Keryn bit her lip. "Probably through the end of August. It depends on if we can sweet-talk the landlord. Remember, our energy bills go up during the summer. But if we miss payroll, we're dead. CypherQuanta *is* our employees. That's your company motto, Grant. The minute you miss payroll, our engineers will be e-mailing resumés. The economy's not on life support anymore. In three weeks, they'll all be gone."

Grant *click-click*ed his pen. "How about if we pay everybody in stock for one month? With a bonus—we'll offer them double their salary-equivalent in stock."

Clifton shook his head. "That ain't gonna fly. If we miss payroll, our stock isn't worth toilet paper."

Dillon nodded slowly. "Grant, it would not be honest to pay them in stock if the stock has no value. If you intend to miss payroll, you are obligated to notify the employees right away."

Grant's eyes narrowed as he looked first at Keryn, then Dillon, then Clifton. "Point taken, people, but before you three bears run off into the woods, Goldilocks here has a little story to tell you." He pointed a stubby finger at Rachel. "Tell 'em, girl genius."

Rachel leaned forward in her chair and her pale green eyes lit up. She pulled Dillon's tablet across the table and held out her hand for his pen. "May I?"

Dillon gave her the pen. He noticed that she had small, clever hands. The nails were polished a light green that matched her eyes, with golden sprinkles the exact color of her hair.

Rachel drew a triangle on the paper and labeled the three corners. *Fast. Cheap. Good.* She looked straight at Dillon. "This is the classic engineering triangle. Even in the best case, you can only choose two of these three. NASA is wrong when they say faster-better-cheaper. You can never have all three, right?"

All of them nodded.

Rachel tapped her pen on the triangle. "Where does Cypher-Quanta stand on this triangle?"

"We're good," Clifton said. "Our quantum encryption is the spiffest thing out there. Nobody does it better, nowhere, nohow. Even God can't do better."

Dillon did not like the way Clifton said this. It was a theorem of quantum mechanics that nobody could do better, but even so, Dillon did not like to place bets on what God could not do.

"And what else are we?" Rachel said.

Nobody said anything.

"We're not faster, that's for sure," Clifton said. "No offense, Dillon. You did the best you could, but we're still only getting kilobits per second. Conventional RSA encryption gets gigabits."

"But our encryption is better," Dillon said.

"Better doesn't always win," Rachel said. "If it did, everyone would have a Mac—and Bill Gates would be shining shoes."

"Which brings us to our other problem," Grant said. "We aren't cheaper either. RSA encryption is practically free. Private users get it for free. Businesses have to license it from RSA, but it's way cheaper than we are."

"But our encryption is *better*," Dillon said. "Quantum encryption is unbreakable. You can prove a theorem—"

"Theorem, shmeorem," Rachel said. "Our competition uses RSA encryption. People *perceive* it to be just as good as ours. *And* it's faster. *And* it's cheaper."

"You're telling us our business model is majorly biff." Clifton leaned back in his chair and crossed his arms.

Biff was one of Clifton's special words. Dillon knew it meant *bad*, but he had never understood why Clifton could not simply say things were very bad.

"It's reality," Rachel said. "Right, Uncle Grant?"

Grant grunted agreement. Then he exploded in laughter. "All right, stop playing with them, Rachel. Give 'em the good news."

Rachel put the pen down in front of Dillon. "In principle, RSA encryption can be broken."

Dillon stared at her, wondering what her point was. "In principle, yes. Everybody knows that *if* you can factor large numbers, you can break RSA encryption."

"Not everybody," Keryn said. "I didn't know that. Can you give me the *Dummies* explanation of what factoring large numbers has to do with encryption?"

Dillon took the pen and wrote down the number fifteen on his tablet. "Any schoolchild can factor small numbers. Fifteen is *what* times *what*?"

Keryn shrugged. "That's easy. Fifteen is three times five."

Dillon nodded. "Correct. But if I give you a ten-digit number, you will find it very much harder to factor."

"Can't a computer do that?" Keryn said.

"For ten digits, yes," Dillon said. "But as you add digits, it gets exponentially harder. For a hundred digits, it takes a long time. And no computer in the world has ever factored an arbitrary two-hundred-digit number."

Keryn still looked puzzled. "Fine, but what does this have to do with us?"

"Everything." Dillon wondered how to explain to her about the Euler totient function. "The RSA encryption scheme depends for its security on the fact that it is easy to multiply two large numbers together, but it is extremely hard to factor the resulting product without knowing one of the original two numbers."

Rachel blew him a kiss. "You get a gold star, Dillon. It boils down to this. If you could factor large numbers, then conventional RSA encryption would be broken. It would still be cheap and fast. But it would be worthless. Which would mean that anyone who needs encryption wouldn't have a choice. They'd have to buy our machines, because we'd be the only game in town. *If* we could factor large numbers, every bank, every brokerage, every government—*anyone* who needs to protect their data in transit—would have to buy our quantum encryption system."

Clifton shook his head. "That's one very bogus *if*. You can't factor large numbers. They use two-thousand-bit keys for RSA encryption. Factoring a number that mondo would take like billions of years."

"Billions of years on a conventional supercomputer." Rachel leaned forward. "Think different. Think quantum."

Dillon felt his heart thump. "There *is* a quantum algorithm to factor large numbers. Shor's algorithm. But . . . you would need a quantum computer with thousands of qubits."

"Whoa, time out," Keryn said. "I'm lost. Thousands of what-bits?"

"A quantum bit," Dillon said. "Q-u-b-i-t, pronounced *cubit*."

Keryn shook her head. "And what are these qubit things used for?"

"It's all very simple," Rachel said. "Our competitors use RSA encryption, which could be broken—if only you could factor very large numbers. In 1994 Peter Shor at AT&T showed that you *can* factor large numbers—if you have a quantum computer with thousands of qubits. In 2001 Isaac Chuang's team at IBM demonstrated that Shor's algorithm worked on a quantum computer with seven qubits. In fact, he used it to factor the number fifteen. It was big in the news. So the only remaining glitch is to construct a quantum computer with a few thousand qubits."

Glitch? Dillon did not see how this could be considered a small matter. "That is like saying you can run a mile in four seconds. All you have to do is run nine hundred miles per hour."

Rachel just smiled at him.

Dillon felt something funny wiggle in his stomach. Rachel had a very nice smile.

Clifton gave a nervous laugh. "Dillon's right. We had a tough time commercializing quantum encryption, and that only needs *one* qubit. Seven qubits is the record, but IBM had fits making that work sorta-maybe-kinda in a *research* lab. It'll be like thirty years before anybody gets a thousand qubits to play together."

Dillon shook his head. "It will not happen in our lifetime."

Keryn's eyes glittered with a look that Dillon could not decipher.

"Tell 'em, Rachel," Grant said.

Rachel reached inside the fanny pack at her waist and pulled out a sealed tube filled with a greenish liquid. "Here are the qubits."

Dillon stared at it.

"That?" Keryn's voice cracked. "That's a computer?"

Rachel shook her head. "Not the whole computer. Just the hard part. The qubits."

"How can a tube of . . . green goop be a computer?" Keryn said. "That doesn't make any sense."

Rachel's face flushed. "The qubits are the nuclei of certain ions trapped in nanoscale ion traps. You manipulate the qubits by radio signals. It's a standard NMR-based quantum computer, not too different from the one IBM built."

Keryn was looking very lost. "NMR?"

"Nuclear magnetic resonance," Dillon said. "Like in MRI machines."

Keryn did not look at all convinced. "A test tube? That's not a computer."

Rachel gave her an intense look that Dillon could not parse. "Listen, Keryn, you just write the checks, okay?"

Grant put a hand on Rachel's arm. "Keryn's not questioning your work, Rachel. It just doesn't look like a regular computer." He turned to Keryn. "You'll have to take this on faith. I realize this is pretty weird looking, but it really is well-established technology."

Dillon raised his eyebrows. "Seven qubits is established technology. A hundred qubits would be extraordinary technology."

"I've got ten thousand qubits," Rachel said.

A rush of adrenaline shot through Dillon's chest. Suddenly, he could not breathe. "Ten . . . *thousand* qubits?"

"Plus or minus a few hundred." Rachel gave him a dazzling smile. "Impressed?"

Dillon could hardly swallow. Ten thousand qubits was impossible. *Impossible.*

"It's only missing one thing," Rachel said.

"What's that?" Clifton's hands were trembling on top of the table.

Grant cleared his throat. "That is the core of an NMR quantum computer. Rachel finished it quicker than we expected, but now it needs NMR hardware to drive it, and software to drive the hardware. Dillon, you're the best hardware/software guy we've got. We need you."

Dillon's tongue felt parched. "New hardware? New software? That could take months of development time. Design reviews. Implementation. Testing."

"We don't have months," Keryn said. "In less than three weeks, we're going to miss payroll."

Grant put his hand on top of Dillon's on the table. "Can you do it?"

Dillon's heart was thumping very hard in his chest. He had a chance to work on something extraordinary. It would save the company. It would keep his friends employed. And it would save Grant's investment. If he could make the device work.

"I . . . I need more information," Dillon stammered. He wanted desperately to think about something calming. The multiverse. Hamlet. Keryn's soft and quiet voice.

"As of today, I want to reassign you to work with Rachel," Grant said. "She's got a bio-lab set up off-site. I want you two working around the clock on this thing. Your first task is to tell me how long it's going to take. Do you want the assignment or don't you? Because if you don't, we're very dead. Nobody else can write code as fast and clean as you can."

Dillon swallowed hard.

"Dude, you the man," Clifton said.

Keryn sat very still.

Rachel gave him an encouraging smile.

Dillon's heart quivered in a way he had never felt before. Rachel was very intelligent. He did not see how he could do this job in only three weeks, but . . . possibly with Rachel's help? And they would have many interesting conversations also.

"Will you do it?" Grant asked. "I'm begging you, Dillon."

Grant was like a father to Dillon. More than a father. The schedule would be almost impossible, but . . . Dillon could not say no to Grant.

Dillon nodded. "I will try."

CHAPTER
THREE

Rachel

Fifteen minutes later, as Grant parked outside the bio-lab, Rachel felt a rush of butterflies. She desperately wanted to make a good impression on the others, her new teammates. She'd been working in isolation for six months now, and it was driving her nuts. But Grant had said he couldn't afford to break security by introducing her to the other employees. Until now. If she went splat, it was going to be horrible. Worse than horrible.

All five of them climbed out of Grant's Lexus.

"Whoa, spiff!" Clifton strode over to Rachel's bright red Miata convertible. The top was down and Clifton ran his hands over the leather interior.

"Like it?" Rachel said. "I got it when I came to San Diego."

"It's very nice," Keryn said in that cool and quiet voice of hers.

Rachel liked watching people, trying to dice out their relationships. She had already figured out that Keryn and Dillon were an item, or an almost-item, or . . . something. They were alike in a lot of ways.

And yet different. Dillon had that delicious Pierce Brosnan look, very mysterious and self-contained. Whereas Keryn was so . . .

dull. Mouse-brown hair, cut to her shoulders and very eighties. Tall, thirtyish, not quite slim, but nicely proportioned. A pleasant smile. Not too quick on the uptake. What *exactly* did Dillon see in her? Or . . . did he? There was clearly some sort of connection between the two of them, but they weren't married and they weren't living together, and Uncle Grant hadn't said anything about them being a pair. Of course, Uncle Grant missed a lot of that kind of thing, but still.

"Come on, people, we can admire the car later," Grant said. "Dillon, I want you to see the bio-lab."

Dillon was staring at the car, frowning.

"Hey, Dillon, check this out!" Clifton said. He was standing behind the car, pointing at the license plate holder.

Dillon didn't move.

Keryn went around to look. Her eyes widened and she covered her mouth with her hand.

Rachel smiled. The plate holder said, *Sometimes . . . I go topless*.

Dillon leaned inside the car and inspected the flashing red alarm light. "This kind of alarm is simple to defeat."

"People, come on!" Grant stood at the top of the stairs, waiting.

"Relax, I've got LoJack," Rachel said. She leaned in next to Dillon, brushing against his sleeve with her bare arm. "Not to mention, that alarm's a dummy. The real one detects tampering and calls me on my cell phone."

"Miatas have a very low theft rate," Dillon said. "Now I understand why. " Dillon said.

Rachel leaned in farther and lost her balance. "Oh!" She grabbed Dillon's arm and caught herself. "I'm sorry."

He helped her stand up. "By the way, your shirt is too short. You should buy the next larger size."

This was so stunningly inappropriate that Rachel stared up at him with her mouth hanging right open. She wanted to laugh, but she didn't dare. There was something not quite . . . right about Dillon.

"People, I hate to interrupt the car festival, but we've got work to do." Grant came down the stairs, wincing each time he put weight on his trick left knee.

"We're coming," Rachel said.

"Right behind ya, Grant," Clifton said. "Great car, Rachel."

Grant turned and hauled himself back up the stairs to the door. He punched in the five-digit security code. "Dillon, I'll give you the code so you can come in anytime. Sorry, Keryn and Clifton, but you don't need to know it, and we're keeping tight security on this place." He turned the knob and pushed the door open dramatically. "Behold . . . the bio-lab! Rachel, go ahead and give us all a tour."

Rachel stepped in past him. The suite was actually two moderately large rooms. In the outer office, she had a desk overflowing with photocopied papers and an empty filing cabinet that was supposed to hold all the papers. A stack of pizza boxes were mounded in the trash can. "Sorry about the mess. I don't eat in the lab because I culture live cells in there. They're not infectious, but still. There's a bathroom over there." She pointed to the corner. "It's kind of a mess in there too. Sorry. I'm not big on cleaning."

Rachel pointed to a pair of metal double doors. "In through here is the actual bio-lab. We maintain it at a slight negative pressure, relative to this outer room. Not enough so you'll notice, but enough to keep stuff from blowing out. Not that anything could actually blow out. I do all the biology work under a hood, and it's vented."

"Biology?" Dillon said. "What does biology have to do with a quantum computer?" Rachel pushed open one of the doors. "Come on in and I'll explain."

The others trooped in. Rachel led the way to a wet bench. "Okay, here's the deal. The problem people have in making quantum computers is that the qubits are small." She grinned at them all. "I hope that's not a surprise."

Grant gave her a big smile. Keryn was gawking around the room. Clifton was sneaking a peek at Keryn's backside. Dillon was looking at the MagTec NMR machine in the corner.

Rachel joined him. "I guess you're familiar with conventional NMR quantum computers, right?"

Dillon nodded. "You control an ensemble of qubits by radio pulses. It is old technology."

"And the problem with that is. . . ?" She touched his arm.

"The problem is that each qubit requires its own resonant frequency," Dillon said. "So if you want thousands of qubits, you will need thousands of resonant frequencies. But since every ion has a characteristic resonant frequency in a given magnetic field, this means that you require thousands of species of ion, and that is impossible."

"Right," Rachel said. "It's a hard problem. I've solved it."

He gave her a probing look.

Rachel felt a shiver of . . . something. She could get lost in those deep, chocolate brown eyes.

"You have solved it?"

"Um . . . right. I decided that if you can't bring Mohammed to the mountain, then you should bring the mountain to Mohammed."

For an instant, Dillon's eyes went blank. Completely and totally blank. Rachel blinked, astonished. What had caused that response?

Grant stepped in. "Say, Rachel, maybe I better explain something to you before you get lost in metaphor-land. Dillon has kind of a special mind. I told you that, right? He thinks different than anybody else."

Rachel vaguely remembered. She'd been too excited on the way to the meeting this morning to pay much attention. "Uh-huh." She had a sudden urge to turn around and run.

A pained expression crossed Dillon's face. "Grant, Asperger's syndrome is not a disease, and you will please not treat me like a cripple."

Rachel felt her mouth drop open. "Um, what's this all about?"

Dillon's face tightened. "I have a form of autism known as Asperger's syndrome. It is named after Dr. Hans Asperger, an Austrian physician who wrote a paper in 1944 describing—"

"Autism?" Rachel said. "You mean like Dustin Hoffman in *Rain Man*?"

"High-functioning autism," Dillon said. "I do not babble, nor do I slobber, nor do I require institutionalization. I am a contributing member of society with a special kind of brain."

"That is so cool!" Rachel said. "Can you count cards like in *Rain Man*?" She put her hand on his arm. "Dillon, now I get it! Uncle Grant told me you were one in a million, but I thought he was exaggerating."

Dillon looked very pleased. "Every autistic is different. I cannot count cards. Very few can. But I have unusual abilities to concentrate. Like Einstein. Like Newton. Both of whom are thought to have had Asperger's."

Grant put an arm over Dillon's shoulder. "Dillon comes up with some amazing out-of-the-box design solutions. But here's the thing. He tends to take things very literally. When you say 'out-of-the-box,' he thinks you're talking about an actual box."

Rachel giggled. She felt terrible for giggling, but . . . it was *funny*.

"You saw his face go blank when you trotted out that thing about Mohammed and the mountain?" Grant said.

Rachel nodded. "You're telling me . . . he thought I was talking about a real mountain and a real Mohammed?"

Dillon's face colored slightly. "My brain is just wired differently. You may think me weird, but in my reference frame, I am being logical and the rest of the world is not."

"I don't think you're weird," Rachel said.

Dillon's face relaxed. "Really?"

"Dillon, you're a stud."

His eyes flew wide.

Instantly, Rachel caught her mistake. "That's slang, sorry. It means you're . . . brilliant. Um, it means you're really, really smart."

Dillon smiled. "Thank you. Now please explain to me about how you solved the qubit problem."

"Um . . . right." Rachel took a deep cleansing breath and tried to get her mind back on track. "I asked myself why we should worry about making thousands of qubits, all different. Why not make them all the same but change their environment instead?"

"Environment?" Dillon looked puzzled.

"You know," Rachel said. "Embed each pair of qubits in a little cage with slightly different magnetostatic properties. Just a small change, but enough to change the value of the applied local magnetic field. In MRI, you vary the applied magnetic field spatially and therefore you get out spatial information from the signal. Here, you vary the magnetic field inside each type of cage, and that lets you drive the qubits in each cage independently."

"Oh." Dillon's face lit up. "I see it. It requires a different external frequency to drive each qubit, even though all the qubits are identical."

"Slow down," Clifton said. "I'm not getting this."

Dillon stepped to the whiteboard and wrote down the equation for the resonant frequency in an applied constant magnetic field. Then he added subscripts to each side. Clifton stared at the equation for a few seconds. "Oh yeah. Right. Hey, that's clever."

"How do you change the magnetostatic properties for each cage?" Dillon asked. "That is a difficult nanoconstruction problem."

"Biological cells do nanoconstruction all the time," Rachel said. "It's kind of a long story but the bottom line . . . I mean, the summary . . . is that I concocted a string of DNA that encodes the pattern for a particular class of proteins that fold themselves into perfect little ferromagnetic cages. I got the idea from rubredoxin, which occurs naturally. My class has millions of degrees of freedom in one particular string of nucleotides, so in principle I could make millions of qubits. I inserted the DNA as an artificial gene into a cell line and forced the cells to express ten thousand different proteins, each in large quantities."

Dillon's face was shining now. "Beautiful. Very, very beautiful."

Rachel felt her pulse speed up. Coming from Dillon Richard, that was quite a compliment.

"Okay, I'm thinking we need to leave you two to work," Grant said. "Dillon, you like what you see?"

Dillon's eyes were looking right at Rachel—or right through her—she couldn't tell which. "Yes."

"Great, then. I want you two to report directly to Clifton. Give him a daily update. If you need anything, ask him." Grant turned to Keryn. "And if they need to spend any money, give it to them. No questions asked."

Keryn's eyes were boring like lasers into Dillon's skull. "Um . . . right, Grant." Her face colored, and she turned toward the door. "Right, let's let Rachel and Clifton and Dillon get to work, and I've got a couple of questions for you outside."

Grant went to the door and opened it. "We need to give Clifton a ride back, remember? We all came in my car. Come on, let's go, Clifton. Rachel, when you lock up for the night, take Dillon back to his car at CypherQuanta, okay?"

"Sure thing, Uncle Grant."

Grant put a hand on Keryn's elbow. "Let's be on our way so the geniuses can work."

"Of course." Keryn had a funny look on her face as she went out the door. Clifton followed her out, his long blond ponytail swishing behind him.

Grant threw a last look inside. "Pedal to the metal, Rachel."

"Vroom, vroom," she said.

Dillon sat down next to the NMR machine. "Tell me what I need to do. I know very little about NMR quantum computers."

"All we need to do is drive my bio-computer with this NMR machine," Rachel said. "This is an off-the-shelf component made by MagTec for biological applications. I've tested it on the bio-computer in manual mode, and I verified that my qubits respond to resonant frequencies spaced out roughly every hundred hertz, over a range of a megahertz. The signal is pretty weak, but it's detectable. That gives us ten thousand qubits. The first thing we need to do is write a calibration program to find the exact resonant frequencies. Then we have to implement Shor's algorithm."

"Actually, I believe the first thing I need is the manuals for this machine." Dillon said this in the same tone of voice that a small boy would use to ask for his dessert first.

Rachel hated manuals and would rather eat crushed glass than read one of the horrid things. She found three thick volumes in the box, tore off the shrink-wrapping, and handed them to Dillon.

Dillon's eyes lit up. "Thank you." He opened the top manual and began reading the preface.

Rachel slumped into a chair. *Great. What am I going to do while he plows through six inches of manuals?*

K e r y n

Keryn marched down the steps and leaned against the hood of Grant's Lexus, folding her arms across her chest. "Grant, I think I'd like an explanation about Rachel."

"Hey, she's some kind of chick, isn't she?" Clifton said. "She's got the mondo right brain. Dillon's got the humungofied left brain." He threw a longing glance at the Miata. "Put 'em together, you've got one well-oiled machine."

Grant grinned. "That's about it, Clifton. Between the two of them, they can do anything. *Anything.*"

Keryn wanted to scream, but she didn't see how that would help. "Grant, my real question is how are you going to pay this girl genius? Last time I checked, Caltech grads were pretty pricey. I've been squeezing the jugular of every penny you've got. Didn't we agree to a hiring freeze?"

"Yes, of course." Grant limped past Keryn to the driver's side. He turned to look at her. "Ready to head on back?"

No, I am not. Behind my back, you've gone and signed on a senior-level scientist, and now you want to go on with business as usual? Keryn wished she dared to yell at him, but she just . . . couldn't. Instead, she said in a very calm voice, "Really, Grant, I need to know how much you're paying her."

Grant shot an uncomfortable look at Clifton. "Keryn, that's not something I want to—"

"Um, Grant . . ." Clifton was looking very interested. "That is a gonzo good question. I don't recall you bringing up a new hire to the board."

Keryn felt her pulse pounding. "More important, you never mentioned her to me, and I'm supposed to be paying the bills. How in the world did you hire her without me knowing? And how much is this costing us that I don't even know about?"

Grant held up both hands. "Peace, okay?" He wiped his sweating forehead on his sleeve. "Keryn, the answer to your first question is that I didn't hire her without telling you. She's been employed by CypherQuanta since last December, and you've only been here since March."

"Oh." Keryn felt deflated. "And how much are you paying her?"

Grant pulled out a business card and wrote a number on it.

Keryn stared at it. "You're kidding me. That's way less than I make, and I only work half-time. That's less than the going rate for a receptionist. How do you expect her to live on that in San Diego?"

Grant took a deep breath. "That's not her annual salary."

Clifton grabbed the card and stared at it. "You're paying her this much per *month*?" He swore at Grant.

Keryn winced. Unbelievable. If that was her monthly paycheck, Rachel was earning more than Grant and Clifton combined. "Grant, how are you cooking the books to do this? It's not possible to sneak that much money past me."

Grant gave them a shrug. "Keryn. Clifton. Listen to me. We *needed* Rachel. She's brilliant. When I talked to her last December, she was ready to quit her research, give the whole thing up. So I . . . took out a loan on my house and put her on the payroll, unofficially. I'm paying her out of my own pocket."

Keryn narrowed her eyes and studied Grant. "You hocked your *house?* You must have been pretty confident."

"No, I was desperate," Grant said. "I've been hearing for months that Lost Angels was looking to break us. Somebody in there hates us, and he's picked up enough votes now to take us to the cleaners. I had to preempt that." He stood up to his full height and gave them a defiant look. "Guys, it worked. Rachel broke the whole thing loose. She's hit it big, and we are gonna be the Microsoft of encryption by Christmas. Bigger than Microsoft. Uncle Bill sells his twerpware for a hundred bucks a pop. We sell ours for fifty K, and everybody's gonna need us."

Clifton began pacing back and forth. "Why'd she come to us? If this is so spiff, why didn't she go to IBM? They're deep into quantum computing."

"They're deep in the government's pocket," Grant said. He looked around and then lowered his voice. "Listen, you may have noticed Rachel's a little unconventional."

"She doesn't seem to live with too many restraints," Keryn said.

Grant gave her a puzzled look. "Whatever. She doesn't care for Big Brother. If she worked for IBM or any of those other bluechippers, anything she created would have wound up at the National Security Agency. And we all know the NSA would use it to spy on us. That's the beauty of CypherQuanta. We make Big Brother impossible. Even God can't break our encryption, much less the NSA sleazeballs. I explained all that to Rachel and . . . gave her a decent offer, and she came here. Now it's paying off."

Clifton was pacing back and forth, his eyes on the Miata.

Keryn still felt furious. She wished she had the guts to yell at Grant. Or quit. Or . . . something. She swallowed her anger. "Grant, you need to keep me apprised of financial matters a little better than that. Okay?" Which was a wimp-out, and she knew it, but she couldn't afford to lose her job right now.

Clifton stopped pacing and came up beside Keryn. "Ditto that on the technical stuff. Rachel's real spiff, but I should have heard about her six months ago."

Grant's eyes glowed with deep inner pain. "Keryn. Clifton. I see things from your point of view and I'm sorry. I just wanted so *bad* to not lose the shirt off my back. Somebody's trying to wreck my company and I did what I had to do to save it. I kept Rachel secret as a matter of security. It was a gamble, because I didn't know how long it'd take her to grow those qubits. Or if she could do it. If word had gotten out . . . Lost Angels would have panicked and found some way to pull funding on us and grab the whole pie months ago. As it was, we kept them on board all the way till the end."

Keryn didn't put much stock in conspiracy theories. "Oh, be serious, Grant. What would Lost Angels do with our technology? They're *investors*, not techies. If they stole that technology from us, they'd have to find somebody else to commercialize it. Why wouldn't they work with us?"

"All I know is what I hear," Grant said. "This is from a source I can't reveal, and all I can tell you is that somebody on Lost Angels wants CypherQuanta drilled right through the skull. I don't know who it is, but he wants the company dead and wants it to look like a natural death. Even paranoids have enemies, right?"

Keryn shook her head. "You've been reading too many of my novels, Grant."

"Just do me a favor, both of you." Grant's face lost all trace of humor. "We need tight security on this thing until Dillon does his magic and gets that thing working. Clifton, you come over once a day and get a report from them, and give it to me, privately. Keryn, I'll keep you abreast of progress, on a need-to-know basis. But I don't want either one of you talking to anyone else about it, not even the other CypherQuanta employees. Got it?"

"Got it," Clifton said. "Loose lips sink ships. Right, Keryn?"

Keryn nodded. She had just realized something.

Six weeks from now, if this thing worked, CypherQuanta could be big. Bigger than Microsoft. Bigger than IBM. And her eight thousand shares of CypherQuanta stock would be worth . . . lots.

At which point, she could retire. Buy a little cottage by the beach. White picket fence. Drop the day job and write full-time.

She could live the life every writer wanted, and all she had to do was stay calm and not yell at Grant.

And make sure Dillon and Rachel worked together like a well-oiled machine.

CHAPTER
FOUR

Dillon

Dillon finished reading the last manual. He snapped it shut and turned to Rachel.

She was pacing by the biology wet bench. When the book snapped shut, her head spun around to stare at him.

"I am finished," Dillon said. "Those were excellent."

Rachel's eyes narrowed. "You've finished skimming through them?"

He shook his head. "I have finished *reading* them. The third one was especially fascinating."

Rachel looked at her watch. "You've only had those horrible things for an hour and ten minutes. What can you learn in seventy minutes?"

"Enough to know how it works and how to drive the hardware. The software has a peculiar interface, and I do not like their naming conventions, but it will be sufficient. Show me your development environment."

Rachel wore a most unusual expression on her face. Dillon found women unreadable at the best of times, but Rachel seemed even more inscrutable than most. She sat down at a Dell workstation and double-clicked on an icon. "I've installed Visual C++ for you. Grant told me that's what you use."

The familiar user interface popped up on the screen. Dillon took ten minutes customizing the environment to his satisfaction. Then he closed the program. "Excellent. Now I need to set up the source control package.

Rachel waved her hand in the air. "I never use source control. It's a waste of time."

Dillon held out his hand. "We need it. Hand me the CD, please."

"I don't have a CD. Relax. We don't need it."

He gave a deep sigh. "Do you drive without insurance on your car?"

"It's not the same thing."

"Rational people insure their cars. Rational programmers use source control."

"There's only the two of us, and we'll be working together on this. We don't need it."

Dillon stood up and went to the door.

Rachel's mouth gaped open. "Where are you going?"

"We are going back to CypherQuanta in your car to obtain a CD of SourceSafe."

Rachel muttered something under her breath and followed him outside. She showed him how to set the alarm on the outside door.

Dillon climbed into the passenger side of her car. He had never ridden in a convertible, and he felt . . . exposed. Naked. He carefully fastened the seat belt.

Rachel hopped in and punched in a combination on a keypad. The engine started. She looked at him and grinned. "Ever ridden in a Miata?"

He pointed at her chest. "You forgot something."

She gave him a very strange look. "That's hardly any of your business."

Dillon could not imagine what she was talking about. "It is illegal to drive in California without a seat belt."

"Oh . . . that." Rachel grabbed the belt and buckled it.

Dillon took sunglasses out of his shirt pocket and put them on.

Rachel put the car in reverse and squealed backward out of the space.

Dillon jammed his foot against the floorboard.

Rachel braked hard, shifted into first, and roared forward. A minute later they were on Miramar Road, speeding west. Dillon saw the speedometer needle spring past 80. The wind roared in his ears, and he put his hand to his sunglasses.

"Like the car?" Rachel shrieked. Her face shone with glee.

Dillon hated it. The car would be completely unsafe in a rollover, and that was not at all improbable, considering the reckless driving style Rachel was using. "Slow down!" he shouted.

"What?" Rachel downshifted into third and veered onto the on-ramp to Highway 805.

"Slow down!" Dillon shouted again.

She shook her head. "Can't hear you!" She punched the gas and the wind rose to a roar.

Dillon gritted his teeth and held on.

Rachel flitted left and passed a couple of trucks and a minivan, then slid across two lanes of traffic and onto the Sorrento Valley Road exit. She downshifted smoothly to the corner and zipped through a right turn without stopping for the red light. She did the same at the next light.

Dillon promised himself he would never, ever ride in a car with Rachel Meyers again. This was beyond reckless. This was foolhardy.

Rachel accelerated under the 805 overpass and flitted into the left lane, skidding through a left turn across the nose of an on-coming Mercedes. She raced down a steep slope, veered left, roared forward, and shrieked to a stop in front of Suite A. She put the gearshift in neutral and left the engine running. "Run on in and get the CD. I'll wait for you out here."

Dillon unlatched his seat belt and climbed out. It was fortunate to learn on such a short trip that Rachel drove like a maniac. He would not make the same mistake again.

After getting the SourceSafe CD from his desk in Cypher-Quanta, Dillon walked out the back door and across the bridge to his parking spot. Slot number 314—his favorite—the first three digits of the number pi. He unlocked his Toyota Siena and buckled himself in, feeling very safe. Minivans had poor gas mileage, but they had an excellent safety record, especially if the driver was cautious. He drove out of the lot and around the building, waving to Rachel to follow him.

Her mouth opened in a big O. In his rearview mirror, Dillon watched her squeal around in a tight U-turn and follow him out. He climbed the hill to Sorrento Valley Road. Rachel roared past him and skittered through a right turn at the stop sign without slowing. By the time Dillon stopped and checked traffic on his left, Rachel's car was disappearing onto the 805 on-ramp.

Ten minutes later, Dillon arrived at the bio-lab. Rachel was leaning back in her seat, her eyes closed, with the sun beating down on her.

Dillon locked his car and walked up beside her. "Excessive exposure to the sun causes skin cancer."

"Your car drives like a tank."

Dillon smiled and patted the roof of his minivan. "Besides its excellent safety record, minivans are rarely stolen."

"I can't imagine why."

Dillon was not sure how to interpret this cryptic remark, but he let it pass. Normals often made illogical comments. It was not important. He unlatched Rachel's door and held it open for her.

"Um, thanks." She gave him another strange look as she got out. "Okay, let's see if you remember how to unlock the lab."

"You forgot to secure your car."

Rachel rolled her eyes and leaned in to punch a number on the keypad.

Dillon did not mean to spy on her, but he inadvertently saw her combination. "Rachel, that is very unwise. You are using the same combination for both your car and the lab."

She stood up and an amused smile covered her face. "So litigate me."

Of course this made no sense at all, since Dillon was not a lawyer, but she was smiling, so he smiled back. If someone was smiling, it was best to assume their meaning was friendly, even if it was incoherent. He went back up the stairs, punched in the combination, and went inside.

Rachel followed him in. "So how long will it take to install SourceSafe?"

He shrugged and pointed at the desk. "Your desk is a mess. It will take less than an hour to clean it, and by then the software will be installed."

Rachel's eyes went very wide, but Dillon could not begin to parse what that might mean. He spent the next half hour installing SourceSafe. When he came back out to find Rachel, the desk was still covered with papers and she was lounging in her chair with her feet on the desk, reading a magazine called *Cosmopolitan*. Dillon had seen this magazine at the supermarket, but it had never occurred to him that an intelligent woman would read such a thing. The cover had a picture of a blond woman in a very immodest red dress.

"All done?" Rachel tossed the magazine on top of the stack. "Okay, let's get to work."

Dillon picked up a plastic garbage bag and emptied the overflowing wastebasket into it. He tied the bag and took it outside to the Dumpster in the side alley. When he went back inside, Rachel was sitting in a chair in front of the computer.

Dillon went to the whiteboard. "What can I erase?"

She blinked twice. "Nothing. Everything on that board is important."

"We need to design the software."

Rachel shrugged. "So design. Have a seat here and let's write some code."

Dillon opened his briefcase and pulled out a white pad of paper. "Writing code is not designing."

"Dillon, we're in a hurry, okay? Let's just skip the retentive stuff and get to work. You've already wasted an hour installing a safety net we don't need. I want to see some code."

Dillon sat down beside her and took the cap off his Uni-ball pen. "The first thing we will design is the class hierarchy for our computational engine. What representation would you recommend for the qubit? Personally, I prefer the—"

"Dillon!"

Dillon looked up at her, astonished. She sounded angry. She looked angry. He could not understand why. If anyone should be angry, it should be him. Rachel had failed to adequately prepare the development environment, causing them to lose an hour. Now she was obstructing work on the analysis and design of the system.

"Put that paper away and let's write code," Rachel said. "Uncle Grant wants us to get this thing done as fast as possible."

Dillon sighed and leaned back in his chair. "Do you speak French?"

She stared at him with a look that told Dillon she thought he was an idiot. "What does that have to do with anything?"

"If you go to France and you do not speak French, what should you do?"

She sighed dramatically. "Speak English and hope somebody understands me, I guess."

"Wrong." Dillon had not expected her to be right. "You take along someone who speaks French."

Rachel stuck out her tongue at him.

Dillon had no idea what this might mean. It was not logical, and therefore it was a waste of time to try to decipher her behavior. "Grant must have told you that I write software very quickly. I know what I am doing and you do not. If you knew what you were doing, you would not need me. Please let me do my job."

"Okay, so *do* your job."

Dillon smiled. Very good. She was going to cooperate. Sometimes people refused to cooperate, and then he could not work with them. This partnership was going to work out excellently.

C l i f t o n

Clifton sat on the beach at La Jolla Shores staring out at the waves. He could not believe how much Grant was paying Rachel. The kid was sharp, sure, but Clifton was no dummy. It was his intellectual property that CypherQuanta was built on. His Ph.D. thesis they'd used ever since they founded the company. He was CTO. He owned six percent of the company, and he held stock options on another four and a half.

All of which would never pay off unless Rachel and the Dillon Dude got that thing to work. Meanwhile, somebody was trying to cut off CypherQuanta at the knees. Bogus, man!

Three girls in bikinis walked by in front of Clifton. He followed them with his eyes for a minute, until they left his field of view. It was just . . . biff, the way Grant was paying Rachel so much. *And* she was getting stock options too. Clifton didn't mind that she got options. Everybody in a startup company got options, even the janitor. But those options would be toilet paper if the company went under.

Whereas cash in the hand was good, CypherQuanta or no CypherQuanta.

Clifton took out his cell phone and flipped it open. He pulled up the list of calls recently received and studied the top number for several minutes. Finally he pressed the Dial button and put the phone to his ear. It rang twice and then . . .

"Ted Hunter."

Clifton cleared his throat. "Yeah, hey, Ted. This is Clifton Potter. You called me this morning."

"Oh, hey, Clifton! Great to hear from you! Are you interested after all in having me look around for you?"

"Um . . . maybe. Just . . ." Clifton swallowed hard. "Just be real discreet, okay?"

"I understand," Ted said. "That's my job, to be discreet. I'll need a little bit of information to get started. You're working for . . . remind me?"

"CypherQuanta."

"I'm not familiar with it. You do what exactly?"

"Quantum encryption. My expertise is lasers. I've got a Ph.D. in laser physics from UCSD and six years' experience."

"Okay, sounds great. What's your job title there at Cypher-Quanta?"

"CTO."

A long pause. "I see. How big is the company?"

"It's a startup." Clifton tried to remember how many people were on staff. "I think we're down to forty-five FTEs. We've had a few financial problems lately and a couple of our engineers left to work for Cymer."

"Right. That happens. Listen, it may take a while to find something at your pay scale. May I ask what you're earning?"

Clifton told him.

Another long pause. "That's not bad in this economy. Ya know, if things keep ramping up in the county, it's not out of the question that you could get something better, but it may take a few months. Are you in any particular hurry?"

"Huh-uh." That was a lie, but Clifton didn't want to sound desperate. Besides, he was just checking. "Look, it's not that big a deal, okay? You just got me thinking this morning when you called and . . . you know, I'm mainly just curious. Not a big deal."

"Gotcha, buddy." The sound of writing. "Listen, I'll check around, and you can rest assured that I'll keep it discreet until there's something definite. Now, maybe you can do me a favor?"

"Sure, if I can."

"Are you guys publicly traded there at, um, CypherQuanta?"

"Not yet." Clifton shrugged. "We were hoping for an IPO in the next couple years, but you know what the climate's like lately."

"Chilly." Hunter laughed. "Things'll get better. Reason I ask, by the way, is I'm always looking for new companies. I invest a little on the side, but . . . if you're not on the Nasdaq . . ."

Clifton snorted. "You want some stock? I can let you have some of mine."

"That bad, huh?"

"Um . . . forget I said that, okay?"

"Right. Look, it's my job to keep things between my ears, so don't worry. I'll be discreet on that. Look, I'll put out some feelers and be in touch if anything comes up, all right?"

"Right." Clifton felt a queasy feeling deep in his gut. He hadn't worked for anyone but Grant for the last six years. And he hoped he wouldn't have to jump ship, but it was always a good idea to keep your options open.

"Oh, one more question," Hunter said. "Can I call you in the daytime? I mean, will it compromise you if I call you at work on your cell phone?"

"I'm in a cubicle," Clifton said. "If you call, I'll just go out in the parking lot and we can talk. Everybody does that. Reception in the building is really biff."

"You're good with that? I don't want to do anything to damage your relationships there."

"I'm good."

"Great. Listen, Clifton, it's been a pleasure talking to you, and I hope I can help you like I did your buddy Kendall."

"Me too," Clifton said. "Catch ya later." He closed his phone and stared out at the waves. His gut felt cold and empty. It was just bogus, thinking about working somewhere else. He'd been loyal to Grant for a long time.

And Grant was paying Rachel Meyers twice what he was paying Clifton. Was that fair? No, it was not.

It was not fair at all.

CHAPTER
FIVE

Rachel

A dozen sheets of white paper lay in Rachel's lap. Dillon was working on the thirteenth, his tongue just poking out of his mouth in concentration.

Rachel had seen a movie once that freaked her out. *Amadeus.* One scene in particular she could not get out of her mind. Mozart stood hunched over a pool table writing music. He would take the cue ball, idly send it rolling against one of the cushions, pick up his quill pen, and write a measure of music. As he wrote the notes, the cue ball bounced off each of the four cushions in turn. As he set down the pen and opened his hand, the cue ball came rolling back perfectly into his fingers. Mozart caught it, then sent it on the next circuit while he wrote the next measure.

Mozart was amazing, a genius, a prodigy, a . . . machine.

Dillon Richard designed software like Mozart wrote music. Rachel could not believe what she was seeing. In a couple of hours Dillon had discussed a complete computational architecture with her, suggested several options, analyzed them for space and time efficiency, made his trade-off decisions, and begun producing a design document.

It was poetry and art and music, and there was nobody to appreciate it but Rachel. It was like watching Mozart compose a symphony that only she would ever hear.

Dillon finished the sheet of paper and tore it off. He handed it to her. "That should finish it. Do you have a stapler?"

Rachel went and rummaged around on her desk for several minutes. Finally, she found her stapler. It was out of staples. She yanked open several drawers. At the bottom of the third one, she found a box and refilled the stapler. She pushed the stack of pages into the stapler, then thought better of it. Better to neaten it up just a little. Rachel straightened all the edges so they were exactly even, then stapled the documents.

When she got back into the bio-lab, Dillon had pulled his chair up to the computer and created a Visual C++ workspace.

"Hey, Dillon, you forgot one thing."

He turned to look at her, and his eyes were two question marks.

She giggled and held out the design document. "You need to sign this."

"Sign it?" Dillon looked at the top page, his face mystified. "I have put our names and the date on the top of every page."

"Dillon, this is a masterpiece. Every artist should sign his work."

He smiled. It was a very nice smile. "Do you . . . like it?"

"It's gorgeous." She pressed it into his hands. "Go on. Sign it."

Dillon uncapped the pen and signed his name at the bottom. His signature was very square and precise, without frills or flourishes.

Rachel sat down in the other chair. "Hey, um, I'm sorry about ragging on you about SourceSafe. You're really good and really fast and . . . I guess I'm learning a lot just watching you."

He smiled again. "Understood. Shall we begin coding?"

"Rock and roll, big guy."

Dillon gave her a completely blank look.

"I mean go ahead." Rachel suppressed a smile. Dillon had a different kind of brain. If there were some things he didn't get, well . . . there were some things at which he was master of the universe.

Dillon reached into his pocket and pulled out his keys. Clipped to the key ring was a small USB flash drive. He inserted it into the USB port on the computer and waited for it to mount.

Rachel leaned forward. "What have you got there?"

"A few libraries I wrote," Dillon said. "Also some software templates for C++ classes." He dragged several folders onto the hard drive of the Dell and unmounted the flash drive.

Rachel stared at the screen, fascinated. "But . . . Visual C++ already has class templates built in. It's got a wizard to write a skeleton of your classes for you."

Dillon returned to Visual C++ and opened one of his template files.

Rachel gasped. The file looked like poetry. She suddenly realized that the auto-generated class files of Visual C++ were unbearably ugly. "That's . . ."

"Better?" Dillon looked at her.

"Yeah." Rachel looked into his eyes. There was depth in those eyes. And pain. She read the hurts laid on him by a thousand people who never saw beyond his pocket-protector geekiness to the soul of the artist that lived inside him. An artist who worked in for-loops and access functions and class hierarchy diagrams.

Dillon's ears turned red, and he suddenly began looking intently at the design document. "I had better . . . start coding."

Rachel felt flustered. Had she embarrassed him? She hadn't meant to, but . . . it was a very nice feeling looking into his deep brown eyes. She stood up. "Hey, I just realized my desk is kind of a mess. Maybe I'll go, um, clean it up a little."

Dillon nodded without looking at her. He began typing rapidly into the document he had opened. Mozart was back at work.

Rachel backed away to the door and pulled it open. She turned around and looked at her desk and suddenly felt very ashamed. Dillon must think she was a pig. She stared at the enormous stack of papers. Revulsion swept through her. And panic. How in the world was she ever going to clear away this mess?

She swore at the stack and then opened the file cabinet. Dozens of empty folders sat there. Rachel took a deep breath. It didn't have to be perfect. Anything would be better than this. She grabbed a handful of papers. Dr. Chuang's reports on his implementation of Shor's algorithm in seven qubits.

Rachel straightened the papers into a neat pile and shoved them into a file folder.

———————

Two hours later, the desk was clear. It was a typical metal office desk. She hadn't seen its Formica surface since last January. It looked naked. Rachel felt a little lost. She liked clutter. Chaos was a good thing, wasn't it? The clean desk made her feel so linear and straight-edged and geeky, she wanted to shriek. She plopped into her chair and put her head in her hands. What was she trying to do anyway? Play Salieri to Dillon's Mozart?

Her cell phone rang. Rachel took it out of her fanny pack and checked the caller ID. It was an unknown caller. She flipped open the phone. "Hello?"

A slight pause. "Um, hi, this is Keryn Wills. Grant gave me your cell phone number. I just thought I'd, you know, check in on you two, see what's happening. How are you getting along? I mean, um, are you making progress?"

Keryn's voice sounded a little higher than normal. Rachel leaned back in her chair. "We're doing great. Dillon is just a *machine* at writing software. He read the manual in, like, an hour, and then he came up with this design that . . . well, you wouldn't understand, but it's, like, brilliant. I mean, it's not like there's anything new there. Just qubit representations and hardware drivers and some high-level algorithms. But . . . it's hard to explain. . . ." Rachel let her voice trail off. Keryn wasn't a techie. There was no way to explain. It was like Einstein's equations. If you didn't know tensor calculus, Einstein didn't make any sense. But if you knew it, then looking at those equations was like looking at Michelangelo's David.

"Hey, sounds great," Keryn said. "Listen, it's getting on toward suppertime, and Grant wanted me to make sure everything's, you know, going smooth and make sure you guys don't work your fingers to the bone, so I was thinking maybe I could bring some pizza over so you won't forget to eat."

Rachel closed her eyes. Pizza sounded great. Keryn sounded uptight about something, but maybe she was just strung tight. She had struck Rachel as kind of a nervy woman today when they'd met. "Actually, I'm getting hungry and pizza would be awesome. I'm a vegetarian, and I like any kind of veggies. Shall I ask Dillon what he likes?"

Keryn laughed. "Dillon likes pepperoni and pineapple. It's kind of a company joke. He always wants the same thing. He's . . . predictable, you know."

"I think it's kind of cute."

A moment of silence. "Um, right, then. I'll call in our order and pick it up on the way over. You want a soda or something?"

"Diet Coke," Rachel said. "Should I ask Dillon—"

"V-8," Keryn said. "It's very nutritious. See you guys in a while." The line went dead.

Rachel sat staring at her phone for a moment, wondering why Keryn was in such a hurry. Whatever. She folded her phone and put it away, then slipped into the bio-lab.

Dillon sat just as she'd left him. She could hear him talking softly. He was dictating C++ to himself and typing it in as he spoke.

Rachel sneaked up behind him and listened.

Dillon's quiet voice muttered on.

Rachel stood there quietly watching him. A feeling of awe settled over her. The bio-lab felt like a cathedral, with Dillon whispering his secret incantations that would turn a string of characters into a program that could tap the power of a zillion universes. It was kind of like one of those Catholic priests who believed he could turn bread and wine into the body and blood of Jesus. Rachel couldn't understand why anyone believed such nonsense. She had figured out that religion was a crock when she was twelve years old.

If you wanted to believe in something bigger than yourself, all you had to do was look around at the universe. You'd see Einstein's God. Truth. Beauty. Order.

Religion was for morons.

K e r y n

Keryn pulled up in the parking lot next to Dillon's minivan. Something funny was going on. When they all came over here earlier today in Grant's Lexus, Dillon had left his minivan back at CypherQuanta. So how had it gotten over here? Keryn climbed out of her car, set the pizza on the roof, and called Rachel on her cell phone.

She answered on the second ring. "Hello. Is that you, Keryn?"

"Hey, Rachel. Yeah, it's me. I'm outside and I don't have the combination. Can you let me in?"

"I'll be right out." Rachel hung up. A minute later the door swung inward and Rachel bounded down the steps. She gave Keryn a golden-girl smile. "Thanks for doing this, Keryn. That's awfully nice of you."

Keryn handed her the pizza box. "I'll get the drinks and lock my car."

Rachel grinned. "That's right, Hondas are one of the most commonly stolen cars in the county."

"Um . . . yeah, I've heard." Keryn went back to her car and got two takeout cups and a pop-top can of V-8. She hurried up the stairs and into the lab and . . .

Keryn stared at the clean desk. "Wow, what happened?"

Rachel opened the box and a puff of steam came smoke-signaling off the pizza. "Oh, I just, you know, got ambitious this afternoon. Dillon was writing code and . . ." She waved her hand at the desk. "I just cleared out a little of the mess. Filed it away."

Keryn set the drinks down. "Good idea." All of a sudden, she didn't feel very hungry. She looked at the door of the bio-lab. "Shouldn't we take the pizza in to Dillon? When he gets coding, he forgets to eat."

Rachel shook her head. "Can't. I culture live cells in there. They're harmless, but it's just a bad idea to take food into a bio-lab. I always eat out here. We'll have to bring Mohammed to the mountain." She went into the lab.

Keryn followed her. Dillon sat at the computer, typing out code in a perfect rhythm.

Rachel went up and touched his arm. "Hey, Maestro! It's chow time. Keryn brought us some food."

Dillon turned around and looked up at them. As always when he came out of his private universe, he looked lost for a moment, as if wondering which Narnian world he had fallen into. Then his eyes focused on them. "Thank you, Keryn. Rachel and I are making excellent progress. We read the manuals and then we worked out a design."

"Oh," Keryn said. "That's great. Really great." She took a deep breath. "Are you hungry?"

Dillon looked at his watch. "It is already six-thirty. Yes, I am hungry."

Keryn wondered if he really needed to know the time before he decided if he was hungry. Rachel didn't wear a watch, and it was a good bet that she just ate when she felt like it. Way different from Dillon. Totally different.

They went back into the outer office. Rachel and Dillon rolled their chairs along with them. Keryn sat in the chair at the desk. Her head felt dizzy, disoriented. This was Rachel's territory, not hers. She grabbed a handful of napkins and handed them to Rachel and Dillon. "Sorry, I couldn't get any paper plates. We'll have to rough it."

Rachel peeled up a long strip of pizza. "Ooh, this looks good! Thanks for bringing this, Keryn."

Dillon was sitting quietly, looking at both of them. "Keryn, shouldn't we thank the Lord for our food?"

Keryn wasn't quite sure how to react. Generally in a group, she didn't make a big deal out of saying a blessing over the food. Rachel didn't seem like the religious type and so why make her feel uncomfortable?

Rachel had a slice of pizza halfway to her mouth. "Um, thank who?"

Somehow, that made Keryn feel better. "Dillon was just suggesting that we say grace over the food. Would you like to do the honors, Rachel?"

Rachel's eyes narrowed and flickered back and forth between Dillon and Keryn. She set the pizza back in the box. "You mean, like, praying?"

"We usually do," Keryn said. A little bit of an exaggeration, since she'd only eaten with Dillon once, at the restaurant last night. Still, it was a tactical advantage and she intended to press it all the way. "Don't you ever bless your food before you eat it?"

A flicker of . . . something crossed Rachel's face. Comprehension, maybe. "No." A tiny smile rosebudded her mouth. "I'm Jewish. You do know that in Jewish tradition, we never bless the food?"

A twinge of anxiety knotted Keryn's stomach. "Um, no, I didn't know that. I thought . . ." Keryn wasn't sure what she thought. Didn't Jesus say a blessing over the food? She could swear she'd seen that in the Bible.

Rachel looked at Dillon. "In Judaism, we bless God, not the food. You knew that, didn't you?"

Dillon's eyes were locked on Rachel's face. "No, that is fascinating. How does the blessing go?"

Rachel closed her eyes and began chanting. *"Baruch attah Adonai, Eloheinu, melech ha-olam, ha motzi lechem min ha'aretz!"*

Dillon blinked twice. "Can you translate that?"

"Of course." Rachel favored him with an innocent smile. "Blessed are you, Lord our God, King of the Universe, who brings forth bread from the earth!"

Keryn felt a sick feeling in her belly. Great. Rachel was stealing the show. She was the kind of girl who was always going to be the center of attention, always floozing it up for the guys. Whereas Keryn . . .

Whereas Keryn was just a dull, mousy little writer who lived her life sitting in a corner with a cup of hot chocolate in her hand, a cat in her lap, and a book in her face. She was boring and Rachel was not, and there was just no changing that.

As they ate, Rachel told them her life story. Her father was a physics professor at Rutgers. Grant O'Connell was a longtime family friend whom she'd known ever since she could remember. For all she knew, Grant really had changed a few of her diapers, as he claimed. She graduated from high school a couple of years early and started at MIT when she was sixteen. Majored in biophysics, but earned enough credits that she could have gotten a degree in either biology or physics. After finishing her undergraduate work at MIT, she went to Caltech, where she'd worked on protein-folding problems, and got her Ph.D. in four years. Then she'd continued on there in a postdoc appointment and discovered a special class of proteins with interesting physical properties.

"And you did not publish it?" Dillon said.

Rachel shook her head, and her curly mane swished her shoulders. "That's when I realized Big Brother was going to want it."

"Big Brother? You mean as in *1984?*" Dillon looked skeptical. "The governing authorities?"

"You bet your sweet bippy." Rachel wiped her mouth and slurped up the dregs of her Diet Coke. "Another few years, they're going to take the whole field black and—"

"Black?" Dillon took a long drink of his V-8. "This is a figure of speech?"

"It means they're going to classify it and we won't have access to it," Rachel said. "The National Security Agency employs more mathematicians than anybody else in the world, and none of them publish. It's all classified, hush-hush stuff."

"They need to," Dillon said. "The NSA handles the federal government's requirements for encrypting sensitive data and decrypting the ciphers of other governments."

Rachel leaned back in her chair. "It doesn't bother you that they have a budget of, like, billions of dollars per year? You don't get a little steamed that for decades the Feds denied the NSA even existed? The joke was that the initials stood for No Such Agency. The exact budget is still classified and they don't allow visitors. The place is a black hole, and I'll be hanged if I let my research go to Big Brother."

"So you came to work for Grant," Keryn said.

Rachel nodded. "Uncle Grant hates the NSA as much as I do. That's what CypherQuanta is all about—putting encryption in the hands of the people. Encryption means privacy. And it happens to be a theorem of quantum mechanics that Big Brother can't break our quantum encryption."

"What about conventional encryption?" Keryn asked. "Big Brother can't break that either, can they? Didn't someone in the government try to keep people from getting access to that? There was a big court case years ago."

"They took Phillip Zimmermann to court," Dillon said. "He created software that he called PGP—Pretty Good Privacy—that made it very easy for anyone to use RSA encryption. The government opposed it because it lets criminals protect their data from the government."

Rachel scowled. "That's completely a smoke screen. A lot of cypherpunks think the NSA has an efficient way to factor large numbers. I betcha the Feds just made a big noise to lull people into thinking PGP is safe to use. In reality, they probably cracked it years ago and they're laughing up their sleeves about our Pretty Bad Privacy."

"But . . . if your machine works, you'll be able to crack PGP too." Keryn had a queasy feeling in her stomach about that.

Rachel smiled. "Correction. If my machine works, *anyone* will be able to do that, and nobody'll trust PGP or any flavor of RSA encryption ever again. That'll blow the cover off the NSA's smoke screen."

"And at the same time it'll make CypherQuanta a pile of money," Keryn said.

Rachel shrugged. "Money is beside the point. Money is nothing if you don't have freedom. And freedom can't happen if you don't have privacy. That'll be my gift to humanity. Privacy forever."

Keryn wiped her hands on a napkin. "I guess that's the sixty-four-billion-dollar question, then. Is your machine going to work? Dillon, what do you think?"

Dillon gave Rachel a look of unrestrained admiration. "The construction of the qubits is pure genius. There are going to be some problems writing the software, but—"

"But nothing." Rachel leaned back in her chair and locked her hands behind her head. "I can't believe how fast Dillon is at writing software. He'll have the drivers done in a few days. Keryn, it's like a work of art. I just wish you understood C++. You'd . . ." She shrugged helplessly. "Sorry. It's like a sonnet. You either know how to appreciate it or you don't."

And I don't. Keryn felt cold. She was on the outside looking in, while these two geniuses got to huddle together, the Dream Team of CypherQuanta. Great. Wonderful. *Spiff,* as Clifton Potter would say.

"Well, hey, I'm keeping Dillon from working." Keryn slapped both hands on the desktop. "I better head on home." She folded up the pizza box and stuffed it in the trash can, then went into the bathroom. The toilet stank and a line of mold ran down the wall from the sink. Gagging, Keryn washed her hands and then came out. "Say, Rachel, have you got any cleaning supplies? That room is *disgusting.*"

Dillon's eyebrows raised. "Really? That is very unhealthful."

Rachel stood up, and her cheeks pinked. "You go ahead and write code, Dillon. Thanks for pointing that out, Keryn. I'll take care of it." Her eyes were lasering into Keryn's heart.

Dillon went into the bathroom and stepped back, alarm scrawled across his face. "That is definitely a health hazard."

Keryn headed for the door. "Want me to go pick up some cleaning supplies at Ralph's? They've got the best prices—"

"I'll said I'll take *care* of it." Rachel took Dillon's arm and guided him back to the bio-lab. "You keep writing code. I'll take care of the cleaning. See you Monday, Keryn, and thanks for catering supper for us drudges."

Keryn slipped outside, but not before she caught a look of silent fury in Rachel's eyes.

Fine, let her be furious. Rachel was all wrong for Dillon. All wrong. The two of them were total opposites. The sooner Rachel figured that out and got over it, the better.

CHAPTER
SIX

Dillon

Dillon sat down at the keyboard and picked up his design documents. It took a moment to remember where he had been before eating. He had finished the pure virtual interface class for the NMR driver. The next part would take more effort. He needed to write an abstract class to do a partial implementation. He had been thinking about the autocalibration function while he ate the pizza, and he thought he had worked out the main algorithm. Of course there would be some low-level details specific to the MagTec NMR machine, but he intended to wrapper those in a concrete subclass so it would be simple to use a machine from a different manufacturer if CypherQuanta decided to change vendors. Then he would only need to write one new concrete subclass and his code would work with the new device.

If manufacturers were intelligent, they would all use the same standard interface for their machines. But they were not intelligent. In the name of competition, they insisted on each creating a different and incompatible interface. They could make life easier for all their users if they would cooperate, but they would never do that.

Dillon took a moment to add some comments to his design

document sketching out the algorithm. Then he began typing. It felt relaxing and soothing to be typing code. He had not felt relaxed or soothed while he was eating, and this puzzled him. Dillon found it very pleasant to be around Keryn. And around Rachel also. Yet eating with both together had not been nearly as pleasant as he had expected, and he could not think why.

Last night had been a wonderful evening. Keryn had invited him to dinner and a play in La Jolla. Dillon liked Keryn very much. She was a friendly woman and she loved the Lord. The books she wrote were very logical mysteries that made Dillon think. And she reminded him of his favorite comic strip character.

On the advice of his counselor, Dillon regularly read all the comic strips in the newspaper. It was supposed to help him learn the slang and double meanings most people understood so easily. Dillon's favorite character was Sally Forth. Sally was a very likeable woman, honest, good, humorous, intelligent. Keryn was like Sally, and she had a quiet way of speaking that made Dillon feel at home. She had treated Dillon well ever since he met her, and that was not usual for a female.

Dillon had three brothers, all Normals, and they had treated Dillon very badly when he was growing up. But his brothers were saints in comparison to the girls he had known in school. Dillon had very bad memories from high school.

But Keryn was different from most females he had known. Keryn did not mind that he was not a Normal. Keryn was a kind person, and her eyes made Dillon feel very warm inside. She asked his opinion about things and then listened. He hoped they could have many interesting conversations together.

Whereas Rachel was something entirely different, and Dillon did not know how to think about her. She . . . excited him, and she terrified him, both at the same time. It was like quantum mechanics, in which a qubit could represent both 0 and 1 simultaneously.

In Dillon's experience, a woman who talked and dressed and acted like Rachel was what Clifton called an airhead. Dillon did not know why such women were called airheads, but he knew that they despised him because he was not a Normal. Yet clearly, Rachel was not an airhead. She did not treat him like a fool. She was interested in his ideas.

Furthermore, Rachel was brilliant. Her solution to the qubit construction problem was clever and profound. How could that be, in a woman so undisciplined, so chaotic? A childish woman who drove like a maniac and lacked the sense to clean the toilet? She was deeply disturbing to everything Dillon believed in. She was chaos to his order, fire to his ice.

And whenever she touched his arm, Dillon felt something hot rush through his heart. He did not understand this, but he felt sure it had an excellent biochemical explanation. He would ask his friend Robert about it the next time they talked on the phone.

A hand settled on his shoulder.

Dillon felt an electric jolt through his body. He did his best to show no reaction. It would be highly inappropriate to react. Highly inappropriate.

"How are you coming along, Dillon?" Rachel took her hand off his shoulder. Its absence felt like the vacuum of deep space.

Dillon took a deep breath and tried to calm his heart. He pointed to the monitor. "I have written most of the autocalibration routine in terms of pure virtual functions that we will implement in the concrete subclasses. When that is—"

"What's this?" Rachel pointed at a line. "You misspelled a word in your comment!"

Dillon felt his ears getting hot. He had spelled "magnetic" as "mangetic." He double-clicked on the offending word and retyped it. "I am very sorry."

Rachel looked down at him and giggled. "It's okay, you know. Nobody's perfect. Anyway the compiler won't care because it's in a comment."

"But I care," Dillon said.

Rachel sat down next to him and flashed him a smile. "That's what I like about you. You *care*. That's really awesome, you know that?"

Dillon felt like a piece of ball lightning had gotten stuck inside his chest.

Rachel leaned back in her chair and locked her hands behind her head. "Most people are such . . . muggles."

"Muggles?" Dillon had never heard this word.

Rachel shrugged. "You know . . . they're so boring, so . . . *normal*."

Dillon's heart double-thumped. "You make being normal sound bad."

"It *is* bad," Rachel said. "It's horrible. I'd hate to be normal."

Dillon did not know what to say, but he liked very much the way Rachel's soft green eyes were looking at him. Finally, he said, "I am very not-Normal."

She leaned forward and slapped his knee. "You're a stud, Dillon."

Dillon's knee felt like it was full of molten metal.

Rachel stood up. "Well, hey, time for you to take a work break. How many lines have you written?"

Dillon opened up his line-counter program and checked his work. "Over three thousand." Had they not lost an hour fetching the SourceSafe program, it would have been over four thousand, but Dillon did not want to say so.

"Rock and roll, big guy."

Dillon smiled and looked down at his design document. After a brief recalibration of his mind, he began typing again. But now he found it much harder to concentrate. *Rock and roll.*

Being around Rachel did something to his mind that he did not understand. Dillon desperately wished that this phenomenon would go away. And he desperately hoped that it would not.

R a c h e l

Rachel would have been happy to sit and watch Dillon write code forever, but at precisely 10:00 P.M. he pulled out his flash drive and inserted it into the USB port on the computer.

"All done for the night?" she asked.

He nodded. "I am making a backup, and then we can go home. We have almost five thousand lines. At this rate, we should be ready for testing in a week."

"A week?" Rachel felt a huge weight lift off her heart. "That's incredible." She opened her fanny pack and took out the vial containing the bio-computer. "I'll just put this in the safe. Come here and watch this. You need to know the combination. It'll reduce my truck factor."

"Truck factor?" Dillon joined her at the safe.

She gave him a sly grin. "Sorry. That's my private slang. It means the risk to the company if I get hit by a truck."

"If you drove a safer car, you could reduce that factor substantially."

"I'm sure you're right." Rachel dialed in the combination and put the bio-computer in the safe. "Did you catch all the numbers?"

"It is the same as the combination for the keypad outside." Dillon sounded very disappointed. "That is a security risk. If somebody can break into one, then they can break into the other."

Rachel flipped the door of the safe shut and spun the dial. "If I used a different security code for everything, I'd have to write them all down, and that's the biggest risk of all."

"Why not just remember them all?"

"Did you encrypt the information on your flash drive?" Rachel didn't want to argue, so she figured the best defense was a good offense.

"Of course."

Rachel shrugged. "Well, whatever. Listen, you're good at that kind of thing. I'm not. So I'm just going to do things the way that works for me, and you do what works for you. Deal?" She stuck out her hand.

Dillon shook it. His hand felt strong and warm. "Deal."

"Great." Rachel looked at her watch. "It's still early. Go home and get a good night's sleep and let's try to get in early tomorrow. What time works for you?"

Dillon gave her an indecipherable look. "Tomorrow is Sunday."

Rachel wondered what that had to do with anything. "Listen, Grant's in a real panic over all this. I'm sure he'll give us some comp time when we get this baby in the bank, but right now we need to work every spare minute till it's done."

Dillon looked offended. "I am not objecting to working extra hours."

Rachel saw that she'd hit a nerve, but she had no idea what it was. "Then what are you objecting to?"

"Sunday is the Lord's Day. I do not work on the Lord's Day."

"Not even in an emergency?"

Dillon sighed. "Do you change your oil every three thousand miles—even in an emergency?"

Rachel gave a nervous titter. "Now that you mention it, I think I haven't changed the oil on my Miata at all."

"If you change your oil on the recommended schedule, your car will last forever. If you give yourself a break on the Lord's Day, your soul will last forever."

Rachel didn't know what to say to that. This was weird, totally weird. "You must really take your religion seriously."

"Yes, I do."

A whole flood of emotions cut through Rachel. Pain. Rejection. Hate. Rage. It shocked her. She wanted so much to be over all that. Fat chance. She had been born right smack in the middle of a religious fault line that was two thousand years old. How was anybody supposed to get over that?

Dillon was still looking at her, and there was concern in those chocolate brown eyes of his. "Are you all right, Rachel?"

"I'm . . ." Rachel wanted to say she was fine, but that would be a big fat lie. And somehow she didn't want to lie to Dillon. She sat down in a chair. "Can I ask you a question?"

Dillon sat down too. "Of course."

Rachel hoped she wasn't going to hurt his feelings, but she really wanted to know. "You believe in science, right?"

"Yes."

"And you believe in . . . God and all that."

"I believe in God. I am not sure what 'all that' is."

"You know. Creationism. The Flood. Jonah and the whale. Water into wine. All that."

"'All that' is a lot to talk about." Dillon's eyes were steady, but Rachel saw pain deep inside them. "Are you really interested or are you just wanting to make fun?"

She put a hand on his arm. "Dillon, I'm not trying to be rude. It's just . . . I'm curious. How do you believe in science and God with the same brain? Don't you worry about all the contradictions?"

"Contradictions?"

"Like Genesis and the Big Bang."

"Contradictions make life interesting."

Rachel gave him her most skeptical look. "Meaning what?"

"Do you believe in Einstein's theory of general relativity?"

Rachel couldn't see where he was going with this. Everybody believed in general relativity. "Well, obviously. The evidence is overwhelming. Gravity. The expanding universe. The cosmic microwave background. General relativity is just about the best-supported theory ever constructed. You aren't going to convince me otherwise, just because Genesis—"

"I do not want to convince you otherwise." Dillon shook his head and he smiled. It was a very nice smile. "Einstein was right. General relativity is true. And yes, I believe in the Big Bang."

Rachel leaned back in her chair. "So . . . um, what's your point?"

"Do you believe in quantum mechanics?"

Rachel blinked. What in the *world* was he driving at? "Of course I believe in quantum mechanics." She pointed at the safe. "If I didn't believe in quantum mechanics, I wouldn't have spent the last six months building that bio-computer. What's this all about? You believe in quantum mechanics. I know you do."

"Yes, I believe in quantum mechanics." Dillon studied her for a long moment. "The evidence for quantum mechanics is overwhelming. It is one of the best supported theories ever constructed. Just like Einstein's general relativity. You do realize that those two marvelous theories contradict each other? They cannot both be true."

Rachel stared at him. "Well . . . yes. Everybody knows that."

Dillon leaned forward. "How can you believe in both of those theories with the same brain?"

"It's . . ." Rachel didn't know what to say. "That's the big unsolved question from the twentieth century. How to arrange what John Wheeler called the 'fiery marriage' of gravity and quantum mechanics. Maybe it's superstrings. Maybe it's quantum loop gravity. Maybe it's something we haven't thought of yet."

"But you believe they can be married," Dillon said. "Why not just throw out one of them?"

"Because they're both true," Rachel said. "I can't give up relativity. It's too perfect. Too good. Too beautiful. And the same goes for quantum mechanics. I *know* quantum mechanics is real."

Dillon's eyes gleamed. "I know God is real."

Rachel shook her head. "Look, God is just some kind of cosmic father figure."

Dillon stiffened as if she'd slapped him. For a moment, something flickered in his expressionless face.

"I'm sorry. That came out wrong." Rachel wished she could just back up and start over. "Listen, I'm not into religion, but everybody's got to find their own truth. You're a Christian, and that's cool with me, but I'm . . . kind of still seeking truth where I can find it." Which was as nice a way as Rachel could think of to say that she was an agnostic and meant to stay that way.

"If you come to church with me, I am sure I can help you find it."

Rachel shook her head. He wasn't getting it. "Thanks, but no thanks."

Dillon looked deeply disappointed. Rachel thought he looked cute that way. She put a hand on his arm again. "Listen, let's both just take a nice break tomorrow. We'll come in on Monday all fresh and rested and we'll jam out some code. Okay?"

"Jam out code?"

"We'll write it really fast." Rachel smiled at him. "You'll write it really fast and I'll watch. Okay?"

"Okay." Dillon turned and picked up his briefcase. "See you Monday."

The way he said that, it sounded like a thousand years. "Right," Rachel said. "Monday."

Driving home on Miramar Road, Rachel let the wind wash through her brain. It had been a weird, weird, weird, whacked-out day.

Uncle Grant was a big teddy bear who didn't want much except to save the world. Right now he'd be lucky if he could save the company.

Clifton Potter was a lech and a half. She'd need to keep an eye on him, because for sure he'd be putting his eyes all over her.

Keryn Wills was a sweet, literary, gracious, backstabbing pain in the rear, who was going to keep butting in every chance she could because she thought Rachel was competition. As if.

Dillon Richard was a big bundle of contradictions—a Mozart of a programmer, a scientist who believed in God. A socially inept guy who just happened to connect very well with Rachel whenever she looked deep into his gorgeous brown eyes.

Working at CypherQuanta was going to be a lot crazier than she had bargained for.

CHAPTER
SEVEN

Keryn

Keryn couldn't think of an excuse to call Dillon on Sunday. Monday morning, she pottered around her home office all morning, unable to focus on her novel. She needed to drill out ten thousand words this week, and it was going horribly. She couldn't concentrate, knowing that Rachel was holed up in that bio-lab with Dillon, getting chummy and doing the well-oiled machine bit.

Around noon, she couldn't stand it any longer and she went in to work early. Grant was on the phone with his door shut, and he didn't look up when Keryn peered in through the little glass square on his door. His forehead looked shiny, and he was scribbling furiously on a pad of paper while he talked.

Nobody else in the company was in on the secret, other than Clifton. It was his job to keep tabs on progress, so Keryn went looking for him. He wasn't in his cubicle, or the coffee room, or the weight room. Keryn poked her head in the assembly room. A couple of engineers were working on a CypherQuanta encryption device. It was the size and shape of a shoebox and was connected to a Dell workstation.

Keryn sauntered in. "Hey, Bill and Jill, have you seen Clifton?"

Both of them turned around. Bill and Jill were twins in their early thirties. Bill had a blond crew cut and Jill had a short brown ponytail tied with a rubber band, but other than that, they looked amazingly alike. They both wore No Fear T-shirts and faded Levi's. Jill had a tattoo on her right arm that said *Bill*. Bill had a *Jill* tattoo on his left arm. They drove identical white Saturns. Keryn had heard they lived in a house they had bought together, which was kind of weird, but whatever.

"I," Jill said.

"Saw," Bill said.

They continued the sentence, alternating words. "Him." "Going." "Outside." "Talking." "On." "His." "Cell." "Phone."

Keryn laughed. Bill and Jill were always trying to do that. Occasionally, they actually made sense. "You two are nuts."

"Thank."

"You."

Keryn went back outside, wondering what it was like to be that in tune with another person. A deep ache settled in her chest. As she reached the door to the parking lot, it swung open.

Clifton Potter stood there. His eyes flicked down for a second, then back up to her face. "Whoa, hey, Keryn. You're in early today. Finished killing off the bad guys already?"

Keryn felt flustered. She wanted to know how Dillon and Rachel were getting on, but she felt awkward asking. "Bill and Jill said you were out here."

"Phone call," he said. "You know how biff the reception is inside."

Keryn knew. "Listen, I came in a little early to talk to Grant about . . . you know. The financials."

Clifton pulled the door all the way open. "Right. Let's step out here, if you don't mind."

Keryn followed him. Clifton plunked himself down at a picnic table looking out toward the gully. Keryn sat across from him. "Listen, there are financial integrity issues we need to deal with. I need to know what the probability is that we're going to do layoffs this month."

Clifton looked all around, his alert blue eyes sweeping the whole parking lot. "I hear ya on that. I'm still chafed that Grant didn't tell us about Goldilocks for six months. We needed to know that. Know what I mean?"

Keryn knew. She hadn't gotten over it herself.

Clifton grabbed his long blond ponytail and held the end of it in his fist. "I mean, this thing Rachel's found is quite the breakthrough. A CTO ought to know about things like that."

"Do you think it'll work?"

Clifton pursed his lips. "Saturday, I wasn't sure. We've never done anything like this before. But I talked to the Dillon Man this morning, and he's on target. Thinks they'll be ready for testing by Friday, next Monday at the latest."

"That soon?" Keryn felt a rush of relief. The less time Dillon was cloistered with Rachel, the better.

"Those two are the Dream Team," Clifton said. "Between the two of them, we're gonna put the wallies of the world on the run."

"The what?"

"The wallies. The doofuses. Like Wally in Dilbert. Everybody's gonna come running to us when they find out about this thing."

"We'd better start gearing up production."

Clifton gave her a look that told her she was missing something. "You got the money to hire another ten thousand Bills and Jills?"

"Ten thousand?"

"Every bank's gonna need a bunch of our machines," Clifton said. "Anyone who transfers money. Every ISP. Every—"

"ISPs?"

"Internet service provider."

"I know what an ISP is. Why would they need one of our machines? Our business plan targets financial institutions, not ISPs."

Clifton just looked at her. "You ever bought a book on Amazon?"

"All the time."

"And you never worried about typing in your Visa number?"

Keryn shook her head. "Everybody does it."

Clifton narrowed his eyes. "You do know that Internet traffic goes through about a bazillion unsecure computers on the way between you and Amazon?"

"Yes, but . . . everybody does it. That info gets encrypted, right?"

Keryn gasped. "What kind of encryption do Web browsers use?"

Clifton gave her a sardonic smile. "Every Web site in the world that does e-commerce uses something called Secure Sockets Layer. Which is just a fancy way of saying RSA encryption. And which we will soon demonstrate can be broken. So every ISP in the country is going to need to come to us to get their quantum encryption. Eventually, every business and every home user. We'll be a commodity."

Karen's heart started pounding. "That means we need a whole new business plan."

Clifton grinned. "Right, I talked to Grant about that this morning. If this thing flies, we'll be the only encryption game in town, and we aren't going to be able to meet the backlog without some *serious* venture-capital money. Which means we are going public real soon now and we'll be sitting on a market cap of a big pile of gigabucks."

Keryn was staring at him in horror. Something terrible had just occurred to her.

"You're looking a little green around the gills, sister. Chill, Keryn! Hey, this is *good*! We're gonna be rolling in green when this takes off. E-commerce moves like a hundred billion dollars a year. The banks and brokerages move trillions. And we'll be sitting there taking our cut."

"Not right away," Keryn said. "You already said we can't gear up that fast. It's going to be months before we can ramp production. In the meantime, everybody will know we've got this technology that makes it all . . ." She was too scared to finish the sentence.

"Makes it all naked as a jaybird," Clifton said. "I thought Grant went over all this on Saturday."

Keryn shook her head. "I didn't realize it went beyond the financial industry. We've been selling a few tens of our encryption units per year. I was thinking that would go up to thousands. You're talking . . ."

"Millions," Clifton said. "Eventually, hundreds of millions."

Keryn was sweating now. "What if it gets into the wrong hands?"

"It won't," Clifton said. "Here's what'll happen. We make a public demonstration. The Feds take it over on grounds of national security. But by then the cat's out of the bag and everybody knows

Big Brother can read their mail, so they switch over to using our encryption. We sell a bazillion machines, get huge economies of scale, and cut the price way low, grabbing market share before anybody else can move. We *talked* about all this, remember?"

"You didn't explain about the ISPs," Keryn said.

"I thought it was obvious."

"And what if somebody finds out about this before we make our public announcement?"

Clifton shook his head. "You mean like Big Brother? Won't happen. Rachel made her crucial discovery back in November. She didn't publish it. Didn't tell anybody at Caltech. Didn't tell her funding agency. She called her daddy, who told her to talk to Grant. The rest is history."

Keryn lowered her voice. "But what if somebody else finds out first? Think like a novelist for a minute. What if organized criminals found out we had this?"

Clifton gave her a sick smile. "I guess we'd have to call the Feddies in on them."

"Don't be an idiot." Keryn felt prickles of fear all over her body. "Before we picked up the phone, they'd kill you, me, Grant, Rachel, Dillon, for this. They'd kill their own mothers. If the crooks find out about this thing . . . we're dead. I mean, literally dead. Large-caliber-bullet-wounds-to-the-head dead. They could use it to rip off the whole world, and nobody would know until they had a few trillion sitting in Swiss bank accounts."

"I didn't think of that." A sheen of sweat appeared on Clifton's forehead. "Makes me wish we could just . . . get Rachel to forget how she made those qubits."

Keryn shook her head. "Grant would never let her do that. Once you know something, you can't unknow it."

Clifton swore softly. "So we've passed the Point of Know Return, is that it?"

"Something like that." Keryn shivered.

The CypherQuanta door burst open.

Keryn jumped and screamed.

"Relax, Earthling," Jill said.

"It is only us Martians." Bill stuck his fingers behind his head like an antenna.

Keryn fanned herself rapidly with her hand. "Sorry, BillJill. I just . . ."

"She was just telling me her latest ghost story and got herself all excited." Clifton studied them. "What brings you two geek-meisters outside in actual daylight?"

"Lunchtime," Bill and Jill said simultaneously.

Clifton looked at his watch. "Oh. Right. Well, don't let us keep you from your appointed rounds."

Keryn watched until Bill and Jill climbed into one of their Saturns and drove away.

Clifton stood up. "Okay, Lit-chick, I think you and I better go have a chat with the Grant Man. He's been paranoid about Uncle Sam finding out, but I don't think he ever considered the commercial appeal to Cousin Vinnie."

Keryn followed him into the building. Her head felt hollow and her skin prickled. She'd written three and a half novels, in which a total of six people got themselves killed and fifteen others narrowly escaped death. She'd often wondered what it was like to be in one of those thrillers. Now she knew.

And she wanted out.

Grant

Within half of an hour of hearing Keryn's fears, Grant was in the bio-lab, pacing back and forth while Keryn and Clifton explained the situation to Rachel and Dillon. This was horrible. The whole thing could blow up in his face. Everything he'd worked for could be taken away from him. An iron fist tightened on his chest.

". . . if organized criminals were to find out about this, we'd be dead," Keryn said.

Rachel's face went white. She was a great kid, and Grant had never meant to put her in danger.

Dillon stood up and his face showed no expression at all. "There is only one solution."

Grant didn't think he was going to like Dillon's solution. "What might that be, Dillon?"

Dillon took out his cell phone. "We need to talk to the FBI. If criminals get hold of this information, it would be a disaster. Nothing would be safe. The whole economy would stop. And an economy is driven by money flow, not by money. Once that flow stops, it can not simply restart. The world economy would collapse."

Grant stepped to Dillon's side and put his hand on the phone. "Dillon, listen. We're not going to call the Feds."

Dillon blinked. "We have to. This is too big for us."

Grant felt sweat running down his sides. He could not let Dillon call in the government. That would ruin everything.

Rachel edged up beside Grant and put her hand on Dillon's. "Give me the phone, okay, Dillon? Just for a minute while we talk."

Grant felt Dillon's hand spasm. His face didn't move a whisker, but he released the phone.

Rachel was wearing a brilliant pink silk blouse today. She slipped the phone inside it and smiled at Dillon. "Listen, the reason I left Caltech was to keep Big Brother from getting his claws in my research. I am not—"

"Big Brother?" Dillon said. "You mean the governing authorities? That is ridiculous. We have a free press. We have the Internet. The free flow of information is the best protection against a government dystopia."

Which was so naive it was pathetic, but Grant didn't want to say so. And anyway he had a hunch Rachel would be a whole lot more persuasive.

Rachel's eyes were glittering. "Dillon, use your head, will you? This technology is going to force people to go all the way with encryption. They'll have to use quantum encryption. They'll get their privacy back."

"Get it back?" Dillon looked skeptical. "What are you talking about? The government does not spy on people. It is a violation of the Fourth Amendment."

"The Fourth Amendment lets them spy on people if they get a warrant," Rachel said.

Dillon was shaking his head. "No, not even with a warrant. If people want privacy, they can use encryption. Until now, RSA encryption has been unbreakable."

"You know that for sure?" Rachel said. "You have a theorem that the factoring problem is NP-complete?"

"Well . . . no," Dillon said. "But it is widely believed."

Rachel gave a harsh laugh. "It's widely believed by gullibles. Before the RSA paper in 1977, it was 'widely believed' that asymmetric encryption was impossible. But you know what? It had already been invented four years earlier. By British intelligence. And they didn't tell a soul. Why not? Because they didn't want us proletarians to have good encryption. All intelligence agencies think alike—they deserve the best encryption, whereas we deserve the worst."

"I don't understand what you're talking about," Keryn said.

Rachel gave a thick sigh. "The British cryptology agency GCHQ discovered RSA encryption in 1973, but they kept it classified. They held it back until years after it was commonplace in the private sector, because they knew people could use it to shut out Big Brother. In 1997 they came clean. You want to know why? Because either their guys or our guys finally cracked the factorization problem. A lot of cypherpunks think so, anyway. The NSA has some of the world's best mathematicians, experts in number theory. If anybody knows a classical way to factor large numbers, it's them. They'd share it with the Brits, but nobody else."

"So . . . what's the problem, then?" Keryn asked. She looked at Grant. "If the NSA already knows how to factor big numbers, they can . . . Oh, I get it."

"They can read our mail," Rachel said. "They can spy on us. Everybody who uses RSA encryption thinks their secrets are safe, but they aren't. It's all an NSA con job."

Dillon looked very puzzled. "Rachel, how can you know this for sure? A great many mathematicians in academia have looked at factorization. None of them have solved it."

Rachel tapped Dillon lightly on the nose with her forefinger. "I can't know it for sure. It's plausible, but there's no way to prove it. So assume the opposite. Assume the NSA can't factor large numbers. If we go to the FBI for protection, they'll turn this over to the NSA and *then* they'll have the secret. And nobody else will know."

"But we could tell people," Dillon said.

Rachel shook her head. "Dillon, that is so absurd. The NSA would make us sign some kind of confidentiality statement. So they can prosecute us if we talk. And if they get really upset with us . . ."

She drew her finger across her throat.

Dillon's lip curled. "That is ridiculous. The U.S. government does not kill its own citizens."

Keryn came and put a hand on Dillon's shoulder. "Dillon, I'm not sure I'd want to bet my life on that."

"Dude, no way," Clifton said. "This nice government of ours could not care *less* if you die. They did all those syphilis experiments on that bunch of black guys in Alabama. You ever heard about that? Plus, they lied about those radiation experiments in Nevada."

"Not to mention they covered up the fact that Elvis is playing checkers with the aliens who landed in Roswell," Dillon said. "It says so in the National Enquirer, so it must be true."

"Be serious," Rachel said. "Dillon, I am not going to let the NSA get my bio-computer. I am not."

"She's right," Keryn said. "The NSA is bad news, Dillon."

"Dude, I'm with the ladies on this one." Clifton began pacing. "Grant, tell him we're not going to the Feds."

Grant coughed softly into his hand. "Dillon, listen. I'm not a conspiracy buff, but I'm cautious about the NSA. Clif and I talked about it this morning. We intend to do an end run on the Feds."

Dillon's eyes went blank. "A what?"

Grant sighed. Dillon could be a royal pain sometimes. "We can beat them at their own game. Here's what we're gonna do. You and Rachel finish this machine up as quick as you can. How much longer do you think it'll take?"

"By Saturday," Dillon said. "If we start testing Friday."

"Fine." Grant thumped Dillon on the shoulder. "Look, there are five people in the world who know about this thing, and we're all in this room. We're all at the same risk. If this secret gets out, we're Alpo and the bad guys are Clifford the Big Red Dog. So we better not talk—any of us. But we can all keep a secret for five days, right?"

Keryn nodded.

"Better believe it," Rachel said.

Clifton's face was so tight you could play a drum on it. "Of course."

"Right, Dillon?" Grant said. "You agree we can keep it quiet for five days?"

"Yes."

Grant felt the tension in his gut ease. "Good, so we test the machine, prove that we can factor a big number."

"And then?" Dillon kept his poker face.

"Then we hold a press conference. We bring in all the honchos and let 'em examine the instrument. We demo the thing factoring large numbers."

Dillon's eyes narrowed. "If the government is as evil as you say, then they will confiscate the machine."

Grant nodded. "Exactly. They take the machine, but then what happens? Then everybody in the world knows that Big Brother really *is* watching them, and they all beat a path to our door to buy the better mousetrap. That's just what we wanted, isn't it? CypherQuanta goes public, we all get filthy rich, and the world gets a decent level of encryption." Grant thumped Dillon on the shoulder. "Now explain to me the downside of that."

Dillon stood motionless, his eyes revealing the wheels turning in his brain. Grant held his breath. Dillon had to see the logic here. He was a smart guy. He had to see that this was the best solution. The only solution.

Finally Dillon nodded. "All right. Five days. If we do not have it working by then, I want us to go to the government."

Grant shook his head. "Nice try, Dillon, but no. You're the bottleneck in this process. You can just stall for five days and then force us to go to the Feds."

Dillon looked shocked. "Grant, I give you my word of honor that I will not stall. Before the Lord, I give you my word."

Which was just about as ironclad a guarantee as Grant could think of. Dillon's religion was more important to him than anything else.

"Five days," Grant said. "Everybody agree on that?"

Heads nodded all around.

Grant felt relief rush through his veins. He had just dodged a cannonball. "Okay, we'll let you get back to work, then. But everybody, remember one thing. This isn't just a business deal we're talking about here. If one syllable of this gets to the wrong ears, we're dead. All of us. Everybody clear on that?"

Everybody was.

"All right, then. Keryn, Clifton, let's get back to Cypher-Quanta." Grant herded them toward the door.

It was going to be a long five days.

CHAPTER
EIGHT

Dillon

By Tuesday afternoon Dillon felt as if he had been flogged. He and Rachel had worked until midnight in the lab on Monday, then come back in at 8:00 A.M. Now his back felt kinked and his brain felt muzzy.

Somebody pounded on the outside door of the bio-lab. Rachel went to answer it and came back with Clifton.

"Hey, Dream Teamers! What's the word on progress?"

Dillon stood up and stretched his aching back. "Actually, we are a little behind schedule. There was a problem with the hardware libraries. Rachel called the manufacturer, and they promised to get a patch to us by tomorrow."

Rachel put a hand on Dillon's shoulder and leaned on him. "It's what they call a 'known problem.' I asked them why they haven't fixed it yet, and they said it only happens when you pulse the machine at rates beyond the spec. Then they wanted to know details about our application and—"

"You didn't tell 'em, did you?" Clifton looked alarmed. "The Grant Man would have a kangaroo if you told them a word. Not to mention that we'd all die in a hail of bullets. Or whatever."

Rachel shook her head. "I told them we're working on a hand-held CAT scan at UCSD and we're gonna miss a deadline for the FDA if we don't get that patch by tomorrow, or Thursday at the latest. I also hinted that our device could double the installed base of NMR machines worldwide as soon as we get FDA approval."

Dillon felt his jaw tighten. It should never be necessary to use prevarication. Unfortunately, Rachel lived life by her own rules, and he had not been able to stop her.

Clifton pointed at the computer. "Can you show me where you're at?"

Dillon's cell phone rang. He checked the caller ID. Robert was calling again from Berkeley. Dillon stepped toward the door. "Excuse me, Clifton, but I need to take this call. My friend is getting married in August."

"Gotcha, dude." Clifton waved him out and sat down at the computer with Rachel.

Dillon stepped outside the bio-lab and opened his phone. "Hello, Robert. How are you?"

"Dillon! Sorry to call you while you're working." Robert's voice sounded wobbly.

"My reception is not very good," Dillon said. "Can you hear me?" He went to the outer door and stepped outside into the late afternoon sunlight.

"I hear you fine," Robert said. "I'm . . . kind of upset."

Dillon felt his stomach tighten. Robert must have had another fight with his fiancée. "Please tell me about it."

Robert spent the next fifteen minutes detailing his latest crisis. For the hundredth time Dillon wondered why people ever got married. It only led to fighting and unpleasantness. Marriage was il-logical.

Finally, Robert finished.

"Have you talked to your priest?" Dillon said. "Ask Sarah to go with you to see your priest."

"She said she'd go see him with me in the morning," Robert said.

"The Lord works all things together for good," Dillon said.

A long silence.

"So did you get that Bank of America thing resolved?" Robert asked. "They can't just send back four machines after they passed the acceptance test, can they?"

Dillon had forgotten about Bank of America. "I . . . we have not gotten back to them on that issue."

"What?" Robert sounded shocked. "I thought that was the deal that put you over the top."

"There has . . . been a change of plans." Dillon looked around, suddenly feeling quite exposed standing outside in public.

"What are you talking about? Sunday you made it sound like a big deal. Now you guys are just going to politely drop it?"

"Robert, I am not able to talk about it." Dillon's heart began thumping. He hated prevaricating.

"What's wrong with your voice?" Robert said. "You sound sick or something."

Dillon felt like a thick rope was wrapped around his neck. "There is nothing wrong. I am working on a tight deadline and I need to get back to work. Please call me tomorrow and let me know if your priest can resolve things."

"Dillon, are you okay?"

Dillon looked around nervously. He had nothing to hide. Nothing except a trillion-dollar secret. He went back inside the building. "I am fine, Robert. I will call you tomorrow."

Clifton burst out of the bio-lab. "Dude, you rock! Rachel showed me your implementation of Shor's algorithm."

"Good-bye, Robert." Dillon hastily folded his phone and slipped it into his shirt pocket. "It is not really mine. I found it on the Web and improved it. But if we cannot solve the hardware problem, we will need another vendor."

"We don't have time for another vendor." Clifton pointed to his watch. "Four more days until we all turn into pumpkins. You'll be done, won't you?"

"Probably."

"Dude, I don't want a probably, I want a yes."

Dillon shrugged his shoulders. "Probably."

Clifton swore and went out, slamming the door behind him.

Clifton

The next day, Clifton burned the whole afternoon with Bill and Jill, going over the failed B of A machines. And there wasn't a thing wrong with them. Bank of America had lied to them.

Bill sat staring at the monitor. "Our data rates meet the spec, Clif." He ran his fingers through his blond crew cut. "They're blowing smoke up—"

Clifton's phone rang. He checked the number and saw that it was Hunter. "Hey, gotta take this outside. Okay, guys?" He strode toward the door without waiting to see if it was okay. On the third ring he flipped the phone open. "Clifton Potter."

"Clifton, *great* to get hold of you!" Hunter had a way of talking that made him sound like a long-lost cousin getting reunited after fifty years. "Are you in a place where we can talk?"

"Gimme about fifteen seconds and I will be." Clifton walked past his cubicle and out through the back door into the late afternoon sun. He continued to the far end of the parking lot. "Okay, I'm away from civilization. What's up?"

"I've been doing a few phone calls," Hunter said. "There's an interest over at Qualcomm."

"Oh." Clifton hadn't expected anything nearly this fast.

"Something wrong with Qualcomm?" Hunter asked. "They took a bit of a tumble way back when, but everybody did. I've got a few ears over there, and I think they're ready to take over the world."

Clifton didn't say anything.

"Hey, you still there?" Hunter said.

"Oh. Yeah, sorry."

"Listen, there's an opening at your level over there. Actually, it'd be a bit of a step up. Where you're at, you're a big fish in a dinky pond. Over at Q, you'd be a pretty big fish in a great big ocean. We're looking at maybe an eighty-percent pay raise, plus some equity options. The options aren't as fat as they were in the dot-com days, but they're real, not vapor. Can you do an interview over there on Friday?"

Clifton felt his heart racing. "I'm . . . kind of busy right now."

"You're busy." It wasn't quite a question, but it wasn't quite a statement.

"Yeah."

A short silence. "Okay, how about Saturday? They're really interested in you, but here's the problem. They were about to make an offer to a guy at Ericsson. It's kind of time-sensitive, but you've got some way innovative stuff in your background. They like that quantum encryption you've been doing."

"I don't think I can make it Saturday."

"Some sort of a crunch over there at CypherQuanta?"

Clifton wasn't quite sure what to say. Either answer was bound to draw more questions. "I can't really say."

Hunter gave a long sigh. "That kind of puts me in a bind. One of the execs who wants to interview you is taking a flight out to Japan Sunday morning. Are you really sure you can't meet with them? What about Thursday? If they scrunch up their schedule, can you make it tomorrow, say, fourish?"

Four was the normal time to talk with Dillon and Rachel. "Sorry, got an appointment then."

"I thought you said you were in a work crunch."

"That's what I mean. A meeting."

"You can't reschedule?"

"No." Clifton could feel every molecule of adrenaline in his body. "Look, it's not a big deal."

Hunter gave a sharp intake of breath that hissed over the line. "Did I not make myself clear? This is the big leagues, Clifton. Qualcomm is a mega-billion-bones company. How much sales revenue are you guys doing over there? Annual?"

"Two." Clifton felt like an idiot.

"You kidding me? Two billion?"

"Million."

Hunter didn't say a word.

An Amtrak train roared by. Clifton waited for it to pass. "Listen, Ted, I'll think about it and get back to you, okay?"

"You'll think about it. That's it, just think about it?"

"Yeah."

A pregnant pause. "Say, Clifton, you still got any stock you want to unload on me?"

"Sorry." Clifton snapped the phone shut and put it in his pocket. An eighty-percent raise. Maybe a few thousand shares of QCOM. It sounded great, but . . .

If the Dillonhead came through by Saturday, that would be chicken feed.

If.

K e r y n

Keryn leaned back in her ergonomically correct chair and rubbed her tired eyes. It was 10:00 P.M. She had been typing for two hours and she had managed 384 words. A page and a half.

Of shlock.

This was not Keryn Wills fiction, this was junk. She was now about twelve thousand words behind schedule and getting further behind every day. A little nagging voice was playing in her head. *Train wreck. You're headed for a train wreck on this one, Keryn. You're going to crash and burn, and no editor will ever buy one of your books again.*

Keryn took a deep breath and stood up and went out to check the front door. The dead bolt was in place. All the windows were locked. The back patio door was locked. The kitchen door was locked. Fine. All secure. No problem. It was Thursday night. Two more days and Dillon would be done doing his magic. And Keryn could quit looking over her shoulder. She *hated* this.

The phone rang.

Keryn jumped.

Smiley meowed loudly from the couch. Keryn gave him a shaky smile and went to check the caller ID. Mom and Dad. She scooped up the phone. "H-hello."

"Sweetheart, what's wrong?" Concern sugared Sunflower's voice.

"Nothing. Everything's fine."

"You don't sound fine, pumpkin." Rusty sounded a little drunk over the speakerphone. Good, if he was only a little.

"I'm fine."

"You aren't acting fine," Sunflower said. "You always screen calls this time of night. Tonight you picked up on the first ring. What's wrong?"

Keryn realized she wasn't going to get anywhere by lying. "I'm just . . . nervous, that's all."

"Well, if you weren't always slicing up people and leaving a trail of corpses in your books, you wouldn't be so jittery."

"It's not that. It's . . ." Keryn remembered something she'd read in the newspaper the other day. "It's just that . . . a woman was attacked the other day. About three blocks from here. Everybody in my neighborhood's a little antsy."

"What does that mean, attacked?" Sunflower said. "You mean raped, say raped. I hate those stupid euphemisms. Anyway, didn't you get a permit to carry pepper spray?"

"Pepper isn't foolproof." Keryn had written a novel in which that was a crucial point. She sat down beside Smiley and began stroking his soft fur. "Anyway, I'm just . . . nervous. What if somebody broke in while I was asleep?"

"So go stay with Kathii and Allen for a few days."

"I don't think so." Keryn closed her eyes and leaned her head back. If it was just her sister, Kathii, that'd be fine. Kathii never asked her about work. But her husband, Allen, was an electrical engineer at SAIC, and he always had a ton of questions about CypherQuanta. Not to be nosy, he was just friendly. And curious. Maybe a little jealous that Keryn was getting great wads of stock options for working half-time at a startup that just might IPO someday and just might pay off a few megabucks.

Keryn did not trust herself to face up to a barrage of Allen's questions about "how are things at CypherQuanta these days?" She wasn't good at evasion. If Allen guessed anything, it would just be horrible if he went back to SAIC tomorrow to speculate with his friends about what breakthrough Keryn couldn't talk about.

"I'm calling Kathii right now," Sunflower said.

"Mom, don't you dare!"

The line went dead.

Keryn wished just once she could find the backbone to stand up to Sunflower. What was wrong with her, anyway? She shouldn't just let Sunflower run over her.

Smiley yawned hugely. Keryn tickled his chin and slammed down the phone. "And how is Mama's big boy today?"

Smiley could have had a Ph.D. in relaxing, he was so good at it.

He rubbed the side of his head against Keryn's hand and looked up at her with his big round Paul Newman blue eyes. Keryn stroked his fur. Smiley was an enormous bicolor Ragdoll cat, twenty pounds of warm, soothing, relaxed pleasure. A massive purr rumbled through his body.

The phone rang again. Keryn ignored it.

Three rings later, the machine in her office picked up and invited the caller to leave a message.

"Keryn! Sunflower just called! Are you all right? Please pick up the phone, Keryn. I'm *frantic*. Allen, she's not answering. You'd better go over there and—"

Keryn picked up the phone. "Hi, Kathii. Sorry, I had Smiley on my lap, and it's hard to get to the phone with a sack of flour across your legs." She tickled Smiley and he meowed in cooperation.

Kathii had this oozy, eager-to-please voice that usually made Keryn feel glad she had a big sister who cared. Tonight it grated on her. "Listen, Keryn, can we come over and get you? It's *really* no trouble. We can have you stay over tonight. Jason and Jordan are in bed already, so you could bring your laptop and write. Really, we'd *love* to have you."

"Thanks, Kath, but no. I'm fine. You know how Sunflower is— always reading in things that aren't there."

Allen's voice came in on the extension. "Keryn, are you *sure* you're okay? I can be there in five minutes and pick you up. Bring Smiley. The boys love him."

"Th-thanks, Allen, that's really nice of you, but I'm fine. I'm already in my nightgown, and I'm not going anywhere tonight. I'll paint Smiley orange and black—anyone who tries to break in will think he's a tiger."

Kathii and Allen both laughed.

Keryn was pretty sure she had won.

"How's the book coming along?" Kathii asked.

"Fine. Just . . . great," Keryn said. "I'm a little behind, but you know, I'm getting all these really exciting ideas and just trying to get it all integrated in my head."

"Things still going hunky-dory at CypherQuanta?" Allen asked.

"Super."

"I'm having lunch with one of your investors tomorrow."

Keryn held her breath. "Um, really?"

"Yeah, one of the honchos over at Cymer. He's got quite a bit of money in Lost Angels. He's coming over to give a talk on some of the new lasers Cymer's using. Anyway, I've been thinking of cashing out some of my equity at SAIC and, you know, playing it somewhere with a little more action. I'm thinking of putting fifty K into Lost Angels and seeing what they can do. What do you think?"

Keryn held her breath. Allen wasn't probing, exactly. Not in an insider-trading kind of way. He was just nervous, that was all. He had socked away all of his money in SAIC stock during the crazy nineties, and that had done just fine, but he had missed the big run-up on all the highfliers. Of course, he'd also missed the bubble popping, but like everybody else who just said no, he was sure he should have said yes, that he would have cashed out at the peak. Now that the economy was turning up again, he was starting to look around for some of that greener grass he had missed the last time.

"Hey, are you still there?" Allen said.

"I'm here. It's just that I'm not allowed to talk about—" She stopped. Good heavens, what had she said?

"Oh." Allen's breathing sounded hoarse. "Sorry. I had no idea you were so close to doing an IPO."

"No, it's not that." Keryn bit her knuckle and wondered how to back out of this.

"Look, if you can't talk about it, I'll understand."

"Thanks. I really can't talk about it. And please don't mention it to anyone, all right? I mean, even the fact that I can't talk about it. Okay?"

"Sure, no problem. Whatever you say." Allen's voice sounded strangely light. Happy.

"I have no idea what you two are talking about," Kathii said.

"You don't want to know." Keryn opened her mouth and forced a yawn. "Listen, guys, thanks for your concern, but I'm fine and I need to hit the sack. I love you both. Kiss the boys for me, okay?"

"Love you!" Kathii said and hung up.

"Sleep well, and . . . thanks." Allen rang off.

Keryn put the phone down so hard that Smiley jumped down off the couch and raced into the bedroom.

Keryn got up and began pacing. "I'm an idiot. I am an idiot. I'm an *idiot.*"

However you sliced it, she had let the cat out of the bag. Majorly.

R a c h e l

At midnight on Friday, Rachel admitted to herself they weren't going to make it. Dillon had been hunched over the computer for nearly sixteen hours, his typing a steady drumbeat. Grant had called about fifteen times on his cell phone and asked in veiled terms if they were "there yet." They weren't. Keryn and Clifton had come by around 7:00 with pizza and drinks and tense small talk. Dillon had taken a few minutes to scarf some food and then zipped back into the bio-lab to continue typing flawless code.

The idiots at MagTec had set them back by two full days. Dillon was racing the clock, but even Mozart was human. He wasn't going to get it done tonight and he needed sleep.

Rachel stood behind him and put her hands on his shoulders. Thick knots stood out on either side of his neck. Rachel kneaded them gently. "Hey, Dillon?"

He continued tapping out source code, dictating it to himself in a low voice.

"Dillon?" She pressed harder.

Nothing.

She tightened her grip on his shoulders. "Dillon!"

"I am listening. You are distracting me." He continued typing.

She came around and stood beside him. "Let's break for the night. You've been at that thing since this morning. Let's go get some shut-eye."

"I could be done in another few hours." Dillon covered an enormous yawn. "We could be testing by three o'clock."

"You're going to give yourself a heart attack," she said. "What's the point? Let's go get some sleep, come back tomorrow, and finish it up."

Dillon looked irritated. "We had a plan. We were going to be testing by this morning. I want to stick to the plan."

She gave him an exasperated sigh. "So plans change. What's the big deal? You've done a miracle already. This is awesomely better than we had any right to expect. We'll be testing tomorrow and wrap things up Sunday . . . um, Monday."

"The plan"—Dillon put on his I'm-the-teacher look—"was to be finished tomorrow. We can do that, but I will need to work all night."

Rachel put both hands on her hips. "What is this nonsense? The plan was an artificial thing. We pulled a date out of our armpit. Saturday. So what's the problem if we slip till Monday?"

"We agreed to work until Saturday and then turn the device over to the NSA if we were not finished," Dillon said. "If I give it less than my best effort, Grant will accuse me of slacking and he will not agree to live by the agreement."

"Dillon, read my lips! We lost two days because that stinking vendor messed us up! Let's just take that two days and add it to our schedule."

Dillon shook his head. "No. We cannot."

Rachel was getting very tired of this stupidity. "Where do you get this *can't* business? Let's call Keryn and Grant and Clifton and tell them we need two more days. They'll give it to us."

Dillon just looked at her.

"Dillon, use your head. They'll give us two more days."

"I am sure they will," Dillon said. "But I will not."

"What do you mean, you won't?"

"When I make a plan, I stick to the plan."

"Is this part of your Asperger's thing?"

"Syndrome. Not thing, syndrome."

"Is it?"

Dillon nodded.

"I thought you people were supposed to be very rational, a bunch of Spocks running around," Rachel said. "Your continuing to work until you keel over, just to stick to the plan, is the most irrational thing I've ever heard."

Dillon looked stung.

She leaned on his shoulder and pointed at the screen. "Look, you're making spelling mistakes again in your comments. You're tired. Get some sleep. Or at least let me type. You tell me what to type and I'll do it."

He shook his head. "I need to do it myself."

"I'm a pretty competent programmer."

Dillon's eyes narrowed. "I prefer to do it my way."

"You like to control things, don't you?"

"I am very good at it."

Rachel was tired of this attitude thing Dillon had. "I bet you there's an error in that function you're writing."

"You bet me what?" Dillon said.

"If I'm right, we go home. If you're right, we stay till it's done."

Dillon reached up his hand.

Rachel shook it.

Dillon held down the Ctrl key and pressed the F7 key. The compiler ran through Dillon's source code. In the message window below, it showed the results: 102 errors.

Rachel dared to breathe.

Dillon double-clicked on the first error listing, and Visual C++ highlighted the error in the source code. He sucked in his breath. "That was stupid. Very stupid." He looked up at Rachel, and she saw red lines of fatigue spiderwebbing the whites of his eyes.

She began massaging his shoulders. "Look, let's just go home and rest a little. We can finish it tomorrow and—"

Rachel's cell phone rang. She checked the display, then flipped it open. "Hi, Grant."

Grant's voice sounded like ground glass on asphalt. "Hey, Rachel, I've got Clifton here on a three-way. How are you two doing?"

"We're shutting down for the night," Rachel said. "We're getting close."

"How close is close?" Clifton said.

"Here, talk to Dillon." Rachel handed him the phone.

He pressed it to his ear. "Grant . . . I am terribly sorry. I wanted to stay all night and work, but . . . I am losing efficiency." He paused, listening. "No, probably not. Rachel wants to extend our deadline to Monday, but that is not part—"

Dillon winced and pulled the phone a couple of inches from his ear. Rachel could hear Grant shouting. Dillon handed her back the phone.

Rachel held the phone in front of her and whistled through her teeth, a long shrill blast.

That shut Grant up. Rachel pressed the phone to her ear. Clifton's voice broke through. "Listen, dudes, let's stay calm. I say we extend to Monday. What say, Grant Man?"

"I guess I'm good with that," Grant said. "Dillon, you good with that?"

"I'm good with it, but Dillon isn't," Rachel said. "But listen, it doesn't matter. We're spinning our wheels right now and we are going home. Right, Dillon?"

He nodded, his lips pressed together into a thin white line.

Rachel rubbed her tired eyes. "We're out of here, guys. We can talk about extending the schedule when we're fresh. It's really close. We might get it done tomorrow. We were just about ready to begin testing, but we're falling-down-on-our-knees tired."

Dillon's eyes shot open and he shook his head.

Rachel turned around so she couldn't see him.

"Go home and get some sleep," Grant said. "Tell Dillon that's an order."

"Roger dodger," Rachel said. "Sleep tight, guys. We'll get there. Monday at the latest."

Grant and Clifton rang off. Rachel closed the phone and put it in her pocket. She turned to look at Dillon.

"We are not ready to begin testing," Dillon said. "You prevaricated. We still have another two hours before we can begin testing."

"Which means we're just about ready," Rachel came back, irritated. "Compared to how much time we've put in, we're there. Grant says to go home. That's an order, sez he."

Defeat washed across Dillon's face. He looked like his firstborn child had just been selected to be sacrificed to the volcano.

"Let's go," Rachel said. "Tomorrow's a big day."

"Big." Dillon's voice sounded thick and tight. "Very big."

Five minutes later Rachel was driving west on Miramar Road toward home, watching Dillon's taillights disappear to the east. She was so tired she could barely drive, but it was okay.

Like Scarlett said, tomorrow was another day. Matter of fact, since it was after midnight, today was another day. Or whatever.

Grant

Grant hung up the phone and stood staring out at the Pacific. Dillon was going to cause problems. He was picky on schedules. Not just picky. Boneheaded. When Dillon Richard made a schedule, he stuck to it or split a spleen trying. And if somebody else made him miss it, he could get downright hostile.

That was the downside of having a perfectionist like Dillon on the job. The upside was that Dillon was practically perfect. The only thing that could stop the guy was a Kryptonite cannonball. The foul-up by MagTec was just an act of God. It was beyond anybody's control. Tomorrow, they'd all gang up on Dillon and talk sense to him until he gave in. If they missed the deadline, they'd just extend it till Monday.

"Honey, are you coming to bed?"

Grant spun around to see Julia in her nightgown.

She gave him a pouty smile that had looked a lot better on her when she was on the short side of thirty. Now she was pressing thirty-five, and the pouting put little crow's-feet around her eyes that the Botox didn't quite erase. "It's after midnight, sweetheart."

"I'll be there in a minute." Grant turned back to stare out at the ocean.

"Who was that you were talking to?" Julia came up behind him and put her hands on his shoulders.

"Rachel."

Julia's hands froze. "Why is she calling you at midnight?"

"I called her, for crying out loud, and she's my niece, practically. I changed her diapers when she was a baby." Grant just did not want to deal with some stupid jealousy thing right now.

"What were you talking to her about at this hour?"

"Work."

"She works at midnight on a Friday night?"

Grant put his thick hands on Julia's. "Yes, she works at midnight on Friday. Matter of fact, she's working with Dillon Richard, and I think she's got a thing for him. You remember Dillon from the Christmas party?"

"How could I forget the three-hour conversation about the multiverse?" Julia giggled. "You can't be serious. What's she see in him? He's so boring."

Grant turned around. "He's also brilliant and handsome."

"But he's nothing like her."

"She's brilliant and beautiful."

Julia grimaced. "She's totally different from him."

Grant shrugged. "Opposites attract. He's yin and she's yang."

"And you think they're doing some hanky-panky?"

"I'm not going there," Grant said. "I don't care if they do the hokey-pokey, as long as they get that machine done before we go belly-up. We get that working and I'm gonna change my name to Trill."

She gave him a strange look. "Trill?"

"You know how Bill Gates is a billionaire? Ever think what he'd be worth if his mother had had the sense to name him Trill?"

"Rachel's machine is worth that much?"

"More. *If* they get it done before our money runs out."

Julia's face tensed. "And what if they don't?"

"Then . . . I'll have to make some layoffs and we'll lose the house and the Feds will get the technology and privacy in this country will go down the toilet. But other than that, no big deal."

"You can't just get a loan?"

Grant stuck his finger to his neck and slashed. "Right, let's just advertise to the whole world what we've got. Counting you, six people know about this, and that is five too many."

And if one of us lets it out to the wrong people, we all get sized for concrete boots.

CHAPTER
NINE

Dillon

Saturday morning Dillon checked his watch when he parked in front of the bio-lab. 10:28 A.M. He had arrived two minutes before his schedule. This made him feel uncomfortable. He had meant to arrive at 10:30, and now he had an additional two minutes that were not scheduled. He sat in his car impatiently tapping his fingers on the steering wheel.

Rachel's Miata was not yet in her parking spot. Dillon had found her unreliable in the matter of scheduling. Some days she came earlier than he did. Other days she came later. Therefore he had already quit giving her a schedule, since she would not meet it. He did not need her until later today anyway. When it came time to test the bio-computer, then he would need her.

Precisely at 10:30 Dillon got out of his car and locked it. He went up the stairs and tapped in the keypad combination and went into the outer office. Rachel's desk had begun to look messy again, but that was not his problem. If it were his own desk, he would be angry, but Rachel could do as she liked with her own workspace.

He went inside the bio-lab and immediately saw that something had changed. His chair was now facing away from the computer.

Dillon never left his chair like that. It reminded him of the story he had liked very much as a child, the Three Bears and Goldilocks. The story had a perfect three-fold structure: a beginning, a middle, and an end, each of which also had three parts having to do with the porridge, the chairs, and the beds, and each of which had three subparts having to do with Papa Bear, Mama Bear, and Baby Bear. It was a perfectly ordered story about a perfectly ordered world, and the only element of chaos was Goldilocks. The three bears easily detected her presence because she brought disorder to their world. Dillon liked Baby Bear, who epitomized the perfect middle ground. He understood that Mama Bear and Papa Bear represented the bounds of permissible behavior. He did not like Goldilocks at all. Goldilocks stood outside the bounds, and this was bad.

Somebody has been sitting in my *chair.*

Dillon knelt beside it, scanning for clues. He almost expected to find a long golden strand of hair, but of course that was absurd. The chair seat did not feel warm. He concluded that it had not been occupied in the past few minutes. Nor were there any other signs, such as food crumbs on the floor. After a careful inspection, Dillon carefully sat in the chair and turned to face the computer.

He pressed the three-key combination—the Ctrl, the Alt, and the Del keys. A log-in dialog appeared.

Dillon sucked in his breath. The dialog initialized itself with the username *rmeyers*. Last night he had been logged in on his own account, not Rachel's. Evidently, Rachel had come in earlier today and logged in. Therefore, she was the person who had left the chair in the wrong position.

Dillon typed in his own username and then typed his password, which was an eight-letter random sequence of characters, of which five were lowercase letters, two were uppercase letters, and one was a numeric digit. This was a very secure combination and could not be guessed by a hacker. He used this password only on this one machine, and he had never used it before. It was very safe.

Dillon double-clicked on two icons, one to start up Visual C++ and one to start SourceSafe. He reopened the workspace he had been working on last night when Rachel had forced him to go home. The files he had been working on automatically opened. The one that had generated 102 errors was the topmost item. Dillon pressed the Ctrl key and then F7.

The compiler started up, and after a few seconds the results appeared in the message window: *0 errors.*

Dillon leaned forward and stared at the screen.

He distinctly remembered that there had been 102 errors last night. One hundred and two was the maximum number of errors that Visual C++ would tolerate before stopping the compiler. It usually meant there was a blunder early in the file that had continuing ramifications throughout the file. Last night, he had seen the cause. It was a simple matter—he had forgotten to type a *#include* statement at the top of the file to import one of the interface files. An easy mistake to correct.

But he had not corrected it last night.

Therefore, Rachel must have done so. Dillon felt a surge of anxiety. Rachel might be a competent programmer. Then again, she might not. Either way, he did not want her making revisions in his code. When speed was so important, he needed to have the entire program clear in his own mind, and this he could not do if someone else was writing part of the code. He had made this clear to Rachel last Saturday.

Dillon pressed the Alt key and the Tab key. The active program switched to SourceSafe. He selected the folder representing the hardware library. A list of the files in that folder appeared in the display window. He pressed the column labeled *Date-Time.* The files sorted themselves in chronological order according to when they had last been changed, with the most recent first.

He saw at once that the file *MagTecNMRDriver.cpp* was at the top of the list. He clicked the right mouse button on this line and a contextual menu appeared. Dillon selected the *Show History* menu entry.

A dialog appeared showing when this file had last been worked on. It showed only three entries. Dillon had created the file on Tuesday and checked it in while still incomplete. He had checked it out again yesterday and checked it back in late last night when he finished.

The file had been checked out again at 2:14 A.M., but it was not checked out by *drichard*.

It had been checked out by *rmeyers*. Which meant Rachel must have done it, because nobody else would know her password in order to log on using her account.

Rage shot through Dillon's veins with such speed he felt dizzy for a moment. Rachel had argued with him and forced him to quit and go home. But it was all a charade. After the two of them had left, she had waited a couple of hours and come back.

She had come back to work on his code secretly. Why?

Dillon selected Version 2 and Version 3 together and then clicked on the Diff button. A window popped up showing the differences between the two files. New lines were marked in red. Dillon saw that Rachel had inserted a *#include* statement to fix the first problem. But there were several other changes. He felt his cheeks burning. He had made a number of elementary errors in his coding. He must have been quite exhausted. Rachel had corrected each one. However, she had not revised any comments, and this was annoying. Now the comments did not match the code. This was bad coding practice and would lead to maintenance problems in the future.

And furthermore . . .

Dillon traced through the program logic and felt a deep ache in his chest. Rachel had made some changes that broke the logic or violated encapsulation. The program compiled, but it would not work correctly. This was inexcusable. It was obvious that Rachel did not know what she was doing, that she was simply guessing. The worst sort of programming. It made him feel sick, to see Rachel ruining the deep beauty of his program.

Somebody pounded on the outside door. Dillon stood up and went to open the door. Clifton Potter was waiting outside. "Dude! Sorry to bother you, but—"

Dillon raised his hand. "I will not work with Rachel anymore."

"Um, what?" Clifton's eyebrows went up. Dillon had learned that this sometimes meant surprise, but it also meant other things depending on something called the social context. His counselor had given him a number of different social contexts and explained what raised eyebrows meant in each one, but Dillon had no time to parse the meaning of Clifton's eyebrows now.

Dillon pointed toward the bio-lab. "Rachel insisted that we should leave last night when I wanted to continue working. Then she came back later and made changes to the code. There is no possible honest explanation for this. Therefore, I do not intend to work with her anymore."

"Whoa, my man!" Clifton looked around. "Let's just go inside and try to sort this out. Sounds like there's some major biffosity afoot. Am I right?"

Dillon did not understand this question, but he stepped back and led Clifton into the bio-lab. He told him about the chair and showed him the changes in the source code, explaining why nearly all of Rachel's changes had actually made things worse, rather than better. Clifton had some skill in programming and he nodded as Dillon pointed out each error. "Biff." "Whoa, that's bonehead." "Bogus City."

When Dillon finished the litany, Clifton sat for a minute holding the end of his ponytail in his hand and staring at it. "What did Rachel say when you discovered this?"

Dillon shrugged. "She was not here when I came in. I have not talked to her yet."

"Dude, when did you get in, then?"

Dillon looked at his watch. "Twelve minutes ago."

Clifton's eyes narrowed. "You came in way later than normal."

"Today is Saturday."

Clifton stared at him. "I know. As in, this is our last day on the nominal schedule. I'd have thought you'd come in early."

"I go shooting on Saturday morning."

"Shooting?"

"I shoot target practice every Saturday morning at nine-thirty. One hundred rounds."

"You couldn't have maybe put it off till tomorrow?"

"I shoot on Saturday." Dillon did not understand why people did not see the value of making a schedule and keeping to it. When you were on schedule, then you felt calm and you did not make mistakes.

"Dillon Dude, listen, maybe a little flexibility would be good. That's why we put Rachel with you on this—"

"I will not work with Rachel anymore," Dillon said. "She did something dishonest."

Clifton stood up and began pacing. "Maybe she had a reason."

"There is no logical reason."

"She's not the most logical chick in the flock. Maybe she had an illogical reason."

Clifton's phone rang. He pulled it out and looked at it. "Hey, Dillon, 'scuse me but I'm gonna step out. Private call."

Dillon nodded and began working at undoing the damage Rachel had done. He did not care what Clifton said. He was not going to work with Rachel anymore.

C l i f t o n

Clifton stepped outside and walked toward his car. His phone rang again. He popped it open. "Hi, Ted, how are you, dude?"

"Clifton, I have three seriously demented Qualcomm honchos on my case." Hunter's voice was very tight. "Are you or are you not going to meet with them today?"

Clifton considered his options. Interviewing with Q wasn't an el slammo, but it was a great shot at a great company. If he passed on this one, Hunter would never talk to him again, and he'd probably pass word on to his headhunter buddies and none of them would give Clifton the time of day either. On the other hand, it was Crisis City here at CypherQuanta. There was a small chance that he could fix things. Small, but the payoff was *huge*. And Clifton wanted that payoff more than anything. It was high risk, high reward, and that was why a guy got into a startup in the first place. If this thing failed, he'd be out of a job, and maybe dead. But if he won . . . well, he'd pretty much own the world.

"Clifton, are you there? Hello?" Hunter sounded agitated.

"I'm here." Clifton took a deep breath and let it out slow. "Listen, Ted, I want you to know how much I appreciate the hoops you've been jumping through on my behalf."

Hunter didn't say anything, which meant he was seriously biffed about this.

Clifton saw no way out except straight ahead. "I wish I could say yes, but I have obligations I need to meet today. I'm just hoping the guys at Q understand that my loyalty is to my company for as long as I'm working with it. So I've got to say no for now, but I'd love to talk to them later, if that's possible."

"It isn't possible, and you are majorly making me look bad," Hunter said. "And it would kind of help if I had an excuse I could toss these guys, because I'm losing credibility. Has there been some sort of major change in your situation that would explain why you've gone all wobbly on me?"

"Oh, hey, listen, my boss just pulled into the parking lot. Gotta go," Clifton said. "Catch you later, okay?" He hung up without finding out if it was okay and put the phone in his pocket. He looked all around him again. Not a soul in sight. The pressure was just getting to him. He felt like somebody was watching all the time, and it was seriously creeping him out.

But there was no *time* for being creeped out. This was a royal biffosity, but for sure he could make things right. All he had to do was sit Dillon and Rachel down in the same room and straighten out the mess and get them back on track.

The sooner, the better.

CHAPTER

TEN

Rachel

Rachel's tires spun on the gravel at the side of the road. She set the brake, armed the alarm, and jumped out of her Miata, slamming the door behind her. Grant was already waiting at the top of the steps, his face a picture of grandfatherly concern.

Rachel stormed up the steps to him. She reached into her fanny pack and pulled out a Ziploc bag containing her bio-computer.

Grant's face went pale when he saw it, and he looked nervously around. "Let's get inside the house before you wave that around." He shepherded her through the massive oak door.

Rachel flounced onto the leather couch and stared out at the Pacific Ocean far below.

"Hey, Rachel, how about if you come back away from the window?" Grant suggested. "They can shine lasers on the glass and pick up what we're saying on the bounce-back signal."

Rachel followed him through the house to the pool area. It was an enormous house, completely surrounding the pool. Grant's wife, Julia, was lying out in the sun on a lounge chair. Rachel knew that she was about thirty years younger than Grant. Grant's first wife had left him for an older man, and Daddy thought that had really got

Grant's goat, to be left for some rich old coot. According to Daddy, Grant had snagged a young bimbo as a way of thumbing his nose at his ex. Rachel guessed Julia was about ten percent saline or silicone or whatever they used these days. She had that scorched-meat look to her skin that a lot of La Jolla people seemed to wear as a badge of honor.

Grant led Rachel to a pair of chairs next to Julia.

"Oh, hi, honey," Julia said in that phony saccharine voice of hers. She was always giving Rachel that weird look, like she thought Rachel was going to seduce Grant or something. As if.

"Hi, Aunt Julia." Rachel sat down in the chair and pretended to be relaxed. Inside, she was trembling with rage.

Grant sat between them. "Rachel, Julia knows all about the bio-computer, so anything you can say to me, you can say to her. Show me the vial."

Rachel took it out again. Most of the contents had leaked out. A few milliliters of it were left. "Dillon left this in the NMR machine upside down and it wasn't stoppered quite tight enough and most of it leaked out on the floor."

"Couldn't you sop it up somehow?" Grant asked.

"There's a slight tilt in the floor. Liquids flow right to the drain," Rachel said. "It's a safety feature."

Grant held it up to the light. "Is this going to be enough to run the tests?"

Rachel shook her head. "I don't think so. I synthesized enough to give a decent signal and no more." Which wasn't strictly true, but that was none of Uncle Grant's business. She had another vial in her apartment as insurance, but she wasn't going to tell anyone about that until she got this resolved.

"And you're sure Dillon spilled it?" Julia said.

Rachel gave an impatient sigh. "There were no signs of forced entry into the lab when I went in this morning. Dillon wasn't there, but I saw that someone had logged on to the computer using my account and was working on the NMR machine. I looked inside and found this. Then I checked the safe where this is supposed to be kept, and it was empty. There are three people in the world who know the combination to the lab. Me, Dillon, and you, Uncle Grant. And I know you didn't go there in the middle of the night."

Grant's face looked pale and moist. "Bet your cookies I didn't. I went to bed after we called you last night."

"I know Dillon did it," Rachel said. "I didn't do it and you didn't do it, so according to Sherlock, that leaves Dillon. And it's real suspicious that he wasn't in when I got there. He was the one foaming at the mouth last night about working till we got it done."

"When did you go in?" Grant asked.

"Ten o'clock," Rachel said. "Maybe a little after."

Grant looked at his watch. "Dillon goes shooting every Saturday morning at nine-thirty."

"Shooting?" Rachel felt her pulse ratchet up. Guns were for . . . criminals. Violent people.

"Right, shooting. He's kind of a gun freak. You know, some Asperger people are weird about trains. They can tell you everything you were ever afraid to ask about trains. They memorize schedules. They obsess on every mechanical detail. Dillon's that way about guns."

Julia gave a nasty smile. "Whatever you do, don't ask Dillon about nine-millimeter pistols at a party. He's even worse about that than the multiverse."

Rachel didn't care about that, but she couldn't imagine why Dillon would take time out of an impossible schedule to go *shooting*. "You're telling me he's shooting while we're trying to get this project done?"

Grant didn't look perturbed. "Listen, Rachel, Dillon is a very weird bird. Yes, he goes shooting every Saturday morning at nine-thirty. He arrives exactly the same time every week, shoots exactly a hundred bullets, and then goes home. It's one of the things in his life that has some order to it. No matter how busy he is, he goes shooting on Saturday."

"And to church on Sunday," Rachel said. "He's some kind of a fanatic."

"He has a brilliant obsessive mind," Grant said. "It takes all kinds, and he's one of the kinds it takes all of. He doesn't think like you and me. In fact, he thinks so far outside the box, he might be in a different universe. But what I care about is that he gets results."

Rachel held up the bio-computer. "Excuse me, but he just waxed six months of my work. That's not the kind of results I want."

Julia looked as if she was going to throw up. An activity she probably had some practice in, judging by her thin, thin waist.

Grant was sweating now. "Listen, innocent until proven guilty, right?"

Rachel leaned forward and let all the fury in her body funnel into her voice. "I don't think you're getting this. We already proved Dillon's guilty. You didn't do it and I didn't do it. Dillon's the only other possibility."

"It couldn't be somebody else?" Julia said. "Maybe somebody else knows the combination to the lab, somehow?"

"And that somebody magically knows my password?" Rachel said. "Dillon knows my password. Even Uncle Grant doesn't know that. So it's Dillon or me, and I didn't do it."

Grant took out his cell phone. "Okay, let's not panic. We need a meeting of the minds. I'm calling Clifton right now, and then—" He swore softly under his breath. "I'm getting shunted through to voice mail. He must be on the line." Grant waited a minute, then left Clifton a message to call back right away. He punched in another number and waited. "Hello, Dillon? I need to see you right away. Where are you?"

Grant listened for a couple of minutes, and his face showed a curious mixture. Surprise. Shock. Puzzlement. "Okay, Dillon, let's not talk about this anymore over the phone. I get the picture, but it's an insecure medium. You and Clifton just sit tight. Rachel and I will be over as quick as we can get there. Do me a favor—call Keryn and have her meet us over there, okay? She needs to be in on this."

Grant hung up and put the phone in the geeky little plastic holster he wore on his belt. He narrowed his eyes and studied Rachel.

"Is something wrong?" she said.

"Real wrong," he said. "More wrong than I want to think about."

Rachel felt her belly tighten into a hard knot. "What is it?"

Grant stood up. "He couldn't say much over the phone, but he did tell me he doesn't want to work with you anymore and that's final."

"Final?" Rachel's voice came out in a squeak.

Grant's lips were white. "And by the way, when Dillon says something is final, it's . . . final."

K e r y n

Keryn paced back and forth in the bio-lab and listened while Dillon explained the whole thing. Clifton kept walking out every two minutes to see if Grant and Rachel had arrived yet. None of it made any sense to Keryn. Why would Rachel send Dillon packing at midnight, then turn around and come back two hours later? What could Rachel expect to do that Dillon couldn't?

Clifton burst in. "Dude, they're here." He put a hand on Dillon's arm. "Listen, buddy, let's just stay calm, okay? I bet there's a rational explanation for it all. Let's give Rachel a chance to explain what she did."

Dillon's face was an unreadable mask.

Keryn had never felt so scared. This was not the *time* for Dillon to go getting principled on them. Time was critical. They needed to just move on and finish the software. A secret this big was too hard to keep under control. And once it got out . . . they'd have no choice but to go to the Feds.

The outer door opened, and then the inner door. Grant strode in, his face gray with determination. Keryn thought he didn't look healthy. Then she saw Rachel, and fear kicked her hard in the gut.

Rachel looked furious. She fumbled in her fanny pack and pulled out a Ziploc bag.

Dillon stared at it with a blank expression. "That is supposed to stay in the safe."

"No kidding," Rachel said. "Is there any particular reason you were testing it in the NMR machine this morning?"

Dillon looked like she'd slapped him. "I was not testing it in the NMR machine."

Rachel pulled the vial out of the bag. "Excuse me, but there isn't any other interpretation of the facts. I came in this morning and—"

"And you interfered in my software," Dillon said. "What possible reason could you have for that?"

Rachel gawked at him. "Don't be stupid. I haven't got any reason to geek with your software. Look at this vial. You put it in the NMR *upside down*. Notice how much there is left? The rest leaked out. Do you have any idea how long it took to synthesize this? There is no excuse for this—"

Dillon stood up and his face looked like a mask. "I did not touch your bio-computer."

She put her hands on her hips. "You're lying. I didn't do it. Grant didn't do it. You're the only other option."

"I do not tell lies." Dillon's face had gone very red.

Rachel scowled up at him. "So you're saying I'm a liar? Or Grant is?"

Keryn wanted to find some way to make peace, but she didn't know how.

Dillon looked at Grant, then back at Rachel. "I do not believe Grant did it. I know I did not do it. Therefore, *you* must have. Furthermore, I have proof you tampered with my software."

"Proof?" Rachel spat out the word. "What proof? I didn't do anything with your software. I wouldn't know how."

"That much is obvious from the bumbling attempts you made to fix it." Dillon sat down in the chair and pulled up a program.

Keryn stepped closer. "Okay, explain all this in slow motion, would you? I'm still not following what happened."

Dillon explained in great detail how SourceSafe worked. It kept a record of all changes that were made to a program. Each time you wanted to work on a file, you had to "check it out" from SourceSafe. When you were finished working, you "checked it back in." SourceSafe kept a record of the changes between the two versions. And it showed who made each change.

One thing was very clear. Rachel had checked out the file at 2:14 A.M. and made some changes that allowed the file to "compile," whatever that meant. According to Dillon, the changes were wrong and had to be fixed again.

When Dillon finished explaining it all, Keryn turned to look at Rachel. She was sitting on a high lab stool at the wet bench with her hands folded across her chest.

Grant cleared his throat. "Um, Rachel, what about these changes here? You made those and—"

"I didn't make them." Rachel stuck her chin at Grant. "Somebody used my account to make those changes. But it wasn't me."

Dillon stood up. "Nobody can do that unless they know your

password. Who knows your password?"

Rachel jabbed a finger at him. "You do, and nobody else does. You're sitting there every time I log in to check e-mail. All you have to do is watch me type it in."

Dillon looked shocked. "You know I would never do that. It would not be honest."

Rachel got off her lab stool. "Oh, excuse me! I would have thought it was perfectly innocent, as compared to sneaking in here at two A.M., logging in under my account, making a bunch of changes under my name, and then playing games with my bio-computer and losing most of the sample."

"Two-fourteen." Dillon said.

"What?" Rachel's mouth hung open.

"It was 2:14 A.M., not two A.M." Dillon pointed at the time stamp. "It says so right here."

Rachel stomped her foot. "I don't *care* what time it was. My point is that spying on me while I type in my password is pretty innocent compared to doing all the rest of it. So don't give me this nonsense about how it wouldn't be honest."

"You are saying I did all that?" Dillon's eyes glowed with anger.

"And you're saying I did it," Rachel said. "Don't give me all that holy-holy stuff. I didn't do it and therefore you did."

Dillon's mouth set like granite. "I demand an apology."

Rachel held up the nearly empty vial. "I demand my computer back. I'm beginning to think it wasn't an accident. What if you stole it—drained it off into another vial and left me a little bit so it looked like an accident? Tough-guy Dillon, coming in to work all night. Sorry, but I'm not impressed."

Dillon turned his back on her.

Clifton stepped to his side. "Dude, listen, I think you're kind of overreacting."

Grant put a thick mitt on Rachel's shoulder. "Rachel, let's not forget why we're in this thing. Privacy for the world. Protection from Big Brother. This is a lot bigger than any of us. I think you two need to just lay this aside for the good of—"

Rachel froze him with a look.

Keryn was sweating now, and praying. *God, help me figure out something. Help me get them back on track.* "Um, guys, could we take a time-out for a couple hours?" She put a hand on Dillon's shoulder. "Clifton, why don't you and Dillon go grab lunch somewhere so you can talk? Grant, you can take Rachel home and do the same. Let's all just cool off and think about what this all means. We're sitting on a really valuable, really dangerous secret. Let's not blow it. We can meet back at CypherQuanta in a couple hours, all right?"

Grant nodded. "Good idea. We need to keep our eyes on the target, people."

Clifton wiped his hands on his T-shirt. "No kidding. Dillon Man, come on. Let's go chow and just talk things through with logic." He led Dillon out of the lab. Dillon looked back and Keryn saw a deep, deep fury in his eyes.

Grant waited a few minutes, until the sound of Clifton's engine had died away. "Come on, Rachel. I'll call Julia and she'll make some of her taco salad. You like that, right? Keryn, you want to come with us?"

Keryn shook her head. "I need to maintain neutrality here. I'll just . . . go home and talk to Smiley and clear my brain. There's got to be an answer."

All three of them went out together. Grant armed the alarm and then got into his car and drove off with Rachel.

Keryn sat in her car with her head on the steering wheel and wondered how she was going to get her novel done when her life was getting deeper and deeper into a story line she wanted desperately to get out of.

CHAPTER
ELEVEN

Dillon

Dillon sat with Clifton in one of the booths at Souplantation, a soup and salad buffet on Mira Mesa Boulevard. It was a very healthful place and on Saturday at lunchtime, it was a calming environment. On Saturday evenings, it was not calming. Dillon never came here on Saturday evenings.

Clifton took another bite of his pizza. "You've been hanging with Rachel an awful lot this week. Tell me what you think of her."

An image formed in Dillon's mind of himself and Rachel hanging together on a gallows. He did not think this was what Clifton meant, but he knew from experience that it was impossible to get a suitable explanation for Clifton's slang.

"I mean, I don't know the chick at all, hardly," Clifton said. "I'm just trying to get a line on her."

"She is very intelligent," Dillon said. "The bio-computer is extremely clever—a major advance. She is paranoid of the government."

"Hey, who isn't?" Clifton said. "With the technology now, they can spy on us and we'd never know."

Dillon shook his head. Such talk was silly. It was foolish to—

Dillon's cell phone rang. He took it out and examined the caller ID. Robert again. Dillon wanted very much to talk with Robert, but he also knew that he must not talk with Robert while he was upset. It would be unhelpful to Robert, and therefore it was illogical to talk with him now. He put the phone back in his shirt pocket.

"I mean, take that cell phone," Clifton said. "You got one of the new ones with GPS on it?"

Dillon nodded. It was a logical feature to have. If you had to call 9-1-1, the cell phone could help the dispatcher find you more quickly and accurately than if you tried to communicate your location verbally.

"So, what I'm saying is, Big Brother can tap into that and they know where you are at all times," Clifton said. "That's information, man. That's power. They could send out a drone to spy on you and you'd never know. They can tap your phone, steam open your letters, read your e-mail. Your whole life is like an open book to your friend, the government."

Be in submission to the governing authorities. "I have nothing to hide from the government," Dillon said.

"Well, it isn't just the government." Clifton took another bite of pizza. "Some fourteen-year-old kid could hack into the networks and . . . va-voom!—he gets your stuff. Steals your ID, or messes with your records, or takes pictures of you naked in the hot tub with your chick and puts them on the Web."

"I do not get in hot tubs naked with women."

Clifton grinned. "Well, maybe you'll get lucky with Rachel. I'll tell you, I wouldn't say no to her. She's a hot little number, isn't she?"

Dillon did not understand this at all. Rachel was not a number, nor was she hot. Therefore, this was some bit of slang that needed parsing, and he had no time for such nonsense. "But you have a girlfriend." Dillon had met her once at a Christmas party. She was a redhead with a mole on her left cheek and her name was Cynthia. Clifton lived with her in a condo east of Highway 5, in a district that called itself La Jolla but was technically part of University City.

"Hey, it's a figure of speech," Clifton said. "I'm just saying, Rachel's kind of cute." He studied Dillon for several seconds. "I would have thought you noticed that, man. Aren't you, like, ever *attracted* to women?"

Dillon did not know how to answer such a personal question. Of course he felt a physical attraction to good-looking women. Just because he was not a Normal, it did not mean that he failed to notice attractive features of women. But it was an embarrassment to speak of such matters.

Yes, he had noticed that Rachel was very attractive. She had a vivacious personality and was very intelligent. When he was around her, Dillon felt as if he were more *alive* than usual. Of course, this was a mere emotional observation. A person was either alive or not alive, and the quality of aliveness was neither enumerable nor divisible nor quantifiable. It was only an emotional reaction to her excellent personality. He had already had several interesting conversations with her on quantum mechanics, and she also believed in the many-universe interpretation. But she did not believe in God, and therefore Dillon was not interested in marrying her. So he felt free to be her friend in a way that he did not feel free with other women, such as . . .

Such as Keryn. Dillon often felt very awkward and shy around Keryn. She was attractive and modest and intelligent. She loved the Lord, and that was a good thing, although she went to a church Dillon did not approve of. Keryn did not make Dillon feel more alive when he was with her. She was not exuberant and vivacious like Rachel. But Dillon thought she had more depth to her character. She was reliable and kind and good, and he felt *calm* around her. *Calm* was not exactly the opposite of *alive*, and yet Keryn was very much the opposite of Rachel. Dillon felt happy when he was with Keryn.

"Dude, I didn't mean to, like, *intrude* or anything," Clifton said. "It's just, hey, haven't you ever been in love?"

Dillon shook his head. From what he had seen, love made people do very foolish things. And this was not merely his own observation, it was universally known to be true. Everyone could see when others made foolish errors of judgment. When a man left his wife and children for a fling with some young woman, all his friends could see that it was a tragic mistake, except he himself. Routinely, such men made extraordinary claims for the strength of their love for the girl. And just as routinely, within a year or two, they saw that they had made a blunder, but by then it was too late. Dillon had known many people who married obviously inappropriate partners on account of this mysterious thing called love. Soon enough, the love was gone and a messy divorce soon followed.

Love made people blind, deaf, mute.

Dillon was not interested in such a thing.

Not interested at all.

R a c h e l

Rachel could not remember ever being so angry at anyone. Dillon had stolen her bio-computer and then had the nerve to call *her* a liar. And Grant wasn't getting it.

". . . need to think of the endpoint of all this," Grant said. "Look, I know you and Dillon are kind of at loggerheads, but you need to just swallow your pride and work with him. Another couple days and we're done and the payoff will be huge. You know how many Miatas you can buy for a billion dollars, Rachel?"

Rachel stuffed in another forkful of taco salad. She couldn't talk with her mouth full, could she?

The phone rang. Julia went to answer it. Rachel kept chewing furiously.

Grant poured some more Diet Coke for her. "And a billion dollars will be chump change after we go public, Rachel. Maybe we'll hire Gates as our gardener, huh? We'll offer him a billion bucks a day to mow our lawn. Wouldn't that be a kick?"

Julia came back. "Grant, it's the people from RediChex again. They are getting *really* antsy because the direct deposits need to go out next Thursday, and that means money needs to be in the bank by then, and . . ." She pointed her thumb at Grant's office. "They're on the line."

Grant huffed into his office and shoved the door shut hard.

Julia sat down across from Rachel. She was still wearing her bikini, and her brick-red skin looked as rough as the corn chips in the salad. Rachel shivered. Some melanoma doctor was gonna put his kid through college someday on Julia's suntan.

"I almost left Grant a few years ago," Julia said.

Rachel washed down her mouthful with a swig of Coke. "Oh yeah?"

Julia looked back toward the office door and gave Rachel that conspiratorial I've-got-a-secret-for-just-us-girls kind of a look.

Rachel leaned forward. Julia was just a dumb bimbo, but scuttle-butt was scuttlebutt. "So, um, spill."

"People think I married him for his money," Julia said.

Well, obviously. Rachel took another drink of Coke, which covered up what was probably a very skeptical look on her face.

"And people think he married me for his trophy case." Julia's eyes were gleaming now, and Rachel saw a look of deep hurt inside her. "Another piece of La Jolla arm candy. Wife 2.0, the new and improved version."

Rachel had never had much sympathy for Bimbo Bambis. She put her hand on Julia's anyway. "That must have been hard."

"Then one night we were at a party and Grant had had a few. When it came time to leave, he couldn't find his car keys, and he insisted he'd given them to me." Julia's face went hard and cold. "I didn't have them, of course. I hadn't brought a purse, didn't have my keys, didn't have his."

Rachel, despite herself, felt some pity for Julia. She'd been in exactly that position a few times, only . . . she was usually the one who lost her keys. She was a little scatterbrained sometimes. That was why she got the Miata fitted with a combination keypad. That way, she never needed keys.

"Anyway, he couldn't find them, and he was a little plastered, and he made a scene." Julia closed her eyes. "By that time, the whole party was watching us. A lot of hoity-toity people who think they're richer than God. Anyway, Grant finally called me a dumb bim—" Julia's voice cracked. She took a deep breath. "A dumb bimbo."

Rachel found she could not breathe. Because she'd never wondered what it was like to be a vanity bride like Julia. Now she could imagine it. People always looking askance at you, measuring you against your thirty-years-older husband, giving you that pitying you-belong-in-diapers look.

"So I called a taxi and we went home," Julia said. "I didn't talk to him for three days, and then I called a lawyer. We have a prenup that gives me practically nothing if I jump out, but I'd had it."

Rachel knew this story must have a happy ending, but she couldn't imagine how. "So how. . . ? I mean . . ."

Julia smiled and opened her eyes. "The hosts of the party found Grant's keys down in the game room. He apparently dropped his keys while playing pool with the men. The maid found them in the crack of one of the chairs, and somebody put two and two together and called Grant."

Rachel narrowed her eyes. "And that's it? That's the whole story?"

Julia shook her head. "No, of course not. Because here's the point. When Grant found out he was wrong, he apologized to me. And he called up every single person at that party and told them he was a jackass and a fool and admitted that he'd been wrong and I was right and that he was wrong to call me a bimbo when I have a bachelor's degree in Cognitive Science and a master's in Russian Literature."

Rachel gaped at her. "You have a . . . what?" She put her hand over her mouth, embarrassed. "I'm sorry."

Julia smiled. "Appearances can be deceiving sometimes. Grant acts and talks gruff, but he's really a big teddy bear. I can read Dostoevsky and Tolstoy in Russian. And sometimes, even when people are in love, they say things they don't mean."

Rachel didn't say anything.

Julia gave her a sly look. "You like Dillon, don't you?"

Rachel sipped her Coke. "No."

"I think Keryn Wills has a thing for him too."

"She can have him." Rachel felt a lump the size of France in her throat.

Julia shrugged and put on an unconcerned look. "Okay, if you say so. Honestly, if you ask me, Keryn's a better fit, anyway. I think they'd be quite compatible. A nice little cottage somewhere, a white picket fence, a neatly mowed lawn, 2.1 kids, a minivan, two cats in the yard. Wouldn't they be happy together?"

Rachel mentally sliced Julia to ribbons with a light-saber.

Julia patted her hand. "But take it from me. People aren't always what they seem. Life is full of surprises, and there ain't no logic in love, honey—you can quote Dostoevsky on that one."

Rachel just looked at her.

"Just try to make up with him," Julia said. "What can it hurt?"

Grant came out of his office and his face looked tight, very tight. "Rachel, look, we have till Wednesday to pull this thing back together again. Do you wanna play ball or don't you?"

Rachel studied the two of them for a long moment, first Grant, then Julia. Finally, she stood up. "I'll play." She moved to the door and waited.

Grant and Julia were exchanging a look that Rachel couldn't begin to read, and she suddenly realized with a deep ache in her heart that she wanted something like that.

Even if it was with a guy who infuriated the guts out of her.

Keryn

Keryn sat on her couch with Smiley in her lap. She had named him after George Smiley, the famous spy in John le Carré's novels. Like his namesake, Smiley was short and very fat and had a truly pathetic love life. Unlike his fictitious counterpart, Smiley never took long walks in the rain.

Keryn ran her fingers through Smiley's long, soft fur. "Rachel says Dillon messed with her bio-computer. Dillon says he didn't, but he claims she made a bunch of changes to his software. Which she denies. It's a mess, Smiley, and we don't have time to figure it out and the whole company's coming unglued."

Smiley meowed and rolled over on his back.

Keryn petted his ruffly white belly. He batted at her hands with sheathed paws. She scratched between his ears. "Oooh, you love Mama, don't you?"

Smiley began purring in that deep rumble of his. All was well in this corner of the universe.

Except that it wasn't.

"Smiley, I realize you don't have any girlfriends, but you're a guy, so I need your advice. Dillon's hard to read. He's a really nice guy, and there's something . . . tender inside that heart of his, if I could only get at it. But he's a great poker player. I can't tell if he likes me, and I can't tell if he likes Rachel. What do you think about that?"

Smiley closed his eyes to flat slits and purred.

"Hey, I'd pay big money if Dillon would purr for me, just once. I was barely starting to get some traction with him when that little chocolate chip cookie butted in on us. It isn't fair, Smiley. She flaunts her itty-bitty little body at him and hangs all over him for fifteen hours a day, and I see him twice a week. I bet she doesn't like Shakespeare. I bet she doesn't read her Bible. She's just going to use him and lose him, and meanwhile, I'm left standing by to get the leftovers."

Smiley yawned hugely.

"I know. I'm boring." Keryn sighed deeply. "Just once in my life, maybe I should do something risky. Something crazy. Act a little more like Rachel. Think that would get Dillon's attention?"

Smiley began purring again.

"I hate to admit it, but I'm . . ." Keryn took a deep breath. "I'm almost glad they've had this big argument. Now he'll see what she really is—a flighty little flirt. And maybe he'll see me for what I really am. I'm calm and steady. Does that make sense, big boy?"

Smiley might have been asleep and he might have been awake. Keryn leaned over and sniffed the bunch of fresh daisies she'd cut from her backyard that morning. She pulled one out of the vase and stared at it idly. A childhood game came into her mind.

She plucked a petal. "He loves me."

Plucked another. "He loves me not."

One by one, she plucked the rest. "He loves me." Pluck. "He loves me not."

When she reached the last two, Keryn saw that she had gotten started on the wrong foot, and now she was doomed. Her heart felt like a brick inside her chest. "He loves me . . ." She pulled on one of the petals.

The other came out with it. Keryn stared at the two petals, stuck together in her hand. She shook the two, but they resolutely held fast. Smiley opened his eyes and looked up at her with all the love a cat could give. Which was not enough.

Keryn showed him the two petals. "Good news/bad news, Smiley. He loves me *and* he loves me not."

PART
TWO

Bridge Over Troubled Water

"Shor's algorithm is extraordinarily simple
and requires far more modest hardware than
would be needed for a universal quantum
computer. It is likely, therefore, that a
quantum factorization engine will be built
long before the full range of quantum
computations is technologically feasible."

DAVID DEUTSCH
The Fabric of Reality, p. 215

CHAPTER
TWELVE

Grant

When they were all inside his office, Grant shut the door and sat down at the round table where they'd all met last Saturday. He could not believe how far they had come in a week. Dillon had worked a miracle. Another couple days and they could put a wrap on this thing.

"Okay, listen." Grant looked around the table. On his left sat Dillon, then Clifton, then Keryn, then Rachel. "I know we all had a little misunderstanding this morning, but I want us to get past that and move on. We have a trillion-dollar opportunity in front of us, not to mention the chance to do a good deed for the world. So let's do it right."

An uneasy silence.

Grant hadn't expected this to be easy. Unfortunately, he wasn't very good at warm fuzzies. He looked at Dillon, whose face showed nothing. Rachel's was a war of conflicting emotions.

"Okay, Dillon, let's start with you," Grant said. "Rachel is sorry for anything she might have done, and—"

"I didn't do anything," Rachel said in a hiss.

Dillon's face was stone.

Grant put a hand on Rachel's shoulder. "Let's pretend like you did. And in exchange for that, Dillon is sorry for whatever he did."

"No."

Grant spun his head to look at Dillon.

Dillon looked perfectly calm, but a muscle was twitching in his cheek. "I did not put her bio-computer in that NMR machine."

Grant sighed. "Listen, I'm trying to mediate a peaceful—"

"With respect . . ." Dillon took a deep breath, as if he was trying to work up his courage. "I do not think . . ." He stopped, and something flickered across his face.

"Go ahead," Grant said. "I hardly ever kill employees anymore since they changed my medication."

Keryn and Clifton cracked smiles at that. Dillon seemed puzzled, as if trying to work his meaning out. Grant kept forgetting that Dillon didn't do irony.

"Uncle Grant, I think Dillon's saying that you're not exactly a neutral mediator." Rachel pressed her lips into a tight line. "And . . . maybe he's right."

Grant hadn't thought of that. Yeah, well, maybe they had a point. He'd known Rachel's daddy and uncles since grad school. She was like a daughter to him, and that didn't make him exactly objective, did it? "All right. That's fine. Somebody else needs to mediate, but it needs to be one of us five, are we agreed on that? Unless we want to let our secret out to one of our twelve hundred best friends."

Everybody nodded.

"Okay, fine. That means one of you two." Grant pointed to Clifton and Keryn. "Anyone got any objections to either of these?"

Keryn was looking a little pale. "Really, I think Clifton would be better at that."

Clifton shrugged. "Whatever. Dillon, you good with that?"

Dillon nodded.

Clifton looked to Rachel. "What about you, Rache? Want me to mediate this thing?"

Rachel's eyes narrowed to slits and she studied Clifton for several seconds. Grant figured she had to say yes. Julia had already picked up on something that Grant ought to have seen himself— namely, that both Keryn and Rachel were kind of sweet on Dillon.

No way in the world would Rachel let Keryn be the mediator.

Rachel shook her head. "If it's all the same to everyone else, I'd rather have Keryn."

Clifton shrugged. "No problem for me."

Grant saw Clifton's eyes flick down to Rachel's T-shirt, and he thought he could guess part of the reason. But it still didn't make sense. He pointed to Dillon. "Dillon, are you okay with Keryn mediating?"

Dillon as usual showed absolutely no emotion on his face. Grant wondered if he could maybe get Dillon some training in negotiation. The guy would be a killer if he could learn how to lie with a face like that.

"I like Keryn," he said.

Grant wondered if that meant what it sounded like. "Keryn, sounds like you're nominated."

Keryn hesitated, and Grant saw right away that she was going to refuse. Which didn't make sense. Furthermore, he could not afford to let her say no.

"Hey, time out." Grant made his hands into a T. "Folks, I want to have a chat with Keryn alone. Five minutes, okay?"

Clifton walked out looking puzzled. Dillon followed him, expressionless as always. Rachel went last, and when she looked back, Grant saw a knowing smile on her face. This did not make sense. It did not make sense at all.

Grant shut the door. "Okay, what's up, Keryn?"

Keryn pressed her hands against the sides of her head, as if doing so would squeeze out some thoughts onto the table. "I'm . . . really behind on my book. Mediating between those two is going to chew up a lot of time, and I'm a half-time employee."

Grant had been afraid it was going to be something *important*. "Listen, Keryn, not a big deal. Your book's due when?"

"The middle of August." Keryn's face looked tense. "I really needed to work on it today."

"Okay, fine. Two months." Grant took out a pen and clicked it a couple of times. "This is going to take a day or two, max."

"I wouldn't bet on it."

"Max." Grant put the pen down between them. "You patch up this little spat and I'll give you paid time off to work on your book until you're done. That sound fair?"

Keryn considered this for about five times longer than Grant would have expected. She had a look on her face as if she wanted to say something, but finally she sighed deeply and nodded. "Okay. I'll try. For a week. After that, it's over and I want the paid time off, success or no success."

Grant didn't know what to say to that. If they got this thing fixed fast, there was that trillion-dollar payday right down the road. If it dragged on for a week, there was not going to be enough left in the kitty to pay a chicken, much less Keryn.

"Deal," he said. "Just remember how much is riding on this, okay? But no pressure."

Keryn got up and went out of the office without saying anything.

Grant sat there feeling a little sick in his gut that he'd lied to her.

The only consolation was that he could tell by the way she'd looked at him that she hadn't told the truth, the whole truth, and nothing but the truth either.

Keryn

Keryn wanted to kick herself. Why, why, *why* hadn't she told Grant her real reason?

Because it sounded stupid and she didn't want to sound stupid, that was why. But she *was* stupid, and now she'd stepped into it with both feet. Rachel, the little vixen, had asked for Keryn to mediate because she believed that Keryn could sweet-talk Dillon to get concessions out of him, whereas she, Rachel, would be immune to all that. Furthermore, Rachel knew good and well that Keryn's intrinsic sense of fairness would make her bend over backward to keep her from steamrolling over Rachel.

Rachel had read the situation and chosen the battlefield for maximum advantage. Now Keryn had to figure out a way to resolve the situation with two strikes against her.

Rachel sat in one of the comfy leather chairs next to Grant's office. Dillon stood stolidly looking out the window. Clifton was looking at the display on his cell phone with a funny expression on his face.

Keryn had no idea what to do next. First, she had to talk to both Dillon and Rachel separately—find out what their nonnegotiables were—and then she had to bring them together and find common ground. It sounded simple, but if negotiations were that easy, the Israelis and Palestinians would have kissed and made up fifty years ago.

Keryn put a hand on Dillon's shoulder. "Do you have a coin?"

He reached into his pocket and took out a quarter. Rachel came over to join them.

Keryn put the coin on her thumb and flipped it in the air. "Heads or tails, Rachel?"

Rachel waited till the quarter reached its apex. "Tails."

It landed on the carpet. Heads.

Keryn picked it up and gave it back to Dillon. "I'll talk with you privately first, Dillon."

He put it in his pocket. "Did you know that in another universe, that came up tails? This whole episode will end differently in that universe."

Keryn led the way to her office and opened the door. "Wish them well. We're stuck in this universe."

Dillon followed her in and they sat down. Keryn had a clean desk, but her computer sat square in the middle, so she rolled her chair all the way around to the other side and sat down next to Dillon.

A big lump formed in her chest. She wanted to reach out and grab his hand. Stick a flag in his head that proclaimed him her possession. Or something. Instead, she just smiled and crossed her legs. "Dillon, we need to get you and Rachel back working together." *Right, that's the last thing I want you doing.* "So, um, I'm not very good at this, but . . . what will it take to get you going again?"

"She lied about me," Dillon said, and there was a note of pain in his voice. "I swear to you, Keryn, I did not tamper with her biocomputer. I did not."

Keryn believed him. Dillon did not tell lies. It was something to do with his Asperger's thing. Even bending the truth weirded him out. Telling a lie put a bend in his universe, and he couldn't stand having any lines that weren't straight lines.

Yet she couldn't see who else could have done it. There were exactly three people who knew the combination to that bio-lab. Dillon. Rachel. Grant. None of them made any sense as the suspect.

Keryn patted Dillon on the knee. "Okay, I believe you. I don't believe you tampered with it. But it couldn't be Rachel either."

"It had to be Rachel," Dillon said.

Keryn felt taken aback. "Um, why?"

"Because she is the only person who could have compiled the program, inserted the bio-computer into the NMR machine, and tried to calibrate the system."

Keryn stared at him. "How could you possibly know that?"

Dillon sighed. "Somebody logged on to Rachel's user account, *rmeyers*, using a password that only she knows. Only Rachel could have done this, unless she has an insecure password. The SourceSafe history shows that at 2:14 A.M. the user named *rmeyers* checked out a file and made several modifications to it. These were incorrect modifications, but this user succeeded in compiling the file and building an executable."

"A what?" Keryn was not following this completely and wished she knew more about software development.

"A program. There is an executable program on the hard drive of the system. It was created at 2:43 A.M. I saw the time stamp on it. Rachel created both a debug version and a release version."

"I have no idea what that means."

Dillon nodded. "My apologies. It is common to make two versions of software. One is optimized to run as fast as possible. This is called the release version. The other version is compiled with special information that lets a program execute it using a debugger. You can then step through the code one instruction at a time and verify that it works. Visual C++ allows you to manage a release and a debug version very easily. Rachel built both versions of the code."

"Did she . . . run them?"

Dillon folded both hands on his knee and stared at his knuckles unhappily. "The program writes a log file every time it runs. It includes a time stamp and the name of the user running the program, as well as a great deal of information to tell if anything went wrong. Rachel ran the release version first, at 2:46 A.M. It ran and failed in the calibration function."

"The what?"

"The computer needs to calibrate the NMR machine, scanning to find the exact resonant frequencies for all ten thousand qubits in the bio-computer."

"You don't know those already?"

Dillon shook his head. "The bio-computer is cleverly designed, but the resonant frequencies cannot be calculated theoretically. The only solution is to scan the frequency domain experimentally and find the resonant frequencies of every qubit. Then we save them in an xml file and the machine is calibrated."

Keryn felt like she was hearing a lecture in Greek. "Okay, I'm following about ten percent of this. So Rachel ran the program and. . . ?"

"It failed. Twice. The third time, she ran it in debug mode and it failed again, but she evidently realized in walking through the debugger that the errors would be too difficult for her to find. She does not understand the deep structure of the program, and she made several blunders."

Keryn compressed her lips. "Why do you think she did all this?"

"I am sure she was merely trying to help. She knew I was exhausted and that I would not agree to extend the schedule. I do not know why she refuses to accept responsibility. Presumably, she is embarrassed about causing the bio-computer to be lost."

"And you're sure it has to be her?" Keryn said. "What if somebody hacked her password?"

Dillon shook his head. "Hackers are not magicians. The password encryption algorithm cannot be broken by brute force unless Rachel chose some simple and obvious password, such as an English word or her name or her birthday. Assuming Rachel has a secure password, then it would not be possible for anyone to hack it."

Keryn decided she had learned enough. Everything pointed to Rachel. Method. A plausible motive. Plus the fact that nobody else had all the information needed to have done it. "Okay, Dillon, thanks for explaining everything. I think you've got enough evidence to convict. Now tell me this. What do you need in order to continue working on this project?"

"An apology," Dillon said. "She made a mistake. She left her bio-computer in the NMR machine and it leaked out. All this I can forgive. I have already forgiven it. But she also accused me of doing it myself and of lying about it." Dillon looked up and—almost—looked Keryn in the eye. "I have a good name, Keryn. I do not prevaricate. Rachel must apologize for falsely accusing me and for calling me a liar."

Keryn felt a rush of hope. She could get an apology. Maybe. Dillon had the evidence cold. She would discuss it all with Rachel. Not accusing. Just laying out the facts, all the while being empathetic and all that. She was a woman. She could do empathy. At some point, Rachel would break down crying. Or she'd quietly admit what she had done. Keryn would not lay any blame on her. It was all understandable, of course. The time pressure. The desire to help Dillon, who had clearly been exhausted last night. Keryn would calmly put her arm around the conniving little ... around the brokenhearted, tearful Rachel. Yes, that would be nice. Rachel, broken and repentant, admitting her guilt. Keryn would help her through that, get her back working with Dillon. No recriminations.

At least not until the machine was working and they were all billionaires. Then she'd lay it all out for Grant and leave the discipline to him. Grant was a fair man. He'd take care of it.

Keryn stood up and opened the door. "Thanks so much, Dillon. I think we're done for now. Maybe you could wait over there in one of those chairs? Rachel, I'm ready to talk with you."

CHAPTER
THIRTEEN

Rachel

Rachel sat down in one of the chairs in Keryn's office. She had expected Keryn to take a lot longer with Dillon. They'd been in the office for only about fifteen minutes. That was good. Keryn had probably laid it on the line for him—that because of him, they were all getting cheated out of gigabucks.

Keryn clicked the door softly shut, sat down beside Rachel, and patted her on the knee. "I'm sorry it's been such a stressful week for you."

That was a surprise. Rachel wasn't quite sure where Keryn was going with this. "So, um, what did Dillon say?"

Keryn gave her an easy smile. There was something behind that smile, and Rachel couldn't figure it out. "Rachel, I'd rather talk about you first, okay? Just kind of find out where you're at. Have you been sleeping okay this week?"

"Fine. I've been sleeping fine," Rachel said. "Dillon's the one doing all the hard work. I just sit there and give him information when he has a question. And I got on the horn to those idiots at MagTec and reamed them out pretty hard. They were giving us the runaround, and Dillon had other things to work on, so I leaned on them till they caved."

"And what happened last night?" Keryn's voice had a soft, almost dreamy quality to it.

Rachel thought she might get to like Keryn . . . eventually. She was different when it was just the two of them. "Dillon was starting to wear down. He's really been working too hard all week, but the guy is a machine, and I just let him. Until last night. Then he was making mistakes. Plus, I could see we weren't going to get it done. I wanted us to be fresh when we wrapped it. Know what I mean? One stupid mistake can cost you a lot of time. So I made him go home, and . . . I guess he didn't like that."

Keryn had been nodding and repeating "uh-huh" and "I see" empathetically throughout the explanation. She patted Rachel's hand gently. "Did you know that Dillon wrote the program so that it contains something called a log file?"

Rachel felt her pulse quicken a notch. This conversation was not going the way she had expected. "I guess that doesn't surprise me. He's kind of A.R., if you know what I mean."

"Dillon says that somebody logged on last night and got the program working, and then they tested it. He has log files for three different runs. Each of those failed."

And now Rachel saw it. The whole clever little trap Dillon had set for her. Which she was *not* going to fall into. She leaned back and folded her arms across her chest. "Tell me about that. Just the facts, ma'am."

Keryn smiled at that. "Right, Joe Friday. Okay, here's what Dillon told me." She talked for several minutes, spinning out the whole string of lies exactly as Dillon had laid them out for her. Rachel thought it was all clever. She couldn't understand the motivation, but it was clever. The whole thing was set up to make it look like Rachel had done it. But there was one thing Keryn didn't know.

". . . third time, the program was run in debug mode and it failed again." Keryn stopped for a moment and looked at Rachel with those big golden brown empathetic eyes of hers. Sweet, innocent Keryn was getting sucked in to something she was incompetent to understand.

Rachel sighed deeply. "And let me guess. I'm betting these log files show my username, just like the SourceSafe history files. Am I right?"

"Um, right." A hint of uncertainty clouded Keryn's eyes. "Do you have anything you want to tell me?"

"You write mysteries, right?" Rachel said.

"Well . . . yes." Keryn was beginning to look seriously confused.

"And you're familiar with the fact that clues often turn up that lead to false conclusions?"

A little understanding began to dawn in Keryn's eyes. "Yes, but . . . I have to say the evidence is pretty conclusive here. Wouldn't you agree?"

"That depends where you sit," Rachel said. "In your chair, with the facts you have, it looks like you've Sherlocked this puppy down to one suspect, right? You're thinking that I'm the only possible person who fits the clues?"

Keryn was clearly trying to keep her nonconfrontational mask in place. "Y-yes."

Rachel leaned forward and put a hand on Keryn's shoulder. "And as a mystery writer, you know that sometimes one new clue can change everything, right?"

Keryn's face turned a couple of shades paler. "Um . . . have you got a clue for me?"

Rachel nodded. "Two clues. Because, remember, we have two suspects besides me. We've got Dillon and we've got Grant. We three are the only people in the world who know the combination to get into the bio-lab. We are the only three suspects."

Keryn bit her lip. "I don't think Grant did it."

Rachel held up her index finger. "Clue number one. Grant is incompetent as a programmer. I don't think he could even write something in Visual Basic, much less Visual C++. If you set him down in front of that computer, he would not have the first clue how to compile the code, much less fix the errors. Furthermore, there's no way he could know my password to log on under my account."

"So basically, you're telling me Grant didn't do it." Keryn didn't look impressed.

"Right." Rachel smiled. "So it's either me or Dillon." She held up her second finger. "Clue number two. Dillon knows my password."

Keryn looked skeptical. "Dillon says he doesn't. But he did say you might possibly have an insecure password that maybe somebody could have hacked."

Rachel ought to have expected some stupid claim like that. "I don't have an insecure password. I can prove it for you." She grabbed a Post-it from Keryn's desk and wrote eight characters on it: *hraK7bwD*.

Keryn stared at it. "That's your password?"

"Yes, and I can prove it. We'll go over to the bio-lab right now and log on to my account using that password. It's a good, secure password. You can ask Clifton or Grant or anyone. Nobody could have hacked that. But I've logged in several times with Dillon sitting right beside me. I can't type capitals and digits very fast. He could easily have watched my fingers and memorized my password. Then the whole story could have happened exactly as he played it out for you, except that he did it, not me."

"So it's your word against his." Keryn looked terribly disappointed.

"Right, and here's the problem. You're familiar with the deconstructionists?"

"Yes. I did a term paper on deconstructionism. I think they have a point, but I don't go all the way with them."

Rachel nodded. "But you agree with the basic point that two people can read the same story and find two different truths in it?"

"I happen to believe there is such a thing as absolute truth."

Rachel wasn't going to go there. Keryn was wrong about that, but she didn't want to waste breath on it now. "Okay, two people can read the same story and, because of their differing backgrounds, viewpoints, worldviews—whatever—they can read the story differently. You agree with that, right? A white Christian reads *Uncle Tom's Cabin* and is awestruck by what a wonderful inspiration Uncle Tom is to forgive his oppressor. Whereas a Black Muslim reads it and is appalled by Uncle Tom's wretched subservient attitude that enabled the white man to keep him in bondage."

"I don't see where you're going with this." Keryn looked at her watch. "Dillon's going to be wondering what's taking so long."

"Here's my point," Rachel said. "You look at the evidence and you see that you have two suspects—Dillon and me. Whereas when I look at the evidence, viewing it through my own experience, which includes the fact that I was in my own bed last night from twelve-thirty until eight o'clock this morning, I can tell you that there is only one suspect—Dillon."

Keryn began sputtering. "But . . . but . . ."

Rachel put her hand up. "Listen, I don't care if you believe me or not. You've got your truth; I've got mine. I'm just saying that my truth is different from yours. My truth is grounded in my experience, which is something you can't share. You weren't in my room. You didn't see me sleeping. You can't know that I'm telling the truth. *But I can.* And my truth is that Dillon did all that stuff under my username. Why he did it, I don't know. You'd have to ask him. But I know I didn't do it."

"And what's his motive?" Keryn said. "You know how picky he is about telling the truth."

"Who knows?" Rachel said. "He didn't want to leave last night, but I made him leave. So I guess he got mad at me and came back to finish the job behind my back."

"But why would he lie about it?" Keryn said. "That's just . . . ridiculous."

"How should I know?" Rachel said. "Of course it's ridiculous. But I know two things for sure. Only two people in the world knew my password last night—me and Dillon. And I didn't come back to the lab. It's a syllogism to conclude that Dillon must have. I don't usually speculate on motives, but if you want one, maybe Dillon's all hot and bothered about not giving the bio-computer to Big Brother right away. But that's a wild guess, and I don't know for sure. Nobody can read minds. Dillon's totally unreadable. If he chose to lie, he could do it with a straight face, couldn't he?"

"I guess," Keryn said. "But he wouldn't."

"You can't possibly know that," Rachel said. "Everybody has secrets. I do. You do. Dillon probably does too."

Keryn looked like somebody had just removed all the oxygen from her environment. Rachel wondered what kind of a nerve she'd just hit. Was there more to Keryn than she'd guessed?

Keryn cleared her throat. "What . . . what will it take for you to, um, continue the work so we can all finish this project?"

Rachel folded her arms across her chest. "I want Dillon to admit he did it and explain why he tried to frame me."

"You don't want much, huh?" Keryn gave her a weak smile.

"Just that," Rachel said. "But it's nonnegotiable." She leaned back in her chair. She knew for a fact that Dillon had done it. Either Dillon would admit the truth or he wouldn't. At this point, Rachel didn't care. She had an extra vial of the bio-computer at home in a safe place. She didn't need Dillon Richard. She didn't need any of them. They needed her a whole lot more than she needed them, and that was a pretty good negotiating position, wasn't it?

Dillon

That evening in his apartment, Dillon inserted his USB flash drive into his personal laptop. It had been a very trying day. Very trying. They had all gone to the bio-lab and verified that Rachel had a secure password for her user account. This eliminated all but the two of them as suspects. But Dillon knew he had not done it, and Rachel insisted she had not. After several rounds of discussions, they had all agreed that they were not making progress and decided to go home.

Rachel had repeated her claim several times that Dillon was guilty. This infuriated Dillon. He wanted his good name back. He thought Keryn believed him, but he could not be sure. Clifton had said outright that he believed Dillon. Grant had not. That stung. Dillon had worked at CypherQuanta for four and a half years, and Grant had always trusted him. Grant had always treated him like a . . .

Dillon took a deep breath and blinked his eyes rapidly several times. This would not be a good time to think about his father. Not a good time at all. He stood up and took several deep breaths as his counselor had taught him. His vision clouded and his head felt dizzy and his heart was pounding. He closed his eyes and thought for a few minutes about the classification theorem for two-dimensional manifolds. It was a beautiful theorem, a very calming theorem. In a few minutes, he felt much better.

Then he remembered the way Grant had looked at him today. Pain stabbed at his heart. Until now, Grant had always treated him the way a father should treat a son. Not like . . .

Dillon's cell phone rang. It was Robert. "Hello, Robert. I am very sorry about not taking your call earlier. I was in a meeting."

"It's okay, buddy." Robert's voice sounded cheerful. "I wanted to tell you that we've talked to my priest again, and I think everything's going to be fine. She's doing a whole lot better, and I think it's resolved. Thanks for your concern and for listening."

"The Lord works all things together for good." Dillon felt very relieved. He had been worried that Sarah would change her mind and back out of the wedding. Women were unreliable. Very unreliable.

"So how are you doing?" Robert said. "I'm so sorry. Here I've been spilling my guts every day, and haven't even asked what's up with you."

Dillon did not like the mental image of Robert spilling his guts, but he knew this was just a figure of speech that Robert used frequently. It meant to explain your feelings to someone else. Dillon did not think he would ever be ready to do something like that. It seemed like a very hard thing. That was why people spoke of it in such violent terms. He walked out to his living room and sat down on his couch. "I am fine, but work is very busy right now."

"Got some new orders in, then?" Robert asked.

"No."

"Working on a new project?"

Dillon did not know how to answer this question. The true answer was yes. But now the project was stalled. Furthermore, Grant did not want anybody to know about the project. Dillon felt his fingers tightening on the phone. "I have been asked not to talk about it."

"Oh." Robert's voice had a peculiar tone to it.

Dillon could not parse its meaning, but he thought he might have offended Robert. "I am very sorry. I will be able to tell you more in a few weeks."

"I hope you're not going to spring it all on me at the wedding." Robert laughed. "Sorry, but I'll have other things on my mind then. Like the mystery of the female mind."

Dillon did not say anything to this. The female mind was something he would never understand. He decided to change the subject. "I am looking forward to seeing Patrick at the wedding." He liked Robert's older brother very much.

A long staticky silence. Finally, Robert said, "Patrick's not coming."

"Is he sick?" Dillon could not remember Patrick being sick very often.

"My folks won't let him come." Robert sounded upset. "You know how my dad is about taking him anywhere."

Dillon felt a sudden tightness in his throat. Patrick was a year older than Dillon, but he had the mind of a six-year-old. Dillon liked him very much. When they were young, none of the neighborhood children would play with either of them, so they often played together. That was how Dillon had become friends with Robert, who was eleven years younger than Dillon. Patrick was the kindest person in the world, and it was because of him that Dillon believed in God.

"So anyway, your folks are going to be there," Robert said. "And I was thinking maybe—"

"No." Dillon knew that Robert meant well, but the answer was still no.

"Just let me finish, okay?" Robert sounded edgy.

Dillon felt panic welling up inside his chest. He did not like this feeling. His counselor had explained that when he felt this sensation, he should calmly extricate himself from the situation. "Have a good evening, Robert."

"Hey, what are you doing?" Robert said.

"I am calmly extricating myself from the situation. I will talk to you later when I am calm." Dillon folded his phone and put it in his pocket. He felt very disturbed. He wished he could be like Patrick. Patrick did not get upset over such things. Patrick was the best person Dillon knew. It was not his fault that he was mentally retarded. To be retarded was not a shame. The only shame was when a family treated such things as a shame.

Dillon's heart was still beating rapidly. He went outside and locked his door and went for a walk and reviewed in his mind everything he knew about Weil's proof of Fermat's Last Theorem. The proof was very difficult and complicated, and Dillon had never been able to follow it beyond the first dozen pages. Today, he could not get past the first page.

When Dillon returned, he felt much calmer. He went into the second bedroom of his apartment, which he used as an office, and sat down. He had followed good procedure on Friday night, and now it would pay off. All of his files were backed up onto his USB flash drive. He could continue working here, bio-lab or no bio-lab. Sooner or later, Rachel would admit what she had done and take back her accusation against Dillon, and then they could continue working together.

It would take some extra time to write a hardware emulator to behave like the NMR machine. He need only make a new concrete subclass of his abstract interface driver class and reimplement the interface. But once he completed this task, he would be able to continue development without Rachel Meyers, without the bio-computer. All because he had followed good design procedures.

A deep sense of well-being settled over him. The man who followed good design procedures could be slowed down by bad fortune, but he could never be stopped completely. Grant would be very proud when he learned how well Dillon had designed the software.

Proud like a father.

CHAPTER

FOURTEEN

Clifton

Late Monday afternoon Clifton returned from the bio-lab and went straight to Grant's office. He shut the door and slumped into a chair at the round table. "Grant, it's looking real bogus between Dillon and Rachel. They are still stuck at Impasse City over at the bio-lab, and Keryn's out of ideas."

Grant's eyes looked huge and hollow, like a panda bear's. "Our bigger problem is cash flow. RediChex gave us till Wednesday to put some beans in for their bean counters. Which is two days from now, if you didn't notice."

Clifton did not know what else could go wrong in his life. Maybe he should have gone to that Qualcomm interview. Except that if there was a chance—any kind of a chance—to make this baby go, he had to try for it. High risk, high reward.

"Here's what I'm thinking," Grant said. "We've got no money for payroll. So we run a snap all-hands meeting Wednesday. We send out word at eleven, set the time for eleven-fifteen."

"Dude, whoa, whoa!" Clifton held up both hands. "When you call an all-hands meeting on fifteen minutes' notice, what does everybody automatically think?"

Grant gave him a dangerous smile. "Layoffs."

"Right. And you panic the troops." Clifton was feeling a big bad lump of lead in his gut. This was horrible and getting more horrible by the second.

"Panic can work for us," Grant said. "Look, think from their point of view. They come in wondering who's getting the ax. We lay out the grim news first—we can't make payroll. Then we tell 'em about our ace in the hole and they perk right up."

"We don't have an ace in the hole. Keryn is, like, striking out majorly." Clifton wondered if Grant was on some kind of medication that was biffing his brain.

"We'll tell them we have something in development that could make us all rich," Grant said.

Clifton shook his head. "Won't wash with the masses, Bossoroni. If we tell 'em that, we have to give details, and we can't do that. Too risky. And if we don't give details, they won't believe us."

Grant smiled. "They'll believe Dillon."

Clifton thought about that. Everybody knew Dillon was Mr. Clean. Back in December the company had paid a fifteen-thousand-dollar fine because the fire marshal had asked Dillon a question and he'd told the truth. People gave him a hard time for a month after that, but Dillon just told them he wasn't going to prevaricate for anyone, that he had to answer to the Lord, yada, yada. Dillon was the company dweebomatic, but one thing was for sure—if Dillon said he had seen the Pope playing poker with Satan, people would believe him. Dillon's word was gold.

"Here's the other thing." Grant leaned forward. "We promise no layoffs. Everyone gets paid in stock, at half the fair-market value. So they effectively get paid double. Plus, we tell them there's an 'event' coming soon that will enable us to go public. We won't say what that event is, but we trot out Dillon to say he's working on it, and—"

"But Dillon isn't working on it," Clifton said. "He's stuck dead in the water until Little Miss Hissy apologizes. Which she isn't—"

"He's working on it," Grant said.

Clifton stared at him. "What are you talking about? They're over in the bio-lab with Keryn right now, ignoring each other. Man, if you want an ice bath, go stand between those two for a few minutes. I say Keryn gets a medal when this is over."

"A medal's fine, but trust me. Dillon's working on it. He has a copy of the software on his machine at home and worked on it till midnight Saturday night. And he'll be at it again tonight."

Clifton stood up. "Hey, that would have been nice to know."

Grant leaned back in his chair. "I just found out at lunch. Dillon told Keryn this morning and she told me."

Clifton felt a surge of emotions. If the Dillon Man was still working on it, there was hope. Not much hope, but a little. But it still depended on getting Rachel back on board. Dillon could only take the software so far without having an actual factual bio-computer to test it on.

Grant stood up too. "We'll do the all-hands meeting Wednesday. Have Dillon here exactly on time, then get him out right away. I don't want people giving him the fifth degree. He's not that great at fibbing, case you hadn't noticed."

Clifton nodded and went out. The all-hands thing was a majorly bogus risk. But what choice did they have? They had no money for payroll. No way of getting money, no backers, no nothing. They couldn't even go spin some kind of fairy tale to the bank, because the only story they could tell was too hot for human ears. Another week of this and Clifton was going to have an aneurysm.

Which was starting to sound like an improvement.

Keryn

"You're going to tell them what?" Keryn's knees almost collapsed underneath her. It was Monday evening, and she was worn out after a long, horrible day of negotiations that had yielded precisely nothing.

Grant pointed to a lounge chair. "Have a seat before you fall in the pool." He turned his head. "Hey, Julia! I think Keryn needs a beer!"

"I don't need a beer." Keryn sat down. Her insides were feeling wobbly and she desperately wanted a long nap.

Julia came out with a bottle of Heineken and gave it to her. Keryn set it on the patio without looking at it. The smell made her feel weak, unbalanced.

"Anyway," Grant said, "my mind is made up. By the way, a few people asked where you were today. I told them you're busy solving a life-and-death puzzle that could change the world. Not my fault if they thought you were home working on your book, is it?"

Keryn gave him a flimsy smile. "Listen, it's dangerously close to fraud, to pay in stock when you know—"

"Repeat after me," Grant said. "Quote—this is a forward-looking statement as defined by the Private Securities Litigation Reform Act—unquote. Standard disclaimer. Nobody reads it, but it basically means—"

"—that you have no idea what you're talking about, but you're sure hoping real hard that things work out." Keryn closed her eyes and massaged her aching temples. This was crazy. This was beyond crazy.

Julia lay down on the lounge chair next to Keryn's. "Any luck with our dynamic duo?"

Keryn shook her head. "It's hopeless. I give up. I can't make them talk to each other. This is not going to work, so let's end it now. They just sit there in the lab and glare at each other. I talk to one. I talk to the other. They say the same things every time. No change."

"So . . . take a break," Julia said.

"What?" Keryn stared at her.

"Take tomorrow off." Julia put her arms behind her head and a sly smile crossed her face. "All three of you."

Grant was looking like he'd swallowed a cow. "Julia, how is that going to help? Every day counts here."

Julia massaged her long, lean calves. "Right now they're stuck in a rut. It's time for something a little . . . unorthodox. Keryn, when was the last time you went to the Del Mar Fair?"

Keryn shrugged. "I go with my sister and her family every year on the Fourth of July."

"Go tomorrow," Julia said. "Grant, go get Keryn some money so she can go to the fair."

Grant mumbled something and padded off into the house.

Keryn was shaking her head. "No, um, really. It's not much fun going alone. My sister can't go because Jason and Jordan have swimming on Tuesdays, and—"

"You aren't going alone," Julia said. "You're taking Dillon."

"Dillon?" Keryn laughed out loud. "That's about the last place in the world Dillon would want to go to. It's so . . . proletarian."

Grant came back with a hundred-dollar bill and handed it to Keryn.

Julia held up both hands like guns and pointed them at Keryn. "They're doing an exhibit of nineteenth-century guns at the fair. That'll get Dillon in the door."

Keryn thought about that. Dillon was a gun freak. He knew everything there was to know about guns. "Okay, so he'll go look at the guns. Is there some point to this?"

"Oh, I almost forgot. You'll need to exert your womanly charms on our boy." Julia winked at her. "If I'm not mistaken, you wouldn't mind a shot at him."

Keryn just stared at her. "My womanly *what*?"

Julia rolled her eyes. "Charms, sweetie. It's time you learned to flaunt what you got."

Keryn had never felt so insulted. "I'm not going to dress like a . . . bimbo."

"Trust me, it's fun to dress like a bimbo—as long as you know you're not," Julia said. "It's time you made a power play for Dillon."

Keryn turned to Grant. "Grant, no. This is silly. This is not going to help the company."

He shrugged. "Well, no offense, but . . . it might help *you*. What have you got to lose?"

Julia sat up and adjusted the straps on her bikini. "Oh, there's one other little thing."

Keryn glared at her. "If you think I'm going to do some sort of jiggle—"

"Do you like any of the rides at the fair?" Julia asked.

Keryn didn't. Mostly. "Well, there's the bumper cars. And . . . The HydroSlide. Jason and Jordan love that one."

Julia pursed her lips and thought for a minute. "Be at The HydroSlide exactly at noon with Dillon. Can you finagle that?"

"At noon? Why?"

"Just do it." Julia chucked Keryn under the chin. "And dress your bimbo best, sweetheart. Just once in your life, do something wild and risky, okay? I want some flouncing and jouncing. Now be a dear and call Dillon right now and invite him to go to the fair with you."

Something told Keryn this was going to be horrible, just horrible. She took out her cell phone, paged down to Dillon's number, stared at it for three or four thousand years, and pressed the Send button.

The phone rang twice, then picked up. "Hello, this is Dillon."

Keryn swallowed hard and then pasted a big smile on her face. She leaned forward as if she were meeting a million-dollar customer. "Hi, Dillon, it's Keryn. I was wondering if you'd like to go see that great gun exhibit at the Del Mar Fair with me tomorrow."

CHAPTER

FIFTEEN

Dillon

Dillon had never been to the Del Mar Fair. He had not realized the fair had anything interesting. But after Keryn called him last night, he had checked through the Fair Special section in the *Union-Tribune* and discovered she was right. They were having a remarkable display of guns from the 1860s through 1890s at the fair.

"Are you sure Grant will not be upset?" he asked Keryn.

"He insisted we go." She was busy slathering sunscreen on the bare parts of her body, of which there were several. Dillon had not realized she was quite so ... unbusinesslike in her life away from CypherQuanta. At work, she always wore attractive business suits. Today, she was wearing shorts and a tight shirt with a V-shaped neckline. Very immodest. Also very unsafe. The sunscreen would screen out UVB radiation, protecting her from sunburn if used properly at the correct intervals. But it would not protect against the UVA radiation, which caused melanoma. Very dangerous.

"Here's our ride!" Keryn seemed in high spirits. A double-decker red bus rolled to a stop in front of them. They had parked at a place called Horsepark, which was free, and which included a free bus ride to the fair. Keryn had said it would be fun. Dillon looked dubiously at the tall bus. It looked unsafe.

The line moved quickly. Dillon let Keryn get on the bus first, which turned out to be a mistake. She led the way up the steep circular stairway to the top deck. Dillon felt a rush of embarrassment. He had never noticed what attractive legs she had. He had not intended to look at her legs. Keryn would feel very bad if she knew he had been looking at her legs, even though it was an accident.

When they reached the top deck, Keryn stopped beside a seat bench. "You sit down first," she said. "Looking over the edge gives me the willies."

Dillon was not sure what willies were, but he slid into the seat. Keryn sat next to him, sitting closer than he had expected. A strange feeling was building in Dillon's stomach. A pleasant feeling, yet very disquieting. He pressed against the side of the bus to give her more room.

"Great day, isn't it?" Keryn said. "Blue skies, no June gloom, perfect breeze."

Dillon nodded, but he felt dizzy in his head. He was used to feeling calm around Keryn, but today he did not feel calm. He felt . . . the way Rachel made him feel when they first met. Fear gripped his heart. If he had realized this would happen, he would not have come.

The bus ride lasted for thirteen minutes. Dillon was almost panicky when they arrived. Keryn led the way down the aisle of the bus to the steep circular stairway. While following her down, Dillon discovered an interesting fact about V-shaped necklines he had not known before. As he stepped onto the sidewalk, he could feel his ears burning and was thankful for the cool breeze against his face.

At the gate Dillon learned he could not take his Swiss Army knife into the fair. A sign said that knives were a security risk. He waited in line to check it at the Will Call window while Keryn went to buy the tickets. The woman at the window took his knife and put it in an envelope. She smiled at him. "Nice tie you're wearing, sir."

Dillon was pleased that she liked it. It was a simple patterned blue tie that matched his gray wool pants nicely. He had noticed that nobody else was wearing a tie to the fair, which seemed very strange. He went back to join Keryn in line. When they went through a metal detector, Dillon had to take off his Italian leather belt and let a man run a wand over it, but they made it past the inspectors without any further problems.

As they went through the gate they met a man handing out programs from inside a cage that was being carried by a man dressed as Frankenstein. Dillon looked closely and saw there was only one man, not two. The legs of the man inside the cage were fake, and so was the upper body of the Frankenstein. The upper body of the man in the cage continued down into the legs of the Frankenstein. It was a clever costume and Dillon studied it for several minutes.

Finally, Keryn took his hand. "Come on, Dillon, you'll get double vision staring at that getup. Let's go look at those guns. It's already ten-fifteen."

Dillon followed her. They spent a very pleasant hour and a half looking at the guns. Dillon explained a number of interesting features of the guns to Keryn. He had never realized before just how much she liked guns. But it was logical that she should like them, because a mystery writer needed to know about such things.

At 11:45 Keryn suddenly told Dillon she was hungry. They went back out onto the mall, which had become very crowded. Dillon disliked crowds and felt grateful when Keryn took his hand and led the way through. She had a nice hand, and Dillon felt very warm inside his chest. It was a feeling he liked very much. He wanted to tell her so but decided it might not be appropriate.

They went past a number of garish food stands selling all kinds of outlandish foods. Fried Twinkies. Apple towers. Pan-fried bread. Roasted corn. Churros. A whole pig roasting on a spit. Hot dogs. Tacos. All of them looked highly unsanitary.

Dillon thought one of these might interest Keryn, but she looked at each of them and shook her head. "Let's keep moving!" she shouted above the racket. Dillon noticed that many of the women were dressed far more immodestly than Keryn. He did not see any men wearing wool pants or cotton button-down shirts or silk ties.

They passed a square red stand that said *Tickets* on one side and *Boletos* on the other. At last they came to a large area with many gambling games and carnival-type rides. There were dart games and many coin-pitching games. Dillon stopped to look at one of the basketball hoops. He saw that the hoop was smaller than regulation and was elliptical in shape, broader than it was deep. The geometry and physics would make it very hard to make a basket. The boy running the booth tossed the basketball to him. "Hey, Silk Tie! Take a shot for free?"

Dillon caught the basketball. Keryn laughed. "Throw it and let's go."

Dillon threw the ball. It missed both the hoop and the backboard.

"Close! Try again!" the boy yelled.

Keryn grabbed his hand and pulled. "Come on, I'm starving. I remember last year there was something I liked around that corner."

Dillon followed. They went past some shooting games. Dillon thought they looked ridiculously easy, but Keryn pulled on his arm with both hands. "Later!" she shouted over the din of bangs, shouts, basketballs, roller coasters, and blaring music. Dillon followed.

They turned a corner and Keryn squealed. "Oh! It's my favorite ride! Look, Dillon, have you ever ridden The HydroSlide?"

Dillon had not. He saw at once that it was a ride in which you were likely to get wet. It was not a good ride if you were wearing wool pants and polished leather shoes.

But Keryn had other ideas. She tugged on Dillon's hand and he followed. When they reached the ride, Keryn stopped and turned to Dillon. "Doesn't it look fun?"

Dillon did not think it looked fun, but he did not know how to say so nicely. "I thought you were hungry."

Keryn shrugged. "Last year they had some great . . . pizza near here. I don't see it. But would you like to ride on the—"

"Yoohoo!" A shrill voice rang out across the mall.

Dillon turned and saw Grant and his wife, Julia. Julia was waving at them frantically. "Keryn! Dillon! Come over here!"

Dillon had never imagined he would see Grant at the Del Mar Fair. Grant wore a huge T-shirt and a baggy pair of blue jeans and a large straw hat. Julia wore . . . very little. She was definitely going to get melanoma. Dillon had warned her about the dangers of excessive tanning at the first Christmas party CypherQuanta held, but she was apparently a slow learner.

Keryn pulled Dillon over to meet them. Julia's eyes were scanning Keryn up and down and she wore a very large smile. Dillon did not see what was funny about Keryn, but perhaps a large smile meant something different in this social context.

"Keryn darling, you look lovely," Julia said. "Doesn't she look lovely, Grant?"

Grant nodded. "Wonderful."

Julia whipped out a camera and took a picture of Dillon and Keryn.

Dillon realized that Keryn was still holding on to his hand. He felt self-conscious.

Julia was staring at their hands and smiling. "Dillon, so nice to see you again. And . . . oh my, here she comes with our tickets." Julia pointed past Dillon.

Dillon turned around and his heart made a funny thumping motion in his chest.

Rachel Meyers was coming toward them. She was wearing sandals and a very short pair of orange shorts and a pink top that did not reach to her navel. She held two sheets of red tickets in her hands.

She was not smiling.

Rachel

Rachel ignored Dillon and Keryn and handed the tickets to Grant. "Come on, let's go on some rides!"

"Rachel, look who came to the fair," Julia said. "Keryn darling, why didn't you tell us you two were coming? We could have all driven together!"

Which was ridiculous. Rachel would not have come in the same car with Dillon. She tugged on Grant's arm. "Let's go ride something scary." She pointed to a ride labeled The Hard Rock. It was one of those twirly things that spun you around on four different axes. "That one looks fun."

"I'm game," Grant said. "Who wants to ride on The Hard Rock?"

Dillon's eyes were shining with horror. Keryn looked queasy.

Julia put her hands on her hips. "Dear, not that one. With your neck the way it is—"

"There's nothing wrong with my neck," Grant said. "How many tickets do we need?"

Rachel squinted at the sign. "Four tickets per rider."

Grant tore eight tiny red squares from the sheet. "We're going. Julia, hold my hat."

Julia put her arms across her chest. "Grant, act like an adult. If that thing throws your neck out, at your age, you'll be—"

"I'm going." Irritation knotted Grant's bushy white eyebrows. "Keryn, can you hold my hat while I—"

"Keryn, he's not going." There was a warning note in Julia's voice that said very clearly that Grant might be Keryn's boss, but Julia was Grant's.

Grant glared at Julia. "I'm going on that ride. Dillon, hold my hat."

Dillon reached out to take it.

Julia knocked it on the ground. "No, Grant. I won't have it. You're always going on about that trick knee of yours, but your neck's in worse shape. Look, there's a warning sign on that horrible ride about neck and back problems. You are not going."

Grant reached down and scooped up the hat. When he spoke, his voice was taut with anger. "Come on, Rachel, let's go get on the ride. I'll leave my hat inside the gate and—"

Julia's hand snaked out and grabbed the hat. She threw it on the ground and stomped on it.

Rachel felt embarrassed to be seeing this. She'd known Uncle Grant a long time and had never seen anyone treat him this way. Aunt Julia was just being an absolute *muggle* today.

Grant swore loudly at Julia. He seized Rachel's hand. "Let's go get in line."

"Rachel, don't you dare!" Julia shouted.

Rachel felt horrible. This was ridiculous. She let Grant drag her into line. He glared viciously ahead at the ride.

Rachel looked back and saw Aunt Julia stomping away. Keryn hurried over to the line. "Um, Grant?"

He grunted something but otherwise ignored her.

Keryn cleared her throat. "Julia said she's leaving, and it looks like she's got the car keys."

Grant swore again. He glared at The Hard Rock for several seconds, then stepped out of line. "Wait for me here, Rachel. Julia gets like this sometimes. I'll go cool her down and be back in a minute." He hurried away, leaving Rachel staring at him, wondering if she should go after him. She decided this was something they'd have to work out by themselves.

It was exactly this sort of idiocy that told Rachel she had made the right decision years ago—she didn't ever want to get married.

Keryn shook her head. "That was really silly, wasn't it?"

Rachel nodded. "Crazy."

"Who's next for The Hard Rock?" shouted the ticket taker.

Rachel turned to look. The ride had ended, and a couple of dozen dazed passengers were staggering toward the exits. Rachel stepped out of line. She'd have to wait for Uncle Grant to get back. Because there was no *way* she was riding that thing alone.

Dillon was still standing back where Grant and Julia had had the fight. Keryn took Rachel's arm. "Um, Dillon looks a little lonely over there, doesn't he?"

Rachel took a good look at him. Black polished leather shoes. Gray wool pants. A white shirt and tie. She giggled. "He really came dressed to get down and dirty, didn't he?"

Keryn gave her a helpless shrug. "That's Dillon. He wanted to look at the gun exhibit."

Rachel gave Keryn the once-over. Twice. "You really came dressed to kill. I had no idea you had anything so . . . provocative."

"Oh, there's a lot about me you don't know," Keryn said in an airy voice. "Come on. We'd better rescue Dillon." She began striding toward him.

A couple of barkers were talking to Dillon, pointing toward their shooting games. Rachel hurried after Keryn. She noticed that Keryn was putting a lot of flounce in her step. Was she making a play for Dillon? That was crazy. Dillon was immune to that kind of thing. Wasn't he? Rachel ran to catch up.

"Uh-oh," Keryn said. "I think they got him."

Dillon was sitting down at a shooting booth. Rachel felt disgusted. She hated guns and everything to do with them.

By the time they reached the booth, Dillon had already paid. It was a competition, where several people tried to shoot a set of targets. Whoever finished first won a prize. Dillon was seated next to a couple of small girls. Keryn went to stand right behind Dillon, snuggling up to him. Rachel didn't know whether to join them or not, so she took a position behind Keryn's right shoulder.

All of a sudden, the competitors all began shooting at once. Rachel had a hard time following it, but Dillon was calmly firing at targets in a steady rhythm, aim and shoot, aim and shoot.

And then it was over and Dillon had won and Keryn was hugging him—in fact, she was all *over* him. Rachel came around on his other side. "Great shooting, Dillon."

He nodded at her curtly. "Yes, it was."

The man behind the counter asked Dillon what prize he wanted. He pointed to a small teddy bear. The man got it down with a long hooked pole and gave it to Dillon. Dillon handed it to one of the little girls next to him. Then he paid again.

Several minutes later Dillon had won another bear. He gave it to the other small girl, spun around on his stool, and stood up.

"Go on, Dillon!" Keryn said. "You could win one of those really big bears if you save your winnings for a few rounds."

Dillon shook his head. "It would not be fair to the others. And besides, you were hungry."

Rachel's cell phone rang and she flipped it open. "Hey, Uncle Grant, did you catch up to her?"

"Bad news, Rachel." Grant's voice sounded furious. "Julia made it to the car before I did and she was in such a hurry she backed right into a minivan. The other driver's having a shrieking match with her right now. We're . . . I'm sorry, Rachel. We're not going to make it back into the fair."

Rachel started walking toward the gate. "That's terrible, Uncle Grant. I'll be right out."

"Not a good idea," Grant said. "Julia's in one of her moods right now, and it might be a few days. It's kind of embarrassing when she gets like this. Can you . . . hang out with Keryn and Dillon? Have a good time and catch a ride home with them, okay?"

"Um . . ." Rachel didn't think that was such a great idea. She was about to say so when the line went dead. She stared at her phone, feeling panic cut through her. The whole thing was ridiculous. Two grown people having a fight in front of everybody and letting it escalate out of control. Now she was stuck here with Keryn and Dillon, dependent on them to take her home. And apparently, they were here on a *date*, and she was the awkward third wheel on the bicycle.

Great, just great.

Keryn held out the two sheets of red tickets to Rachel. "We have to give these back to Grant."

"He's not coming back," Rachel said. "He . . . well, Julia had an accident in the parking lot, and Grant said they're going home." She looked from Keryn to Dillon. "I guess . . . I'll be seeing you tomorrow at work."

Dillon was not looking at her at all.

Keryn shook her head. "Didn't you come in Grant's car?"

"I . . ." Rachel bit her lip. She had no idea how to get home from here. "I can take a taxi home."

"That's crazy," Keryn said. "It'll cost you fifty bucks. At least."

Rachel hadn't brought her wallet. Julia had told her not to bother bringing money, that Grant was paying. But it would be just way too awkward to butt in on a date, especially with things the way they were between her and Dillon.

Keryn touched Rachel's arm. "Listen, you two. We came here today to have fun. So let's have fun. We'll call a truce, okay? Just for today, we can forget about what happened at work. Okay, Dillon?" She grabbed his arm and clutched it. "Cease-fire?"

Dillon was looking very dazed, which was natural the way Keryn was floozing all over him. "I can do that," he said.

Rachel backed away. "Um, no. I'm willing to call a cease-fire, but you guys are here on a date and . . . I don't want to butt in on that."

Dillon's face showed puzzlement. "A date? That is not true, is it, Keryn?" He turned and looked at Rachel. "We came to look at guns. Keryn is very interested in nineteenth-century guns."

Keryn was nodding like a monkey. "Right. Guns. That's all. Just, you know, looking at guns and . . . more guns and . . . a lot more guns, and then we got hungry and came over here."

So it was a half-date. Keryn thought it was. Dillon thought it wasn't. He was just so . . . dense about things. Rachel tried to bite back a smile, but she couldn't help herself. She began giggling.

Keryn looked mortified. Dillon seemed utterly confused.

Rachel covered her face with her hands and just laughed. She laughed for a long time, until she was all laughed out. At some point, she noticed that Keryn was laughing too. Dillon was looking at them both with an expression that could have meant anything.

"So you'll stay?" Keryn finally said.

Rachel nodded. "If you'll go on some rides with me."

Keryn blanched. "I don't do scary rides."

"That's all I do," Rachel said. "Dillon, I'll join you two, but I need somebody to go on the scary rides with me."

Dillon stood thinking for a long minute. Rachel could almost see the wheels computing in his head, weighing the risk of going on an unsafe ride against the risk of sending her off on her own with no way to get home.

Finally he nodded. "I will go on the rides with you. On anything but The Hard Rock."

"Deal," Rachel said, thinking that Dillon was just too nice for his own good.

CHAPTER
SIXTEEN

Keryn

They rode on The Cliffhanger first. It was a simple ride that looked like a hang glider. Three people could ride abreast on each one, and it swung you up in a big circle. No loops, no spinning, nothing fancy. It looked safe even to Keryn. Dillon rode in the middle, with Keryn on his left and Rachel on the right. They swooped up and down, round and round. Halfway through the ride, Keryn noticed that Rachel was clutching Dillon's right hand very hard and her knuckles were white. Keryn took his other hand.

When the ride ended, their glider settled in smoothly to rest. Keryn hadn't been afraid at all. It was a very tame ride. As they got off the glider, she saw that Rachel was breathing hard, and her face was very red.

"Rachel, are you okay?" Keryn said.

Rachel took a deep breath. "I'm fine. It's just . . . I'm scared of heights."

Which did not make any sense. "If you're scared of heights, why are you going on rides like that?"

Rachel was staggering just a little, but after a few paces she seemed to recover. "I'm not going to go through life running away from my fears." Her face became giddy. "What shall we ride next? Keryn, you choose!"

Keryn chose the bumper cars. She had always liked them, and it was pretty hard to get hurt in bumper cars. And Rachel wouldn't have the heights thing to worry about there. They all got in separate cars and put on the absurdly inadequate safety straps.

When the electricity started, Keryn jammed her foot to the floor. Her car wouldn't start. She spun the wheel, but she was backed up against the curb and it just would not—

"Whooheeeeee!" Somebody slammed into Keryn from the side. Keryn's car bounced loose. She pressed the accelerator and saw Rachel roar away, waving gaily and having the time of her life. Just like a little kid. It was almost funny.

Keryn bounced off a few cars and then broke free of the pack. Over in the corner, Dillon was whizzing around in a tight circle by himself. He wore a serious expression on his face, as if he were writing software.

Keryn cut across in front of him and swerved right sharply to bump him. His car bounced off hers and stalled. Dillon looked shocked. Then a smile spread across his face.

"Wheeeeeeee!" Rachel sailed up from behind and slammed into Dillon's car at full speed. His car leapt away and began spinning in a tight circle. One and a half revolutions later, Dillon came roaring back. Rachel had reversed direction and was madly fishtailing her car backward, screaming in a voice that would have put a banshee to shame. She rammed into the main pack and stalled. Dillon pounded into her car and she bounced in her seat.

Dillon had a big grin now. Keryn wheeled around in a circle and sideswiped him. Dillon bounced sideways, then whipped around and roared off, snaking through the pack. Rachel followed him, whooping with glee. Keryn pursued them both but got stuck in traffic. When she finally broke through the pack, Dillon and Rachel were racing toward each other at top speed.

They met in a tremendous collision and bounced back. Rachel was laughing hysterically. Keryn drove her car into the crack between them. All three cars whacked into the end curb. Keryn's car twisted around to face Dillon and she stopped short, astounded.

Dillon was laughing.

Way too soon, the ride ended. Keryn got out of her car and found that she was laughing so hard she could hardly walk. Rachel staggered out of her car as if her legs were rubber, but she hooted and threw an arm over Keryn's shoulder. "That was fun! What are we going to ride next?"

"It's Dillon's turn," Keryn said. "Let him choose."

Dillon chose The Teacup. This was a deceptively safe-looking ride. Keryn knew from experience that you couldn't get hurt in the teacups, but you could lose your lunch. Which she still hadn't had. The three of them sat in one teacup and grabbed the center wheel. Dillon was in the middle. Keryn wedged in on his left. Rachel slid in tight against him on the right.

The ride began tamely enough. There was a little up-and-down motion and the teacup swiveled left and right.

Then Rachel swung hard on the wheel and the teacup spun full around. Rachel shrieked like a little girl. Keryn wished she could feel free to scream like that. To just have fun, to let go, to be . . . crazy.

Rachel spun it hard again, and the teacup roared through another full circle. Keryn felt herself pressed up against Dillon. She grabbed his arm. "Having fun?" she shouted.

He took the wheel and spun it hard the other way and now they were whipping through turn after turn after turn. Rachel was screaming nonstop. Dillon was laughing out loud and turning, turning, turning. Keryn began to feel dizzy. She wished Dillon would slow down. It was fun, but it was . . . too much.

They screamed through another circle and all of a sudden, Keryn knew she was in trouble. Her stomach was heaving. She leaned forward and retched. Nothing came out, but she felt horrible and she retched again.

"Keryn!" Dillon stopped spinning the wheel. He put an arm around her shoulder. "Keryn, are you all right?"

She shook her head, feeling weak. "Uh-uh."

"Rachel, no more spinning," Dillon said. "Keryn is vomiting."

Keryn covered her mouth for the rest of the ride. Finally it was over.

Keryn stumbled out of the teacup and bent over. She retched again, several times. Dry heaves. It felt terrible.

Dillon patted her back gently.

Rachel knelt beside her. "Gosh, Keryn, I'm so sorry. I didn't mean to make you sick."

"It's . . . it's okay," Keryn said. "I'll be fine. Let's just . . . go sit down for a bit."

Rachel and Dillon guided her out through the gates and to a bench. Rachel put her arms around Keryn's shoulders and talked quietly. Dillon went away and came back shortly with some bottled water. He twisted the cap loose. "Can you drink? Will that help?"

Keryn took a sip of water and swished it around in her mouth. The cool wetness refreshed her. "Thanks, guys. I'm . . . feeling better now."

"No more rides," Dillon said. "We can go look at the gun exhibits some more and then have lunch."

"Um . . . no." Keryn didn't think she could handle walking around anymore. "I think I need to be off my feet for a while. We've still got some tickets. You two go on some more rides, okay?"

"Your turn to choose, Rachel," Dillon said.

Rachel stood up and looked around. "What's left? Ferris wheels are boring. I don't like roller coasters. The merry-go-round is for little kids." She looked again at The Hard Rock.

Keryn studied the ride. It was *horrible*. There were two arms reaching out horizontally from a central axis. You locked yourself into seats in the arms and then the whole thing starting spinning around. Then the arms tilted up at an obscene angle. And the arms also spun around their long axis. *And* they rotated around a vertical axis at the center of each arm. The whole thing was grotesque.

Rachel turned her back on The Hard Rock. "There's got to be something we can go on."

"The Sleigh Ride looks fun." Dillon pointed to something that looked like a merry-go-round on steroids.

Rachel shook her head. "That's just speed. I want something . . . high. High and scary."

"Try The Rocket." Keryn pointed to a tower. You strapped into chairs and they raised up a good hundred feet in the air. Then the whole thing came plunging down and braked to a stop amid a chorus of screams.

"Half a second of scare," Rachel said. "Not enough." She shaded her eyes and walked fifty yards down the pavement. When she came back, her face was glum. She hunched onto the bench beside Keryn. "Maybe we should get something to eat."

Dillon had been pacing back and forth while Rachel looked. His hard leather shoes gleamed in the bright sun. When she sat down, he kept pacing. Back and forth. Back and forth. Finally he stopped.

Reached out a hand to Rachel.

She looked up at him, her eyebrows raised in surprise.

"I will take you on The Hard Rock," he said.

Rachel's face lit up with joy. Then panic replaced it. Keryn stared at her, fascinated. Rachel was absolutely terrified of this thing. Drawn to it. Scared to death. She took Dillon's hand, and her arm was quivering. "Okay, l-let's go."

Keryn watched them walk away together and realized that somehow, someway, she had lost. Rachel, who was scared of heights, knew how to live, in a way that Keryn never would.

Dillon

Dillon had watched The Hard Rock several times by now, and he knew what to expect. He did not think it was particularly dangerous. Of course it would be unpleasant. Spinning around on four different axes would make him dizzy, and he did not like being dizzy. But the ride had been in operation for a number of days and nobody had been killed. It would be more dangerous to cross Jimmy Durante Boulevard in the crosswalk than to ride The Hard Rock.

Furthermore, Rachel wanted to ride it and it was her turn to choose and she could not go alone because she was afraid. It was only polite to take her on the ride.

They paid their tickets and went through the gate. Rachel led the way. The seats were arranged in groups of four. The innermost of the four would experience the least centrifugal force. The outermost would experience the most. Rachel pointed to the outer one. "Do you want the good seat?"

Dillon shook his head.

Rachel jumped up into the cage and nestled into the hard plastic seat. Dillon sat beside her. Signs warned them to keep their feet in. An attendant came by and helped them pull down the thick plastic safety harness. Dillon felt very enclosed, trapped. He could not back out now, even if he wanted to.

A hydraulic arm pulled the top of the cage down around them, and a foot bar popped up to latch against the floorboard. Dillon rubbed his wet palms against his pant legs. A speaker began blaring very loud rock music. Slowly, the arms of The Hard Rock began rotating on two axes—around the main vertical axis and around the long axis of each arm. All Dillon's weight pressed against his safety harness. The turn continued and now he was upside down, inches above the platform.

A hand fumbled for Dillon's. He twisted his head and saw Rachel. Fear covered her face. He gripped her hand.

They spun faster. The arms continued rotating on the two axes. Soon they were spinning very fast. They began to tilt upward.

Rachel screamed.

Dillon squeezed her hand. "We will be quite safe." He could not hear his voice, so he repeated the words, shouting this time. He could see Rachel's eyes, wide and white in her slick face. As they rolled forward, her hair flopped this way and that.

The arms were now pointing up at a steep angle and the centrifugal force alternately crushed Dillon's chest against the harness and his back against the seat. He felt blood rushing into his face, then out of his head. He wished the ride were over.

Then the arm began rotating on its fourth axis. Dillon felt fingernails digging into his hand. Rachel was screaming again, so loud it hurt his ears. Now there was no predicting the motion. It had gone chaotic, and Dillon felt unseen forces sucking him first one direction then another with no discernible pattern. The sun blazed into his eyes, then disappeared. The sky, the ground, the machinery, the sun, the crowd below—all flashed past his eyes in a sickening dizzy sequence.

"Oh my gosh, Dillon, help!" Rachel cried. "This is horrible! Help me!"

Dillon could do nothing. Her hand clutched his like a vise grip. She screamed again.

Dillon knew the ride should last for two minutes and thirty seconds. Something must be wrong. They had been swirling now for many minutes. Again and again he felt twice his body weight pressed against the safety harness, crushing the breath out of him. He hoped his tie would not get wrinkled.

After a very long time, the tilt of the arms began to decrease. The rotation around the fourth axis stopped. The arms flattened out until they were inches above the platform, still rotating. Slowly the ride came to an end. Dillon could not believe anybody would be so foolish as to ride this terrible ride. The arms lurched to a stop. The foot stop clicked open, the cage opened, and the safety harness unlatched.

Dillon pushed up the harness with his left hand. Rachel still clung to his right. He stepped out, feeling woozy and dizzy and relieved that it was over. "Rachel! Are you all right?"

Rachel's face had gone completely white and a mask of sweat covered it. Dillon pushed up her safety harness.

She lurched out of her seat and fell forward, grasping at his arms. "Oh my gosh, that was . . . awful!" Rachel clung to him.

Dillon saw that most of the other riders had cleared the platform. "We have to leave, Rachel." He led the way.

She staggered along, hanging on his arm, her breath coming in deep sobs. Somehow, they got out of the gate. Dillon helped her stumble over to where Keryn sat on the bench.

"Have a good time?" Keryn said.

Rachel collapsed onto the bench and wiped her face on the sleeve of her shirt. "That was . . ." She fanned her face with her hand. "That was . . . wonderful!" She seized Dillon's hand. "Didn't you love it? Let's go again!"

Which only verified something Dillon had long believed.

Women were irrational and there was no understanding them.

Rachel

Somewhere during the most horrible, blood-gushing, joyful, terrifying, exciting ride she'd ever been on, Rachel realized that she had misread Dillon. Yes, he was obsessive. Yes, he was wrapped up in rules. Compulsive, irritating, schedule-possessed.

But he was a rock.

Dillon had ridden out The Hard Rock without any kind of fear. He had something she did not have—a quiet strength. She looked up at him now, thinking how incredibly *fun* it had been to scream through the whole ride while clutching his hand. "What do you say, Dillon? What shall we go on next?"

"I need to use the men's room."

"We passed one back that way." Keryn pointed toward the main strip that led to the gate.

Dillon nodded and strode away.

Rachel sat for a minute, still trying to catch her breath after The Hard Rock. "Keryn, can I have some of your water?"

"Um, sure. I'm done with it."

Rachel took a swig from the bottle. The water was tepid. She spat it out on the ground. "Yuck! I think we need another cold one. Can I borrow a few bucks off you?"

Keryn gave her a ten, and Rachel went looking for a concession stand. She finally found one and stood in a long line. After about a six-year wait, she bought three ice-cold Aquafinas at three dollars a bottle. She left the change in the tip jar and headed back.

The Hard Rock was spinning out a fresh crop of shrieks when she walked past. She stopped to watch it. Four axes. Something inside her was burning to ride that thing again. And she would, if she could get Dillon to go with her.

She could see Dillon and Keryn sitting on the bench together on the far side of The Hard Rock. Keryn had her eyes closed and her hands behind her head, which was tilted back. Keryn was getting a little sunshine and strutting her stuff, all at the same time, all very innocent, of course. Rachel felt disgusted. Keryn was such a . . . Church Lady, most of the time. Today, she had come loaded for bear, and . . .

The bear wasn't looking.

Rachel suppressed a smile. Dillon was sitting right next to Keryn. It would be so natural for him to just turn his head and take a peek at her. But he wasn't doing it. Rachel stood watching for a few minutes and Dillon kept looking straight ahead. He was talking to her. Rachel couldn't hear a thing, of course—but she could see his mouth moving, could see Keryn answering him.

Watching them, Rachel felt . . . jealous. Dillon and Keryn would make a good match. Keryn was a very prim and proper Church Lady. Well, not so prim today, but today was an anomaly. She was putting on a different persona, and it wasn't working. Keryn probably felt like an idiot and tomorrow would go back to normal. Dillon was so old-fashioned. He wouldn't sneak a look at a woman even when she put herself out on display and practically begged him to look.

A guy like that had integrity.

Rachel felt sick to her stomach. She'd been so furious at Dillon on Saturday that it hadn't penetrated her skull that something was very wrong. Something did not compute.

There were certain things that you either had or you didn't have. Like virginity. Someone like Keryn—obviously, she was saving herself for marriage, and was proud of it.

And then there was integrity. You either had that or you didn't. And Dillon had it. There just wasn't any lie in the guy. He didn't show his emotions. He had a fabulous poker face. And yet . . . he couldn't tell a lie to save his life. Wouldn't tell one.

Which meant that if Dillon said he hadn't messed with her bio-computer, then there was only one possible conclusion.

Dillon hadn't messed with her bio-computer.

Rachel put her hand to her mouth, feeling suddenly nauseated. She had wasted days accusing Mr. Clean of being dirty. Meanwhile, the clock was ticking and the real work wasn't getting done. She was an idiot. A king-sized moron.

Dillon hadn't done it, any more than Uncle Grant had done it.

Which meant that somebody else had. Somebody knew about what CypherQuanta was cooking and had found a way to break in and check it out. Somebody clever enough to steal her password.

Rachel felt very cold. She strode around The Hard Rock and hurried toward Dillon and Keryn.

Dillon looked up at her in surprise. "Rachel! Where have you been? We've been wondering where you were."

"Long line." Rachel handed Keryn and Dillon each a bottle and sat down beside Keryn. She opened her bottle and took a long, long swig. "Listen, guys, I have something to say."

Keryn's eyes narrowed. "What's up?"

Rachel took Dillon's hand and stared at it. "Dillon, I was really ticked off at you Saturday. Really mad. That's my baby in that vial. I've worked on that for six months and . . . it meant a lot to me and—"

"I did not take it," Dillon said.

"I know that now." Rachel looked up at him and felt hot tears spilling up out of her eyes. "Dillon, you're . . . the most honest guy I've ever met, and I'm really, really sorry I accused you of taking it. I was just so mad that I couldn't think straight. But I'm convinced now. You didn't take it. I know for sure Uncle Grant didn't do it either. And I didn't do it. You've got to believe me. I didn't do it."

Dillon's face twitched. "If that is true, then we have a problem."

Keryn looked like she was going to throw up again. "You guys are telling me somebody broke into the lab, cracked your safe, hacked your password, and . . ."

"And stole most of the bio-computer," Rachel said. "I don't know how they could possibly have done all that, but they did. They made the spill look like an accident, like it had just leaked out on the floor, but I bet they took it. They tested the software and it didn't work, but they probably made a copy of that too, hoping to make it work. They could have burned a CD and walked out with all our secrets."

"Not all," Dillon said. "There was a fundamental problem with the software. It will not work."

Rachel felt her heart double-thump. "How do you know?"

He pulled his flash drive out of his pocket. "I had a backup. I continued working on it Saturday night and last night. There was a serious problem."

"What kind of problem?" Rachel had been so sure her bio-computer would work. It had to work.

"My calibration function was too slow, by a factor of about eighty thousand," Dillon said. "I have completely rewritten it using a new algorithm, and now it should take only fifteen minutes."

"How long would it have taken with the old software?" Rachel drank another swig of water.

Dillon smiled. "More than two years. The fundamental idea was wrong."

Keryn cleared her throat. "Guys, we still have a problem. The bio-computer is gone. Dillon, you could have the best calibration thingie in the world, but if it takes Rachel six months to rebuild that bio-computer, we aren't going to make it. Whoever stole it is going to come back for us and—"

Rachel leaned in close to both of them. "Well . . . no. I haven't told Grant this. I haven't told anyone, because I didn't trust anyone. But I trust you two. I have another bio-computer."

"You have . . . what?" Keryn's jaw dropped. "Where?"

"Shhhh." Rachel looked all around. "It's in my apartment. When I made the original, I kept back a vial of it. You know . . . insurance. In case something went wrong."

Dillon's eyes gleamed. "This means we can test my software."

Rachel nodded. "But here's the thing. I don't know who to trust anymore, other than you guys. I guess I trust Grant and Clifton—mostly. But we've got a leak somewhere. Maybe Grant, maybe Clifton, maybe one of us let the cat out of the bag to one of our friends. Have either of you talked about this to anyone?"

Keryn swallowed visibly. "My brother-in-law was asking some questions the other night, but I put him off. I swear, I didn't spill it to him."

"Don't tell him a word more," Rachel said. "What about you, Dillon? Any confessions? Is there anybody who asks you about your job?"

Dillon's face hardened. "Only my friend Robert. He is a graduate student in physics at Berkeley."

Rachel sucked in her breath. "If he asks again, tell him we've given up on the project."

Dillon shook his head. "I will not prevaricate."

Rachel bit back her exasperation. "Then don't talk to him."

"But his wedding is in August," Dillon said. "We have many things to talk about."

"Change the subject if he brings the project up," Keryn said. "Ask him if he's getting cold feet. That'll distract him."

"Cold feet?" Dillon's eyes went completely blank for several seconds. "Oh. You mean last-minute fears."

"Right." Keryn's eyes closed and her face tightened. "Do we know we can trust Julia? She's quite an operator, behind that bimbo exterior of hers."

"I don't trust her." Rachel took a deep breath. All of a sudden she was scared. "Look, I want no more leaks. Right now only the three of us know. We can't tell Grant or Clifton or Julia or anyone. If we get another leak, that'll narrow it down to one of us three."

"We have to tell them something," Keryn said. "They're going to see that you two aren't squabbling anymore."

Rachel tried to concentrate. "Okay, here's a plan."

"I am not going to prevaricate," Dillon said.

Rachel nodded. "We're not going to lie. Keryn, tell them Dillon and I made up today at the fair. Tell them . . . we're working together again. Tell them Dillon's working on the software and I'm making another vial of that bio-computer, but it'll take me a month to get it finished."

"I am *not* going to prevaricate." Dillon's hand tightened on Rachel's.

"That's right, we're not going to lie," Rachel said. "Because you *will* be working on that software, which should be done in a few days. And I *will* be starting up another batch of that bio-computer—which will take a month to cook up if everything goes right."

"But that is not the whole truth," Dillon said.

"No, it isn't," Rachel said. "But it's true as far as it goes."

Dillon looked very unhappy.

Keryn sighed heavily. "Listen, Dillon, in Nazi Germany people sometimes had to lie to save Jews. Like Oskar Schindler. Lives could be at stake here. If word of this leaks out, we could all end up dead, and a lot more people besides us. But we're trapped. We can't walk away from this. The genie is out of the bottle. I think we need to do what we have to. A week from now, we can tell the world the whole truth. Until then, we *have* to keep it quiet. Does that make sense?"

Dillon didn't say anything.

Rachel reached deep into her brain and pulled up one of the fragments she had heard from her cousin. "Hey, you know, there's an old Jewish principle that applies here. They call it *pikuach nephesh*. It means *the saving of a life*. When lives are in danger, it's considered okay in Jewish law to tell a lie."

"Who told you that?" Dillon said.

"My cousin Rivka." A wave of sadness washed through Rachel. "She's dead now, but she was studying all that before she died."

"I am very sorry," Dillon said. "How did she die?"

"Trying to save the world." Rachel felt her eyes misting. "She was kind of like a big sister to me. Anyway, she told me that most everybody agrees it's okay to kill in self-defense. So it stands to reason that it's okay to lie to protect your life. Right?"

Keryn was nodding her head. "That makes sense to me. Which means it ought to be okay to withhold the truth in order to protect your life." She put her hand on Dillon's arm. "Okay, Dillon?"

A long silence. "I am not so sure, but . . . okay," he said. "For one week."

Rachel leaned forward and planted a kiss on his cheek. "You're a stud, Dillon."

CHAPTER
SEVENTEEN

Grant

On Wednesday morning Grant stood at the podium in the large conference room, watching the stragglers hurry in. Nobody was ever late to an all-hands meeting announced on fifteen minutes' notice. Work had probably come to a screeching halt during the past quarter hour, but that was okay. There weren't any new machines contracted right now, so there wasn't a whole lot to do, anyway.

Clifton stood at the door with a clipboard checking off names. He nodded to Grant. "Everybody's here, Grant. Go ahead and get started."

"Where's Keryn?" somebody asked.

"Oops, she's coming." Clifton opened the door.

Keryn Wills came in holding a big stack of papers hot off the copy machine. She was wearing a nice suit in a muted green color and took a seat in the back. All around the room, everybody was looking at that stack of papers in her hands.

Clifton shut the door. "I just called Dillon and he's on his way over. Hit it, Grant."

An uneasy silence shrouded the room. Forty-odd pairs of eyes studiously avoided Grant's. He let the tension hang there for a few seconds. Best to scare them up good before giving them good news.

"Okay, people, we've had a tough little development." Grant took a pen out of his pocket and clicked it a few times. "I guess you all know B of A reneged on the contract."

A hiss of fear rippled through the room.

Grant waited for silence, then took a deep breath. "There's bad news and there's good news. I'll give you the bad news first. Lost Angels is claiming we're short on the terms for the second tranche, so they're withholding the money. Which puts us in a bad situation with the cash flow, because we spent money on those machines B of A rejected." He shook his head and put the right amount of regret into his voice. "Keryn will verify this for you, but I've been taking stock in lieu of salary for the past six months."

Heads turned to look at Keryn. She nodded. "It's true."

"Things are about to turn around," Grant said, "but we are temporarily short on cash. Which means I need to ask you for something. In exchange for that, I'm going to give you something."

Nobody was breathing now.

Grant licked his lips. "Here's the deal, and it's a good one for you. First, there aren't going to be any layoffs. None."

A murmur of relief ran around the room.

"Second," Grant said, "I'm asking each one of you to take stock in lieu of salary for one month. Just one month, and because of the sudden nature of this announcement, I'm offering it to you at half the market rate. Which means you get twice as much."

He waited a few seconds to let the shock of this work its way through their heads.

Bill whispered something in Jill's ear, and then they raised their hands together and started alternating words in that obnoxious way they sometimes did. "Two." "Times." "Zero." "Is." "Zero."

Nervous laughter around the room.

Grant raised his hand for silence, and he held up three fingers. "Third—and this is the kicker—we are working on a surprise technology announcement that should put us on the way to an IPO later on this year."

Nancy, the frizzy-haired redhead who handled database work, stood up. "Exactly what kind of surprise are you talking about here?"

Grant was sweating. He needed Dillon *now.* "Um, I'm not at liberty to say, exactly."

All around the room, eyes narrowed. Grant could see behind those eyes, could see the inward concentration that meant that four dozen resumés would be hitting the wires by this evening. Unless he did something right away.

Clifton coughed and looked at his cell phone. "Hey, Grant, looks like Dillon just pulled in."

Grant nodded. He stepped back from the podium. "Um, people, stay calm for just a minute. I've asked Dillon Richard to say something."

Total silence smothered the room. Grant could feel a bead of sweat running down the back of his head.

Footsteps outside. Hard leather shoes on linoleum.

"Dillon Dude!" Clifton pushed the door open.

Heads turned to look.

Dillon strode in, his face as expressionless as ever.

"Come on up here," Grant said.

Dillon came up and stood next to Grant. He looked down at his hands. "I . . . was asked to say a few words about our financial situation."

Every eye was locked on Dillon. Grant could have stripped off all his clothes and gone running out naked, and nobody would have looked.

Dillon took a deep breath. "I am working on a project that should guarantee us a number of new contracts within weeks and an IPO by the end of the year. I understand that Grant is offering each of you the same offer he made me—stock in exchange for salary for the next month. I am taking the offer." Dillon licked his lips. "If any one of you does not want the stock, please sign it over to me, and I will pay you fair market value for it. I will pay cash."

Grant's head snapped around to stare at Dillon. That last part wasn't what he had told Dillon to say. Of course, it made it just that much more believable, but if people took him up on it, Dillon would be out a lot of money. "Say, Dillon, I'm not sure that's legitimate. Keryn, is that legal? Can he do that?"

Keryn's face was a mask of astonishment. "I . . . I think so. I can't think of any reason why not. It's just . . . a little unprecedented."

Grant cleared his throat. "Okay, we've got a kind of a short time fuse on this, so Keryn's going to pass out the paperwork now. I'm asking each of you to sign it by close of business tomorrow. Unless you want to take up Dillon on his . . . his generous offer."

All of a sudden everybody was on their feet, crowding around Keryn, grasping at the papers she was holding. Grant had been part of four startup companies, and he could smell it—IPO fever. In any company, there always came a turning point when it became clear that the beast was going to make it, that it would be going public for big bucks. That's when employees would scratch out their mothers' eyes if it got them another thousand shares.

Dillon remained standing quietly at the podium. Grant stepped up beside him. "Okay. Thanks, Dillon that was great. You can get back to the bio-lab now." He whacked him on the shoulder. "Nice bluff. That was a stroke of genius."

Dillon just stared at him. "Bluff?"

Grant narrowed his eyes. "Do you have the beans to pay off on that offer you made?"

Dillon nodded. "Do you know what the biggest winner on the Nasdaq was in 1999?"

Grant remembered. If he'd cashed out at the end of that year, he'd have earned back thirty to one on his investment. But he hadn't cashed out. "Qualcomm."

Dillon shrugged. "And do you remember when I came to work for you?"

Grant remembered that too. December 1999. "So what are you telling me?"

"In some universes, I kept the stock and lost a large amount of money when the Nasdaq collapsed." A faint smile curved Dillon's lips. "But in this universe, I sold."

Grant swore softly under his breath. "You're telling me you could have financed payroll out of your own pocket for the next month? Why didn't you *say* something? We could have avoided this giveaway here."

Dillon shook his head. "It would not have been honest for me to take all the profit. This way, everybody has a fair share."

Grant wanted to shake Dillon by the scruff of the neck. Him and his confounded *honesty* could get them all killed. "You better get back to work, Moneybags. Is Rachel gonna have that bio-computer done in a month?"

"Nothing could be more certain." Dillon turned and walked quietly out the door. The door clacked shut behind him. Clifton had a tense smile glued on his face. He came over and joined Grant. "Think they're gonna get it done?"

Grant shrugged. "The software, sure. Dillon should have that done this week. It's that bio-computer that's giving me fits. Rachel took six months to synthesize it the first time. Now she's got a month."

Clifton cracked his knuckles. "There is, like, no margin of error on that schedule. She showed me the timeline and it's mondo tight."

"She'll come through." Grant hoped it was true. Because if it wasn't, a whole bunch of nice kids were signing papers right now for some very expensive toilet paper.

K e r y n

At 6:00 Keryn took a box of pizza over to see how Dillon and Rachel were doing. Rachel came outside and let her in.

Keryn laid out the food on Rachel's desk.

Rachel opened the door to the bio-lab. "Chow time, Dillon. Keryn's brought some goodies." She rolled a chair out to the desk. "Keryn, we changed the combination on the outside door so even Grant won't be able to come in. Want us to tell it to you?"

Keryn shook her head. "No. If somebody comes in and steals that bio-computer again, I don't want you thinking it was me."

Rachel shrugged. "There's nothing to steal in here. When we leave at night, Dillon copies the software to his flash drive and erases it off the computer. And the bio-computer goes home with me in my fanny pack."

"But in a few weeks, you'll have more synthesized." Keryn pulled drinks out of the paper bag and set them out on the desk. "What if somebody steals that?"

"Won't happen." Rachel shook her head. "I have a phony

schedule that *says* it'll be done in a month. Reality is that it won't be done for eight weeks at the earliest. Grant would have a cow if I told him, so just smile if he asks how we're doing. Dillon's already testing the software and it looks good. I bet we'll be running Shor's algorithm tomorrow. Friday at the latest."

Dillon came out of the bio-lab wheeling a chair. He left it at the desk and went into the bathroom to wash his hands. When he came out he sat down and rubbed his neck. "Keryn, would you say grace?"

Keryn prayed over the food and they all dug in. "How's the software coming, Dillon?"

He took a large bite of pepperoni and pineapple. "Very well. I am teaching Rachel how the program works now. In case something . . . happens to me, she can carry on."

A chill cut through Keryn. "Nothing's going to happen to you."

"We hope not, but it is always wise to be prepared," Dillon said. "Right now I am on the critical path. If anything slows me down, the project slows down. Rachel is helping me in many small ways, and this speeds up the project."

Keryn was beginning to feel like an extra hand on a clock. "Is there anything I can do to help?"

Rachel patted her hand. "You're doing it. Thanks for bringing the food by. And for keeping the bosses happy. They are gonna be *so* surprised when we show them this thing running on Saturday."

"It might take longer," Dillon said. "It is possible we will finish as late as Monday. I will know tomorrow."

Rachel popped the tab on her Diet Coke. She opened Dillon's V-8 and Keryn's Sprite. "A toast!" she said. "To Dillon Richard, Chief Studly Officer."

Keryn raised her Sprite, but a sick feeling settled at the root of her stomach. She had helped negotiate an end to the impasse. Her reward was that she was out of the loop again.

And Rachel was right in the center of it.

C l i f t o n

Clifton parked next to Keryn's car and bounded up the steps to the bio-lab. He knocked loudly several times and waited.

Footsteps inside. The door opened and Keryn stepped back.

"Hey, Clifton! Come on in. There's one slice of pizza left if you want it."

Clifton didn't want pizza. He wanted news. Desperately. That crazy headhunter had called him again, and Qualcomm was asking one more time if he wanted an interview. They needed an answer tonight. Which meant Clifton needed an answer now.

He surveyed the scene. "Dudes! Grant is like majorly stressing over the schedule. We bought ourselves a month, but there isn't anything in reserve." Clifton pointed to Dillon. "You're good on the schedule, Dillon? You'll be done in a week, am I right?"

"Yes, I guarantee it," Dillon said. "If I had the bio-computer, I could be testing in a day or two and it would be done next week."

Which was all hunky-dory, but there was that massive *if* hanging up front of that sentence. Clifton jabbed a finger at Rachel. "Tell me again about your schedule, Rachel. Grant's gonna have a heart attack if it isn't done on time. Are you double sure you'll grow that new bio-computer by the end of July?"

Rachel nodded solemnly. "Tell Grant to relax. I synthesized it once by trial and error. Now I know the steps cold. I'm a hundred percent sure I'll have a bio-computer ready for testing by then."

Clifton began pacing. "The schedule looks tight."

"It is tight, but I'll make the deadline. I guarantee it." Rachel went to the bio-lab. "Do you want a demo?"

Clifton shook his head. "Not if it's going to take time away from you working."

"Well . . . it would," Rachel said. "But it's okay. Half an hour isn't going to break the schedule."

Which was just the kind of attitude that broke schedules. Clifton shook his head. "Look, here's what I'd rather see. You in the lab. Dillon at the computer. Keryn making the food runs."

Keryn stood up. "Well, actually, we're done with supper. Dillon, Rachel, I think you've got work to do, right?"

Dillon rolled his chair back into the bio-lab. "We do. Rachel, you are the bottleneck in the schedule. If you run into any problems, let me know and I will help."

Rachel remained seated in her chair. She pushed off from the desk and rolled into the bio-lab. "Wheeeeeee!"

Clifton could have done with a bit less fooling around and a bit more sniffing the grindstone, but he didn't want to alienate the troops. When Dillon and Rachel shut the door of the bio-lab, Clifton helped Keryn fold up the pizza box and stuff it in the trash. The trash bag was full, so he tied it off and lugged it outside to the Dumpster. When he came back, Keryn was just coming out the door.

"Don't shut that!" Clifton said. "I need to call Grant, and my cell phone's battery is biffed out."

Keryn held the door and Clifton squeezed through. He looked at her pensively. "So, Keryn, whaddaya think? Is the golden girl going to make it?"

Keryn nodded. "I don't see how she can miss."

Clifton did. He could see a lot of ways. "Okay, I'll call Grant and tell him we're on track. You have a good night and write some scary stories, all right?"

Keryn nodded and headed for her car. Clifton waited until he heard her engine start and the car pull away. He stepped to the inner door of the bio-lab and peered in. Dillon was hunched over the keyboard typing. Rachel was doing something under the hood of the wet-lab.

Clifton tiptoed to the desk and sat down in the chair. He picked up the phone and wedged it under his chin, in case one of them came out. Then he pulled open the middle drawer of the desk and reached inside. Far inside . . .

There. His fingers closed on a small device the size of a cigarette lighter. He pulled it out and slid it into his shirt pocket next to his cell phone. He eased the drawer shut and stood up, setting the phone back in its cradle.

He walked to the outer door of the bio-lab and let himself out silently. It was a long shot, but he needed to score here.

Half an hour later, Clifton was driving north on Highway 5, somewhere around Carlsbad. He turned off the voice-activated electronic recorder and concentrated on traffic.

The bad news was that his crew was lying to him and Grant. For no reason Clifton could see, they were lying, pretending that Rachel was busily growing herself a new bio-computer. That was biff, but not majorly so. He could deal with his team lying. Everybody lied.

The good news was that Rachel had made a backup bio-computer. Which only made sense, now that he thought about it.

The good news majorly outweighed the bad news. The only way things could go wrong was if they missed the schedule. That was the sixty-four-trillion-dollar question that Grant was asking, like every ten minutes: *"Are they gonna make the schedule?"*

And the answer was yes. They were gonna make it real soon.

Clifton pulled off at the next exit and swung around over the overpass and drove toward the coast. He parked and got out of his car and went to look out over the Pacific Ocean. The sun hung above the horizon, just turning to orange in the sky. It was a perfect day in paradise.

Clifton looked around and saw that, yes, he was really alone. He took out his cell phone and selected a number from his electronic phone list.

One ring and then . . . "Ted Hunter."

"Hey, Ted, this is Clifton Potter."

"Clifton! Great to hear from you! Have you got a time the big boys over at Q can meet with you? Man, this is a real break, Clifton."

"Tell them I'm not interested," Clifton said.

"You . . . what?" Hunter's voice trailed off. "Clifton, what is this? I went to the wall for you on this one and they finally caved."

"Hey, and I appreciate that. Believe me, I appreciate it." Clifton felt like a jerk. This was the second time Hunter had gone to bat for him, and the second time he had pulled the rug out. "Listen, I'm sorry about this, but things have changed."

"You mean, like, in the last hour?" Hunter sounded exasperated. "You said you were interested this afternoon."

"Yeah, well, something came up," Clifton said.

"Big?" Hunter said.

Clifton didn't say anything.

"Hey, not trying to get you to disclose anything, but . . . if you guys at CypherQuanta need to staff up, you know who to come ask. Am I right?"

"Maybe." Clifton felt relieved that Hunter didn't sound too

upset. Typical headhunter. "How many heads are you dealing these days?"

"Well, you know, the market's still a little soft. I've got about thirty names on my hot list and another fifty warm contacts. Will that do you?"

Clifton laughed. "Not a chance. Are you hooked into some kind of network?"

"Yeah, sure." Hunter's voice sounded strained. "Can you give me some kind of line on what kind of people you're interested in? Programmers? Electronics guys? Optics?"

"All those, plus some physicists," Clifton said. "Probably a lot of physicists."

"Any particular branch?"

Clifton decided he'd said enough. "I'll call you when I know more. Monday, how's that? I'll call you Monday."

"Sounds good, dude. Good luck on your IPO."

"Hey, no hard feelings on the Qualcomm thing?" Clifton said.

"I'm not gonna bleed over it, bro. Talk to you Monday."

"Gotcha." Clifton hung up and put the phone away. His hands were quivering with excitement. It had been a long time coming, but the payout on this thing was gonna be a monster.

A monster.

CHAPTER
EIGHTEEN

Dillon

Dillon's phone rang at 9:13 that evening. He was working at home on his laptop and thinking about Rachel and Keryn, and his first thought was that one of them was calling. For some reason, he felt just a little breathless. Through the first three rings he waited for his heart to stop pounding. Then he went and picked up the phone. "Hello, this is Dillon."

"Yes, am I speaking to Dillon Richards?"

"Richard." Dillon shifted his weight and tried to remember the last time a telemarketer had called him. The national Do Not Call Registry kept most of them away, but there were a few loopholes.

"Oh, sorry about that, Mr. Richard. My name is Ted Hunter, and a mutual friend of mine suggested you might be interested in speaking with me."

Dillon doubted that. "Which mutual friend?"

"I'm sorry, but I need to keep that information confidential."

"I do not talk to people who will not tell me who referred them," Dillon said. "Good night, Mr.—"

"Clifton Potter."

Dillon sat down. "I know Clifton."

"I'll get right to the point," Hunter said. "I advise people who are making career transitions and—"

"Clifton told you I might be interested in switching jobs?" Dillon shook his head. "No. Why would he tell you that?"

"I'm not entirely sure," Hunter said. "He gave me your name a couple of months ago. I met him at a party and we got to talking. I understand there's a sort of crisis at your company and—"

"There was no crisis at our company two months ago."

"I'm sorry, perhaps you've misunderstood. I *met* Mr. Potter a couple of months ago. I've not kept in touch with him, but I have heard through the grapevine that there are problems at Cypher-Quanta now, and I remembered that Clifton had given me your name. Tell me, are you happy with your job?"

Dillon sat quietly trying to process all this information. He did not see the connections, and that made him feel uneasy. A person should make the proper connections when he spoke.

"Hello, Dillon, are you there?"

"If I was not here, then to whom would you be speaking?"

Hunter laughed nervously. "Hey, that's a good one, Dillon. I'm sorry about what's going on at your company, and I'd just like to let you know that I'm here to help if you need it."

"You are a headhunter."

"Right."

"Ted Hunter the headhunter." Dillon laughed out loud. "That is quite funny. Ted Hunter the headhunter." It had a nice ring to it. He wondered if Hunter had become a headhunter just so he could make a pun on his name. He had once known a Dr. Proctor, who was a proctologist. But Ted Hunter the headhunter was funnier.

"You're a funny guy, Dillon." Hunter cleared his throat. "I know you can't talk about internal problems at your company, but—"

"There are no internal problems at CypherQuanta."

"Oh." A long silence. "I'm sorry, maybe I've been given wrong information. Isn't it true that your payroll is processed by a company named RediChex?"

"Yes." Dillon felt sweat rolling down his sides.

"And isn't it true that CypherQuanta is missing payroll this month?"

"That kind of thing is confidential information," Dillon said. "If you tell me who told you that, I will make sure they are prosecuted."

"Um, that . . . won't be necessary. I'm not interested in prosecuting anyone. I'm interested in helping you."

"I do not need help." Dillon wondered if he should just hang up. But he owed it to Grant to find out as much as possible. Somebody was spreading stories about CypherQuanta, and that somebody needed to be taken to justice.

"Are you independently wealthy, then?"

"I do not need help. Who told you about the payroll?"

In the silence that followed, Dillon realized he had just confirmed something for Hunter. That might be the point of the phone call in the first place. Ted Hunter might not be a headhunter at all. He might be a journalist. Or an industrial spy. He might be anything. He might not even be named Ted Hunter.

"Let me phrase that a little differently, Dillon. Do you see any need for some . . . career options?"

"No. I am loyal to Mr. O'Connell and I intend to keep working for him until I retire."

"Even if he doesn't pay you?"

"He is paying me." Dillon realized he had just said more than he intended.

"In equity? IOUs?"

"If you would like to talk to him, I can give you his home phone number, Ted Hunter the headhunter. Would you like to talk to him right now?"

"Dillon, please. You're in a crisis and—"

"I am not in a crisis and neither is CypherQuanta."

"I understand you just lost a contract with Bank of America and your angel investors backed out on you."

"Who told you that?" Dillon was angry now, furious. Somebody was telling Ted Hunter the headhunter things they should not.

"Is there any chance you might have some new technology?" Hunter said.

Dillon felt his chest seize up. For a few seconds, he could not breathe. He could not think. Then he slammed down the phone and sat listening to his heart pound against his chest.

He should call Grant.

No, Grant had enough problems right now. He would panic and

then he would want reassurance. He would ask when was the earliest the project could be finished, and Dillon would have to tell him it could be done next week. It was too dangerous. Dillon had promised to keep Rachel's secret and so he had to keep it.

Dillon picked up his phone and tried to think whom to call. Rachel or Keryn. Keryn or Rachel. He desperately wanted to hear Keryn's soothing voice on the line. Keryn made him feel calm. She was like a vortex of peace in a storm. Dillon liked Keryn very much.

And yet he also wanted to hear Rachel's voice. Rachel was not soothing but she made Dillon feel happy. When he talked with her, he felt optimistic, excited about life. Everything seemed possible when he was with Rachel. Together, they made an excellent team. Rachel had many interesting and stimulating things to say about such things as the multiverse and quantum mechanics.

Dillon could not think which of them he should call. He had a quantum-mechanical coin flipper on his desk. It was a small electronic device that CypherQuanta salesmen used to demonstrate the physics used in quantum encryption. Inside the device were two polarizing filters set at an angle of forty-five degrees. The first allowed a single photon of light through, polarized in a particular direction. The second filter either stopped the photon or passed it through with a forty-five-degree change of polarization. One or the other, with each event happening with equal probability. This was Einstein's famous dice, which he claimed God did not throw.

If the Copenhagen interpretation was right, then Einstein was wrong and God did not know in advance what would happen.

But if the multiverse interpretation was right, then Einstein was right, because the universe split into two. In one universe, the photon passed through. In the other universe, it was stopped. God knew there would be two universes, identical in every respect except for the state of that one photon. In this picture, there were no dice, and God's foreknowledge was preserved. That was the kind of universe Dillon believed in—a universe that made sense.

He pressed the button and somewhere deep inside, one single polarized photon was created.

Keryn

Keryn had been battling writer's block for two hours when the phone rang. This was ridiculous. She never had writer's block. She taught at writers' conferences on how to avoid writer's block. Furthermore, she couldn't afford to be blocked. She had a deadline in less than two months, and she was so far behind she was practically hyperventilating.

The machine picked up. "Hello, this is Keryn Wills. I'd love to talk to you, but I'm out. Leave a message and I'll call you back as *soon* as I can."

"Girlfriend, why aren't you answering my messages?" Sunflower sounded frantic. "I swear, if you don't pick up right now, I'm going to send Kathii over there to see if you're dead."

Keryn dug her nails into her palm and snatched up the phone. "Hi, Sunflower."

"Honey, where have you *been*? You haven't answered your cell phone all day, and I left you two messages at home this afternoon."

"I . . ." Keryn didn't want to admit she'd been ignoring the calls on her cell phone. "I guess I forgot to check my machine." That was true. She'd been so eager to get to work, she just hadn't checked. "I'm sorry. Is something wrong?"

"Wrong? You're not answering my calls—that's what's wrong. Where have you been?"

Keryn's stomach contracted into a small knot. She daydreamed all the time about standing up to Sunflower, but somehow she never could do it in real life. What was wrong with her, anyway?

Rusty's voice mumbled something in the background.

"Shut up," Sunflower said. "I'm trying to get two words out of Keryn. Honey, you've been acting strangely lately. Now you just tell me what's going on. Is it that man you've been seeing?"

"I . . . no." Keryn felt like an idiot.

"What? Speak up. You don't sound right. Are you drunk or something?"

"I don't drink."

"Listen, there's nothing to be ashamed of in having a beer once in a while. Don't lie to me. I've known you too long to lie to me. Are you getting sloshed again?"

"I'm not drinking. I'm doing fine. Everything is fine."

"Have it your way, then." Sunflower's voice cracked. "Keep your secrets. Lie to me." A long pause. "Are you still seeing that man? Tick, tick, tick."

Keryn didn't know what to say.

"Spill it, sister! When was the last time you saw him?"

"I saw him at work today."

"I'm not talking about work, girlfriend! When was your last date with him?"

Keryn desperately wanted to just slam the phone down. "Yesterday."

"A weeknight? You went out on a weeknight? I thought you were so busy writing."

"It was in the daytime. We went to the fair."

"The daytime? You stole away from work in the middle of the day for a secret rendezvous at the fair? Sweetcakes, tell me more!"

Keryn felt like screaming. "It wasn't any big thing. Rachel was there, and—"

"Rachel? Who's Rachel?"

Keryn took a deep breath and decided to just spill. "Rachel Meyers is a twenty-five-year-old girl genius who has the hots for Dillon and dresses like a little floozy. We all went to the fair and rode bumper cars and I got the heaves on The Teacup and then the two of them rode together on The Hard Rock while I watched. Satisfied?"

"Rusty!" Sunflower hollered. "Get on the phone and talk to this girl. She's gotten herself mixed up in some kind of a weird triangle, and I think she's drunk again."

Keryn set down the phone, knowing that it would ring again in two minutes. Knowing she would pick it up. She put her head in her hands. She'd made things sound as crazy as she could but . . .

The reality was crazier still.

R a c h e l

Rachel was soaking in a bubble bath, thinking about Dillon.

The whole thing was absurd. She was his exact opposite. They had nothing in common. As a teenager, Rachel had spent a lot of time reading up on the Myers-Briggs personality profiles. She was an ENFP, an Extravert-Intuitive-Feeler-Perceiver. Whereas Dillon was an ISTJ, an Introvert-Sensor-Thinker-Judger. The books said an SJ could do fine with an NF, but Rachel wasn't kidding herself. There was no way in the world she could ever get along with him.

Dillon was some sort of legalistic Christian. Whereas she was . . . what? She didn't know. She was nothing. Her father was a Jewish agnostic. Her mother was a fundamentalist true believer. Rachel had seen enough about religious differences growing up to run shrieking at the thought of it. Growing up, she had felt split right down the middle. Home was a battlefield and she was the prize.

Which was why she had bagged on religion. A week before she was supposed to do her Bat Mitzvah, she had just bailed on the God thing. Her father wasn't religious, but a Bat Mitzvah was a big deal to him, and he had almost disinherited her. Her mother had cried for three weeks straight when Rachel told her she was glad Jesus died and gladder that he was still dead, and she hoped the rest of the Christians would die out too.

Rachel still felt that way. Christians were snots, and she was just fed up with all those lies about how they were the prodigal son who came home and Jews were the self-righteous older brother doomed to die in their hypocrisy. Most of the Christians she had met were the biggest hypocrites around. She had lost her virginity one Saturday night when she was sixteen with a nice Baptist boy who sang in the choir the next day and was always doing that See-You-at-the-Pole rot. And the only difference between him and her was that he felt guilty about it and she didn't. Where was the advantage in that?

So what was it about Dillon that was dragging her toward him? It couldn't possibly work. He was her exact opposite. He was everything she wasn't.

He was everything she needed.

The phone rang.

Rachel didn't want to bother answering it. She leaned back in the water and let its bubbly fragrance soothe her.

After four rings, the machine picked up and played her message in a breathy voice. "Hi, this is Rachel and I was just thinking of you! Please leave a message and I'll get back atcha." *Beep*.

"Rachel, this is Dillon."

Rachel sat up, straining her ears. Dillon sounded . . . scared. Well, maybe nervous.

"Please call me right away," Dillon said. "I think we have a problem." Then a dial tone. Something was terribly wrong. Dillon sounded totally freaked.

She could feel her heart pulsing inside her chest, could feel the sweet rush of adrenaline. Fear was kicking her right in the gut and . . . she was enjoying it.

Rachel kicked the lever to start emptying the water and stepped out of the tub. She wiped her feet, grabbed her terry cloth robe, wrapped it around her wet body, and walked into her bedroom. Dillon had called barely three minutes ago. She scooped up the phone and punched in his number.

He answered after one ring. "This is Dillon."

"Hi, Dillon," she purred. "I was in the tub when you called. What's up?"

Dillon told her. Ted Hunter the headhunter. RediChex. Rumors of a crisis at CypherQuanta.

"It's just a rumor," Rachel insisted. "This Ted Hunter guy doesn't know anything. He was just guessing."

"He sounded like he knew about the stock in lieu of salary." Dillon's voice sounded very tight.

"Well . . . at least he didn't know about our special project."

A short silence. "He . . . he asked if we had any kind of new technology."

All of a sudden, Rachel thought her insides were going to melt. *Please, please no.* If one *word* of that got out . . . "You didn't tell him anything, did you?"

"I hung up on him."

Rachel gasped. "Just like that? You didn't feed him some line and then hang up gracefully?"

"I just slammed down the phone. I was very upset."

"Dillon, that told him an awful lot!"

"I am very sorry. I am not good at prevaricating."

"He didn't ask about the bio-computer, did he? Or Shor's algorithm?"

"No, of course not."

"All he asked about was new technology? That's all? Just a vague kind of fishing question?"

"He sounded like he knew more than he was saying."

Rachel shivered violently. "Dillon?"

"Yes?"

"I'm scared."

"We should talk to Keryn," Dillon said.

"I'll talk to Keryn," Rachel said. "And while I'm doing that . . . could you do me a favor?"

"Anything."

"Could you . . . come over for a while?"

"Come over?" Dillon sounded shocked. "Rachel, it is very late. It would not look right. Your neighbors might misinterpret."

Rachel couldn't care less what her neighbors thought. She wanted a man in the house. All night. "You could sneak in. I'll turn off my porch light. Nobody's going to know if you come over for the . . . for a few minutes."

A long silence. "*I* will know," Dillon said. "I would not feel right about it."

"Dillon, I'm scared to death!"

"I could come over and sit in my car and watch your door."

"Oh, forget it. I'll just lie here awake all night waiting for somebody to come in and murder me."

Dillon sighed. "Rachel, nobody is going to murder you."

"If they know about that bio-computer, they will. We're sitting on dynamite. Nuclear-powered dynamite."

"Then we should get a good night's sleep so we can finish the software. We will be testing the calibration tomorrow and factoring large numbers by Friday."

"Dillon, *please* come over!"

"I . . . cannot do that. People might think something is going on."

"Fine!" Rachel snapped. "If I'm dead in the morning and that bio-computer's been stolen and the whole world economy comes crashing down, well, at least my neighbors can take comfort that nothing is *going on*." She slammed the phone down so hard she chipped a nail.

Rachel lay in bed for a minute, waiting for her heart rate to come down to normal. Finally, she went out to the living room and checked that her dead bolt was locked. She left on all the lights in the apartment and checked that all the windows were locked. When she was satisfied that the place was secure, she went back into her room and hid the bio-computer in the bottom drawer of her dresser.

Then she turned off the bedroom lights and crawled into bed, wishing desperately that Dillon were there. She hadn't snuggled up with a guy since she'd left Caltech, and she wanted a guy's arms around her now.

Not just any guy.

Dillon.

She felt safe around him. Valued. Respected.

But not loved.

It was horrible, horrible, horrible having a crush on a guy who didn't know the first thing about love.

CHAPTER
NINETEEN

Grant

Grant was just getting ready to leave for work when his cell phone rang. One look at the caller ID told him it was trouble. Ron Lord, one of the three board members from Lost Angels. Grant sat down on his couch and flipped open his phone. "Hey, Ron, long time no see! How are ya?"

"Grant, did you just issue a special round of stock to your employees yesterday?"

Grant took a deep breath and looked out at the Pacific Ocean. "Is there some problem?"

"I don't believe you had board approval for that."

"Well, I can set your mind at ease on that question. I *know* I didn't have board approval. So if that's your question, you've got an—"

"Don't play cute with me," Ron said. "You need board approval and you know it."

"I don't think so. I wrote the Stock Option Adoption Agreement back when the board was me and Clif Potter and our lawyer." *Back before you were a bad dream, buddy.* "I have broad discretionary powers in granting stock options to employees."

"Stock *options*. You made a stock *grant*."

Grant felt a sick jab in his gut. "Ya know, in the heat of things, I didn't think much about the distinction. Isn't there something in the charter about stock grants?"

"That's the problem, Grant. That power is reserved to the board."

Grant was sweating now. "My mistake, I guess. Listen, maybe I was hasty on that. We can get the paperwork changed. We gave everybody until close of business tonight to—"

"Grant, we're having a board meeting in San Clemente at ten. You need to be there."

Grant looked at his watch. He had a bit over two hours to get there. "Right. Thanks, Ron, I'll be there. You take care now, you hear?"

"See you at ten." The line clicked dead.

Grant flipped his phone shut. Great, just great. On top of all the fun stuff today, the board was calling him on the carpet. *Say, Grant, you don't look like you've been reamed out enough lately.*

"Grant, are you okay?" Julia plopped on the couch and scootched up to him.

"No. Got an emergency board meeting in San Clemente. Apparently, I don't have enough flaming torches to juggle."

She leaned over and nibbled on his ear. "Well, don't forget, we've got a secret weapon. So tell those goons whatever they need to hear. Next month, they'll be singing a different song."

Grant squeezed her knee and then stood up. "Right. Too bad I can't tell 'em what's in our back pocket. The only thing I hate about this thing is that making us obscenely rich is gonna make those creeps at Lost Angels obscenely richer."

"Maybe." A grim smile slid across Julia's face. "Are you thinking what I'm thinking?"

"Yeah. It may be time to take that cyanide I've been saving." Grant went outside and climbed into his Lexus. The board was going to play rough today. He'd have to find a way to play rougher.

K e r y n

Late in the afternoon, Keryn pulled out her cell phone and dialed Dillon's number, still staring at the e-mail she'd just gotten.

He answered on the second ring. "Hello, Keryn."

"Dillon, I just got a company-wide e-mail you should know about. From Grant. He's calling another all-hands meeting in fifteen minutes in the main conference room. He made it clear that all employees need to be there, which I assume means you and Rachel."

"I'm very busy right now."

"Then Julia called me on my cell phone right after that. She said Grant called her from his car while he was driving down with Ron Lord."

"Ron Lord, the board member?"

"Right." Keryn's lips felt very dry. "Julia said she's really worried. She wants you to make a backup of your software and reformat the hard drive on your computer before you leave."

"Why?"

"I don't know. I'm just telling you what she said. And she said for Rachel to bring any lab books she has."

"She does not use lab books. She keeps it all in her head." Dillon sounded very disapproving.

"Then bring her head. Julia says to leave her in the parking lot—don't bring her into the building."

"Do you have any idea what this is about? We just finished testing calibration. This is very inconvenient."

"Dillon . . . I don't know, but I think something horrible is happening. You've got twelve minutes. Can you make it?"

"I will be a little late," Dillon said. "I am copying the latest version of the source code now."

"See you in a few minutes."

"Good-bye, Keryn." Dillon hung up.

Keryn folded her phone and sat for several minutes in her chair thinking how nice it was to hear Dillon say her name.

———

At exactly 4:45, Keryn heard the door of the meeting room

open. Grant walked in with a couple of men in suits. She recognized Ron Lord, one of the investors from that horrible Lost Angels group. The other man, she didn't know.

Grant walked to the podium and just stared at the assembled employees. His face looked gray and sweaty.

"Go ahead, Grant," said the man Keryn didn't recognize.

"I don't think everybody's here," Grant said. His voice sounded hoarse and raspy. "Clifton, can you check? Is Dillon here?"

Clifton got up and went outside. A slow minute ticked by. Footsteps out in the hall. Clifton Potter came back in with Bill and Jill and . . . Dillon. All four sat down in the back.

Keryn found that she could not breathe.

Grant looked around the room. "As you all know, I took some drastic action yesterday to ensure that there would be no layoffs on my watch while we're going through this rough spot in our finances. Unfortunately, the board didn't quite approve of my methods." Grant threw a poisonous look at the two men behind him.

Keryn felt a knife in her gut. She saw it coming now, as huge and horrible as a truck in the night.

Grant cleared his throat. "I've been ordered to do this by the board in an effort to save the company. The following people are notified that you are laid off, effective immediately: Ann Blodgett, Pete Cramer, Jacqui Darling . . ."

A shocked hush ran around the room. Keryn was clenching her fists so tight her nails felt like they were going to snap.

". . . Rachel Meyers, Ron Pettis, Clifton Potter, Dillon Richard, Renee Smythe, Chuck Tillich, Ed Vandeventer, and . . . Keryn Wills." Grant looked up from the paper in his hands, and his eyes were mournful. "Those of you whose names I called, you have ten minutes to clear the building. You are advised that effective immediately, you are not to take any physical objects from your workspace, download any data, or remove anything from the building unless it happens to be on your person at the moment. The board has also asked me to resign, and I am doing so . . . now." Grant took a handwritten note out of his pocket and handed it to the board members. "I'm sorry, people. You know I did my absolute best to save the company. If any of you need references, just . . . call me." Grant's voice cracked and he stepped away from the podium.

Keryn felt light-headed. She bent over, trying desperately to keep from crying. She was laid off again. This was the second time in five months, and she didn't want to think about looking for a job.

All around her, Keryn heard the buzz of voices. Somebody was shouting at Mr. Lord. Grant's voice rumbled nearby, telling people to clear the building if they were laid off. Keryn staggered to her feet and stumbled toward the exit. Dillon. She had to find Dillon. He was in the back, and his face looked like he'd seen a corpse. When Keryn reached him, she heard Bill asking Jill who Rachel Meyers was. Keryn grabbed Dillon's arm. "Let's get out of here," she said.

Dillon helped her to the door. Quiet strength seemed to flow out of his arm into her hand. She admired that. Dillon was so strong, so calm.

"This way." Dillon pointed toward the exit sign.

"I need my purse," Keryn said. "It's in my office."

"Is that allowed?"

"Of course it's allowed." Keryn pulled him down the hall and into her office. Her purse was in her desk drawer. She grabbed it and a picture of Kathii and Allen and Jason and Jordan. "Come on, let's go."

Out in the parking lot, Clifton Potter was in the middle of a big crowd of people. "Okay, listen, everybody! Let's go drown our sorrows at Karl Strauss. I'm buying." He waved to Keryn. "You coming, Keryn?"

Keryn shook her head. "I . . . better not. I don't drink." And besides, Rachel was parked over in the parking lot on the other side of the gully, and there was no way she could go to Karl Strauss. Everybody would want to know who she was, and that would raise some difficult questions.

"Coming with us, Dillon?" Clifton shouted.

Dillon shook his head. No explanation necessary. Dillon wasn't the most sociable guy in the world. Keryn doubted that anyone would miss him. She clutched his arm. "Let's go tell our friend what's up."

Dillon nodded and led the way. They walked down to the bridge and across into the main parking lot. Dillon's minivan was parked in space number 314, and Rachel's Miata was right next to it. She had the top of her car down and was stretched back with her eyes closed, listening to her CD player at high volume. "Dust in the Wind," by Kansas. Which somehow seemed fitting.

Keryn leaned down next to Rachel's car and looked back to make sure nobody had followed them over from the main crowd. "Listen, bad news, Rachel. We've been laid off."

Rachel's eyes flew open. "Who has?"

Keryn tried hard to swallow the brick in her throat. "Most of the company. You and me and Dillon and Clifton and a raft of others. Grant just resigned. The board forced him out and they're shutting down to a skeleton crew."

"We've got to go back to the lab," Rachel said.

"The lab?" Dillon shook his head. "We cannot. That is owned by CypherQuanta. We are forbidden to go there."

Which explained Julia's strange request to reformat the hard drive on the lab computer. "Dillon, you brought a copy of your software, right? And Rachel, you've got your bio-computer?"

Dillon smiled. "Grant explicitly said that anything we have on our persons belongs to us."

"But . . . the NMR machine," Rachel said. "We can't run the software without that."

"NMR machines are everywhere," Dillon said. He pulled his key ring out of his pocket. His flash drive dangled on the end of it. "The software is finished. This and Rachel's bio-computer are all we really need."

Keryn's phone rang. She checked the incoming number and flipped it open. "Hi, Grant."

"Keryn, are you doing all right?" Grant's voice sounded low and guarded.

"I'm fine. What's wrong with your voice?"

"I'm in a stall in the men's room. Listen, I'm gonna be in a debrief meeting with these clowns for a couple hours, and then I'm taking Julia out on the town to decompress, but I want to see you and our friends ASAP about . . . a business opportunity. Did they bring out what Julia asked?"

"Yes."

"You know that, legally, they can't go back to the lab. Anything that's over there is a loss, is that clear?"

"We figured that out already." Keryn heard an Amtrak train approaching, and she turned and walked away toward the gully, poking a finger over her other ear.

"There's one other—"

Grant's voice cut off suddenly. Keryn heard the sound of flushing and then a dial tone. It was a good bet he'd been interrupted by the board creeps. She put the phone in her purse and went back to join Dillon and Rachel. "Grant called."

Worry creased Rachel's eyebrows. "Did you tell him about the bio-computer?"

"On the phone? Not a chance." Keryn didn't have a lot of confidence in the privacy of a cell phone.

"What did he say?" Dillon asked.

"He said something about us meeting him to discuss a business opportunity," Keryn said. "I'm guessing he'll try to form a new company to take advantage of what we have."

Rachel gave her a very strange look. "I don't think you understand, Keryn."

Keryn didn't like her condescending tone. "What don't I understand?"

Dillon put a hand on Keryn's arm. "Without CypherQuanta, we have *no* legitimate business opportunities for the bio-computer. Now the only purpose we could use it for is . . . stealing."

"Or spying on people." Rachel's face glistened with sweat. "Guys, this is bad. We don't have a reason to keep working on that thing."

"Of course we do," Dillon said. "We could finish the project, announce it to the world, and sell it to the NSA. It will force people to switch to secure encryption. That will give CypherQuanta a second chance, and we could get our jobs back and save Grant from losing his investment."

"We are not going to give my bio-computer to the NSA!" Rachel snapped.

"Sell." Dillon's voice sounded even and tense. "I said sell, not give."

"I'd rather die than let Big Brother have that technology," Rachel said.

"That is absurd." Dillon's face turned red. "Rachel, you should read—"

"Guys, not now." Keryn held up two hands. "I can't handle another fight right now—not when I feel like somebody just kicked me in the face. Let's do something together tonight, shall we? Go to dinner maybe. Grant said he was going to do that with Julia—decompress. Let's have a good time, just the three of us."

Which was crazy, of course. Keryn didn't want a threesome. What had *possessed* her to suggest that?

"I'm game," Rachel said. "Dillon, shall we adjourn this discussion till tomorrow? We can treat ourselves to one decent meal. How's that? What's your favorite restaurant, Keryn?"

"The Star of India just reopened in La Jolla," Keryn said.

Rachel grabbed Dillon's arm. "Perfect. Say yes, Dillon."

He shrugged. "Yes, with two provisos. I am driving and I am paying."

"Deal." Rachel looked up at Keryn. "Deal, Keryn?"

Keryn didn't want it to be a deal, but she didn't seem to have much choice.

"Deal," she said.

Crazy, crazy, crazy.

PART
THREE

Dust in the Wind

"The opposite of a profound truth may very well be another profound truth."

NIELS BOHR

CHAPTER
TWENTY

Keryn

Keryn would not have guessed that parking would be so difficult on a Thursday night in La Jolla. Dillon was driving with his usual maddening precision, and they had circled for the third time from Prospect Street up to Ivanhoe to Silverado to Girard and back around again on Prospect. Keryn was wearing shoes with sensible two-inch heels, but Rachel had on a pair of four-inch spikes that would not survive a long walk. Finally Dillon decided to drop them off at the restaurant and find a parking spot farther away.

They watched Dillon drive off alone. Rachel turned and gave Keryn's dress an appraising look. "Wow, daring!"

Keryn couldn't tell if Rachel was being sarcastic. It was a basic black sheath dress that she mostly wore to awards banquets. The only thing even slightly daring about it was a smallish peekaboo slit running down from the neckline. Not a big deal. Keryn was pretty sure Dillon wouldn't be doing any peeking. By La Jolla standards, this dress was about as tame as you could get. It wouldn't draw attention to Keryn, and that was just the way she wanted it. Whereas Rachel . . .

Rachel looked spectacular. The Star of India served the finest

Indian cuisine in San Diego, and Rachel seemed determined to pass for a native. She was wearing a brilliant orange sari that showed a lot of skin in the back. On most women, the outfit would have looked ridiculously gaudy. Rachel made it look . . . perfect.

"You look great," Keryn said, wishing she could be that bold.

Rachel smiled. "Let's get a table. Our reservations were for eight-thirty and we're a little late."

They went inside and let the maître d' find them their table. It was perfect—small and private in a little alcove in the far back corner. Rachel immediately excused herself and *tap-tapp*ed her way to the bathroom. Keryn sat at the table feeling very lonely. Ten minutes later, Dillon showed up, impeccably dressed in a charcoal suit pinstriped in light gray. He wore a white shirt and a light blue solid-color tie. He reached the table and stood there, looking puzzled at Rachel's empty seat. Keryn thought he looked very nice, for a guy with a hopelessly tame idea of fashion. A striped tie with a dash of red or yellow would—

"I'm back!" Rachel sang out. She threaded her way through the tables, turning heads all across the room.

Keryn could not imagine how a person could be so outlandish and so stunning, both at the same time. When Rachel reached the table, Dillon pulled out her chair and seated her. He sat down and looked at both of them. "This restaurant was a good idea, Keryn."

Keryn felt a rush of warmth in her chest. "I'm hoping we can forget our problems for a while."

The waiter came by, and after ordering their drinks they opened their menus. "Have you been here before?" Rachel said. "What's good for a vegetarian?"

"All the vegetarian dishes are marked," Keryn said. "Do you like hot food? You can order it on a scale of one to ten. I usually ask for a six."

"I'll take a nine." Rachel looked over at Dillon. "Do you like it hot too?"

"I am very sensitive to spices," he said. "I had better take a one."

It took fifteen minutes to choose their dishes and make their orders. Rachel kept changing her mind. It didn't help that she wanted to know every ingredient that went into every dish and insisted on asking the Indian pronunciation of everything.

The waiter patiently answered all of her questions and scratched her order half a dozen times.

"What part of India are you from?" Rachel asked when she finally handed him her menu.

He gave her a little half bow. "Chicago."

"Chicago." Dillon grinned as if that were extraordinarily funny. "I am from Chicago too. Maybe we were neighbors." He shook his head. "Chicago."

Keryn looked carefully around the restaurant. The lighting was dim and the mood relaxed, and the other diners were far enough away that she felt comfortable talking about CypherQuanta. "Well, guys, have you thought about what we're going to do next?"

Neither Dillon nor Rachel said anything. They looked at each other with wary eyes.

Keryn forged ahead. "I wish we could just forget about you know what, but I don't think we can. It's a secret for now . . . I think . . . but it won't be for long."

"Exactly," Dillon said. "Right now six people know about it . . . and possibly more if none of us tampered with the lab. That number cannot decrease."

"Unless one of us gets . . ." Keryn didn't want to say it, but it was a very real possibility. They were sitting on top of a secret so valuable it could get them all killed.

Rachel shivered and leaned forward. "Are you guys as scared as I am?"

Keryn nodded. "I'm scared out of my skull."

"Isn't it . . . delicious?" Rachel said. "It's like riding one of those rides at the fair, but taken to the nth power. I *love* this feeling."

Keryn hated it. She liked writing stories in which her characters were in terrible danger. But she didn't like it herself.

"This secret is too big for us," Dillon said.

Rachel leaned back and crossed her arms across her chest. "I'm not going to give it to the NSA. That defeats everything Uncle Grant has stood for all these years. That's why he founded CypherQuanta—to give people back their privacy. To take it back from Big Brother. If Big Brother tries to take this thing, I'll flush it down the toilet." She put a tiny orange handbag on the table.

Keryn hadn't noticed it yet because it blended so well with her sari. "You brought it *with* you?" she gasped. "Rachel, put that away."

Rachel pursed her lips. "Nobody's going to know what's in here."

"Put it out of sight," Dillon said. "You should have left it at home."

"I'm not letting it out of my sight," Rachel said. "Somebody stole the first one. It wasn't Grant and it wasn't Clifton, so therefore somebody else has it. I bet they don't need this one. If you want my opinion, the real danger is that somebody will get hold of your software, Dillon."

"They will not." Dillon shook his head. "I reformatted the hard drive in the bio-lab and erased everything from my personal laptop. There is only one copy left—on my USB flash drive."

Keryn put a hand on his arm. "Do you have it in a safe place?"

Dillon looked all around the room, then leaned close to her. "Right here on my key chain."

A heavy shroud of silence settled around them.

The waiter appeared with their plates of food and set them out. "Enjoy your meal."

When he disappeared, Dillon looked around the table. "Shall we thank the Lord for our food?"

Rachel shrugged. "Sure, go ahead."

"You pray, Dillon," Keryn said.

Dillon took each of their hands in his and said a blessing over the food. When he finished, Keryn squeezed his hand. She was scared to death, but she knew Dillon wasn't afraid. He would take care of them all, would set this situation straight.

Dillon tore off a chunk of the Indian flatbread and wrapped it around a chunk of lamb. "Rachel, the problem is that this secret will not go away. It will get out and then it will be too big for us to handle."

"So we'll make it public before it leaks out." Rachel wrapped a carrot in a section of bread and popped it in her mouth. Her eyes went wide. "Wow!" she gasped. "I think they gave me a twelve." She gulped a big swallow of beer.

Dillon shook his head. "We have nothing to make public. The complete system requires the bio-computer, the software, and a functioning NMR device, all integrated, tested, and ready to demonstrate the factoring of large numbers. Until we have that, we cannot hold a press conference. We would look like those scientists who announced they had performed cold fusion in the lab but were unable to reproduce the results. That would be the worst possible situation. Most people would label us fools, except for the criminals, who would consider it worth spending a few bullets to determine if we were telling the truth."

Keryn's throat suddenly felt very dry. "So you're telling me we can't hide the secret and we can't unload it either? We're hanged if we do and hanged if we don't?"

Dillon thought about that for several seconds. Keryn could almost see him parsing the sentence in his head. Finally, he nodded. "That is correct, Keryn. Our only option is to keep it secret, finish it as rapidly as possible, and give it to the governing authorities."

Rachel

Rachel hated hearing that kind of talk. "Dillon, that's nonsense. We've always got options."

Keryn leaned forward. "Can't we just make it go away? Rachel, you could flush the bio-computer down the toilet. Dillon, you could erase your flash drive. Then we'd be back where we were."

"That is not an option," Dillon said. "We cannot erase what is in Rachel's mind—the secret to creating the bio-computer. We cannot erase the software design from my mind. And we cannot change the fact that it is likely somebody outside CypherQuanta broke into the bio-lab, tampered with my software, and stole the bio-computer. That person knows that a secret exists that is worth trillions of dollars. When that news reaches the wrong ears, Rachel and I will be kidnapped and all that we know will be forced out of us. We *must* go to the governing authorities."

Rachel couldn't stand it any longer. "I'd rather die than go to the government."

Dillon gave her a scorching look. "You may get your wish. Unfortunately, Keryn and I would also be killed. If you will not go to the governing authorities, I will."

Rachel narrowed her eyes. "You'll look pretty silly without a bio-computer to prove your claims."

"Not for long. I will send them to speak with you."

"I'll flush it down the toilet," Rachel said. "Big Brother won't get it."

"Then criminals will," Dillon said. "We have already established that."

Rachel glared at him. "Your problem is you see everything in black and white. Everything is a logic puzzle for you. Either/or. Black or white. True or false."

"Some things *can* be reduced to two possibilities," Dillon said. "The coin lands on heads or it lands on tails."

"You're not thinking quantum," Rachel said.

"I am . . . what?" Dillon looked deeply offended.

"Some things can be both/and. They don't have to be either/or. A qubit can be both one *and* zero simultaneously. That's how quantum computers work."

"I know how quantum computers work." Dillon leaned back in his chair. "You are reasoning by analogy, and such reasoning is flawed. You have not demonstrated that our situation bears any meaningful resemblance to a quantum mechanical system. You have simply asserted without proof—"

"Guys, we aren't getting anywhere," Keryn said. "I think you're both right. If we take it public the way it is now, we'll be cold-fusioned. Then it's just a matter of whether the crooks believe us or the government—"

"Same difference," Rachel said.

"The governing authorities are not criminal." Anger flashed across Dillon's face. "They are there to help us."

Rachel could not believe anybody could be so gullible. She gaped at him, trying to come up with a truly devastating response.

"Time out, you two," Keryn held up both hands. "I'm sorry, I shouldn't have brought it up. We're not getting anywhere. So let's just drop it for a while, okay? Let's talk to Grant as soon as we can and get his thoughts. He said he wanted to discuss a business opportunity with us. Until then, how about if we forget about it and think about something fun?"

Rachel glared at Dillon for a few seconds and then realized Keryn was right. They weren't getting anywhere. They'd been strung too tight for almost two weeks. No wonder they were scratching each other's eyes out. She reached out her hand across the table. "Truce?"

"Truce." Dillon shook her hand.

Rachel drank the last of her beer and signaled to the waiter for a refill. "Say, Keryn, this Ambari is really good. Want one?"

"No." Keryn's words came out clipped and tight.

It reminded Rachel of the way Mother used to act when people offered her a drink. "You seem kind of tense tonight. Want some wine to take the edge off? We could order a bottle."

"I said no."

Rachel saw that she had hit an artery. Which was just fine. Keryn was so . . . obnoxious, it would be nice to take her down a peg. "Can I ask you something?"

Keryn just looked at her.

"I know some Christians are really uptight about alcohol. And you don't drink, so I'm wondering—"

"Some of the people in my church drink alcohol," Keryn said. "It's not a big deal in my personal theology."

But something was a big deal. Rachel could see it in the strained look on Keryn's face. Somehow, Rachel had struck a nerve and she didn't know why. "Any particular reason you don't drink?"

"It's very simple," Keryn said as a hungry look slid across her face. "It's because I'm an alcoholic."

Rachel stared at her. "*You're* an alcoholic? But you're so . . ." She wanted to say *dull* but she managed not to. "You're so nice."

Keryn's face was burning now. "A lot of nice people have wretched pasts."

Rachel didn't know what to say. Finally she patted Keryn's arm with her hand. "Well, I'm sure you never killed anybody."

Tears sprang out on Keryn's face. She suddenly stood up and hurried away to the ladies' room.

CHAPTER
TWENTY-ONE

Keryn

Keryn could not believe she had just *cracked* like that. It wasn't fair. She was stressed out, had been stressed out now for months with the new job and the book deadline and this horrible bio-computer thing and . . . now that little vixen had busted her. In front of Dillon.

Keryn wiped her eyes and stared into the mirror. She looked awful. Not as awful as she felt, but awful enough.

The door creaked open. An orange sari blurred into view in the mirror.

"Keryn?" Rachel's voice was soft. "I'm sorry. I didn't mean to pry."

"It's okay." It was not okay and Keryn knew it, but she was not going to give Rachel the *satisfaction*.

Rachel took her hand and squeezed it. "I told Dillon I'd be gone awhile. If you want to talk, I'm here. And if you'd rather that I just took a long walk off a short pier, well, I can do that too, but I'm a pretty good swimmer, so it's not a very good way to get rid of me."

Keryn froze her with a blast of silence.

Rachel sighed deeply. "Sorry. I'm an idiot. I'll just . . . go back out there and leave you alone." She opened the door.

Keryn took a deep breath. "Wait, I'll come with you."

Rachel turned to look at her. "You don't have to."

"I want to. I'm ready." Keryn followed Rachel back to the table.

Dillon was sitting there with very wide eyes. "Keryn, we can go home if you are not feeling well. I can go get the minivan—"

Keryn shook her head and sat down. "Um, maybe I could just talk a little, okay?" Dillon might as well know what kind of person she was. He wouldn't approve of her, but she had been fooling herself, anyway, if she thought she had any kind of future with him. Eventually, she'd have to introduce him to her parents and then her whole past would come out. She couldn't run away from it forever. It was forgiven. She knew God had forgiven her. But she was still an alcoholic. Would always be one.

Rachel put a hand on Keryn's arm and stroked it gently. "You're with friends, Keryn."

Dillon leaned forward. "Rachel and I are good at keeping secrets."

Keryn swallowed the cannonball in her throat. "Okay. This is . . . kind of hard. Nobody here in San Diego knows any of this. Well, except my sister. And her husband."

Keryn fumbled for her glass and fortified herself with a gulp of ice water. "My parents are a little bit weird," she said. "They're . . . hippies. They never did get married. They got together in 1967. You know, the Summer of Love. Anyway, they had a couple of kids, my sister, Kathii, and me, and just hung out in Santa Cruz. They never let us call them Mom and Dad. It was always Sunflower and Rusty. They're kind of party animals. Not so much now, but when we were kids . . . a lot."

Keryn bit her lip. So far neither Dillon nor Rachel had freaked out. But she hadn't gotten to the bad part yet. "Anyway, I just kind of grew up thinking all that was normal. Parties every weekend. People getting drunk and throwing up on the kitchen table. Couples sacked out in sleeping bags in the yard. By the time I was eight, they were giving me beer at parties and blowing pot smoke in my face to get me high. And I liked it. I was getting drunk by the time I was eleven. I went all the way with my boyfriend in the back of my parents' VW bus when I was fourteen. Maybe thirteen, I don't remember very well."

Keryn had her eyes closed now. It was easier to talk that way. "And it just got worse through high school. The drinking and drugs and . . . boys and all that. I went to UC Santa Cruz and . . . moved in with my boyfriend. We had a party every weekend that pretty much lasted the whole weekend. And in the spring of my sophomore year . . ." Keryn's voice cracked. She clenched her fists tight and breathed in and out, in and out.

"One weekend we had a party at our apartment with a bunch of friends. We had a keg of beer and . . . I caught my boyfriend throwing up on the coffee table. I was pretty rocked, but I got mad and told him to go do that on the balcony. I yelled at him and . . ."

Keryn felt tears streaming down her face. She covered her face with her hands. "And he went out and leaned over the balcony and heaved out his guts and . . ."

Keryn didn't want to say any more. Couldn't say any more.

Rachel's soft hand touched Keryn's face. "Keryn, did he . . . fall?"

Keryn nodded. "The police report ruled out suicide and homicide. They said it was an accident."

"It *was* an accident," Dillon said.

"I know that, but I . . . contributed to it." Keryn felt the old familiar numbness in her chest again, the cold fingers caressing her heart.

"And that's when you turned your life around?" Rachel said.

"Right." Keryn dried her face with her napkin and opened her eyes. "My sister had just gotten involved with a group called InterVarsity at UCSC. She got me to come to it, and both of us decided we needed God. Kathii made me go to AA and I got cleaned up and . . . I've been sober ever since. But Rusty and Sunflower still don't understand. They're so . . . embarrassed that Kathii and I rejected everything they stood for. It's really hard to go home because they don't understand about the alcohol. They don't get it that one taste of beer would put me right back where I was. I used to hate them for raising me like that, but I forgave them years ago. Now I just feel sorry for them."

Keryn stared at her hands. "I don't know why I told you guys all that. It's kind of heavy, but . . . I guess not everybody is what they seem to be." She risked a look at Dillon.

Stark horror covered his face.

Keryn felt completely and utterly humiliated. She had blown it. Blown it big time.

D i l l o n

Dillon realized that his face had given him away. Rachel and Keryn were both staring at him with strange expressions he could not parse. He did not know what social context applied in this situation, but he could not remember all the meanings of the expressions, anyway.

"Dillon, did I upset you?" Keryn said. "I'm so sorry. I shouldn't have laid all that on you. Now you know what a terrible person I am and—"

"I do not think you are terrible," Dillon said. "You did not choose the way you were raised. You made a clean break with your past. And the Lord forgave you."

"You're not disgusted with me?" Keryn asked in a small voice.

"No, why would I be disgusted with you?" Dillon's throat felt very tight and his chest felt hot.

"I don't know," she said. "I just . . . that expression on your face. You looked horrified."

"I . . . was horrified," Dillon said in a very quiet voice. "Horrified with myself."

The two women sat looking at him in silence. The waiter came by. "Would you like the check?"

Rachel glared up at him. "We're busy. We'll let you know when we want the check."

The waiter backed away with his mouth hanging open.

Rachel leaned forward. "Dillon, maybe this is true confessions night. If you want to spill your guts, go ahead."

Dillon shivered. He did not like the expression "spill your guts." It gave him a bad mental image. Very distasteful. He had never spilled his guts to anyone. Robert did it all the time, and he said it made him feel better, but Dillon had never felt he could trust another person enough to do so, not even his counselor.

And yet . . . he felt he could trust Keryn. He had always thought of her as a righteous woman, and now she had spilled her guts and he found that he respected her even more. She would not judge him for the wrong he had done. Nor would Rachel. He looked around the restaurant and saw that they were alone.

Dillon took a deep breath and told them the one fact they needed to know in order to understand it all. "I have three brothers who are Normal." He then leaned back to let them work out the details.

Rachel and Keryn looked at each other for several very long seconds and then both of them began giggling.

Dillon did not know what was so funny. He had just explained his entire terrible childhood, and they thought it was a matter for laughing?

Rachel began playing with her napkin. "Say, Dillon, I think we need a little longer true confession than that."

"Is it not obvious?" he said.

Keryn shook her head. "Pretend we're stupid. Give us the long version."

The heat in Dillon's chest expanded. His head felt very light. He did not feel calm. Not calm at all. He wanted very much to talk about something calming. "There have been some interesting results on the Poincare conjecture lately," he said.

"Dillon!" Rachel reached over and put a hand on his arm. "Forget the Poincare conjecture! Tell us about your three normal brothers."

Dillon's whole head felt as if it were filled with cotton candy. He thought the answer to the Poincare conjecture would have a very long-lasting impact on Western history, but he could see that neither Rachel nor Keryn thought so.

Now his secret seemed to be rising up inside him, and he could not hold it down for one more second. "My brothers are all older than I," he said. "They are Normals. One of them was student body president in high school. All of them lettered in track. My second brother also lettered in basketball and football." Dillon stopped, feeling that to say another word would make him explode.

"I bet you didn't letter in anything, did you?" Rachel said.

Dillon stared at his hands. "I was in the chess club. Normals do not join the chess club."

"And just what exactly is a Normal?" Keryn asked.

"Whatever I am not," Dillon said slowly. "Whatever my brothers are."

"Are you angry at your brothers?" Rachel asked.

"No."

"Your mother?"

"No." Dillon felt sure he would faint. It was terribly disloyal, and now he had betrayed a family confidence.

"Your father, then." Rachel's voice sounded soft and warm. "You're angry at your father."

Dillon swallowed hard. "It is a sin not to honor your father and mother."

"You hate your father," Rachel said.

Dillon felt something deep and hot rising inside him. He could not speak. He could not think. It was wrong to hate. It was a sin.

"I do not hate . . ." Dillon could not say it. It was wrong to hate your father, but it was also wrong to prevaricate. He wanted to scream, to vomit. This spilling of guts was very painful. He put his elbows on the table and covered his face with his hands.

"When was the last time you talked to him?" Keryn said. "I know from experience that if you talk about it, you can work through it."

Dillon did a calculation. "Thirteen years ago."

Rachel gasped and put her small hand on his arm. "Dillon . . . you haven't talked to your father in thirteen *years*? What do you do when you go home?"

"Sometimes you cannot go home again," Dillon said. "Sometimes there is nothing to go home to. He has been embarrassed of me since I was four years old. I was clumsy. I could never catch the football. He said I threw like a girl. I tripped and fell when I was getting my high school diploma. He refused to come to my college graduation because he did not want to be embarrassed again. I have not gone back home since then."

Keryn's eyes were gleaming. "I'm sorry, Dillon."

"I think he'd be proud of you now, if . . . you'd give him a chance," Rachel said.

Dillon did not think so. He did not want to find out. He would make Grant proud of him instead. That was possible. To make his father proud of him . . . that was not possible. He reached for his glass of ice water and drank. Slowly, the water chilled the rage in his heart. The rage was not gone, but now it was back the way it had been before.

In a frozen place in his heart where he could control it.

"Are you feeling better?" Keryn said.

"No." Dillon dared to look at her eyes. "But now you know that I am not what I seem either."

Keryn's eyes looked very warm. "Maybe nobody is. But Jesus can heal the hate, if you let him." She raised her hand and signaled to the waiter. "Check!"

Rachel's grip tightened on Dillon's hand.

He looked up at her. Her face had twisted like a knot. Dillon did not need to know the social context to realize that she was angry. Very angry. "Rachel, is something wrong?"

She yanked her hand away. "Not at all. Let's go."

Dillon felt certain she was prevaricating, and he could not imagine why.

The waiter arrived with the check. Dillon looked at the bill. He took two fifty-dollar bills out of his wallet and handed them to the waiter. "Please keep the change. We will be staying to talk for a few more minutes."

"As you wish, sir." The waiter was smiling and looking at the two bills. "Whatever you wish, sir. Have a very good evening, sir."

Rachel stood up.

Dillon did not move. "Rachel, you are upset. Please sit down."

She glared at him. "I'm ready to go home."

"I am driving and you are not," Dillon said. "Unless you intend to walk all the way home in those absurd shoes, you will sit down and explain why you are angry."

Keryn leaned forward. "Rachel, I'm so sorry if I said something to upset you."

Rachel's eyes flicked between the two of them. "You won't like what I have to say."

"Please dump your guts," Dillon said.

Rachel gave a very loud sigh and sat down.

CHAPTER
TWENTY-TWO

Rachel

Rachel took a sip of her Indian beer, wondering how to begin. There was no way they would understand. Finally, she said, "Wow, it's nice to hear you both had happy childhoods."

Dillon looked confused. "We did not have happy childhoods. We just told you—"

Rachel put up her hand. "That was irony, Dillon, sorry. I'm just saying, by comparison to mine, your childhoods were idyllic."

Dillon nodded.

Rachel stared into the depths of her beer, but there was nothing there. "I told you guys I'm Jewish. That's half true. My father is Jewish. Not religious, just Jewish. My mother wasn't religious either when they got married. She was raised in this uptight fundamentalist church, but she rebelled and bagged religion when she went off to Princeton. She and Daddy lived together for a couple years, then they got married and started making babies."

Rachel wasn't sure how to explain the next part. She'd never understood it herself. "They had a little boy and named him Aaron. After Daddy. I've seen pictures of him. He was cute."

Dillon appeared to be holding his breath, his face was so still. Keryn's eyes were glistening.

Rachel put both hands flat on the table and studied them intently. "My brother, Aaron, died when he was six weeks old. SIDS. They never did know what caused it. But it freaked my mother out. She decided God was punishing her, so she . . . decided to get right with God."

Rachel looked at Dillon and took a deep breath. "Ever notice that when somebody gets right with God, they usually get wrong with everybody else?"

"I had not noticed that," Dillon said.

"I'm sorry, Rachel," Keryn said.

"My mother became the Church Lady from hell," Rachel said. "It wouldn't have been so bad if she just picked a normal church. But she only knew one kind of church. Uptight fundie. So that's what she went back to."

"So you were raised *Christian?*" Keryn said.

Rachel gave her a twisted smile. "I wish. That would have made it simple. When I was born, Mother told Daddy that she was going to raise me 'right,' meaning her way, and Daddy told her no, I was Jewish and he'd see me dead before he saw me growing up Christian. So they fought about that for several years and finally got a divorce when I was five or six—I forget exactly. I wound up in joint custody. Mostly with Mother, but every other weekend with Daddy."

"Rachel, I'm so sorry." Keryn scootched her chair over and wrapped a hug around Rachel. "That must have been horrible."

"Yeah." Rachel's voice felt thick and viscous in her throat. "Yeah, it was horrible." She daubed at her eyes with her twisted napkin. "One weekend I'd be in Sunday school learning all about how Jesus condemned the Jews for being legalists. Then the next weekend I'd be with Daddy, and I knew he was Jewish, but he wasn't a legalist, so I got very confused. Daddy didn't even go to the synagogue, so how could he be a legalist? About the only thing he did was have a Passover Seder every year. If anyone was a legalist, it was Mother."

Neither Dillon nor Keryn said anything.

"Then I'd go back to church the next week and learn about how the Jews killed Jesus, and that was really confusing because they never said which Jews. They just said Jews. It said so in the Bible. And I knew Daddy was Jewish and I was Jewish, and I knew we didn't kill Jesus."

Keryn's breath caught in her throat. "You didn't kill Jesus, Rachel."

Dillon's hands clenched on the table. "No, you did not kill him."

"And then . . ." Rachel felt the anger rising in her heart again. "And then I'd go to Daddy's house the next weekend and he'd tell me about what Christians did to Jews in Europe for hundreds of years. How they killed Jews for being Christ-killers. How they said we put the blood of Christian children in our Passover matzohs."

Dillon looked like he was going to be sick.

Keryn's face had gone completely white. "How long did all this go on?"

"Till I was twelve," Rachel said. "It was a war between Mother and Daddy, and I was the prize. They fought like tigers whenever one of them came to pick me up from the other. Then when I was twelve, Daddy secretly enrolled me in Sunday school."

"Sunday school?" Keryn said. "I think I'm missing something."

"When a girl turns thirteen, she's supposed to have a Bat Mitzvah. You have to read from the Torah and the Prophets. In Hebrew. Usually, it takes months to learn to do that, to say all the prayers and stuff. Daddy did that when he was a kid and he wanted me to do it too. Not a religious thing. Just culture. Most synagogues have a special school that meets on Sunday mornings to train kids in Hebrew and all that. Sunday school. When Daddy put me in that, Mother went nonlinear."

"It wasn't fair, what they did to you," Keryn said.

Dillon shook his head. "It was not logical."

"I hated it," Rachel said. "It was the worst thing in the world. I was twelve years old, and I was stuck in this war zone with no way to do the right thing. The rules changed every weekend."

"And that's why you hate your mother?" Keryn said.

"I don't hate my mother. We made our peace a long time ago. I feel sorry for her."

Keryn looked confused. "But . . . you call your parents 'Mother' and 'Daddy.' Sounds partial to your father."

Rachel sighed. "I identify more with Daddy than Mother. But I don't hate either one of them."

Keryn's eyes narrowed. "It sounds like you're still harboring some kind of . . . grudge."

"Oh, you better believe I've got a grudge," Rachel said. "But I don't hate Mother or Daddy." She closed her eyes because she didn't want to see their faces when she told them. "It's Jesus I hate."

A gasp.

"Oh, Rachel." Keryn's voice was almost a sob. "Don't hate Jesus."

"Jesus was . . . Jewish," Dillon said.

"That's why I hate him." Rachel took a deep breath. "Jesus was Jewish, but he went and started his own religion. He was always calling the Pharisees hypocrites and legalists, but they weren't! I read up on them. They were great men. They were the best Jews there were. Rabbi Hillel and Rabban Gamliel were leaders of the Sanhedrin and were good and kind men. It was the Christians who were the arrogant ones. As soon as they got the chance, they started persecuting Jews and they never quit. They called us Christ-killers and told lies about us and they murdered us. So who are the hypocrites?"

Keryn put her hand on Rachel's shoulder. "Rachel—"

"I didn't kill Jesus, but I'm glad somebody did," Rachel said. "He ruined life for every Jew who ever lived, and he ruined my life too. He told all those hateful stories. I learned all about them in church. In his stories, Jews are the bad guys and the Samaritan is the good guy. Jews are the wretched overseer who killed the son of the land-owner and will get punished. Jews are the hypocritical older brother who didn't rejoice when the prodigal son came home. Jesus hated Jews. I *hate* Jesus!"

Shocked silence.

Rachel wiped her eyes. "Sorry, but when I hear people saying that Jesus fixes things, it just drives me right up the wall. Jesus didn't fix my life—he ruined it."

"I'm sorry," Keryn said. "I didn't have any idea. Jesus means so much to me . . . I didn't realize he'd mean something awful to you."

"It was not your fault that you were raised like that," Dillon said. "We will not talk about Jesus with you again."

"Thanks, guys," Rachel said, feeling a little better. She had known all along she'd have to tell Dillon this eventually. Tonight was probably the best possible time to get it out in the open. All of them had a dirty little secret, and who could say whose was worst.

"Well," Keryn said. "It's getting late. Maybe we'd better be going home."

Rachel saw that they were the only diners left in the restaurant. The waitstaff were busy cleaning tables and pulling linen table-cloths.

Dillon stood up. "I'll go get the car and pick you ladies up outside in a few minutes." He walked outside and strode away up the street. Rachel and Keryn sat down on a couch just inside the door. They looked at each other and both of them cracked a guilty smile.

Keryn shrugged. "I guess we both shot ourselves in the kneecap, huh?"

Rachel felt a very large lump in her throat. "I guess."

Dillon

Dillon drove up to the curb and stopped. The door of the Star of India opened and the maître d' ushered Rachel and Keryn out. He was staring at both of them as they walked toward the minivan. Dillon did not like men who could not control their eyes, but there was nothing he could do to make the maître d' stop staring. Dillon shut off the engine and hopped out to open the door for the ladies and help them in.

Rachel took his hand first and stepped up inside. Dillon's heart thumped again in that strange way that seemed to happen whenever she was around. Dillon felt very sorry that she hated Jesus. Then she was inside. Dillon gave Keryn his hand and helped her in too. Her hand felt very warm and soothing. He felt very sorry that she was not a virgin. There was a hollow feeling deep inside his stomach that he did not understand.

Keryn settled in beside Rachel. Dillon closed the door of the minivan and got back in the driver's seat. He buckled his seat belt and looked back to be sure the ladies were both belted. Earlier in the evening, when he had picked them both up at Keryn's house, he was forced to argue with Rachel to make her buckle up.

Dillon started the car and drove carefully down Prospect Street toward Torrey Pines Road. The streets were nearly empty. The clock on the dashboard told Dillon that it was 11:52, but he knew that this clock was nearly two minutes fast. He made a mental note to adjust it when he got home. He did not feel calm when his clocks told different times.

Dillon saw a pair of headlights zooming up from behind at a very unsafe speed. The headlights switched into the right lane and came up alongside him, slowing down so that they matched his speed. As they passed under a streetlight, Dillon saw that the car was a gray Ford Taurus with dark windows.

One block ahead, the traffic light turned yellow. Dillon took his foot off the gas.

The Taurus squirted ahead and cut much too close in front of Dillon. Then it braked fiercely. Dillon jammed on his brakes. Rachel screamed. The antilock brakes began hammering, but a minivan cannot stop as fast as a Taurus. At the last second Dillon spun the wheel to the right. His left front bumper nicked the back of the Taurus just before the minivan shuddered to a stop.

In the sudden silence Dillon felt his heart pounding very fast. He looked back at the ladies. "Are you hurt?"

"I'm fine," Keryn said.

"I . . . I . . . I'm okay too." Rachel looked like she had just swallowed a goldfish. "What happened?"

"He cut me off." Dillon looked outside. A well-dressed man in a suit had gotten out of the Taurus. He was shaking his head and looking at his back bumper. Dillon shut off his ignition and took the keys out. He reached into the glove compartment and took out his registration papers and proof of insurance card. "I will talk to the man. Please stay in the car."

He stepped out of the minivan and closed the door. As a precaution, he pressed the remote. All the door locks clicked. He put his keys in his pocket and turned to face the man. "I'm very sorry, but—"

The man in the suit had a gun pointed at him. "Give me your wallet."

Dillon stared at the gun. It was a Sig Sauer nine-millimeter pistol. He could not tell if it was a Model P225 or P226.

Three more doors of the Taurus flew open and more men jumped out. Each of them had a Sig Sauer.

"Give me your wallet!" the first man shouted.

Dillon put both hands out where the men could see them clearly. "My wallet is in my front left pocket. I am taking it out now."

He moved his left hand very slowly into his pocket and eased out his wallet. He held it up to the light so the men could see it, then dropped it on the ground and stepped back several paces.

One of the men came forward and picked up the wallet. He pointed his gun at Dillon's heart. "Your car keys too. We're taking the car."

"It is a minivan."

"We're taking the minivan. Give us the keys now." The man looked surprisingly calm. Dillon thought that if he himself were committing a carjacking, he would be much more nervous than these men. They must be professionals.

"My keys are in my right front pocket," Dillon said. "I am removing them now." He slowly put his hand in his pocket. Then he remembered that the women were still in the minivan. "Excuse me. I have some passengers." He stepped to the window of the minivan and tapped on the glass with his left hand. "Keryn! Rachel! Please come out! They want the minivan."

Dillon stepped back two steps and slowly pulled his keys out of his pocket.

The minivan door rolled open. Rachel came out first, and her face was sweating in the dull yellow sodium lights. "Dillon, what's going on?"

"They are carjacking my minivan."

Rachel looked terrified.

Keryn came out next and her mouth was hanging open. "Dillon, they can't do this."

"They are doing it. I refuse to argue with Sig Sauer. He usually wins."

The man holding Dillon's wallet pointed his gun at Rachel. "Give me your handbag. And you there, in black. Give me your purse."

Rachel held her little orange bag out at arm's length. The man snatched it away. Keryn took her cell phone out of her purse and threw the purse on the ground. The man picked it up, then pointed his gun at Dillon. "Now the keys, sir, if you please."

Dillon set them on the roof of the minivan and stepped back. "Keryn. Rachel. Stand behind me."

Headlights appeared three blocks back.

The men snapped into action. Two of them jumped into Dillon's minivan. The other two leaped back into the Taurus. Both engines roared to life. The vehicles sped away, racing through a red light and turning left onto Torrey Pines Road heading toward Highway 52.

Dillon found that he had been holding his breath. Keryn and Rachel threw their arms around him, and Dillon felt their bodies shaking.

"Dillon, they got your car keys," Rachel said. "They got your flash drive."

Dillon's heart was still pounding in his chest. He looked all around. The headlights behind them had vanished. They were alone at midnight in La Jolla.

And Rachel's bio-computer was in the little orange handbag the men had stolen.

CHAPTER
TWENTY-THREE

Keryn

Keryn had never felt so scared. She was trembling and wanted to throw up. This whole thing had turned into one of the stories she liked to write. Except that she didn't want to be inside the story. She wanted to be safely outside, twisting, twisting, twisting the plot, leaving the reader gasping with every twist until it reached that trademark Keryn Wills ending, bittersweet and clever and haunting, with a final surprise in the closing sentence.

This was clearly not going to be that kind of story. Rachel's whole body was shaking. Dillon was a shelter in the storm. Keryn felt his hand patting her gently on the back. "Rachel, Keryn, we are safe. They took our things, but we are alive. Now we need to call somebody to come get us. And we need to call the police."

Somewhere deep inside Keryn's brain, a neuron jiggled. Something in one of John le Carré's spy novels. *There are no coincidences.* "Um, Dillon? Rachel?" Keryn's voice felt shaky and weak. "I . . . I'm wondering if this was just a simple carjacking."

Rachel pulled away from her and Dillon. "You're not suggesting . . ."

Dillon looked completely puzzled. "Suggesting what? Those men planned this very well. They trapped us out in the open and stole our money and my minivan."

Keryn looked nervously around, wishing she could speak openly, afraid of who might be listening in the night. "That's not all they stole. I think we were followed. I think somebody knows who we are and what we . . . had, and now they've stolen it."

Rachel's green eyes were round and huge. She unclipped her cell phone from a thin belt at her waist. "I'll call Grant. He'll come get us. Oh my gosh, he's going to be so upset." She punched a button.

Keryn and Dillon leaned close. The phone rang four times and then Grant's answering machine message came on. "Hello, this is Grant O'Connell. I'm terribly sorry I missed you—"

Rachel snapped the phone shut. "Maybe he and Julia went somewhere. We can't leave a message. This is too sensitive."

"Call his cell phone," Dillon said. He pulled his own phone out of his shirt pocket. "I'd better call the police. They can set up road-blocks and stop the minivan before it gets far."

Keryn didn't think that would do any good. If this was the kind of operation she thought it was, Dillon's car was parked somewhere three or four blocks away, already abandoned. The men hadn't come for the money and the minivan. They had come for the bio-computer and Dillon's key ring. "Go ahead and call them. We'll keep trying to get through to Grant."

Dillon stepped away a few paces.

Keryn stayed with Rachel. "Call Grant on his cell phone."

Rachel pressed some buttons and held it up so they could both hear. The line didn't even ring once but switched to voice mail right away.

Keryn felt frustrated. Grant must have turned off his cell phone. She opened her own phone. "Here, I'll call Clifton. He lives some-where in La Jolla, doesn't he?" She selected his number in her phone list and pressed Send. It rang four times and switched to voice mail.

"Try his landline," Rachel said.

Keryn shook her head. "Clifton doesn't have a landline. He uses a cell phone for everything."

Dillon was still talking on his phone. From the sounds of things, he had some dim-witted sergeant on the line. He was reading off the vehicle identification number from his registration papers. His face looked calm, but his fists were clenched very tight. Keryn felt horrible. There was nothing Dillon could have done. You didn't argue with four men with guns.

"Who do we call now?" Rachel said. "We've gone through all the people who know our secret."

"I can call my sister," Keryn said. "She could send her husband out to pick us up."

"I could call my aunt Esther," Rachel said. "She goes to bed early, but she'd come get me."

Keryn shivered. "I think we need to stay together tonight. Kathii can put us all up. It'll be safer that way."

Fear lit up Rachel's eyes. "Okay, call her."

Keryn punched a number and heard the phone ring four times. The answering machine message started up. Keryn knew the answering machine was right by Kathii's bed and the phone would have woken her up and she would be listening right now, so she just started talking. "Kathii, this is Keryn, and I'm really, really scared. I was out with some—"

"Keryn, what's wrong?" Kathii sounded groggy and frantic.

Keryn felt so relieved that she had reached a real human being that she almost couldn't breathe. "Kathii! Oh, thank God you picked up! We were carjacked. I'm stranded in La Jolla with two friends of mine. Can you—"

"Of course. Hang on a second. Allen, wake up! Keryn's in trouble! Wake *up*! Keryn, where are you?"

Keryn checked the signs at the nearest corner. "We're in La Jolla on Prospect Street, just north of Torrey Pines Road."

"Allen'll come get you in a few minutes. Keryn, are you hurt? Is everyone okay?"

"Yes, we're fine, but . . . we got robbed too."

A gasp. "Oh, Keryn, I'm sorry. Thank God you're alive. Did you lose much?"

Keryn felt a deep pain stab through her chest. *Only a few trillion dollars.* "Quite a bit."

"He's on the way, Keryn. Stay on the line. I'm gonna pray for you right now. Thank you, Lord, for protecting Keryn and her friends. Please, Jesus, just keep her safe until Allen gets there."

Keryn closed her eyes and clung to the sweet voice of her sister. God was going to take care of them. God had to take care of them. God could fix this awful mess they were in.

Rachel

Rachel felt numb in her brain. This was horrible, simply horrible. Dillon finished talking to the cops and joined her and Keryn. Keryn still had her phone to her ear. Rachel could hear the voice of Keryn's sister praying. Thanking Jesus. Rachel clung to Dillon's arm and fought the nausea welling up inside her.

Within minutes, a white Toyota Camry turned right at the light and headed toward them. Keryn raised her arm and waved frantically, still talking into the phone. "He's here, Kathii! Allen just turned onto our street. Thank God!"

The Camry passed them and flipped a U-turn and pulled up next to them. A man in his late thirties jumped out and raced to Keryn and hugged her tight. "Keryn, it's okay, it's okay. You're fine. I'm here." He patted her back, then reached a hand over Keryn's shoulder toward Dillon. "I'm Allen Russell."

Dillon shook his hand. "Dillon Richard. This is our friend Rachel Meyers."

Rachel nodded toward him.

Allen stepped back. "Okay, listen, you're all in shock. Hop in the car. I'll take Keryn to our house and then I can take you all wherever you need to go."

Keryn hesitated as she placed her hand on the door handle. "Uh, Allen, would it be possible for us all to stay at your house?"

Rachel watched as Allen flicked a glance at Keryn, but he didn't question her request. "Um . . . sure, Keryn. We can find room."

They all piled in. Rachel and Keryn sat in back. Dillon sat in front with Allen.

Rachel closed her eyes and saw in her mind's eye the faces of the men who had robbed them. They would come back. She knew they would come back. Next time, they would kill her. She knew it.

Keryn's soft hand patted Rachel's cheek gently. "We're going to be okay, Rache. God's going to take care of us."

"Sure." Rachel turned and looked at Keryn. "I'm sorry I got you into this mess. This thing has just . . . exploded in our face."

"It's okay," Keryn said. "Just relax. Allen and Kathii will help us."

Rachel wasn't sure she wanted two more people in on the secret, but it didn't look like she had much choice.

A few minutes later, they took the Genesee exit off of Highway 52 and headed north into University City. It was the same exit Rachel would have taken to go home. They turned right on Governor and hung a left soon after that, and Rachel was lost. After three turns, they pulled into a driveway and sat waiting for the garage-door opener to grind its way up.

Then they were inside and the door was shut and they were safe. Sort of.

A tall woman in a bathrobe was waiting inside the garage. She yanked open the back door of the Camry and smothered Keryn in a huge hug. "Keryn! Oh, thank God!"

It took a few minutes to get settled inside the house. Keryn and Dillon and Rachel sat in a row on the couch. Allen sat in a big leather easy chair. Keryn's sister, Kathii, went to make hot chocolate. Keryn told the whole story of the carjacking—leaving out their speculation about the carjackers' motives.

Allen nodded quietly until she finished. "I'm sorry. It was just . . . bad luck."

"It was not bad luck," Dillon said.

Rachel stiffened. "Dillon."

Keryn leaned forward. "Rachel, Dillon, I think we need to tell them. It doesn't make much difference anyway. They stole . . . it."

Dillon nodded. "Yes, it is out of our hands now."

Rachel felt her heart breaking. No, she didn't want to tell anyone this awful secret. But yes, it was out of their hands now. She sighed deeply. "Okay, tell them."

Dillon explained about the bio-computer and the software they had been developing. Allen's eyes grew steadily larger. Kathii came in with steaming mugs of hot chocolate. "Marshmallows, anyone?"

Nobody wanted marshmallows.

Kathii sat down on the arm of Allen's chair. "So they got the software and the bio-computer? I guess that means you're out of danger, right? I mean, now you can just call in the FBI and it's out of your hands."

"Not exactly." Dillon stood up slowly and reached into his pocket. He set the contents on the coffee table. A Swiss Army knife. A pair of fingernail clippers. Four quarters.

A flash drive.

Rachel screamed, shocked, terrified. Keryn gasped and fell back against the couch.

"I unclipped it in my pocket before I pulled my keys out of my pocket," Dillon said. "I stalled for a minute by tapping on the window and telling the ladies to come out."

Allen leaned forward and picked up the flash drive. "So . . . you're telling me they only got half of what they need? They have the bio-computer but not the software to use it?"

"I am afraid so," Dillon said. "When they find that out, they will come back looking for us."

Rachel felt very hot all over. This was unbelievable.

Keryn let out a low moan.

Dillon turned to her. "Keryn, are you all right? I am sorry, but . . . it was just instinct to keep the flash drive."

Rachel was trying hard to breathe.

Keryn finally leaned forward. "Dillon, I have something to show you."

Dillon's eyebrows shot up.

Keryn slipped her thumb and forefinger inside the keyhole slit in her dress, reached down, and pulled out . . .

Rachel's bio-computer.

D i l l o n

Dillon turned his head away, feeling deeply embarrassed. His ears had gone very warm. He felt a jolt of fear, hot and molten, in his stomach. "The criminals got . . . nothing." He could not believe it. "How. . . ?"

"As soon as I saw the guns, I knew they were going to rob us all," Rachel said. "I took out the bio-computer and was going to hide it in the car. Then the man told you to give him the keys and I knew they were going to take your car. This sari is skintight and I didn't dare try to tuck it inside and . . ." She shrugged. "I couldn't think what to do. Then Keryn just grabbed it and popped it down her front and you opened the door—just that fast. I was scared to death, but I hopped out first and hoped she had time to smooth herself out."

"They're going to come back for us," Keryn said.

Dillon felt dizzy. "They have my keys, my wallet, my credit cards, my driver's license, everything. They will go to my house and search it."

"Mine too." Rachel looked defiant. "They won't find anything. I don't have another bio-computer."

"If they go to my house, they won't find anything there either," Keryn said. "Just my novel, and that's backed up online. And—" She gasped and stood up. "Allen, can you run me over to my house? Smiley's there all alone."

Dillon stood up too. "No, Keryn, you cannot risk it. If they are watching your house, they will grab you or follow you back here."

"But . . . Smiley." Keryn put her face in her hands. "I can't let anything happen to him."

Dillon looked at his watch. "Keryn, no. It is unsafe. Do you have a neighbor with a key who can check on your cat tomorrow?"

"Oh!" Keryn's mouth broke into a smile. "Of course! Hold on, I'll call them now."

"It is already after midnight," Dillon said.

"Not a problem." Keryn opened her cell phone and punched in a number. A short pause, and then . . . "Hi, it's Keryn. Still up working on your novel?"

She listened for a couple of minutes. "Oh, I hear you, I hear you. I'm behind on mine too. Listen, I'm not able to get back home tonight, and I might be gone for a few days. Could you be a dear and take care of Smiley until I get back? I know he loves playing with Zephyr."

Another pause. "That'll be great. Big hug to Eunice and the girls. Night, night!"

Keryn closed the phone. "He was still up writing. He'll go get Smiley right now and keep him until I get back. They've got a Ragdoll cat too, so they know how to take care of him. We trade cat-sitting. I keep Zephyr for them when they go out of town."

Dillon felt impatient to deal with the real issue at hand. "This thing has become dangerous. We need to call in the governing authorities."

"I'm not going to let Big Brother have it," Rachel said. "I'd sooner flush it down the toilet."

"That'll get us killed!" Keryn said. "Somebody has been tracking us. They've probably already discovered they didn't get what they were looking for. They're going to come looking for us, and the absolute worst thing we can tell them is that we're very sorry but we flushed a trillion dollars worth of bio-computer down the sewer to feed the sharks. They're not going to believe that, and they'll play hardball."

Dillon did not want to think about what the next time would be like. "We need protection. We can call the police and—"

"You talked to the police already, didn't you?" Rachel said.

"Yes." The policeman had taken all Dillon's information in a bored tone that suggested he was probably surfing the Web at the same time.

"And did they, offer to come protect you so you won't get carjacked again?" Rachel asked.

"No, of course not. We would have to tell them about the . . ." Dillon leaned back and closed his eyes. It would be the worst sort of logic to tell the police about the bio-computer. The police would smile and politely promise to do something. No action would be taken, but the word would leak out. In days, instead of one group after them, there would be several. The police would do nothing, but the criminals would act swiftly.

"Guys, we have to go to the government," Keryn said. "Unless we want to just wait for the crooks to come back so we can hand it over nicely."

"Or terrorists," Allen said. "If terrorists got hold of this, they could shut down the economy. Sort of like a financial 9/11—and it would be global. Once you shut down the flow of money, it doesn't start up again. Money flow has momentum, kind of like water flow. If you shut the valve for even a short period of time you damage the system. Catastrophically."

Rachel grabbed hold of Dillon's arm. "That's bad, but the alternative is no better. If you give it to Big Brother, then you've got the heel of the government grinding itself into your face, forever. I can't live like that."

Dillon had read *1984*. He thought it was nonsense. But he could not make Rachel give the bio-computer to the governing authorities. If she thought Big Brother would get it, she would destroy it, and then they would all be in mortal danger. Rachel might be willing to die to keep the bio-computer away from Big Brother, but Dillon was not.

"We need Grant's opinion on all this," Keryn said. "He financed this thing. When I talked to him today, it sounded like he had some sort of plan."

Kathii yawned. "Let's sleep on it, shall we? It's getting late, and tomorrow morning the boys and I are going to church camp."

Dillon opened his eyes. "You are going out of town?"

"Sort of," Kathii said. "Up the coast a ways. Our church is having a weekend campout at the YMCA camp. It's got a little lagoon there, with canoeing and windsurfing and swimming and things. Allen's going to work all day and then he'll join us tomorrow evening. Keryn, were you planning to go?"

"I was going to work on my novel," Keryn said. "But I guess that's not going to happen until it's safe to go back home again. Can we . . . stay here for a few days?"

Dillon shook his head. "We cannot do anything here except sit. And we have no transportation. My car is gone. Your car and Rachel's are parked in front of your house, and it is unsafe to be seen there. Somebody is probably watching your street around the clock."

"And we're broke," Rachel said. "My money, my Visa card, my license were all in that handbag."

Keryn shivered. "Mine too, in my purse. I'll have to go to the DMV and get another license tomorrow."

"Not safe," Dillon said. "They will be watching the DMV."

Allen leaned forward. "Listen, we can spot you guys some money, but I think what you really need is a break until you talk with Grant and figure out what he has in mind. How about if you join us for church camp?"

Dillon did not think that was a good idea. "What kind of church do you belong to?"

Keryn shrugged. "Nondenominational. It's a neighborhood church here in University City."

Dillon did not know what a nondenominational church was. "Are you Calvinist or Arminian?"

Rachel punched him on the arm. "Hey, chill, Dillon. I'm the pagan, remember? If they're gonna try to convert anybody, it'll be me."

"Guys . . ." Keryn had a funny look on her face. "Nobody's going to try to convert either one of you, okay? I'll tell them you don't want to be converted. But listen, I think it would be good for us to get away for a few days. The bad guys won't have a clue where we are, and we can take a break from this . . . thing we're locked in. As soon as we get hold of Grant and Clifton, they can come pick us up. Okay?"

"I'm game," Rachel said. "Come on, Dillon, it'll be a blast. Ever been windsurfing? I'll teach you."

Dillon had no desire to go windsurfing. But it sounded like Keryn and Rachel were going to this church camp. It would not be logical for the three of them to get separated.

"All right, I will go," he said.

In any event, they could have many interesting conversations on quantum mechanics. It would help calm them all down after a terrible and exhausting week.

CHAPTER
TWENTY-FOUR

Keryn

In the morning Allen went off to work, and everyone else piled into Kathii's minivan with an enormous load of camping gear. Keryn wore some jeans and a T-shirt she had borrowed from Kathii. Her sister had offered clothes to Dillon and Rachel, but they declined—since they were going to be stopping at a store for supplies anyway—and wore the same clothes they'd worn to the restaurant last night. Jason and Jordan, who were eight-year-old twins, were bragging about how they would take a canoe and paddle it all the way to Alaska. Kathii drove up to Carlsbad, where they stopped at a Target to go shopping.

Keryn picked out some underwear and casual clothes and then tried on several swimsuits. She wanted something that would be modest, but . . . not too modest. She finally settled on a one-piece Lycra suit, electric blue with white diagonal stripes. When she finished shopping, Dillon was waiting quietly in the sporting goods section reading the directions on a box containing a pup tent. Rachel was playing some sort of video game with Jason in the electronics section. Jordan was sitting on a bike, twisting an imaginary throttle, and saying, "Vroom! Vroom!"

They all went through the checkout line and Kathii paid with her Visa card. The bill came to over three hundred dollars. Keryn winced. "Thanks, sis. We'll pay you back as soon as this thing's over."

Kathii smiled. "Take your time. I've got no balance and a twenty-five-day grace period on this card, so it's no big deal."

Keryn thought it must be nice to have a Visa card with no balance on it. They drove up to the next exit, crossed the overpass, and turned left onto a gravel road. After a long jouncing ride, they reached the campground.

It wasn't noon yet, but a few families were already there. The pastor's wife, Gloria, greeted them all and assigned them spots for two tents. Gloria was about four foot ten, and she might have been that far around too. She wore a huge pink top and flowered pants and a smile as big as her heart. Keryn always felt very welcome around Gloria.

"Who's your friends?" Gloria said, taking in Dillon's suit and Rachel's sari without showing any hint that they were dressed oddly.

"Co-workers," Keryn said. "This is Dillon—he goes to a Presbyterian church in Mira Mesa. This is Rachel and she's Jewish. Guys, say hi to Gloria, who pretty much runs the church when her husband isn't looking."

"How lovely to meet you!" Gloria waded into Rachel and wrapped her up in a hug.

Keryn winced. When Gloria hugged you, she left no doubt that you had been hugged. Severely.

Gloria fingered Rachel's sari. "This makes your eyes look so green! It's beautiful."

Rachel gave her a five-hundred-watt smile.

Gloria turned her attention to Dillon. Keryn held her breath. She did not think a bear hug would sit well with him.

Gloria looked him up and down, taking in his pinstriped suit, his silk tie, his hard leather shoes. Then she stretched out a hand. "Dillon, you've got taste. I'd like you to teach my husband how to shop sometime." She wrapped up his hand in both of hers and shook it. "Welcome to camp!"

Dillon looked as if he wanted to ask whether she was a Calvinist or an Arminian, but he shook her hand and even gave her a shy smile.

"Okay, guys, maybe you better get changed," Keryn said. She gave Gloria a shrug. "We went out to eat in La Jolla last night and got robbed, so we're a little overdressed for this party. Kathii bought us some clothes. . . . I guess we'll just . . . go get changed." It sounded lame and Keryn knew it.

Gloria gave her a knowing smile but didn't ask any of the obvious questions. "Go on, then! Get changed, then come back and get your tent up!" She shooed them away with her hands, then turned and bellowed at the twins. "Jason! Jordan! You need to wait till you've got an adult to take you in that canoe!"

Keryn grabbed the Target bags out of the minivan. "Here, Dillon. Take this one, Rachel. There's bathrooms over there where you can get changed. I'll get started with Kathii on the tents."

Dillon and Rachel disappeared into the bathrooms. Keryn joined Kathii, who was struggling to unroll the two tents they had brought. They spent the next five minutes spreading out the tents and laying out stakes at the corners and the midpoints. Keryn rummaged around in the minivan and found a rubber hammer.

Dillon came out of the rest room carrying a bag and turned to look out at the lagoon. He had put on a pair of khakis and a polo shirt and running shoes, and he looked . . . excellent. Kathii gave Keryn a little nudge. "Sister, you better be glad I'm married or I'd be horning in on your game."

Keryn sighed. " 'Fraid I already ruined my chances last night. I told him about Rusty and Sunflower and . . . everything."

Kathii just looked at her. "I did all that stuff too and Allen's okay with it. Forgiven is forever."

"Yeah, well, Dillon's kind of fussy." Keryn sighed. "He likes things just so. Orderly. I'm afraid I shocked him."

"Well, just remember, it ain't over till the fat lady—" Kathii sucked in her breath. "Good heavens!"

Keryn turned to look and saw Rachel coming out of the women's bathroom wearing a bright orange bikini. Three itty bitty triangles of cloth. She had a trim, lithe body that made Keryn want to shriek.

"Sister . . ." Kathii's voice came out in a hiss. "I think you've got competition."

Keryn felt like somebody had punched her in the stomach. "I . . . no. I'm not in that game."

Kathii reached over and pinched Keryn's cheek. "Listen, I don't want to see you roll over and play dead. You always do that. I want to see you fight fire with fire."

"I am not going to prance around in three little Band-Aids," Keryn said.

"I'm not talking about Band-Aids," Kathii said. "But what have you got against flaunting it a little bit?"

"I think Dillon's impervious to flaunting."

"Sister, there isn't any man alive who's impervious to flaunting. Tasteful flaunting. If you want something, sometimes you need to fight for it."

"I'll fight, but Rachel's not fighting fair. Somebody should talk to her. That is just so . . . indecent. When the men get here from work, we're gonna have a wives' revolt on our hands."

Kathii thought about that for a minute. "Well, we've got a few hours yet. I betcha Gloria will have a little chat with her by then. Look, Dillon's coming this way now. Did you see that? He didn't even look at her."

Keryn was surprised. In her experience, it was a rare guy who wouldn't at least take a quick peek. Dillon's face was unreadable as he approached them. He put his Target bag in the minivan and then came over. "Can I help with the tent?"

"Are you good at pounding spikes?" Keryn held up the hammer. "I'm not."

Dillon took it and squatted beside her. He studied the tents for a minute, then spent the next five minutes adjusting their layout so the edges were exactly parallel. He pounded in the first spike, made some fine adjustments, then went from corner to corner, pounding in the spikes rapidly.

Keryn stood watching him with one eye. With the other, she enjoyed the sight of Gloria having a quiet discussion with Rachel by the water's edge. Kathii came back from the minivan lugging a large sackful of the metal framing for the tents. Keryn helped her spread out the tubes on the grass. She was feeling better now. Gloria would set Rachel straight, and then it would be a fair—

"Yoohoo!" Rachel's voice sang out.

Keryn turned to look.

Rachel was sauntering back toward them, with the twins jumping around her, looking like they had just been given a year's worth of allowance.

Rachel put her Target bag in the minivan and came up next to Keryn. "The boys want to go canoeing, and Gloria thought maybe Dillon could take them out. Would you like to do that, Dillon?"

Dillon didn't look up. "I need to help with the tents."

Kathii didn't hesitate for an instant. "We're fine, Dillon. Go ahead. The boys'll love it. We can manage here."

Dillon stood up and looked over at Keryn.

"Go," she said. "The rest of this will be easy."

Jason and Jordan came running over and began jumping around Dillon. "Can we? Can we, Mr. Richard?"

Dillon shrugged. "Okay." He still hadn't so much as looked at Rachel.

The boys began shrieking with glee. Each of them grabbed one of Dillon's hands and began tugging him toward the dock.

Keryn and Kathii followed to help get them launched. Kathii made a fuss about putting huge orange life vests on the boys just so. Dillon had a hard time putting his on. Keryn wondered if he'd ever worn one before. She watched him fumble at the straps for a while and finally decided she'd better help.

"Here, let me show you." Rachel appeared from nowhere and rearranged Dillon's vest. She rethreaded the straps, cinched them down, and squared him away. "Perfect! Here, boys, I'll help you into the canoe." She gave Jason a hand in, followed by Jordan.

Dillon didn't take the hand she offered. He clambered in, but then his foot slipped and he nearly fell into the water. He crept forward past the boys until he reached the middle of the canoe, where he took a seat and grabbed a paddle. He turned and smiled at Jason and Jordan. "Are we ready, boys?"

"Bye, Dillon!" Keryn waved.

"Have fun, boys!" Kathii said.

"Don't you worry, we'll take good care of them!" Rachel slipped past Keryn and hopped into the tail of the canoe. "Save some lunch for us!" She pushed off and the canoe slid silently away from the dock.

Keryn's mouth fell open and she could not even think what to say.

Rachel was already paddling away with swift, sure strokes. The boys were splashing the paddles in the water and hooting with laughter.

"I don't believe that!" Kathii's voice was shaking with rage. "Keryn, she hijacked your guy! Go get her!"

Keryn was too angry to move. That little . . . hussy!

Quiet laughter rippled over the dock.

Keryn turned and saw Gloria's whole frame shaking. "Well! She outfoxed us all, didn't she? Time to make some serious battle plans. I'd like to win this war before any man-flesh gets here."

Rachel

Rachel hadn't been canoeing in ages, but from the way Dillon handled the paddle, it looked like he'd never done it in his life. The boys were no help. Their ropy little muscles strained at the paddles, but they were doing more splashing than anything else. Rachel pushed the canoe forward, enjoying the heat of the sun and the cool breeze. "Having fun, boys?"

Both of them shrieked in glee. Dillon kept paddling doggedly. He hadn't even looked back yet or said a word. Rachel realized she'd made a tactical error. He was in front of her. She should have taken the front seat. But it couldn't be helped now. She had him and Keryn didn't, and that was victory enough. They paddled north along the shoreline, then turned east when they reached the north end of the lagoon. When they came to the east end, they turned again south. By now Rachel was bored of hugging the shoreline, so she stuck her paddle in the water and steered them around west, on a heading across the middle of the lagoon back toward the dock.

As they reached the midpoint, one of the twins lost his paddle in the water. Rachel leaned over to grab it. Out of the corner of her eye, she saw an orange streak. A huge splash hit her in the face.

"Aughhh!" A boyish scream gurgled as it went underwater.

"Jason!" yelled the other boy. "Jason, get back in here!"

Rachel made a grab at Jason as the canoe swept past him, but he was thrashing so wildly it was impossible to get a grip.

"Jason!"

Dillon turned to look and his face went white—he seemed immobilized with panic. Rachel calmly stood up and dove into the water. Jason was churning up a regular Niagara—arms flailing like a helicopter and yelling his head off. Rachel swam toward him in a few strokes and circled around behind him.

She lunged at him from behind and wrapped him up in a hug, pinning his arms. "Jason! Calm down. You're safe. I've got you. Everything's going to be fine. Just fine."

Jason was hyperventilating and crying at the same time. Rachel wiped the water out of his face. "It's okay, Jason. You'll be fine. They'll be back with the canoe in a minute. Just settle down."

Jason finally got calmed down to a low blubber. Rachel watched the canoe make a long, leisurely circle and head back to them. Dillon knew enough to point the canoe to one side, rather than driving it right over the top of them. Unfortunately, he didn't seem to know how to slow down. As the canoe pulled alongside them, Rachel saw that it was going too fast.

She made a grab at the side, hoping to slow it down. Dillon leaned over and latched onto Jason's arm. Jordan reached out and got the other arm. Then physics took over. The canoe tilted and veered around sharply, and Dillon and Jordan tumbled into the water.

There followed several minutes of thrashing around while the canoe drifted away. The boys and Dillon couldn't make any kind of progress in their clumsy life vests. When Rachel was sure they were all floating safely, she corralled the paddles and swam up alongside the canoe, which was almost completely full of water.

It had been a long time since Rachel had emptied a swamped canoe, but at one time she could do it in about thirty seconds. She faced it broadside and grabbed the gunwale with both hands. Shoving the gunwale sharply beneath the water, she frog-kicked forward, pushing the canoe straight ahead and taking advantage of the water's inertia. At just the right instant, she tipped the gunwale back up to keep water from sloshing back in. She repeated this maneuver again and again in quick succession. Her timing was a little off. It took her almost a minute to get most of the water out.

She looked back to check on Dillon and the boys. "Doing okay, guys?"

"Wow, that was cool!" one of the twins shouted. "Did you see that, Mr. Richard?"

Rachel swam around to the stern of the canoe and gripped the top with both hands. She kicked up hard, pulling down with her arms in one swift move that lifted her on top of the stern, straddling the canoe and sitting on her hands. She pulled her legs inside the canoe.

Behind her, she heard the twins hollering with glee. Rachel sat down on a bench and pulled the paddles into the canoe. She stroked the canoe around and glided back to the guys. Back-paddling the last few strokes brought it to a perfect stop beside the soggy trio.

Jason and Jordan were whooping and shouting and generally having a fine time. Dillon looked a mess. Rachel couldn't read his expression. With his help, she hauled in Jason first, then Jordan. The two of them immediately huddled in the back of the boat, shivering in the cool wind.

Rachel turned to Dillon. "Okay, you're next. Hop on."

Dillon grabbed the side of the boat and tried to haul himself in. The canoe tipped dangerously. "Whoa!" Rachel shouted. "Hold on, you'll tip us all over. Boys, let's get on the other side and try to counterbalance it so Dillon can get in."

The three of them leaned to the other side. Dillon tried again, but he could not pull himself in. Not in a bulky life vest and a shirt and pants and shoes.

Finally Rachel shrugged. "Grab onto the end of the canoe, Dillon. I'll just have to tow you back to shore."

"Perhaps we can be of assistance?"

Rachel turned and saw another canoe gliding toward them.

Gloria sat in the back, paddling serenely, all eight thousand pounds of her. Kathii was in the front, her eyes glued on the boys. Keryn sat in the middle. She was wearing a dazzling blue-and-white swimsuit, and filling it out *wretchedly* well. As they pulled up alongside, Keryn grabbed Dillon's hand. Kathii and Gloria inched to the other side of the canoe to balance it.

Keryn reached over and tugged Rachel's canoe closer, then

stepped across so she had a foot in either boat. "Okay, we're stable. Pull yourself on up, big guy." She leaned down and grasped his hand.

Dillon grabbed the side of Keryn's boat with his free hand and lunged up and inside it. He looked a horrible, soggy mess. Kathii hopped across to Rachel's canoe and scuttled down the length of it to the twins. "You boys scared me to death! Are you okay?"

"That was fun!" Jason shouted. "Boy, Mrs. Meyers can really swim! Did you see her? She swims like a shark!"

"It's Miss Meyers." Kathii looked at Rachel and her face broke into a grateful smile. "Rachel, thank you so much."

Rachel shrugged modestly. "It was nothing." She felt the canoe shudder and turned in time to see Gloria sitting down in the rear of the canoe, brandishing a paddle.

"Bye, guys!" Keryn shouted from the other canoe. "See you back at the dock!" She dug in with her paddle and accelerated away.

Alone with Dillon.

Dillon

After getting dried and changed, Dillon came out of his tent to find that it was lunchtime. He had put on a pair of baggy swim trunks and a T-shirt but he still felt ridiculously underdressed. Even with sunscreen, it was dangerous to expose one's skin to the sunlight in such a way. His only consolation was that he would not be the first to die of skin cancer.

Rachel would. Dillon had never seen such a small swimsuit on a grown woman. Not that he actually saw it, of course. He was doing his very best not to look at her at all. The only problem was that when he was trying to not look at Rachel, Keryn somehow drifted into view. Her swimsuit covered more of her than Rachel's did, but it was still very embarrassing. Very immodest. Dillon felt a strange sense of panic in his chest. He was surrounded by attractive women who seemed so very ignorant of their own attractiveness. It was hard to think righteous thoughts when surrounded by such things. He focused carefully on his corn chips and potato salad and thought about quantum mechanics.

There was a famous experiment in physics that Dillon had seen for the first time in college. A beam of laser light was allowed to shine through two parallel slits onto a screen. If you covered up one of the slits, the light shone through the other slit and made a fuzzy slit-shaped pattern on the screen. This suggested that light was a wave, since diffraction through slits was a property of waves.

If you uncovered both slits, then something more interesting happened. The pattern on the screen was not the simple sum of the two hazy slits. Instead, it showed a sequence of light and dark bands—an interference pattern. This proved beyond all doubt that light was a wave. The dark and light bands were caused by two waves that either canceled or reinforced each other.

Except that light could also be shown to be made of particles—photons. You could reduce the intensity of the light source until only a single photon was emitted each second, a photon that moved in straight lines like a bullet and could be seen with the naked eye or a photomultiplier tube.

This photon could go through one slit or through the other, but of course it could not go through both. A particle could not be in two places at once. If you replaced the screen with a photographic film and waited a long time for many photons to go through the slit, you would create an image on the film—a series of alternating bands of light and dark.

That was extraordinary. You *still* got an interference pattern, even though you knew with certainty that each photon could go through only one slit or the other. The only conclusion was that the photon was a strange beast that was not quite a particle and not quite a wave. It traveled in straight lines, like a particle. But it created an interference pattern, like a wave.

A photon was a particle that could interfere with itself.

Dillon felt like this photon. When he was working with Keryn, he felt very calm and peaceful, but he did not feel excited. When he worked with Rachel, he felt very happy and excited, but he did not feel peaceful.

When he was around both of them together, he did not feel calm or peaceful and he did not feel happy or excited. He felt a strange and terrifying inner turmoil. In some mysterious way, it was like there were two Dillons who were interfering with each other.

It was a terrible feeling and he hated it and he did not know what to do about it. It was bad enough last night at the restaurant, when both of them were adequately dressed.

Today at the campground, it seemed ten times worse. It was too embarrassing to speak about. Both women would be astounded and outraged if they knew how attractive he found them. Obviously, they had no idea, or they would not dress so provocatively. Dillon's whole head seemed to be buzzing, as if it were filled with hundreds of horseflies. He chewed his food and swallowed, but he could not taste it.

Finally lunch was over. Dillon hurried to his tent and got his toothbrush and brushed his teeth in the mildew-smelling bathroom. He had bought dental floss also, but his dentist had told him to floss only once per day—after supper—so he did not floss now. When he returned to the tents, he saw that Rachel was chasing a volleyball that one of the twins had kicked into the trees, and Keryn had gone with her sister to greet another family that was just arriving.

So Dillon walked to the dock and threw a life vest into one of the canoes and stepped in and quietly paddled away into the lagoon. He paddled all the way across and through the channel that went under Highway 5 into a smaller bay on the other side. He experimented with paddling different ways. After much practice, he found the most efficient way to power himself.

The surface of the water was very still, but Dillon did not feel calm and he did not feel happy.

He felt very alone—and for the first time in his life, he did not like it.

Keryn

Around 5:00 Keryn finally heard from Grant. She had left a terse message on his cell phone voice mail that morning. "Grant, it's me. Call me as soon as you can."

When he called, he sounded nervous. "Keryn, what's up?"

She filled him in on the carjacking, taking care not to say too much over the phone. ". . . and we think they were after more than just our money and our car."

"Did they get the you-know-what?" Grant's voice crackled with tension.

"No."

"Where are you?"

"I'd rather not say on the phone. Where've you been all day?"

"Mexico. Julia and I decided to go to Tijuana for dinner and we stayed the night. Got a great price in the Camino Real. We're still here."

"We need to talk when you get back. Where's Clifton?"

"No idea," Grant said. "But tell me something. Did Dillon scrub that hard drive in the bio-lab?"

"Julia said to reformat it, so that's what I told him to do."

"Not good enough. Any idiot with good data recovery tools can read the hard drive if you just reformat it. You have to scrub it. You overwrite it with random ones and zeroes a bunch of times."

"I . . . didn't know that. Julia said to reformat it, so I would guess that's what Dillon did."

Grant swore softly on the phone. "Listen, you kids stay in hiding for a couple days. I don't want you out in public. I'll sneak over to the bio-lab and scrub the hard drive myself."

"You can't get in," Keryn said. A hot rush of embarrassment swept over her. "We . . . we changed the keypad combination a few days ago and didn't tell you. And I'd rather not tell you the combination over the phone."

"Hey, Keryn, not to worry. That keypad lock is configured for multiple combinations. I've got one for my private use, and you can't change it."

"Oh." Keryn felt like an idiot.

"I'll get over there tomorrow morning early and scrub the hard drive. Then I'll slap the ultimate security lock on it."

"What's that?"

"A sledgehammer," Grant said. "Five or six whacks with one of those and God himself won't be able to read that hard drive."

"Talk to you tomorrow," Keryn said. "Call me as soon as Clifton turns up."

She closed the phone and stared out at the lagoon, where a small canoe skittered across the water. Her insides felt like she'd just drunk a gallon of ice water. The hard drive in the bio-lab was not secure. And she didn't dare go near it.

Late in the afternoon, a marine layer of chilly gray fog rolled in. Keryn changed into warmer clothes. Rachel put on a tight sweatshirt and some low-cut jeans over her bikini. More families arrived, as did most of the men who'd been working all day. Dillon paddled his canoe in, docked it, and rejoined the human race. Keryn was dying to ask him where he'd been all afternoon, but she decided to give him some space. Rachel sat next to him at suppertime. Keryn sat with Kathii and did a slow burn.

After supper there were marshmallows to roast over the fire and s'mores to eat. Around 9:00 Gloria stuck a silver police whistle in her mouth and blew out a long blast. "Story time!" she bellowed.

The kids came running and gathered around her in a big circle near the fire. The adults followed, but they took care to stay on the outer fringes. Gloria's stories were famous. Or infamous. She was good at embarrassing people without meaning to. Keryn sat down with Kathii and Allen behind Jason and Jordan.

"All right, kids," Gloria shouted. "Tonight's story is called 'The Prodigal Papa'. Who knows what the word *prodigal* means?"

Hands shot up all around the circle. A little girl named Charisse stood up and said, "It means 'bad.'"

Gloria pressed her lips together. "Does it, now?" She looked all around the circle. "How many think that's what it means?"

The show of hands she got were about as close to unanimous as a Cuban election.

"How many think that isn't what it means?" Gloria shouted.

Keryn raised her hand. Nobody else did.

Gloria pointed at her. "What does our famous author think it means?"

Keryn felt her cheeks flushing. "It means 'wasteful.'"

"We have a winner!" Gloria hooted. "A prodigal person is a wasteful person. You win a marshmallow." She took one out of a bag and tossed it to Keryn. It landed in the sand. Jason dusted it off and ate it.

"Now then, this story has three characters in it," Gloria said. "The first one is the Prodigal Papa, and I'm going to play that role. Now I need two volunteers. I need a Big Brother and I need a Little Brother. Who's good at acting?"

A dozen hands went up. Jason and Jordan jumped up and waved frantically. "Me! Me!"

Gloria looked around the circle and an enormous smile wreathed her huge face. "Wonderful! I see just the two I need!" She pointed toward the back. "You there, and you! Come on up! I promise you'll both win a prize for participating!" She bounded into the crowd to apply a little persuasion on her reluctant volunteers.

Jason and Jordan flounced back into the sand, complaining. Keryn turned to see who Gloria's victims were.

Gloria came wading back through the sea of faces, clutching the arms of two very unhappy-looking campers.

Rachel and Dillon.

Keryn saw in a flash what was going to happen. She wanted to dig a hole in the sand. All the way to China.

Rachel, dressed like a little floozy, was going to be the prodigal son, Little Brother. And Dillon, stiff and shy, was going to be the uptight Big Brother. They were perfect for their roles.

And they were going to *kill* Keryn for getting them into this.

CHAPTER
TWENTY-FIVE

Keryn

Keryn wanted to run up and stop the whole thing. She wanted to, but she didn't know how. Didn't dare.

Gloria planted Dillon and Rachel behind her and turned to face the children. She apparently didn't see Keryn's wide-eyed look of dismay.

"Once upon a time there was a Jewish farmer who had a great big farm!" Gloria said. "And on this farm he had horses and cows and camels and donkeys and sheep and goats and pigs!" Gloria had a funny little hand motion for each of these animals, and Keryn marveled that she could say this litany of animals in perfect meter and not miss a single motion. The motion for pigs involved billowing her arms out in front of her to make her enormous perimeter even bigger.

"Oops!" Gloria slapped her head. "Did I say pigs? That's a mistake! Because this was a Jewish farmer, and Jewish farmers don't raise pigs. How many of you knew that Jewish farmers don't raise pigs?"

Almost nobody raised their hands. Keryn raised hers just a little. She had known that, sort of. Behind Gloria, Rachel had a "Well, duh" expression on her face. Dillon's face was unreadable.

"And this Jewish farmer also had two sons, and they had very strange names," Gloria said. "One of them was named Big Brother and the other one was named Little Brother. And both sons worked all day long on Papa's farm, feeding all of his horses and cows and camels and donkeys and sheep and goats and pigs!" Again, the perfect litany of hand motions.

Jason jumped up. "You said he didn't have any pigs!"

"Oops!" Gloria bellowed. "That's right, he didn't have any pigs. My mistake. So as I was saying, Big Brother and Little Brother spent their whole day feeding all those animals and telling them, 'Eat more food! Eat more food!'"

Keryn had never heard the story told quite this way before. Dillon would probably say it wasn't theologically correct, but . . . oddly enough, she didn't care.

Gloria began pacing. "Now, one of those brothers didn't like spending his whole life feeding those animals. Can you guess which brother that was?"

"Little Brother!" Jordan shouted.

Gloria shook her head. "Where'd you get that idea?" she hollered at Jordan. "You must be thinking of somebody else's story. This is my story and I'll tell it my way. And in my story, it was Big Brother. So as I was saying, one day Big Brother told Little Brother that he wanted to leave that farm with all its horses and cows and camels and donkeys and sheep and goats and pigs."

"No pigs!" somebody shouted.

Gloria looked thunderstruck. "Did I say pigs? What a dummy I am! Of course, there weren't any pigs! But Big Brother was tired of telling all those animals, 'Eat more food!' every day, and he told Little Brother he wanted to ask Papa for his half of the inheritance and go far away. Who knows what an inheritance is?"

The little girl, Charisse, waved her hands in the air. "It's when somebody dies and then their children get all their money."

"That's right!" Gloria said. "You don't get an inheritance unless somebody dies. Big Brother wanted his inheritance early, because he couldn't even wait for Papa to die. In fact, he would have been glad for his papa to die just so he could get that inheritance. And that was a terrible thing, wasn't it? Who knows what happened next?"

By now Keryn felt off-balance. She had thought she knew this story cold. But Gloria had bent it beyond all recognition. Nobody ventured a guess.

Gloria smiled. "Big Brother was too afraid to ask his papa for his share of the inheritance. So he did nothing. But Little Brother got to thinking about that, and one day he went to Papa and told him he wanted his half of the inheritance right now. So what do you think Papa did? Do you think he took Little Brother over his knee and spanked him like he deserved?"

Dead silence. Anything could happen in this strange universe of Gloria's.

"No!" Gloria hollered into the night. "That silly, wasteful Prodigal Papa *sold* half of his farm and half of the horses and cows and camels and donkeys and sheep and goats and pigs, and—"

"No pigs!" shouted several of the children.

"Oops! That's right, he didn't sell any pigs," Gloria said. "But he sold the others and he got a great big bag of . . . money!" Gloria held up a large bag of marshmallows. It gleamed orange in the flickering firelight.

Gloria turned around and looked at Rachel and Dillon. "Then Papa went and *gave* all that money to Little Brother." Gloria held the bag toward Rachel. Rachel reached out a tentative hand. Gloria yanked the bag away. "Not you, Big Brother. This money is for Little Brother." She thrust the bag into Dillon's hands.

Dillon's jaw dropped. A murmur of surprise ran around the circle.

Gloria took Dillon's elbow and pulled. "And Little Brother went on a long, long journey to a far country." She led Dillon away from the fire, threading her way through the crowd all the way to the back.

Everybody turned around so they see.

Gloria waited while the rustle of bodies subsided to perfect silence again. Dillon towered above her, his face a mask of stone. Keryn could not remember ever being so embarrassed. Dillon was never going to speak to her again. She was sure of it.

Dillon

Dillon had never liked having people looking at him. He felt self-conscious around people, especially those he did not know. Whenever he found himself in a large crowd of people, he developed a peculiar kind of tunnel vision. His field of view closed up so that he could see only a few faces. Now, in front of a sea of darkened faces, he could not see anybody. Only the fire, and the dark shape of Rachel, backlit by the flames. He clutched the bag of marshmallows in a sweaty grip and wondered how he had gotten into this strange situation with this woman of very dubious theology.

Gloria jabbed her finger into the bag of marshmallows. "Now when Little Brother got to that far country, he felt very free! Little Brother found lots of friends. One day, he threw a party for all his friends. He had food and wine and music and dancing girls, and he gave away lots of money to all his friends."

Gloria reached into the bag and grabbed a handful of marshmallows and threw them out into the crowd. Many of the children shrieked. Dillon winced at the sound. He did not like loud noises.

"And the next day, Little Brother threw another party with food and wine and music and dancing girls, and he gave away lots of money to all his friends." Gloria threw another handful of marshmallows out at the children.

"Can you guess what he did the next day?" Gloria shouted.

"A party!" somebody hollered.

"That's right!" Gloria grabbed two handfuls. "With more food and wine and music and dancing girls and lots more money for all his friends." She heaved the marshmallows high in the air. "Little Brother was wasting all his money. Where do you think he learned how to do that?"

A stunned silence.

Gloria put her hands on her hips. "You're not thinking! What's the name of the story?"

"The Prodigal Papa," said a small girl.

"That's right!" Gloria grabbed more marshmallows and flung them at the girl. "Little Brother learned it from his Prodigal Papa!"

Dillon was sweating now. This was all wrong. Very unsound theology. Very unsound.

"Finally, one day, Little Brother threw another party, and guess what he discovered?" Gloria grabbed the bag and turned it upside down, emptying its contents in the dirt. "That's right, he discovered that he had spent all his money." Gloria flung the bag up in the air. It floated down in a sad little flutter that made Dillon feel . . . empty.

"Then Little Brother went to all of his friends and do you know what he discovered?" Gloria began backing away from Dillon. She motioned with her arms to those nearest Dillon. They moved back, back, back, leaving Dillon . . .

Alone.

Something cold and hollow seemed to have gotten stuck in Dillon's throat. He did not like crowds. Did not like them at all. But he did not like being abandoned either. Gloria went all the way back to the fire and everybody turned their backs on Dillon.

He saw that he could walk away now. If he simply went back to his tent, he would be done with this foolish story. The cold lump in his throat spread to his chest, then to his stomach.

Dillon found that he could not move.

Gloria was pacing back and forth in front of the fire. "Little Brother went looking for a job. He couldn't find work in the city, so he went out of town to a village. He couldn't find work in the village, so he went out of the village to the farms. He couldn't find work on the farms, so he walked down the road until he came to a horrible little pigsty. And he saw some men feeding the pigs, saying, 'Eat more food! Eat more food!'"

Gloria stopped pacing and turned to look straight at Dillon, and something gleamed in her eyes. "Little Brother was a nice Jewish boy who had never touched a pig, but he was so hungry, he was so desperate for food, that he waited for those men to go away and then he jumped into that pigsty and fell down—glop—in the pig poop and he crawled past those pigs and he ate their food."

A hush settled over the crowd. Dillon felt numb all over his body. He could not imagine being so hungry that he would fight a pig for its food.

Gloria seized a tube from a roll of paper towels and held it up in the air. "Meanwhile, back at home, Papa bought himself a telescope. And every morning, Papa tied on his running shoes and went up on the roof of the house and set up his telescope"—she placed the tube to her eye—"and looked down the road, and guess what he saw?"

Nobody said a word.

"Nothing!" Gloria shouted. "Papa didn't see anything except horses and cows and camels and donkeys and sheep and goats and pigs."

"No pigs!" all the children shouted.

Gloria nodded and her face looked very solemn. "That's right, Papa didn't see any pigs. But Little Brother did. Every day, Little Brother went down the road until he found a place that had pigs. And every day, he had to wrestle with the pigs. And every day he fell down in the pig poop. And every day he stole food from the pigs."

A great deep silence settled down on the crowd. Dillon found that he could not breathe, could not feel, could not . . . think.

"Then one morning, Papa tied on his running shoes and went up on the roof and looked down the road with his telescope, and guess what he saw?"

"Little Brother!" shrieked one of the boys.

"That's right!" Gloria dropped the telescope and began running. "Papa saw Little Brother walking down the road, and his shoes had pig poop on them and his clothes had pig poop on them and his face had pig poop on it and—"

Gloria came churning around the circle of people and barreled into Dillon at full speed. Dillon staggered backward, desperate to keep on his feet. Gloria threw her arms around him and engulfed him in a vast and powerful hug. Then she reached up and pulled Dillon's head down and kissed him on both cheeks. One side, then the other. Again and again and again. "Oh, Little Brother, I've missed you! Welcome home, Little Brother! Papa loves you so much, Little Brother, Papa's glad you've come home."

Something hot broke loose in Dillon's chest. He gasped and staggered to one knee. Gloria hugged him again. "Welcome home, Little Brother! It's time for us to have a *party*!" She pulled him to his feet and led him through the people back toward the fire.

Shouts and cheers rang in his ears. Dillon felt grateful for Gloria's thick hand leading him through the crowd because he could not see a thing through the blur in his eyes.

R a c h e l

Rachel watched Gloria lead Dillon back toward the fire. She knew this parable backward and forward. Knew what was coming next. Big Brother was the jerk of this story. Which meant Gloria was going to make a fool out of her.

Gloria made Dillon stand in front. He was grinning like a monkey and . . . crying. Rachel stared at him, astonished. Dillon Richard, crying.

Gloria took a deep breath and turned to face the children. "So Papa called in all his friends and threw a party, with food and wine and music and dancing girls, and they roasted a nice big fat juicy pig—"

"No pigs!" the children roared.

Gloria put her hand over her mouth. "Oops, I meant a calf! A nice big fat juicy calf, and everybody was happy."

A pregnant pause. Rachel felt sure all the children were staring at her. She crossed her arms across her chest, furious. This was more horrible than she had expected. Keryn must have set this up.

"Oops!" Gloria said. "Did I say everybody? I meant everybody except Big Brother. Big Brother was angry when he saw what happened. He knew that Little Brother had done exactly the things he wanted to do, only he hadn't dared and Little Brother had. So Big Brother refused to go in to the party. He went out to the barn and shouted at all the animals. 'Eat more food! Eat more food!' And he went through the whole barn, feeding all the horses and cows and camels and donkeys and sheep and goats and pigs."

"No pigs!" shouted the children.

Gloria gave a sly grin. "That's right. No pigs. Big Brother stayed out in the barn feeding the animals and hollering, 'Eat more food! Eat more food!' And guess who came looking for him."

A hush. A little boy waved his hand. "Papa?"

"No!" Gloria said. "*Prodigal* Papa went looking for Big Brother. Prodigal Papa, who wasted half his farm on Little Brother and who roasted a nice big fat juicy calf out of Big Brother's inheritance.

Prodigal Papa went out to the barn and saw Big Brother shouting 'Eat more food!' at all the horses and cows and camels and donkeys and sheep and goats and pigs."

"NO PIGS!" screamed the children. "NO PIGS!"

"Oops!" Gloria rapped her forehead. "I'm sorry, I keep forgetting. No pigs. And Prodigal Papa went up to Big Brother and he said, 'Big Brother, come into the house. We're having a party for Little Brother.' But Big Brother was angry and he said, 'No, I'm not going to that party.'"

Rachel glowered at Gloria. She didn't have to pretend to be angry. She was furious.

Gloria's face went very solemn and sad. "Then Prodigal Papa said, 'Big Brother, why won't you come to the party?' And Big Brother said, 'You know why.' And Prodigal Papa said, 'No, I don't.' And Big Brother said, 'Yes, you do.' And Prodigal Papa took Big Brother's hand and said, 'I want you to tell me.'"

Gloria's eyes were big and soft as she took hold of Rachel's hand. Rachel wanted to scream at her that it wasn't fair that Dillon got the good role in this stupid story and she got the lousy one. Dillon was the hero and Rachel was the villain, and she hadn't even had a chance to choose.

Gloria's eyes filled with pain and her voice nearly broke when she spoke. "So Big Brother told him. 'That rotten Little Brother went and took half the inheritance and went off to a far country and had fun! He had parties with food and wine and music and dancing girls every day, and I was stuck here feeding all these horses and cows and camels and donkeys and sheep and goats so I could earn my inheritance and—'"

Gloria raised her hand and black silence fell like night. Rachel felt hot rage in her veins. Here it came now. Big Brother was the Jews who were going to hell because they were legalists. She had seen it coming a mile away.

Gloria's voice came out in a whispered roar. "Then Prodigal Papa said, 'What did you say? So you could earn what?' And Big Brother said, 'So I could earn my inheritance.' And then Prodigal Papa laughed. He said, 'Big Brother, you can't *earn* your inheritance! Your inheritance is free!'"

Rachel's mouth dropped open. Gloria was changing the story line again.

A huge smile spread across Gloria's face. "Big Brother said, 'It's . . . free?' And Prodigal Papa said, 'That's right! Your inheritance is free!' And Big Brother said, 'Are you sure it's free?' And Prodigal Papa said, 'Of course it's free! There's nothing you can do to earn your inheritance. It's free, it's free, it's free!'"

Rachel felt like she'd been hit in the face. No, this was wrong, all wrong. The story did not go like—

Gloria threw her arms around Rachel. "Then Prodigal Papa gave Big Brother a big hug, and Big Brother was so happy, he starting yelling, 'Woohoo! My inheritance is free!'"

Gloria stood up on tiptoe and kissed Rachel on both cheeks, first one, then the other. Over and over.

Rachel's insides felt like they were melting, and all of a sudden she couldn't see.

Gloria put an arm around Rachel and guided her over toward Dillon. She threw an arm around Dillon and squeezed them both in her vast embrace. "And Prodigal Papa killed another nice big fat juicy calf and they had another big feast, with food and wine and music and dancing girls, and everybody was happy, because Prodigal Papa got back *both* of his sons that day."

It wasn't the way the story was supposed to go at all.

Rachel wept.

CHAPTER
TWENTY - SIX

Dillon

Dillon slept deeply and woke up early feeling better than he had in a long time. He was in the tent with Allen and the twin boys. Allen was snoring and the boys were sleeping the sleep of the innocent.

Dillon took out his cell phone and called his home phone number. He pressed the code to access his answering machine remotely and found only one message. The police department had called yesterday to say that his minivan was recovered and he could pick it up at an impound yard in Point Loma. It made no sense that they would tow it all the way to Point Loma, but Dillon did not expect the police to act sensibly.

Dillon hung up and checked his watch. 5:47 A.M. His cell phone said it was 5:48. He took a minute to reset his watch to the correct time. His hair felt very oily, so he pulled on his clothes and took a towel and soap and shampoo and went to take a shower in the bathroom. By 6:02 he was washed and dressed. Nobody else in the camp was up so early.

Dillon went and sat down on the dock and stared east. The red sun hung above the horizon. His cell phone rang. He flipped the phone open. "Good morning, Grant."

"Dillon, what did you do with the hard drive?"

Dillon's heart lurched. "What hard drive?"

"The one in that computer in the bio-lab. The one you were writing all that software on."

"It is still there. I copied the data to my USB flash drive and reformatted the hard drive as Keryn told me."

"It's gone." Grant's voice sounded very peculiar.

Dillon could not guess what that tone of voice meant. He did not know this social context at all. "How could it be gone?"

"I went in this morning to scrub the drive and smash it." Grant was breathing heavily now. "The case was open and the drive was gone."

Dillon felt like he had been punched in the face. "Rachel and Keryn and I have been together since we were laid off. None of us took it."

Grant let loose with a string of words that took the name of the Lord in vain.

Dillon winced. "Maybe Clifton went to rescue it?"

"He doesn't know the combination to the bio-lab," Grant said. "You guys changed it, remember? And I have my own combination, but even Julia doesn't know it. Whoever . . . stole the bio-computer in the first place came back and got the software."

Dillon knew that any hard-disk recovery service could recover most of the data on that drive, reformatted or not. He had made a critical error leaving it there. He had not known they would be laid off when he left, and he had been too shocked afterward to think of it. It would have been against the rules to go back to the bio-lab, but he might have been willing to break the rules. Except that he had not thought of it in the first place.

"Are you guys in a safe place?" Grant said.

"Yes, for now."

"How far along were you with that software?"

Dillon felt a wave of sadness wash through him. "We were ready to begin testing. We need that NMR machine in the bio-lab."

"Testing?"

Dillon realized he had just said much more than he should have.

"Dillon, listen, I don't want a direct answer on an insecure line, but I need to know if there's something very important that Rachel may have forgotten to tell me."

Dillon felt sick to his core. They had deceived Grant and now he would be angry. "Yes," he said in a very quiet voice. "I am sorry, Grant, but—"

"Sorry?" Grant's voice was a yelp. "Are you telling me—no, don't tell me. I think you're telling me you need an NMR machine right now, is that correct?"

"Yes. Grant, we made a terrible mistake not telling you."

"Actually, I'm not surprised," Grant said. "I should have guessed, now that I think about it. But it might turn out for the best that I didn't. If I'd known, I could have fought off the leeches. As it is . . . the leeches have the shell and we've got the meat. Am I right?"

Dillon had no idea what Grant was talking about.

"What kind of NMR machine do you need?" Grant said. "Do you need any special connectors or cards or drivers to . . . to test your software?"

"We were using a MagTec NMR machine with a FireWire connector," Dillon said. "And I need a computer with a FireWire port."

"I don't want you going anywhere near the bio-lab," Grant said. "For one thing, it's illegal for you to use that equipment. For another, it's dangerous. Somebody's probably watching that place."

"Then they saw you." Dillon felt a rush of fear. If anything happened to Grant . . .

"Listen, nobody's gonna bother me. I don't have anything. It's you they want. You need to finish testing your . . . software. I bet you can borrow an NMR machine from a university around here. I'll make some calls and get back to you on that."

"We can call people. Rachel knows people at Caltech."

"No." Grant's voice sounded thick and tired. "Caltech's too obvious. Everybody knows Rachel got her Ph.D. there. Listen, you people are in danger. I want you to stay where you are and turn off all your cell phones. If your phone is on, the cell company knows where you are and somebody could conceivably tap into that and track you down. Borrow a clean phone Sunday night and call me at the Camino Real Hotel in Tijuana at eleven sharp, and I'll tell you what to do next."

"Have you talked to Clifton?"

"No, I've got no idea where he is. His cell phone is turned off or he's out of service. I haven't been able to get hold of him since that all-hands meeting."

"Grant?"

"Yeah?"

"I . . ." Dillon didn't know how to tell Grant he loved him. "You have been like a father to me."

"Thanks, Dillon. I've always been proud of you."

An uncomfortable silence.

"Oh, say, Dillon, there's one more thing you should know."

Dillon held his breath.

Grant lowered his voice. "I looked at the manual for the keypad combination box this morning. I hadn't realized this, but there's an option to see how many combinations have been created."

"How . . . how many?" Dillon was afraid to hear the answer.

"Four. You and Rachel created one. I created two of them. Somebody else created the fourth."

"Do those come with time stamps?"

"Yeah." Grant hesitated. "Two were created last December. I did those, one for me and one for Rachel. Rachel's was disabled on Wednesday morning, and another one was created at the same time."

"That was the new one Rachel and I created," Dillon said. "I am very sorry. We wanted to be able to rule you, and everybody else, out as a suspect . . . in case there was another break-in."

"It's okay," Grant said. "You didn't show me yours and I didn't show you mine. We're even. But I wanted you to know that the other combination was created a week ago Friday night. Actually, a week ago Saturday morning. At four forty-five A.M."

Dillon tried to process that. "It was created by whoever broke in and stole the bio-computer."

"Has to be," Grant said. "They must have been in the lab for a few hours. I don't know what it all means, but that's where we're at. Keep yourself safe, okay? I'm heading back to Mexico right now. Julia's still there, and . . . I've got some things to do. Call me tomorrow night. And hug the girls, will you?"

Dillon did not think it was likely he was ever going to hug either

Keryn or Rachel. A deep hollow filled his stomach. "I will call you if we have any trouble."

"Fine. Just turn off your phone and have the girls do the same. If *they* track you down, I can't help you. Understand?"

"Good-bye, Grant." Dillon hung up and powered off his phone and stuck it in his pocket. He felt very alone again. He was trapped in a small and shrinking box with two women he did not understand. Somebody out there was stalking him.

He did not feel calm and he did not feel happy.

K e r y n

The weekend passed in a blur. Rachel's bikini mysteriously disappeared Saturday morning, and Keryn noted a certain smugness in Gloria's smile. She overheard Dillon having a long discussion with Allen and two other engineers at lunchtime on why all Christians ought to believe in the Big Bang.

Keryn desperately wanted to talk to Rachel and Dillon about Gloria's story, but she couldn't find an opportune moment. Sunday morning during church service, Gloria told an outrageous story about Peter walking on the water and ended up getting her husband completely soaked. Church camp ended Sunday afternoon without any further disasters. Dillon rode home in Allen's car with the boys, while Keryn and Rachel returned with Kathii in the minivan.

At 11:00 P.M. on Sunday, with Jason and Jordan safely in bed, Keryn and Rachel and Dillon and Allen and Kathii huddled around the phone in the guest bedroom in Kathii's house. Dillon dialed the number for the Camino Real in Tijuana and asked to be connected to Grant O'Connell's room. The phone rang once and then . . .

"Hello." It was Grant's gravelly voice, very tired and very wary.

"Grant, it's me," Dillon said. "We are all here on speaker-phone."

"Hi, Grant," Keryn said.

"Are you okay, Uncle Grant?" Rachel asked.

"I'm fine. I've found a lab you guys can test the you-know-what, but they can't let you have it till Thursday. And I've got some goodies for you. I took your photos to a place here in TJ and got some driver's licenses made."

"Mexican driver's licenses?" Dillon said.

"California. Don't argue," Grant said. "They're not legal, but they look pretty good. They aren't your real names, but they are your real photos. In case you need ID. I also got you each a clean cell phone, not traceable to you, and some Visa cards. Do not drive your own cars anywhere; do not go back to your homes. Stay incognito. Got it?"

"Grant, you're acting like we're criminals," Keryn said.

"You're the good guys, trust me," Grant said. "But somebody out there hates your guts."

"We should take it to the governing authorities," Dillon said.

"I swear, I'll drink that thing before I let Big Brother have it," Rachel said.

"We're not gonna give it to them until we've demoed it in public," Grant said. "Then if Big Brother gets it, they can't hide the fact that they have it. Okay, time's wasting and I want to meet you guys tonight and give you your goodies. Don't use your cell phones again for any reason. Keryn, does your sister have a cell phone that I can call you at when I get across the border? I'll have you go out driving and give you directions on the fly, so we can meet somewhere safe."

Kathii handed Keryn her cell phone with the phone number displayed.

"Yes," Keryn said. "Got a pen? Here's the number." She read off the digits and Grant read them back to her.

"Okay, it'll take time to get across, even at this hour," Grant said. "Be ready to go for a drive when I call. And one more thing. Tomorrow, I want Rachel and Dillon to get separated, each of you with half the goods. In case they track one of you, they won't get the other. You can both rent cars tomorrow and just go somewhere, but don't tell each other where, okay? Keryn, you can stay wherever you are, as long as you don't go home. Any questions?"

Nobody had any.

"We will await your call," Dillon said.

"Bye, kids," Grant said. "I love you—ya know that?"

The line went dead.

———

They waited for more than two hours before Kathii's cell phone rang. Keryn swallowed hard and answered it. "H-hello?"

"It's Gandalf," Grant said. "Sorry, it took a while to get back into Mordor. You guys ready to go fight the Dark Lord?"

Keryn laughed nervously. "I guess so."

"I assume you've got transportation. Wherever you are, get on Highway 5 and head north. Watch to see if anyone's following you, got it?"

"Got it."

"Call me back at this number when you get north of 52." Grant hung up.

Keryn closed the phone. "Let's go."

She climbed into the passenger seat of Allen's Camry. Allen was driving, and Dillon and Rachel were in the backseat. The garage door opened and they rolled out into the night. "We need to head north on Highway 5," Keryn said.

Allen drove out to Governor's Drive and turned right. He barreled through a yellow light when they got to Genesee. Keryn kept an eye behind them and saw nothing. No headlights, no nothing.

At Regents Road, Allen made an illegal left turn through the red light.

"Allen, please, it is not wise to do that," Dillon said.

"Nobody was watching," Allen said tightly.

"I was watching," Dillon said.

"Oh, Dillon, cut him some slack." Rachel sounded scared. "Let's just get this over with."

Allen drove down the hill and took the on-ramp onto Highway 52 west. Minutes later they were on Highway 5 heading north. Keryn pressed the dial-back button on Kathii's phone.

Grant answered on the first ring. "Any pursuit?"

"I don't think so," Keryn said. "We're heading north."

"Take the Sorrento Valley exit and wait for sixty seconds at the stop sign. Then call me." Grant rang off.

Keryn passed this on to Allen. He shrugged and moved into the left lane and pressed the accelerator until they were whizzing along at ninety. Keryn was pretty sure nobody was following them. At the Sorrento Valley exit, Allen veered across four lanes and barely caught the off-ramp. They roared down a long lane and screeched to a rest at the stop sign.

Sixty seconds passed in breathless silence. Keryn called again. Grant picked up. "Any sign of Black Riders?"

"Nothing," Keryn said. "Nobody changed speed, nobody tried to catch our exit, nobody's come down this exit in the last minute."

"Go across the railroad tracks and turn right." Grant hung up.

Keryn shook her head. This was just too crazy. "Turn left here, Allen, then cut right and go across the tracks and then right again on Sorrento Valley Road."

Allen hit the gas and followed her directions.

"This is crazy," Rachel said. "He's directing us straight to the CypherQuanta building. It's too obvious."

Keryn was sweating now. This wasn't safe.

The phone rang in her hands. She stared at it stupidly for a few seconds, then flipped it open. "This is, um, Arwen."

"Get on Highway 805 going south," Grant said. "Call me when you pass the Governor's Drive exit."

Keryn flipped the phone shut. Allen was slowing down for the turn to the CypherQuanta building. "Don't turn, Allen. Go straight and take the on-ramp to 805 south."

Allen gunned the engine and roared past CypherQuanta and up the long ramp onto the highway. Keryn had her eyes glued behind them. Nothing but blackness. They drove in silence for a few minutes. As they flashed past Governor's Drive, Allen scowled. "He's got us driving in circles."

Keryn dialed Grant. "Me again. What's next?"

"Next exit, take a right," Grant said. "Then I want you to solve a riddle. What's the only illegal place in San Diego that Dillon approves of? I want you to go there and call me." The line went dead.

"Allen, turn right at the next exit," Keryn said.

Allen smoothly veered onto Highway 52 heading west. Again. "Crazy," he muttered.

"Okay, Grant's getting nervous," Keryn said. "He gave us a riddle. There's an illegal place somewhere in San Diego that Dillon approves of. Grant wants us to go there."

Silence.

The car roared west through the night. They passed the Genesee exit, then Regents Road.

"What do I do now?" Allen said as they approached Highway 5 for the second time that night.

Keryn shrugged. "I have no idea. Dillon, any ideas? This riddle's about you."

"There is no illegal place that I would approve of." Dillon sounded deeply offended.

"Guys, I need to know!" Allen said. "Do I take this exit north or south?"

"Straight," Rachel said. "Move left one lane and go straight."

"Into La Jolla?" Keryn said. "There's nothing illegal in La Jolla."

"Just do it."

Allen lane-shifted left and punched the gas. The Camry flew up the long ascent and merged into La Jolla Parkway and on over the pass into La Jolla. Keryn looked back and saw a pair of headlights behind them. "Guys, there's somebody on our tail."

Allen's knuckles glared bone white in the dim glow of the dashboard. "Okay, now what? I need a little guidance here."

"Straight," Rachel said. "You guys, this is way obvious."

Keryn had her eyes on the headlights behind. They were closing. "Allen . . . hurry."

Allen accelerated as they began the descent. "I need some more guidance here, Rachel."

"Right lane and slow down for a right turn onto Torrey Pines Road," Rachel said.

Allen moved over one lane and began braking.

Keryn was so scared she wanted to shriek. The lights behind were catching up fast.

Rachel leaned forward. "At the next intersection, turn . . . left! Now! Turn left!"

Allen swung the wheel hard and cut across two lanes into the left-turn lane. And stopped at the red turn arrow.

Brakes squealed behind them. A horn blared. Headlights fishtailed past them through the green light. Keryn was hyperventilating, she was so scared. "They almost hit us!"

"Turn left now!" Rachel ordered.

The left-turn light was red, but the intersection was empty.

Allen punched the gas and turned onto Hidden Valley Road. Dillon didn't say a word.

"Straight up the hill," Rachel said. "Don't you guys get it?"

It hit Keryn like a brick in the face. Yes, it was obvious when somebody pointed it out. "The Mount Soledad Cross!" she said. "Grant wants to meet us up there. It's isolated and he can be sure nobody else is there."

"No, that is incorrect," Dillon said. "We have not solved the riddle."

Keryn turned to look at him. "It's the only possibility," she said. "The Cross is illegal. The city keeps losing lawsuits. Sooner or later, they're going to have to tear it down."

"I hope they do," Dillon said. "It is a violation of the separation of church and state. We have not solved the riddle at all."

Keryn thought he was probably the only Christian in San Diego who thought that way.

Allen kept driving up the twisting hillside. "Dillon, does Grant know you don't approve of the Mount Soledad Cross?"

"I have never discussed it with him," Dillon said.

"Drive," Rachel said. "It's right up here on the left. . . ."

Allen slowed the car to a stop and they all stared at the small road leading to the Cross. A metal gate barred the way.

"It closes at ten." Rachel pointed at the sign.

"We were supposed to call when we got here." Keryn flipped open the phone and dialed Grant.

It answered on the first ring. "Gandalf speaking."

"Arwen here. Listen, we're at the gate, but it's shut. How do we—"

"Turn off your headlights and take a right and go three tenths of a mile," Grant said. "When you see three towers on your right, watch for a Dark Rider on your left." He hung up.

Keryn had no idea what that meant, but she repeated it all. Allen cut off his lights and they crept forward along La Jolla Scenic Drive. The eerie yellow glow of the low-pressure sodium lights made the whole street look like a creepy *Nightmare on Elm Street* kind of place. They passed a trio of radio towers on their right.

A parking lot opened on their left. As they rolled past it, Keryn saw a pair of parking lights flick on and off just once. She pointed.

"Stop! Back up! There's our Dark Rider."

It was a Ford Explorer sitting in the middle of a deserted church parking lot. Allen pulled into the lot and drove slowly toward the SUV. The window on the driver's side descended. A shadowy figure sat in the driver's seat.

Allen pulled closer.

Closer.

A small penlight flicked on inside the SUV. Grant's bushy white eyebrows sprang out, sharp and clear. Behind him, Julia's anxious eyes glittered in the dark.

Allen rolled down his window and began braking.

Grant tossed a packet through the window and started his engine. "Go!" he said. His engine revved, and he shot forward past them toward the exit of the parking lot.

Allen spun the wheel in a tight circle and hit the gas. They lurched forward and out of the lot.

Keryn grabbed the packet out of Allen's lap and clutched it to her chest.

"Crazy," Allen said again.

Nobody said anything else for the fifteen minutes it took to get home.

CHAPTER
TWENTY - SEVEN

Dillon

Monday morning after breakfast, Dillon transferred all the phone numbers from his cell phone to the new one Grant had given him. He did not feel calm today. Grant had given him a driver's license and a Visa card in the name of Jake Scanlon. Dillon did not feel like a Jake. He felt like a fake.

Keryn sat down next to him on the couch. "Have you decided where you're going?"

"I have a friend in Berkeley, and I thought—"

"Berkeley?" Keryn narrowed her eyes. "Is that the friend who's a physicist?"

"He is in graduate school in physics. I would not call him a physicist yet."

"You were talking to him last week though, right?" Keryn was studying her hands.

"Yes, I talk to him every week."

"Listen, call me paranoid, but . . . just how well do you know him?"

Dillon did not like this question. "I trust Robert completely. I have known him since he was born. His family lived next door to us in Chicago."

"Okay, I know you trust him, but I don't. Pretend he's somebody with a secret past. Pretend he's a Mafia guy. Now think. Did you . . . did you tell him anything at all about the bio-computer?"

Dillon tried to recall his conversations with Robert. "I told him I was working on a special project. And . . ." Dillon stood up and began pacing. He had just remembered something.

"Dillon, what's wrong?"

Dillon sighed. "Robert may have heard something. I was at the bio-lab, talking to him on my cell phone. I was about to say good-bye when Clifton came out talking loudly about Shor's algorithm."

"Remind me, what is Shor's algorithm?"

Dillon stared out the window. "It is the algorithm we use on the bio-computer to factor large numbers."

"Is there anything else Shor's algorithm is used for?"

"No." Dillon felt cold.

"Would Robert know what it is?"

"Maybe." Dillon shook his head. "Yes. He would know what Shor's algorithm is."

Keryn stood up and put a hand on his arm. "I don't think you should be going to see Robert anytime soon."

Dillon's heart skipped a beat. "I have to. He is visiting his fian-cée's family in Mission Viejo this week, and I promised to drive up and meet them this weekend."

"This weekend?" Keryn's voice rose half an octave. "Dillon, you can't possibly meet these people this weekend. We won't be testing the bio-computer until Thursday, and there's no way we can hold a public demonstration of it on Friday. Not till next week at the ear-liest. You can't come out of hiding before then."

"I told you I have to go. I gave my word." Dillon felt sick. Rob-ert was not the one who had leaked word of the bio-computer. He could not be.

"Dillon, if you go, you'll be putting yourself at risk. And Rachel and me. You shouldn't be out in public any more than you need to."

Dillon sat down and put his head in his hands. He had not thought of that. He was not used to this life of hiding, of prevari-cation.

Keryn sat beside him. "I really, really don't want you to go. Robert and his fiancée will probably be busy anyway, planning the wedding."

"That is why I need to go," Dillon said. "I am the best man."

K e r y n

An hour later Keryn was driving north on Highway 5, trying to keep Dillon in her sights. Dillon had agreed to let Keryn follow him up in Kathii's car and meet Robert. If she didn't like him, Dillon would then turn around and go back to San Diego. Keryn was a good judge of character. If Robert was shady, she believed she would know it. Unfortunately, meeting with him meant that both she and Dillon had to come out of hiding, but Dillon had to go somewhere anyway. Grant wanted Dillon's software separated as far as possible from Rachel's bio-computer. Rachel had called her aunt, who came and picked her up.

Up ahead, Dillon's rented Dodge Caravan signaled to take the Alicia Parkway exit. Keryn was a couple of hundred yards behind. She watched closely to see if anybody else made the same move.

Three cars took the same exit. Keryn followed them. Her heart was hammering now. The novelist part of her brain was sitting back taking notes furiously. This was what it felt like to be in an international intrigue. She had always thought it would be *exciting*. It wasn't exciting. Part of her wanted to heave and part of her wanted to die and part of her wanted to shriek. If this were a novel, instead of real life, she'd be tempted to reach right out of the computer and wrap the mouse cord around the author's neck.

Dillon's car came to a complete halt at the end of the off-ramp. The car behind almost hit him. Either that driver was expecting a California rolling stop through the red light or he was thinking about carjacking Dillon. If anyone tried that, Keryn would just drive up alongside and Dillon would jump in the car and . . . she'd find out what a real-life car chase was like. She gripped the steering wheel so hard her fingers ached.

Dillon turned right and drove sedately down Alicia Parkway. Keryn had a Yahoo map on the seat beside her showing exactly where they were going. There was a Denny's restaurant just off the highway. Dillon had agreed to meet Robert there and introduce him to Keryn. From there, Keryn would play it by ear.

Right now she wanted to kidnap Dillon and just take him home. Forget meeting Robert's future in-laws. Forget the stupid bio-computer. They had phony ID. Tomorrow they could be in South America or New Zealand or . . . wherever. They could start a new life in a galaxy far, far away, find jobs, settle down together in a little cottage by the sea, where she could write under a pseudonym and Dillon could find some sort of techie job.

Dillon's car turned left onto Charlinda Drive and then immediately left into a shopping center. Nobody followed him. Keryn drove on to the next light, made a U-turn, came back. Nothing looked out of the ordinary. Dillon had parked in the main parking lot of the shopping center, not in the Denny's lot. He hadn't got out of his car yet. Keryn parked in the Del Taco lot across from Denny's and dialed Dillon's cell phone. "I'm here. Go on in and find him. I'll watch your back."

Dillon got out of his car and locked it. Keryn noticed that he made a point of walking all the way around the minivan, looking at all four tires. A rental car that had probably been gassed and oiled and pressurized that morning.

Dillon completed his inspection and went into the Denny's. Keryn sat watching. A couple came out of the restaurant, each holding the hand of a small blond-haired girl. Keryn felt an ache in her throat.

Her cell phone rang. Keryn answered it. "Yes?"

"I have found Robert. We are in a booth in the corner."

"I'm on my way." Keryn closed the phone and hopped out. She locked the car and went into the Denny's.

A greeter assaulted her with a huge plastic smile and menu. "Table for one?"

"I'm meeting someone." Keryn pointed toward the back corner. "Those two back there." She took her time walking to the table. Dillon was sitting with his back to the wall, talking to a tall man with sandy hair. Keryn felt her heart racing. There had to be something she could find wrong with Robert. She did not want Dillon hanging around with him. A guy from Chicago. A guy with ties to the physics community. Was he the leak?

Dillon said something to Robert when Keryn arrived. Robert turned around and saw Keryn and stood up.

Keryn looked him in the eye. "Hi, I'm Keryn. You must be Robert."

"Glad to meet you," he said with a puppy-dog grin that was either really, really sincere or a great act. His eyes fixed on her face. "Dillon's a lucky guy."

Keryn felt her cheeks heating up. She wasn't sure what Dillon had told Robert about her, but she doubted very much that he had said they were an item. She stuck out her hand. "Glad to meet you."

He shook it and then they sat down. Dillon scooted over in the booth so Keryn had plenty of room.

Keryn studied Robert carefully, looking for something, anything wrong with him. "So . . . you're getting married in August?"

Robert grinned and his eyes lit up with that special glitter that was impossible to fake. "That's right, and this is my first trip to Mission Viejo. My fiancée's got a big family and she's been wanting me to meet them all. Her little sister will be maid of honor, and she really wants to meet Dillon."

"Do you have a picture of your fiancée?"

Robert pulled out his wallet and folded out his photos. "This one. And this one."

Keryn looked at the two pictures. Robert's fiancée had a great mass of curly blond hair and startling blue eyes. And a smile that could light up the whole state of Illinois. "She's a cutie," Keryn said. "What's her name?"

"Sarah."

Keryn nodded. A guy who was in love had a special way of saying his girl's name. Robert was in love. In love bad. He was a nerdy-looking guy with a goofy grin, and Keryn would bet he was a terrible liar. Whatever else Robert was, he wasn't an enemy. She pushed the photos back to him. "Congratulations."

Robert grinned back at her. "Listen, we'd love to put you on our guest list. We just . . . well, Dillon didn't tell me about you." He shot Dillon an accusing look.

Dillon didn't say anything and Keryn didn't dare look at him. She pursed her lips and looked at Robert. "I don't think Dillon can come to your family get-together this weekend."

Robert's eyes narrowed. "I would think Dillon can decide that. Listen, if you're . . . worried, Sarah's sister already has a boyfriend."

"That's not the problem," Keryn said. "I can't tell you much, but Dillon's life may be in danger. Mine too, for that matter. We absolutely have to keep him in hiding for the next few days. That's the only reason I let him meet you here. But he can't be meeting a lot of people until we get something resolved, and that's probably not going to happen before the weekend."

Robert's face looked as if she'd just jabbed him with an ice pick. "What's going on? Shouldn't you call the police?"

"We're planning to," Keryn said, "but if we do it too soon, it'll be crying wolf and they won't believe us. We're waiting for the last little bit of evidence to come in. That will be Friday at the earliest, but . . . more likely next Monday. You can see what kind of a bind that puts us in."

Robert looked very puzzled. "I don't understand."

Which was good. The only way he could understand would be if he knew more than he should.

Dillon leaned forward. "This will all be over within a week, and then we can explain. I promise I will be there for your wedding. Nothing will keep me from that."

Robert sighed. "I'll tell the family you're sick."

"Please do not prevaricate," Dillon said.

Robert did not look happy. "You don't know Sarah's mother. She likes to be in control of things." He pulled out his backpack and rummaged around inside. Finally, he pulled out a wedding invitation. "Keryn, I'd love for you to come to the wedding. It would really make the day special. First Saturday in August. Can you make it?"

"Well . . . I can try. I've got a book due in the middle of the month and I'm way behind." Keryn studied the invitation. The photo showed Robert in a suit and Sarah looking radiant. Keryn felt a tear ball up in her eye, and she brushed it away with her finger. "You two look like you were made for each other."

Robert grinned.

"There's one more thing," Keryn said. "Right now Dillon and I need to keep out of sight as much as possible. We have fake IDs, credit cards in a phony name, the works. Dillon needs a place to stay until Thursday, and I'm thinking it might be safer if you can find him a hotel room without him needing to use his bogus stuff. I'm not sure how good that ID is or how long it'll last. Can you put him in a hotel room somewhere?"

"Sure, sure!" Robert's face showed raw concern. Just that—concern. "I'll get another room in my hotel. He can stay there as long as he wants." He looked at Dillon. "You must be in a lot of trouble, buddy. Is there anything you can tell me? Anything I can do to help?"

Keryn shook her head. "Have you got some phone numbers I can reach you at?"

Robert pulled out a business card and handed it to her. "That's got my cell phone number on it. I don't remember the hotel number, but you can call Dillon when you get back to San Diego and he can give it to you."

She studied the card for a moment. The name on the card was not Robert, it was Bob. Come to think of it, he looked like a Bob, not a Robert. His last name looked utterly unpronounceable. "How do you say your last name?"

Robert grinned. "Sorry, it's kind of tricky, isn't it? Put the accent on the first and third syllables. Kaganovski. My friends call me Kaggo."

"I'd better be getting back home." Keryn stood up. "Take care of Dillon, Kaggo. And congratulations on Sarah. She's a lucky girl."

Keryn spent the long drive back to Kathii's house wondering if she was ever going to get lucky.

CHAPTER
TWENTY-EIGHT

Rachel

"D avey's home from UCLA for the summer, so you can sleep in Rivka's old room." Aunt Esther led the way back to a small bedroom decorated in pastel pink colors.

Rachel dropped her Target bag on the floor. "Thanks for coming to get me, Auntie. Where's Davey?"

Aunt Esther shrugged. "I think he went surfing at La Jolla Shores today. Don't you have any more clothes than what's in that little bag?"

Rachel shook her head. "I . . . I'm in trouble, Auntie. I didn't want to talk about it on the phone, but I can't go back to my apartment. We think people are watching it and . . ." Rachel felt so exhausted and frightened she didn't know what to say. She had been trying to be strong for the last two weeks and now she was all alone and she just wanted this nightmare to be over. If she thought it would help, she'd throw the bio-computer away. But that would just make it worse. She desperately wanted a strong pair of arms to lean on. And the only strong arms she knew of had gone up to Mission Viejo. She had never felt so alone.

Aunt Esther put her arms around her. "Come sit down. I'll make some tea and you can tell me about it."

Rachel spent the next half hour in the kitchen explaining the whole story over a pot of tea.

Aunt Esther listened with very wide eyes. She patted Rachel's hand when she told about the carjacking. Finally, Rachel finished.

"You like this boy, Dillon?"

Rachel smiled. She hadn't said so, but Auntie was good at picking up certain things.

"He's not Jewish." Aunt Esther made it sound like a fatal disease.

"Auntie, I'm not Jewish either. Not according to the rabbis. My mother isn't Jewish."

"I know, I know, but Jewishness is more a state of mind. You're Jewish." Aunt Esther sighed deeply. "You're welcome to come to Beth Simcha anytime you want."

It was a standing offer, but Rachel had never seriously considered it. Auntie went to some weird kind of a synagogue. Jews for Jesus or something. Daddy said they were a crock. Mother said it sounded cultish.

"You don't have to," Aunt Esther said. "I don't mean to pressure you. I just want to help."

Rachel smiled. "I'll think about it, okay? I've been . . . thinking about a lot of things lately. Oh! Guess what? I decided I don't hate Jesus anymore."

"Really? That's wonderful!" Joy filled Aunt Esther's face. "People have done such horrible things to us in his name, but he's not like that at all. Yeshua was one of us."

Rachel remembered that Rivka had always been adamant that the real name of Jesus was Yeshua. Whatever. It was hard to win a debate with Rivka. Rachel usually didn't care, anyway, so she had always just agreed and changed the subject. Rachel sipped the last of her tea. "I miss Rivka so much."

Aunt Esther's eyes filled with tears. "I miss her too. She was . . . doing what she loved best."

"It's been how long now? Four years?"

Aunt Esther nodded. "I haven't had the heart to change anything in her room."

Rachel cleared the cups and the teakettle from the table and put them in the sink. Aunt Esther didn't have a dishwasher, so Rachel washed them and left them to dry in the drainer. When she finished, she saw that Aunt Esther hadn't moved, but two tracks of tears gleamed on her face.

Rachel hugged her tight. "Maybe . . . maybe you'll see her again, Auntie."

Aunt Esther looked up at her. "Do you believe that or are you just saying it?"

Rachel had no idea. She was so confused and mixed up right now, she didn't know what she believed and what was just California dreaming. "You believe it, Auntie, and that's enough."

"I wish you believed it too." Aunt Esther wiped her eyes.

Rachel didn't want to talk about that. Not now. Maybe not ever. She needed time to sort things out. "Could I use your washing machine? I'm almost out of clean clothes."

Aunt Esther led her back to Rivka's bedroom and opened a door in the far wall. It led into the garage. "The washer and drier are right back here." She turned to look at Rachel and hesitated for a very long time. "You're in trouble and . . . Rivka would want to help you. Look and see if there's anything you can wear." Aunt Esther opened the closet. "And there's some underthings in the dresser over there."

Rachel yawned mightily. "Could I . . . would it be rude if I took a nap for a while? I've had a really hard couple of weeks and I'm awfully tired."

"You go right ahead, honey."

Rachel stretched out on the bed. Aunt Esther gently closed the door.

———

When Rachel woke up, she felt groggy and ratty. She had dreamed that Dillon was getting married to Keryn and she was one of the bridesmaids, and when the preacher gave that blah-blah about speaking now or forever holding your peace, Rachel had started screaming, and Jesus came down out of one of those stained-glass pictures and dragged her out of the church by the hair and stole her bio-computer and gave it to Satan.

Rachel got up and rummaged around in the dresser and closet

for some of Rivka's clothes. After a long hot shower, she felt better. Rachel brushed her thick, curly hair and came out feeling almost alive. She went out to the kitchen and found Aunt Esther sitting there with a box full of things. A backpack. A wallet. Some cutoffs and T-shirts.

"What's this, Auntie?"

Aunt Esther's lip quivered. "It's all the things they sent back from Israel after Rivka . . . passed. This is her backpack and some of her clothes. I've never been able to go through it all."

Rachel opened Rivka's wallet. There were pictures of Aunt Esther and Uncle David and their son, Davey. There was another picture of Rivka's biological father—Uncle Leonard—Daddy's brother. Rachel knew vaguely that Auntie had divorced him a long time ago. She didn't know the details, and she didn't want to know. Uncle Leonard had remarried several years ago, to a young bimbo who wore gaudy makeup and had been through enough surgery to start a plastic factory. There was no picture of her in Rivka's wallet.

Rachel leafed through and found an expired Visa card, a worn Blockbuster card, and . . . a driver's license. Rivka was three years older than Rachel, with straight black hair, gorgeous brown eyes, and a dusky complexion. Unlike Rachel, she actually looked Jewish. The only thing they had in common was a perky nose that was decidedly not Jewish. Nobody would ever mistake either of them for Barbra Streisand.

Rachel reached in her pocket and pulled out the fake driver's license Grant had gotten for her in Mexico. It had her picture but a bogus name—Sally Swigert.

"What's that you've got, dear?" Aunt Esther stood up to look.

Rachel showed her. "My boss made it in case I needed some ID."

A VW bug roared up outside. Rachel saw a surfboard roped to the top.

"Oh my, Davey's already home." Aunt Esther scooped up all of Rivka's belongings and stuffed them back into the box. "Dear, could you put this back in Rivka's room? We'll sort through it tonight or tomorrow and throw away some of these old things. It's . . . time to put the past behind us."

Rachel carried the box back to her room and plunked it on Rivka's desk. She felt oddly glad that she'd been forced to come visit

Aunt Esther. Maybe, between the two of them, they could sort out the shredded pieces of their lives and make some sense of it all.

Keryn

On Tuesday morning Keryn called Dillon on her cell phone and made sure he was safe. He still sounded very unhappy about not getting to meet Robert's fiancée. Keryn didn't care. The most important thing was to survive for the next few days.

On Thursday Rachel and Dillon would get access to an NMR machine over at Mesa College and they could finish testing and then try to run Shor's algorithm. Nobody knew how long that would take. A day or so if all went perfectly. Then Grant would arrange a press conference and the world would see the proof.

After that . . . Keryn couldn't guess what would happen. The NSA would probably swoop in and grab the bio-computer. But they could not take it black. A black project, by definition, was one the world didn't know about. If the NSA used it to spy on people, well, people would know about it. There was a cure for that—the machines made by CypherQuanta. The world would be a better place and Keryn's stock would make her rich enough to quit working and write full-time.

All she had to do was survive until Thursday.

Keryn decided to pass the time working on her book. She was so far behind now that there was no hope of making her deadline. She'd have to call her agent and get her to wangle an extension from her editor. Agents were good at being bad cops.

Kathii got Keryn set up on a computer in the family room and then left to go food shopping. Keryn downloaded her files from her .Mac account on the Web and began typing. Jason and Jordan were playing a noisy game of checkers out in the living room, but within minutes, Keryn was in a universe of her own.

She kept coming back to the problem of how to kill Josh and make it look like an accident. Modern chemistry was too good. Even the tiniest traces of poisons could be detected by forensic investigators. She had been planning to use botulism, but just how believable was that?

Or did it matter? Every day things happened that were totally absurd. Ridiculous. Unbelievable. Take 9/11. Using jets as bombs. Clancy had been ridiculed for writing a scenario just like that in *Debt of Honor*. The difference between the fiction and the reality was that Clancy's idea was so much more plausible than bin Laden's.

Lots of things that happened in real life were absurdly improbable. People often did illogical things for no reason at all. Real life didn't have to make sense. But you couldn't get away with any of that in fiction. Fiction had to be plausible and logical, and it had to make sense.

"Aunt Keryn?"

Keryn turned and saw Jason standing behind her. "What is it, sweetie?"

"There's a man here who wants to innerview you."

Keryn's heart clawed its way up into her throat. "Interview me? Who would know I'm here?"

"He's at the door right now." Jason tugged on her hand. "Jordan's showing him a magic trick."

Keryn stood up. Jordan shouldn't be talking to some strange man at the door. She hurried out to the living room.

A man in a dark suit stood outside smiling at Jordan's attempts to yank a string through his neck. When he saw Keryn, he held up a badge. "I'm Rod Greene with the FBI. I believe you're the sister-in-law of Allen Russell?"

"What's this about?" Keryn said. "How did you know I was here?" She snapped her fingers at Jordan. "Come inside right now."

"Ma'am, is there a problem?" Greene said. "Mr. Russell is being considered for a higher security clearance over at SAIC, and he listed you as one of his references. We called your home on Friday and yesterday but got no answer, so we went by your house. Your neighbor happened to be out watering his lawn."

"Since when does he water anything?" Keryn narrowed her eyes. "And his lawn is nothing but weeds."

Greene shrugged. "He told us to let you know Smiley and Zephyr are doing great together. And he guessed you were at your sister's house. So we came over here."

"We?" Keryn peered past him. "Who's 'we'?"

"My partner is Hector Gonzales. He's over at the neighbors'. They're also listed as references and—"

A Hispanic man in a suit came down the walk, shaking his head. "The Websters aren't home. Did you find Miss Wills?"

Greene nodded. "She's here." He held up a clipboard with an apologetic smile. "Is this a good time to answer just a few questions about Mr. Russell?"

Keryn had gone through this once before when Allen first went to work at SAIC. That was years ago, and the agents had spent almost an hour asking all sorts of absurd questions about Allen. "Mind if I look at your badges and call your main office?"

"Please do," Greene said. He held up his badge for her inspection.

Keryn looked at it. The picture on the badge matched his face.

"Here's my card, ma'am." Greene handed her a business card. "Hector, just give Miss Wills a look at your badge and one of your cards. She'd like to check us out."

Gonzales showed her his badge and gave her a card.

Keryn took both cards and stepped back into the house. She shut the door and twisted the dead bolt. Jason and Jordan were staring at her with enormous eyes. "Were those real FBI men?"

"That's what I'm going to find out." Keryn went back to the family room and grabbed the phone and dialed the number on the card.

"Federal Bureau of Investigation, Security Clearance Department." It was a young female voice.

"Yes, I have two men at my door, Rod Greene and Hector Gonzales." Keryn read off their badge numbers from the cards. "Are those men in your division?"

"Yes, they're doing security clearance interviews this morning on Allen Russell."

"Thanks, that's all I needed to know." Keryn hung up and sighed with relief. Okay, fine, so she was paranoid. But even paranoids had enemies. She had a right to—

The back patio door gritted open behind her.

Keryn spun around. The two agents sprang inside, lunging for her. Keryn screamed.

Agent Greene wrapped his arms around her, pinning her arms to her sides. Gonzales yanked a hood over her head.

"Get away!" Keryn stomped down hard, trying for Greene's instep.

He swore at her and lifted her off the floor.

She kicked out in the air with both feet. Hands grabbed them, lashing them together with some kind of twine.

Raw terror washed through Keryn. If they weren't real FBI agents, then she was in extreme trouble.

And if they *were* real FBI agents, she was in even bigger trouble.

A sickly sweet odor assaulted her nostrils. Keryn tried not to breathe, but she knew that tactic would only last about fifteen seconds. She relaxed her body, letting her limbs go limp. She took a small, shallow breath and held it as long as possible. Her mind began slipping, sliding away.

Relax. Play dead.

All the world went black.

When Keryn came to, she felt sick and dizzy. Several slow and lazy minutes passed while she tried to get her bearings. Why was it so dark? What was that dull roar?

Slowly the world of reality pressed in around her. She could feel that her legs were tied. The men. The horrible FBI men. Or were they? Her hands were tied in front of her with rough twine.

Keryn brought both hands up to her face and found that the awful hood was gone. She raised her hands and thumped against something hollow and metallic. As the muzziness in her brain cleared, she suddenly realized that she was in the trunk of a car. She felt around and identified the locking mechanism. After playing with it for a minute, she realized that she was not going to unlock it.

She rolled the other way and by twisting around awkwardly, she pressed her ear up against the hard inner wall of the trunk.

Voices.

By listening hard, she could make out the voices of three men. Greene. Gonzales.

And Clifton Potter?

Keryn felt like somebody had shoved an icicle through her heart.

Clifton! She tried desperately to make out his words, but that was impossible.

She rolled back away from the seat back and began gnawing desperately at the twine binding her wrists. Slowly, slowly, it began to come undone. Obviously, they hadn't expected her to come to so soon or they would have tied her better. At last she got the knot loose enough to slip her hands free.

Keryn took a deep breath to calm herself. She had read a news article not long ago about a kidnapping victim locked in a trunk who worked loose the taillight and stuck her hand out, eventually attracting the attention of somebody. Keryn felt around with her hands, but she couldn't see anything. She pawed for the light switch in the trunk. There!

She flicked it.

Nothing happened.

Keryn wanted to scream. Then she remembered she had put her cell phone in her pocket. Had the men found it? It had the numbers for Dillon and Rachel encoded. Keryn held her breath and reached into her pocket. Her fingers wrapped around . . . a small metallic phone.

"Thank God." Keryn brought it up to her face and flipped it open. Blessed light nearly blinded her. She selected the phone list and toggled down to Dillon's number. But Dillon was an hour away in Mission Viejo. Keryn sighed deeply and selected Rachel's number. Rachel was here in town. She could . . . do something. Call the cops. Get the phone company to triangulate on her signal. Whatever.

Keryn pressed the Send button.

CHAPTER
TWENTY-NINE

Rachel

Rachel was watering Aunt Esther's roses in the backyard when her cell phone chirped. She yanked it out and saw that Keryn was calling.

"Hi, Keryn, what's up?"

Keryn's voice came in a whisper. "Rachel! Help me! I've been kidnapped."

Rachel dropped the hose and ran into the house. "What! Say that again!"

"I've been kidnapped. I'm in the trunk of a car. We're driving somewhere."

Rachel's heart was pounding so hard, she was afraid her ribs might crack. "I'll call the cops! Do you have any idea where you are? What kind of car?"

"Wait!" Keryn's voice hissed across the line. "The men might be FBI agents."

"What do you mean, they *might* be?" Rachel fell onto the couch and put her hand on her heart, willing it to slow down.

Aunt Esther came in from the backyard. "Rachel, the hose is going full blast on the—" She gave a little shriek when she saw

Rachel lying on the couch. "Oh my! Are you all right?"

"No," Rachel said. "One of my friends has been kidnapped. Wait, Keryn, say that all again. My aunt came in and I couldn't hear you." She motioned to Aunt Esther to come close so she could listen.

"Two men came to Kathii's house," Keryn whispered. "They said their names were Rod Greene and Hector Gonzales." She spent five minutes explaining what had happened.

"And you think they might be real FBI?" Rachel said.

"I don't know," Keryn said. "But listen! They've got Clifton in the car with them. I heard his voice up there. I can't hear what they're saying, but it's normal conversation. They're not interrogating him or anything."

Rachel wanted to die. Clifton Potter. She never had liked him. This explained a lot.

Aunt Esther's face had gone white. "I'll call the police."

Rachel grabbed her hand. "Don't you dare! If the FBI are in on this, then the cops are too, and they'll trace the call back to this address."

"Rachel, can you call Dillon?" Keryn's voice quivered with fear.

"Hang on a second." Rachel studied the buttons on the phone. Dillon had shown her the other night how to do a three-way on these gizmos. She pressed a small button labeled Conference and was rewarded with a dial tone and her phone list. Rachel toggled down to Dillon's number and pressed Send.

Three rings and then . . .

"Hello, Rachel." Dillon's voice came through the line, strong and true.

"Dillon, they've got Keryn. Hold on and I'll try to patch her back in." Rachel held her breath and pressed Conference again. "Keryn, are you there?"

"I'm here." Keryn said. "Did you track down Dillon?"

"Keryn, what's happening?" Dillon's voice roared through the earpiece.

"I've been . . . kidnapped," Keryn said. "I'm in the trunk of a car. There are two FBI men and *Clifton* up in the front."

"Hang on, Keryn," Dillon said. "I'll be there as quick as I can."

"Dillon, no!" Rachel shouted. "Stay where you are! There's nothing you can do down here."

Rachel heard the sound of feet running.

D i l l o n

Dillon raced out the door and down the hall. When he reached Robert's door, he pounded on it many times. "Robert! Open up!"

Several doors opened up and down the corridor.

Dillon kept pounding. "Robert!"

The door swung suddenly inward. Robert looked very annoyed. "I'm trying to talk with Sarah. What's—"

Dillon pushed his way in. "I need my car keys."

Robert shook his head. "Keryn made me promise to keep them so you wouldn't go anywhere until—"

Dillon slammed the door shut. "Keryn has been kidnapped. Now give me the car keys."

"Kidnapped?" Robert stared at him. He ran to the phone and scooped it up. "Sarah, I'll call you later." He threw the phone on the cradle and went to the small refrigerator by the minibar, and pulled Dillon's car keys out of the freezer. "I'm going with you."

"Give them to me!" Dillon shouted.

"I'll drive," Robert said harshly. "You're in no state. Now move!"

Dillon jerked open the door and ran. Robert's footsteps thudded behind him.

Two minutes later they were southbound on Highway 5. Robert slipped the minivan over into the left lane and pegged the speedometer to the far right. It was very unsafe. Dillon did not care at all.

Dillon cradled the phone in his hands. He had closed it when he ran to get Robert and had lost the connection. He tried to dial Keryn, but her line was busy. Likewise Rachel. He closed the phone and waited, filling Robert in on what little he knew.

After a couple of minutes, the phone rang. Dillon flipped it open. "Keryn?"

"Dillon, I'm so scared." Keryn's voice rasped in the earpiece. "Dillon, I think . . . I think it really is the FBI who took me. Don't call the cops, please. If the cops are in on this, it won't do any good to call them and they'll just track you and Rachel down. If they aren't in on it, the FBI will just lie to them and use them to find you."

Rachel's voice cut in. "Keryn, do you know what direction you're going?"

"No. They chloroformed me or something and . . . I woke up in the trunk. I can't see a thing and . . . I'm scared. Guys, listen. Get out of Dodge. Both of you. Call Grant and get as far away from here as you can. Don't try to save me. There's nothing you can do. I'm sure they've got guns, and they're probably hoping to use me to get to you. If I break the connection, don't call back and don't answer any calls from me. They'll try to trace back to you somehow."

Dillon felt dizzy and sick in his belly. He leaned forward and moaned softly.

Robert swerved into the next lane and passed a Porsche that was going a mere ninety.

"Hang on, Keryn," Dillon said.

"Be careful!" Rachel's voice sounded full of tears.

"Dillon?" Keryn's voice was very small.

"Yes?" Dillon felt a buzzing in his head, and a great warmth filled his chest at the sound of her voice. "Yes, Keryn?"

"I . . . if I don't see you again, I just wanted to say that . . . I love you."

Dillon felt something huge rise up in his heart. He wanted to say something. Wanted to tell her that . . . that she was a most excellent friend. That he admired her. That . . .

"Oh my!" Keryn's voice squeaked with fright.

"Keryn, what is it?" Dillon saw a sign flash by that said *Entering Oceanside.*

"I . . . we're slowing down." Keryn sounded very out of breath. "We're bumping over some kind of rough road."

Dillon felt his heart crashing against his chest. "Please, Lord, keep Keryn safe."

"Jesus, help me!" Keryn said. "The car just stopped. I hear voices. They're getting out. Oh, Jesus, please, please, please!"

Dillon could not breathe. He simply could not breathe. Black spots danced in front of his eyes.

"I hear a key in the lock!" Keryn said. "Jesus, help me!"

A thud.
A scream.
A gunshot.
Silence.

PART FOUR

The Grand Illusion

"As I have said, there is no practical prospect
of factorizing 250-digit numbers by classical
means. But a quantum factorization engine
running Shor's algorithm could do it using
only a few thousand arithmetic operations,
which might well take only a matter of
minutes. So anyone with access to such a
machine would easily be able to read any
intercepted message that had been encrypted
using the RSA cryptosystem."

DAVID DEUTSCH
The Fabric of Reality, p. 216

CHAPTER
THIRTY

Dillon

Dillon felt like his brain had exploded. He leaned forward and retched.

The minivan swerved violently. "Dillon!" Robert shouted. "That sounded like a gunshot!"

A scream shivered through the earpiece. "Keryn!" Rachel shouted. "Keryn, are you there?"

Nothing.

Hot tears welled up in Dillon's eyes. He closed his eyes tight and moaned.

"What's happening?" Robert shouted.

Dillon pressed the earpiece to his ear. Rachel was wailing, but there was something else.

Men's voices.

"Is she dead? Shoot her again to make sure." Clifton Potter's voice.

Another gunshot.

"Dillon, hang up!" Rachel said. "They'll trace back to us."

Dillon slapped the phone shut. He wanted to die. Right now, to die and . . . go where Keryn was. To the arms of the Lord.

Robert braked gently to a more normal speed. "Dillon, what's going on?"

Dillon's voice cracked. "She . . . they . . . shot her." He fell back in the seat and wept. Evil men had killed Keryn. Sweet, innocent Keryn. A dull hollow pain welled up in Dillon's chest.

Robert swerved into the right lane and took the next exit. Dillon felt the minivan slow to a stop. Heard the engine cut off. Footsteps outside. The door yanked open.

Robert's strong arms. "Come on, Dillon. You need some air."

Dillon did not want air. He wanted to die. Life without Keryn was like . . . life without air. He could not imagine living without her calm, gracious presence. Her soothing pastel colors. Her subtle perfume.

Robert unlatched Dillon's seatbelt. "Dillon, I'm so sorry."

The phone rang in Dillon's lifeless hands. He had no strength to open it.

It rang again.

Robert grabbed the phone. "The caller ID says it's from someone named Rachel. Should I answer it?"

"Yes." Dillon squeezed out a whisper. His ears seemed to be filled with a roaring sound.

Robert opened the phone. "Hello?"

Dillon vaguely heard Robert talking to Rachel. Explaining who he was, that he was a friend of Dillon, that they were just south of Oceanside.

"Hold on one second, Rachel," Robert said. The phone pressed up against Dillon's ear. "Dillon, Rachel wants you to tell her I'm not the bogeyman."

Dillon took a shallow breath. "Rachel, Robert is my best friend. He was driving me when . . ." He couldn't say it.

"Dillon, get hold of yourself!" Rachel said. "I'm scared out of my wits and my aunt Esther is freaking out. I need you! I'm going to call Grant and tell him what happened. He'll know what to do. Are you there? Answer me, Dillon, I need you!"

"I . . . I am here." Dillon felt like his body weighed a thousand pounds. "Tell me how to find you."

Rachel gave him directions to her aunt's house in Clairemont, then rang off.

Dillon closed his eyes. "Robert, we need to go to Rachel."

The door slammed. A few seconds later, Robert hopped into the driver's side. "Just tell me where, buddy."

"South on five," Dillon said.

The engine roared. "We're on the way. You just . . . pray for her soul. I'll drive."

Dillon had no worries about Keryn's soul. Yes, she had been a sinner as a young girl, but the Lord had forgiven her. If anyone would go to heaven, it was Keryn.

The miles hummed by. Somewhere near the 805 fork, Dillon wiped his tears away and opened his eyes.

Robert put a big strong hand on his shoulder. "She was so right for you."

Dillon did not know what to say. He had been so blind. Robert was right. Keryn was perfect for him. He had not realized it until now, but she was perfect for him.

"The minute I saw her, I thought what a lucky guy you were," Robert said. "I could see how much she loved you."

Dillon felt numb. "Do you . . . think she meant what she said?"

Robert turned to look at him. "What do you mean? What did she say?"

"Just before . . . the end, she told me that she . . . if she did not see me again, she wanted to say that . . . she loved me. Do you think she meant that?"

"Well . . . of course. I mean, you two were going together, weren't you?"

"Going where?" Dillon tried to look at Robert, but all the world was a smear.

"Wasn't she your girlfriend? I just assumed . . ."

"She was a good friend. I liked talking with her very much."

"And whenever you were with her, you felt like she was the only woman in the world? That you could tell her anything?"

"Yes."

"And whenever she wasn't there, you were thinking about her and wishing she would call?"

"I . . . yes." Dillon wiped the tears out of his eyes. "Is . . . is that what love is?"

A light pickup cut in front of them. Robert braked sharply.

"Dillon, you're telling me you were in love with a gorgeous woman and you didn't know it?"

It hit Dillon like a punch in the face. He had not known. Had not imagined. He buried his face in his hands and wept. He had not merely lost a good friend.

He had lost the love of his life.

Rachel

"Auntie, calm down, please. It's going to be all right." Rachel fumbled with the phone, finally toggled down to Grant's number. Tears stood so thick in her eyes, she could hardly see. She brushed them away madly and pressed the Send button. On the third ring, it picked up.

"Hello, Rachel," Grant said. "Everything okay?"

Rachel took a deep, deep breath and let it out slow. "N-no."

Grant swore. "I hope Dillon isn't planning anything stupid. Keryn told his friend he can't go to that thing this weekend, right?"

Rachel felt her whole insides caving in. "Uncle Grant?" Tears started rolling again. Until now, she'd been able to pretend it wasn't real. But she felt that as soon as she formed the words, it would be true. "You better sit down. Something . . . awful has happened."

A muffled grunt. "Okay, I'm sitting. Now what could be so wrong? Everybody's still in one piece, right?"

Rachel sucked in her breath and started wailing.

"Rachel! What's happened? Are you hurt?"

"I'm f-fine, but . . . they got K-Keryn."

"Got her? What do you mean, *got* her?"

"They kidnapped her. And . . . killed her." Rachel couldn't say any more, she was crying so hard. It was true now. She had wanted so bad for it to be a lie, but it was true.

Uncle Grant sounded like he was having a seizure.

Rachel was almost hyperventilating now. "Some m-men with FBI badges came and kidnapped Keryn and took her somewhere. She . . . called me from the trunk of the car. Then they stopped and opened the trunk and . . . shot her. And . . . Clifton was there! He told them to shoot her again to make sure she was dead."

Grant's voice was husky with emotion when he finally spoke.

"Rachel, this is horrible. Keryn was . . . I just can't believe it." A long silence. "And . . . I'm sorry I ever got you into this mess. If anything happens to you, I'll die."

"What are we going to do, Uncle Grant?"

A long silence. When he finally spoke, Grant sounded like he was going to be sick. "I think we'd better get out of town. All of us. Does Dillon know yet?"

"He was on the line too," Rachel said. "He heard it all."

"Tell him to get his butt back to San Diego," Grant said.

"Where are you?" Rachel said.

"Downtown in a hotel. Julia's out shopping right now. I'll track her down and we'll scoot over to the airport. I'll buy us some tickets. Meet me there as quick as you can."

"Where are we going?" Rachel said.

"I'm not sure. I'll figure it out. Call Dillon and have him meet us there."

"Uncle Grant? I'm . . . really scared. Can I have Dillon pick me up here?"

"Sure. Call me when you get to the airport. Travel light. We're on the run. And bring the bio-computer."

"See you soon."

"Bring that phony ID," Grant said. "You can't fly without a picture ID. I'll get you a ticket in that name." He hung up.

Rachel folded the phone and put it in her pocket. "Auntie, don't worry. Uncle Grant's going to get me out of town. As soon as Dillon gets here, we're leaving."

"You should call the police." Aunt Esther was locking the window in the living room.

Rachel shook her head. "It's too dangerous. I don't trust anybody. The FBI killed Keryn. We've got to leave town. Uncle Grant is going to meet me at the airport with tickets."

"Can't the FBI track passenger names on the airline computers?"

"He'll get the tickets in phony names—the same names he put on the fake driver's licenses."

Aunt Esther went and locked the back patio door. "When is your friend coming?"

"Soon." Rachel went to Rivka's bedroom and looked around, trying to decide what she should take. She checked that the bio-computer was still in her fanny pack. But what else should she take? Underwear? Clothes? She riffled through the box of Rivka's things, but she was so scared she couldn't think. Forget packing clothes. Wherever she was going, she could buy things. She had a Visa card. Best to just travel light.

Rachel grabbed Rivka's wallet and staggered back out to the living room and sat down in Auntie's rocking chair. Slow breathing. In and out. In and out. *Think calming thoughts.*

Clifton had betrayed them. Rachel felt nauseated at the thought. How could a guy do that?

More importantly, how *had* he? Unless Rachel answered that, she might be the next one killed. Or Dillon.

Dillon. Rachel's heart began hammering as the answer fell into place. Dillon was the key. The men had kidnapped Keryn. If they knew where Keryn was, they must know where Rachel was, but they hadn't come for her. They came for Keryn instead. Why?

Because they already had a bio-computer.

It was so obvious, Rachel wanted to scream. Dillon was the target, not her. They had kidnapped Keryn to lure Dillon back because he had the software they needed to make the bio-computer work. Which meant that Clifton was the one who broke into the bio-lab. Clifton must have stolen the bio-computer. He had taken the software too, but then he found out it wasn't ready yet.

Rachel closed her eyes and imagined the scene. Clifton must have seen her or Grant keying in the combination earlier that week. On Friday night she had called him to say that they were close but were quitting for the night. Around two in the morning Clifton had just walked in and logged in under her username. He must have seen her log in once. He could have seen her password. Then he tried to compile Dillon's source code, but it failed. He found the obvious bugs, fixed them to make the code compile, but he didn't really understand the code and didn't realize that his fixes wouldn't work. He opened the safe—it had the same combination as the door—and took out the bio-computer. He tried to test the software, but the code crashed. After three tries, he gave up. He drained the bio-computer into a flask, set it up to look like it had accidentally leaked out, and left.

Then he just played dumb the next day. And now she remembered that he was always taking phone calls at weird times and going off somewhere private to talk. Which meant he was working with someone else. He'd probably bugged the office, their phones, everything. If he had some buddies in the FBI, that would explain it all. He'd offered them a few billion to help. Or something. Most people had a price, and it usually didn't have that many zeroes behind it. Rachel had heard once that seven percent of all Americans would kill somebody they didn't know for ten million dollars. For ten trillion dollars . . . just about anybody could be bought.

Clifton Potter had sold his soul for a shipload of money.

That was the only explanation. Clifton knew Dillon had that flash drive on his key chain and he had tipped off his friends. The carjackers stole Dillon's car just so they could get his keys. They probably didn't even know Rachel had the bio-computer. They didn't care because they didn't need it. Dillon was the target all the time.

Rachel took the idea apart and put it back together twice in her mind. It explained all the facts. And the clincher was that Clifton was right there with them when they killed Keryn. Clifton told them to shoot her again. Clifton, in cold blood. The filthy, evil, lying—

"Somebody's here!" Aunt Esther said.

Rachel shot out of her chair. "What kind of car?"

"It's a white minivan."

Rachel almost collapsed in relief. "Thank God! That's Dillon's rental car!" She threw her arms around Aunt Esther. "I'll call you when I'm safe."

"Like fun you will. I'm coming to the airport with you."

"No, it isn't safe."

Aunt Esther was shaking, but she held Rachel's hand tight. "Rachel, honey, Yeshua will take care of me."

"He didn't take care of Keryn."

"I'll . . . I'll pray for Keryn."

"And what good will that do?"

Aunt Esther put her arms around her. "Rachel, honey, if God wants to raise Keryn from the dead, he can do it."

Deep bitterness filled Rachel's heart. If there was anything in the world she hated, it was blind, stupid faith.

"Honey, I'm coming with you." Aunt Esther picked up her purse.

A knock on the door.

Rachel yanked it open.

Dillon stood there, a rock of calm.

Rachel rushed into his arms. "Dillon, I'm so glad you're here. Grant wants us to meet him at the airport."

"When?"

"Now." Rachel squeezed Dillon around the waist. "I've been so scared."

He stroked her hair gently. "The Lord will protect us."

Rachel didn't say anything. Keryn had believed that, and now she had a bullet in her brains.

"We have to find Grant." Dillon released his hold on her.

Rachel didn't want to go anywhere. Didn't ever want to leave the quiet strength of Dillon's arms.

Aunt Esther put a hand on Rachel's back. "Let's go, already. Yeshua watched over Rivka. He'll watch over you."

Which was exactly what Rachel was afraid of.

CHAPTER
THIRTY-ONE

Dillon

O n the way to the airport, Dillon sat with Rachel in the middle
seat of the minivan, hoping the darkened side windows would
give them slightly better concealment. Rachel seemed terrified. She
clung to Dillon and explained her theory about Clifton.

By the time they reached Harbor Drive, Dillon was shaking with
rage. He had trusted Clifton. To betray a friend—that was evil, pure
and simple. To kill Keryn for the love of mammon was beyond evil.

Dillon took out his cell phone and dialed Grant.

It answered after one ring. "This is Russell."

"Russell?" Dillon's heart began hammering. Who was Russell?

"Is that you, Jake?" Grant's voice was a dry rasp. "This is Russell."

Dillon realized that Russell was the name Grant would be trav-
eling under. "This is . . . Jake." He hated speaking a lie. It felt bent.
Evil.

"I'm in Terminal 2, across from the American Airlines counter,"
Grant said. "Have you heard from my wife?"

"Julia?"

"Teresa!" Grant snapped.

"Sorry." Dillon again felt a twist in his heart. This was wrong, all wrong, this business with false names. It was wrong to bear false witness. "No, I have not heard from her. I am with . . ." He tried to remember Rachel's false name. "I am with Sally now. We are on Harbor, just turning in toward Terminal 2 right now. We have friends with us to help."

"Good. Walk behind them and keep your heads down. Did you bring any kind of disguise?"

Dillon felt his heart lurch. "You think they will be watching for us?"

"I have no idea what they'll be doing." Grant's voice sounded tight, exhausted. "It may be just a few rogue agents—that's my guess. Or it could be the whole U.S. Army. I don't know. I'm wearing a Padres cap and some reading glasses I bought at a drugstore on the way here. And I'm hiding behind a copy of the *Union-Tribune*."

"We will be in shortly." Dillon hung up. "Robert, no, do not park. Just drop us at the curb at the American Airlines sign."

Robert growled something and chugged to a stop at the short-term parking entrance. He lowered the window and pressed the button for a parking slip.

A minute later they had parked and were walking toward the terminal. Rachel's aunt walked in front with Robert. Dillon followed close behind Robert, keeping his head down. Rachel clutched Dillon's arm and kept her face pressed against his shoulder as if she were his girlfriend saying good-bye. Dillon felt a peculiar burning sensation in his belly.

As they crossed the drop-off lanes, a policeman turned and began walking toward them. Dillon felt his mind contract into a hard knot. He heard a whistle blow.

"Keep going," Rachel whispered. "They whistle all the time. Odds are he's whistling at some goofball who's double-parked."

Another whistle. Dillon began feeling dizzy. They reached the terminal and walked in through the automatic doors. A uniformed man appeared in front of them.

Dillon's heart felt like melted cheese.

"Carry your bags, sir?" said the porter.

"No bags," Robert said. "But thank you very much."

"You have a nice flight, sir."

Dillon breathed again. They turned left and hugged the outer wall of the terminal, passing little shops selling San Diego sweatshirts and baseball caps and cheap paperbacks. A newspaper rustled. Dillon saw the bill of a Padres cap behind it. "Robert, stop. He is here."

The newspaper lowered, and Grant's bushy eyebrows peeked up at them. He pointed to Dillon and Rachel. "Sit down, quick. Have your friends stand in front of us."

Dillon sat on one side of Grant. Rachel sat on the other. Rachel's aunt and Robert took up positions that Dillon was sure told everybody in the world they were trying to hide criminals from view.

"I still haven't gotten hold of Julia," Grant said. "I don't dare leave a message. Too risky." He pulled three tickets out of his pocket. "Jake Scanlon, going to Baltimore-Washington International via St. Louis on American." He looked at Dillon. "You brought your ID, I hope?"

Dillon pulled everything out of his pocket.

"You can't take that pocketknife on the flight," Grant scolded. "You trying to get arrested?"

"It is my letter opener," Dillon said.

"I'll keep it for you." Robert took the Swiss Army knife out of Dillon's hand and pocketed it.

Dillon held up the driver's license. "Jake Scanlon."

"What's your birthday, Jake?" Grant asked.

Dillon did not know. He looked at the card and read it off.

"Memorize that," Grant said. "Keep telling yourself, 'Jake Scanlon, Jake Scanlon.' I don't want you standing there with your mouth open when the stewardess calls you Mr. Scanlon, okay?"

Dillon sighed. "I will try."

Grant picked the flash drive out of Dillon's hand. "You haven't made a copy of this, right?"

Dillon shook his head. "This is the only copy in existence."

"How close is the software to working?" Grant asked.

"Close," Dillon said.

"If anything happens to you, could Rachel get it finished?"

Dillon nodded. "Unless there is some major design flaw, any competent programmer could. It is just a matter of walking through it in a debugger and verifying the logic in the calibration function and—"

"All right, all right, I don't need a C++ lesson." Grant closed Dillon's fingers. "Guard this with your life, all right? When we meet up in Baltimore—"

"Meet up?" Dillon's heart thumped. "Are you not coming on our flight?"

"We're all flying separately," Grant said. "Less risky that way. They'll be watching for us. I'm sure they're expecting us to have phony names, so they'll look for a pattern. Three people flying together with the right age profile on the same flight—they'll be monitoring the computers. Rachel's flying Continental to Houston and then on to BWI. She leaves a little before you do."

"When is your flight?" Dillon said. He did not like the idea of each of them flying alone. Especially Rachel, alone with that bio-computer.

"Mine's in half an hour," Grant said. "I'm going first. If anything goes wrong, I can press a couple buttons on my cell phone and send you a text message to bail out. I'm flying America West to Phoenix, then on to BWI. I'll scout the area and check for suspicious activity. When you land, turn on your cell phones right away and check for voice or text messages. If anything goes wrong, don't go into the terminal. Try to sneak down the steps off the breezeway onto the tarmac and get away somehow. We'll meet up if we can."

"Why are we going to Baltimore?" Dillon asked.

Grant turned to Rachel. "Rachel, honey, good luck. Here's your ticket. I'm gonna have to go now or I'll have a heart attack running for my flight. Make your daddy proud." He leaned over and kissed Rachel on the forehead.

Rachel hugged him fiercely. "Bye, Uncle Grant. See you when we get there. Are you going to have Daddy meet us?"

"Sure." Grant stood up, adjusted his cap down as far as he could, and strode off.

Dillon felt terribly alone. A black sheet of depression settled over his mind.

Rachel

Rachel watched Uncle Grant stride off. She felt very tired. "Auntie, don't you want to sit down? Here, Dillon, scootch over this way and let Auntie have your seat." She grabbed Dillon's hand and pulled him over.

Aunt Esther sat down on his other side. Robert moved to stand directly in front of Dillon. "What time are your flights?" he asked.

Rachel looked at her ticket. "An hour and ten minutes."

Dillon held up his and stared at it with a vacant expression on his face.

"Dillon, what time is your flight?" Robert said.

Dillon shook his head slowly, and a tear wandered down his face.

Rachel grabbed his ticket. "Dillon, get hold of yourself. Looks like your flight isn't for another two hours."

Robert knelt in front of Dillon and gave Rachel a savage look. "Would you mind? He's still in shock over losing her."

Which just made no sense at all. "Hey, I lost her too," Rachel said. "She was as much my friend as his."

Robert looked at her as if she were a child. "It hardly compares."

Rachel glared at him. "What hardly compares?"

Robert fished a handkerchief out of his pocket and handed it to Dillon.

Rachel wondered what kind of a geek actually carried a handkerchief in his pocket. Were they still actually *making* hankies? "What hardly compares?" she demanded. "You don't think I cared about Keryn? She was a good friend of mine."

Robert looked at her with an expression of slight revulsion. "I certainly *hope* you weren't in love with her too."

Rachel felt her jaw drop right open. In love? Great.

An awkward silence descended on them all. Rachel felt empty and cold.

"Rachel, honey, why are you going to Baltimore?" Aunt Esther asked. "Wouldn't it be easier for your father to pick you up in Newark?"

Rachel hadn't thought of that. Uncle Grant had been in such a hurry, he hadn't really explained what they were going to do when they got there.

"I assume you're going to Fort Meade," Robert said. "Isn't that the obvious place to go?"

No. Rachel's mind refused to accept that. It made no sense at all. Uncle Grant wouldn't sell them down the river like that.

"What's in Fort Meade?" Aunt Esther said.

"The NSA." Rachel spat out the words. "No Such Agency."

"It is the logical thing to do." Dillon put a hand on Rachel's shoulder. It burned like liquid nitrogen. "If we give this thing to the governing authorities—"

"I am *not* giving it to Big Brother!" Rachel snapped. Acid fury burned in her heart. Never, ever, ever. Anyone who trusted the government was a fool. Every government abused its power. Therefore, you gave it as little power as possible and watched it like a hawk. Rachel was not going to give Uncle Sam anything with this much power.

"Rachel—"

"No!" Rachel stood up and slapped Dillon full on the face. "What part of 'no possible way' do you not get?"

He took her hand in his. "Rachel, please—"

"For the last time, no!"

"Rachel, sit down!" Aunt Esther said. "You want that people should look at you?"

Rachel flounced into her seat and turned her back on Dillon. She yanked out her cell phone and dialed information for the airport. It took her ten minutes to make a reservation in the name of Sally Swigert for a flight to Newark. She slammed the phone shut and jammed it into her pocket.

Aunt Esther knelt in front of her. "Honey, are you going home, then?"

Rachel nodded. "Daddy will know what to do. But he won't give this thing to Big Brother." She threw a scowl at Dillon, then stood up and hugged her aunt. "My flight's in Terminal 1. I'm going over there and wait inside the security area. I'll call you when I get to Daddy's house."

Aunt Esther held her tight. "Go with Yeshua. I'll be praying for you."

Rachel kissed her fiercely on the cheek. "Thanks, Auntie." She marched away without looking back at Dillon.

CHAPTER
THIRTY - TWO

Dillon

Dillon stood up to follow Rachel.

Robert moved to block his way. "Dillon, she's not going to go to the NSA."

Dillon felt like he had swallowed a ten-star pepper from the Star of India. Heat burned in his heart. "That woman is so . . . infuriating."

Robert shook his head. "Reminds me of Sarah. She's Irish, you know. Kind of hotheaded."

"So why are you marrying her?" Dillon did not understand what any man could see in a woman like that.

Robert smiled. "I guess . . . opposites attract. She's a lot of things I'm not. Sarah kind of completes me. I don't know what I'd do without her. She's so lively, so . . . fun."

Dillon slumped down into his chair and looked at his watch. "My flight leaves in an hour and forty minutes." Despair washed over him. What was the point of going to Baltimore now? He had the software but no bio-computer. If they caught him, he was dead. His only hope was that bio-computer. And Rachel's only hope, whether she liked it or not, was his software. If they caught her, they would kill her too. He and she were two halves of a puzzle, and neither half had any value without the other.

Rachel's aunt put a hand on Dillon's arm. "Dillon, I'm Rachel's aunt Esther. I'm sorry she didn't formally introduce us."

"Dillon Richard." He put out his hand. "Actually, for the time being I am Jake. Fake Jake until I can get rid of this terrible burden."

"You two need each other," Esther said. "You and Rachel."

Dillon nodded. "I am no good without her. She is no good without me."

"You know why she's so angry, don't you?" Aunt Esther had a funny expression on her face.

Dillon sat trying to parse this social context for a quarter of a minute, then shook his head. "I am not good at understanding people."

Esther smiled. "Dillon, honey, it's as plain as anything. She *likes* you."

"Likes me?" Dillon did not see the point of this comment. "I like her too—most of the time. She is a good friend."

"Dillon, don't be dense. She's attracted to you." Esther pinched his cheek. "And I can see why. You're everything she isn't. She's flighty—you're a rock. She's one of those right-brained wonders—you're left-brained as all get out. Plus, you're a handsome devil."

Dillon felt a hot current in his cheeks. "I am not handsome."

"You're humble too. Even better."

Dillon did not want to contradict her anymore. He sat there trying to understand this puzzle.

Esther shook her head. "I'm terribly sorry about the other girl. Were you going together long?"

"I . . ." Dillon swallowed hard. "We were not going together."

Robert squatted down beside him. "Actually, you already said it, ma'am. Dillon's kind of dense about women. He didn't know he was in love with Keryn. And he had no clue she liked him."

Esther collapsed in laughter.

Dillon could not imagine what was so funny.

"Oh, Fakey Jakey, you are such a case!" Esther wiped her eyes. "If you weren't in such danger, I'd take you home and frame you. Good heavens, you're telling me you've had two beautiful young girls after you and you didn't have a clue?"

Dillon stared at her. "You are telling me . . ."

"You didn't notice?"

"I am sorry," Dillon said. "I have been trying to learn more about social contexts."

"Social what?" She looked at him with an expression Dillon could not read.

Robert grinned at her. "Dillon has a funny kind of autism, ma'am. Asperger's syndrome. It means he's not completely human, the best I can tell. We always thought he was just weird when we were kids, but . . . they diagnosed him a couple years ago, and he's had a counselor helping him learn the language the rest of us speak. He's getting better at figuring us out, but you've got to understand, he just thinks about things in his own way."

Esther pursed her lips in thought for a couple of minutes. "If I could make a suggestion here, there's an angry young woman heading to Newark in about . . . forty-five minutes, and I think you two need each other. And not just because of those wretched computer things either. She could help heal your heart, and . . . you might heal hers too."

Robert stood up. "Dillon, she's right. It's no good you going to Baltimore without her. For better or worse, you need to be with Rachel." He yanked on Dillon's arm.

Dillon stood up. "But—"

Esther jumped to her feet and slapped him hard on the buttocks. "Go, you silly goose! Run!"

Robert pulled on Dillon's arm. Dillon followed him out into the bright sunshine.

The two of them ran.

———

When they got to Terminal 1, Dillon raced to the United Airlines desk. There were a dozen people in line, and he had thirty minutes to make the flight. Robert stood waiting beside him, fidgeting and looking around anxiously.

"Is something wrong?" Dillon said.

"I'm just thinking." Robert turned his head to both sides, eyeing those around them. "You'll be buying a second ticket for almost the same time and under the same name as the one Grant bought you. If I were watching the computers, that would be a red flag."

Dillon knew that a red flag meant a danger signal. "It will be much worse if I use my real name. But I cannot do that, because I do not have my driver's license. The carjackers stole it."

Robert looked all around them, then slipped his hand into his pocket. He drew his hand out and gave Dillon his wallet. "Use my driver's license and my Visa card. Just study the signature on the card and try to scribble like I do."

"I . . . I cannot do that." Dillon felt a vise grip on his heart. "I have dark hair and you have light hair."

Robert grinned at him. "Not to worry. Nobody looks like their driver's license. We're both nerdy white males. I'm a little taller than you and a little heavier. It's close enough."

"I am eleven years older than you."

"I don't see a date stamp on your forehead."

"Robert, I cannot do this. What if they ask why I do not look like my picture?"

"They won't. Beat them to the punch," Robert said. "Give them an ironic smile and ask if you look like your picture."

"What?" Dillon stared at him. "That is crazy."

"Try it. Stay here in line alone. I'll wait by the security gate." Robert strode away.

Dillon's heart was jackhammering against his ribs. This was insanity. But Robert was right that he could not buy another ticket under the name of Jake Scanlon. He might be caught if he used Robert's ID, but he would certainly be caught using Jake's. The line dwindled slowly, and there were only twenty minutes till flight time when his turn came.

Dillon strode to the counter and held up Robert's license and Visa card. "Round trip to Newark with no specific return date. I would like to get on the 1:10 flight if I possibly can. My father had a heart attack an hour ago and . . . he may not last till I get there tonight."

"I'm very sorry about your father, sir." The woman at the desk took Robert's Visa card. Dillon sweated through seat assignments. Then she picked up Robert's driver's license and held it up.

Dillon had no idea how to give an ironic smile. "Do I look like my picture?"

"Yes, sir, but you look much better in person," the clerk said in a practiced tone that told Dillon she had answered this question five hundred times. "Sign here and hurry, sir. Your flight leaves in fifteen minutes."

Dillon signed something that looked like R-squiggle K-squiggle, grabbed his ticket, and ran.

At the security gate, Dillon handed Robert his wallet and got in line. Robert looked in the wallet and gave Dillon his license. "You'll need this to get on the plane." Then he gave Dillon his Visa card too and thumped him on the arm. "Good luck, buddy. On . . . everything." He turned and hurried away.

Dillon shoved the license and credit card into his pocket and waited.

As he approached the security area, Dillon took off his shoes and belt. He put his cell phone and flash drive and fingernail clippers in a tub and sent them through the X-ray machine.

It suddenly occurred to him to wonder how Rachel was going to get that bio-computer through the X-ray machine. It was in her fanny pack, which she could not wear through security. He scanned the area beyond the machines but saw nothing. He checked his watch. They were certainly boarding already. He would have to run to catch the flight.

Then it was his turn to go through. He walked through slowly, arms well away from his body. No lights, no beeps, no suspicious glances. Dillon reclaimed his pocket contents and belt and shoes and reassembled himself. He checked his ticket. Gate 22. Six minutes. He rushed out of the security area and ran.

Seven minutes later he reached the gate. A flight agent was standing all alone, holding a microphone. "Last call for Flight 524 to Denver." Dillon handed her his ticket and held up Robert's driver's license. She barely looked at the license and zipped Dillon's ticket through the machine. "Have a nice flight."

Dillon strode down the breezeway and into the plane. He looked at his ticket stub. Seat number 8A. It was the first row behind first class. The flight attendant greeted him. "Please take a seat, sir. We'll be leaving momentarily."

Dillon nodded and rushed to his seat. It was a window seat with no legroom. He turned around and craned his neck, hoping to catch sight of Rachel. Nothing. Given her height, that was not surprising.

The intercom buzzed with static. "Ladies and gentlemen, we'll be leaving momentarily. Please fasten your seat belts and make certain all your luggage is stowed securely in the overhead bins or under the seats. . . ."

Dillon listened carefully, then buckled his seat belt and settled in for takeoff.

The plane did not move.

The intercom buzzed again. "Ladies and gentlemen, this is your captain speaking." A low chuckle. "Seems we have a special announcement for a *very* special young lady. This message comes to you from a young man in love."

More static, and then . . .

"Sally, this is Jake. Please, please, please forgive me."

Dillon's head shot up, and every hair on his body quilled out like a porcupine. That was his voice coming over the intercom. *His voice.*

"Sally, I was wrong. I'm sorry for what I said . . . and I want you back. Please forgive me. I . . . I want you to share my life. Sally, please take me back." The voice broke.

Whoops rang out all up and down the aisles. A woman shouted, "Take him back, Sally!" An old man hollered, "Throw the bum out!" More laughter. Another woman shrieked, "Sally, if you don't want him, I'll trade you for mine!"

Hoots of laughter. Dillon could not understand what was happening. That was his voice, begging Rachel to take him back. Somebody was trying to draw her out. Somebody who knew Rachel was on this plane. Under the name Sally Swigert. Sweat poured down his sides. He wanted to shout a warning, but that would only give him away too. *Please, Lord, do not let her take me back.*

The laughter continued for close to a minute before it subsided. Rachel did not appear.

Two men in suits came through the curtain from first class. One of them held a picture of Rachel out to Dillon and his two seatmates. "Have any of you seen this woman?"

Dillon shook his head.

The FBI man moved on to the next row.

Dillon leaned back in his seat and tried to breathe. They were searching the plane row by row. There was no possible way Rachel could evade capture. They would take her off the plane. Would take the bio-computer.

Would kill her.

Hot fear roiled in Dillon's stomach. He had not been able to save Keryn. He could not save Rachel either, but . . .

He would not let her die alone.

When they dragged her screaming down the aisle, Dillon would stand up and fight them.

And let the devil take the software.

Dillon unbuckled his seat belt and waited.

CHAPTER
THIRTY - THREE

Rachel

After Rachel had left Dillon and Robert, she had run all the way to Terminal 1 in a white fury. Dillon was such a . . . wimp! Ready to go to the government every time there was trouble. That was not acceptable. Not acceptable at all. The line at the ticket counter had a dozen people in it, and Rachel only had forty-five minutes before her flight. She didn't want to wait, so she walked up to a guy in a Princeton shirt near the head of the line and threw a flirty smile at him. "Hi, mind if I cut in with you? I'm late for my flight and . . . oh my gosh! Are you at Princeton too?"

"I'm . . ." He looked her up and down and grinned. "Yeah."

She touched his arm. "Oh, that is so cool! What's your major?"

"Philosophy."

"Really? Like, wow! I'm in math. What do you think of Gödel's Theorem?"

His eyes opened wide and then his grin broadened. "I'm undecided."

Rachel giggled as if that were original. She had a well-practiced giggle for airhead moments like this. "You are so funny! Oops, it's your turn at the counter!"

He looked over at the counter. "You go ahead of me. You're in a hurry."

Rachel backed toward the ticket agent and blew the guy a kiss. "Thanks, you're a stud!" She spun around and pulled out her driver's license. "I'm Sally Swigert," she said. "No relation to Jimmy Swaggart."

The agent picked up the license and typed in her name. "May I see your credit card?"

Rachel pulled out her Visa card and handed it to him. Minutes later, she had a seat in row 37 and a ticket. She hurried toward the security checkpoint. Fear shot an arrow through her heart.

The X-ray machines! She could not take the bio-computer in her fanny pack through the X-ray machines. But she couldn't carry it in her hand either.

Rachel hesitated just a minute and then hurried past the line into the ladies' room. She locked herself in a stall, opened her fanny pack, took out the bio-computer, and stared at it. They would make her empty her pockets in line. Maybe take off her shoes. Unfortunately, Keryn's hideaway trick wasn't an option. Rachel put her foot on the toilet, lifted one leg of her jeans, and shoved the bio-computer down her sock. She flushed the toilet, zipped shut her fanny pack, and went out.

Ten minutes later, she was through security and still had almost thirty minutes before flight time. They'd be boarding soon. Rachel decided to do like Uncle Grant and buy a bit of disguise. She stopped in one of the little shops and bought a thin blue silklike scarf and some horrible pink sunglasses and a huge sweatshirt with a picture of a panda bear on the front and the words *San Diego Zoo.* At the next bathroom, she ducked into a stall and recovered her bio-computer from her sock and put it in the fanny pack. She covered her hair completely in the scarf and pulled on the sweatshirt, which was so big it made her feel like a walking tent. Finally, she put on the sunglasses and went to check herself in the mirror.

It wasn't much, but it would have to do. The important thing was that she had neutered her hair. That was the first thing people noticed, her blond curls. Now those were buried under blue silk. The sweatshirt made her look fat.

Rachel checked her watch and saw that she now had only fifteen minutes till her flight. Time to rock and roll. She grabbed her ticket out of her back pocket and strode out.

As she approached the gate, Rachel paused to reconnoiter. Just to be sure. There was a ticket agent with a microphone announcing which rows could enter. Rachel's row had already been called, so all she had to do was walk up there and—

A man in a dark suit.

He was standing near the gate and he was not holding a ticket. In his hand he held something. A stiff piece of paper that looked like a five-by-seven photo. He was wearing dark glasses and studying passengers as they walked past the ticket agent.

And Rachel thought she had seen him before. He had a mole next to his nose. The last time she'd seen a man with a mole like that, he'd been standing under a streetlight pointing a gun at Dillon.

He was one of the carjackers.

Rachel stuffed her knuckles into her mouth to keep from screaming. She didn't dare look around to see who else was there. Didn't dare turn and run. After fifteen seconds of jagged panic, she decided that the only thing she could do was leave.

Slowly, Rachel turned around. She looked at her watch, then began walking with a determined pace back toward the exits. They had tracked her. She had bought a ticket by phone less than an hour ago, and they had detected it. How? Nobody knew Sally Swigert from Adam. Uncle Grant said the ID was safe.

A sick feeling filled her stomach. Of course. She was an idiot. They had checked the computers and seen that two tickets were bought in the same name on two different airlines. That tipped them off that Sally Swigert was somebody to watch for.

Which meant that both her tickets were useless. They would have put men at both gates to watch for her. If she got on either plane, they'd take her and kill her.

Rachel ducked into the nearest rest room and hid in a stall. It was still ten minutes till her plane took off. She waited fifteen minutes, just to be sure. Then she ducked out and hurried toward the exits. She didn't see anyone in dark suits, or anyone holding stiff pieces of paper. When Rachel reached the exit of the terminal, she breathed in deeply. Freedom. Thank God for fresh air. For life.

She looked at her watch. Grant was safely away and Dillon's flight would go out in forty-five minutes.

Dillon.

All of a sudden she wanted his strong, calm presence. Dillon wasn't afraid. He was being stupid about going to the government, but . . . even Uncle Grant was being stupid about that. She didn't have to go. Anytime she felt like it, she could break the vial and all the king's horses and all the king's men couldn't put Humpty together again. Dillon couldn't stop her. She could make him listen. Make Uncle Grant listen.

Though Rachel hated to draw attention to herself, she started to run. She was sweating by the time she reached Terminal 2 but didn't want to take off her sweatshirt. Even if it was a crummy disguise, it was all she had.

She found an ATM just inside the terminal. Her Sally Swigert Visa card was the kind that let you take a cash advance. She got the limit, five hundred dollars. Which would probably cover a flight to the East Coast. Uncle Grant had said Dillon was flying American Airlines through St. Louis to BWI. Rachel bit her lip.

And decided.

She reached into her pocket and pulled out the driver's license of her dead cousin, Rivka Meyers. The license had expired last October. Rachel got in line clutching the license and cash and wondered if now would be a good time to think about maybe considering the possibility of praying.

The ticket line was horrible, and it took twenty-five nerve-wracking minutes to get a ticket on Dillon's flight. The idiot at the counter gave Rivka's license a careful examination that lasted a full five milliseconds before he gave her a ticket. Rachel saw that she had twenty minutes to make the flight. If she called Dillon on his cell phone, he could stall the people at the gate, but she didn't want to risk him calling attention to himself. She'd just have to hurry.

The next barrier was the X-ray machines. Rachel did her trick with the bio-computer in her sock again. The line in this terminal took forever. She got through security five minutes before the flight. It took her two precious minutes to find a bathroom and get the bio-computer out of her sock.

Then she ran.

She made the gate just as they were shutting the door.

Waving her ticket, Rachel raced up to the ticket agent. "Sorry!" She grinned at him. "You know how long the line in the rest room is."

"I'm terribly sorry you were inconvenienced." He ran her ticket through and took her driver's license.

Rachel waited, feeling her heart doing horrible gymnastics.

His face tightened. "You realize this license expired last October?"

"I know." Rachel looked at her shoes repentantly. "Last night I was out with friends in the Gaslamp and we got robbed. I lost my license and all my credit cards and . . . I'm going to Johns Hopkins to start my residency in ophthalmology, and my mother convinced me to just use my old license from when I was studying here at UCSD. I'm sorry. I know it was wrong." She brushed away a real tear that had formed in her eye. "I'm gonna be an eye surgeon, and I really need to get back to Baltimore before tomorrow."

A long silence.

"Go on, then." The agent handed her back her license. "Have a nice flight."

"Thanks!" Rachel hurried through the door and down the breezeway and into the plane. People were still standing in the aisles jamming oversized carry-on luggage into overhead bins. Rachel had a seat over the wing in row 14.

Rachel plunked into the window seat and buried her nose in the in-flight magazine.

Shortly, things settled down and she heard the dull *thunk* of the main door being closed. There followed a pause, and then the doors *whoosh*ed open again.

"Ladies and jellybeans, this is your captain speaking. I know it isn't Valentine's Day, but there's a very persistent young lady on board who wants to say something to a lucky young man."

Rachel found that she was holding her breath.

"Jake, it's me—Sally! Please, I'm sorry. I'm such a jerk. I want you back. I'm sorry for what I said. Jake, I'm crazy about you and I want to go wherever you go. Take me back and I'll never leave you again."

· Rachel thought she was going to get airsick right there. It was her voice. *Her voice.*

A chorus of whistles greeted this. "Go for it, Jake!" "Take her back!"

Rachel waited for Dillon to call out, but nothing happened.

Shortly, two men came down the aisles showing pictures of Dillon and asking if anyone had seen him. Rachel took a good look and shook her head earnestly.

Cold fingers of fear caressed her body. It was a photo of Dillon taken at the Del Mar Fair with Keryn. Rachel saw right away that this was the same photo that had been used for Dillon's phony driver's license. It had been cropped down very tightly for the license, but Dillon wore the same squinting-into-the-sun half smile. Only one person in the world could have given them that photo.

Uncle Grant.

CHAPTER
THIRTY-FOUR

Dillon

When he reached Denver, Dillon found a quiet spot and called Grant's cell phone. No answer. He tried Rachel's phone. Still no answer. Finally, he tried Julia.

Three rings and . . .

"Hello?" Julia sounded frantic.

"Julia, this is Dillon. Where are you?"

"Dillon, what's going on? Are you in the Caymans already?"

"I am in Denver." Dillon's throat felt tight. "What are you talking about?"

"I was out shopping and forgot to turn on my cell phone. When I got back, Grant was gone. I tried to call him and found that he'd left me a voice mail saying that you were all flying to the Caymans."

"The Caymans? No." Dillon did not want to believe this. "Grant met us at the airport and bought us tickets to Baltimore. He got on a flight just ahead of us."

"What's happening? Why are you all leaving?"

Dillon realized that she did not know. His voice buckled. "They . . . kidnapped Keryn." He turned toward the corner and let the tears flow. "Rachel and I were on the phone with her and . . . they shot her."

Julia shrieked and then began crying.

Dillon waited until they both calmed down. "Rachel was supposed to be on my flight, and they came for her, but she was not there. I do not know where she is."

"Where are you going?" Julia said.

"Newark. Rachel's father teaches at Rutgers."

"Call me when you get there, honey. Something's fishy."

"Julia?"

"Are you thinking what I'm thinking, Dillon?"

"I believe Grant has been . . . prevaricating."

"Oh, Dillon, I'm so sorry."

"If Rachel calls you, tell her . . . I am sorry and that I want to make peace with her."

"Call me when you get to Newark."

As Dillon hung up, he wondered if it was possible that the person he had just spoken with was not really Julia.

Rachel

Rachel sat with her face turned toward the window all the way to St. Louis, trying to grapple with the horrible truth.

Uncle Grant had betrayed her. Betrayed them all. There was no other explanation. He had been running a giant con on them the whole time. It was evil—that's what it was. He had let them kill Keryn. Had put Dillon and Rachel on separate flights. Why? So they could be taken separately, with no fuss? It didn't make sense. Was Julia in on it? Clifton?

Rachel couldn't be sure. Julia might have been waiting at the gate while Uncle Grant met with Rachel and Dillon and gave them his sweet talk and lies. As for Clifton . . .

Everything Rachel knew about Clifton, every point against him, could be explained away. She didn't know for sure he had broken into the bio-lab—that was inference based on the assumption that it couldn't be Uncle Grant. She didn't know with certainty that Clifton had stolen the hard drive from the computer or added a new alarm combination on the door. She had deduced it from what Grant had told her.

Furthermore, she couldn't even trust her own ears. Sure, she had heard Clifton over the phone, telling them to shoot Keryn. But she had heard her own voice on the intercom of the plane begging Dillon to take her back. Somebody had some really good speech-synthesis gear. Good enough so it sounded real over a scratchy plane intercom. They had faked her voice, and they might just as well have faked Clifton's over Keryn's cell phone. And they could probably fake Dillon's. Rachel took out her phone and stared at it. She could not use it when she landed. How could she trust the voice on the other end? Grant and his accomplices could spoof anybody, and she would have no way of knowing.

A cold hard knot formed in Rachel's belly. She closed her eyes and pretended to be asleep, but she did not think she would ever sleep soundly again.

———

Rachel had a tight connection in St. Louis and had to run to catch the second leg of her flight. She wanted to call somebody, anybody, but she had no idea whom she could trust.

Nobody bothered her on this flight. There weren't any agents showing pictures of Dillon. Nobody doing phony speech-synthesis tricks to fake her voice. When she reached the Baltimore-Washington airport, she took stock of her cash. She had five dollars and change. A look at her watch told her that she had landed twelve minutes after she would have if she'd gone to Newark.

Rachel took out her cell phone and wished she dared call home. But what if they were already there, waiting for her to call, with Daddy duct-taped to the chair? She would have no way to authenticate—

The phone rang in her hand. The caller ID said it was Dillon, but that didn't mean a thing. If they'd captured Dillon, they could spoof him. It rang again. Again.

Rachel took a deep breath and opened the phone. "Yes?"

"Rachel, thank the Lord I got through to you! They can synthesize our voices."

"I know." Rachel paused. "How do I know you're Dillon?"

"We will have to authenticate both ways," Dillon said. "Quickly now, what is the only illegal place in San Diego that I would approve of?"

Rachel backed out of the foot traffic to a quiet corner. "I don't know. If you're really Dillon, then it isn't the Mount Soledad Cross, because you think that cross violates separation of church and state."

"Good. Your turn. Authenticate me. Ask me something only I could know."

Rachel closed her eyes and thought for several seconds. "Who did I take a dive for?"

"Jason. He wore a lot of orange. You wore . . . a little."

Rachel laughed. "Okay, you're Dillon. Where are you?"

"We will have to talk in riddles, Rachel. I am assuming they can listen in on this conversation."

Rachel checked again that nobody was watching her, then turned back toward the corner. "Okay, let's make this simple. I don't need to know where you are, because I don't have any money and I can't go anywhere. The Visa and driver's license Grant gave me are probably compromised. I've got another ID they don't know about, but I've only got five bucks cash. You'll have to come to me, and I can't tell you where I am."

Silence for thirty seconds.

"I am assuming you are in an airport," Dillon said. "There are hundreds around the country and each has a unique three-letter designator. San Diego is SAN. Los Angeles International is LAX. Do you know the three letters for your airport?"

Rachel stared at her ticket. BWI. "Yes."

"All right, you need to think of three words. Each word starts with one of the three letters. Do not tell me the words. Just give me a clue that only I would know that I can use to guess each word."

Rachel thought for a few seconds. "How many brothers do you have, Dillon?"

"Three."

"No, you have a fourth one. What's his first name? That's the first clue."

A very long silence. Rachel hoped it was obscure enough, but not too obscure.

"If Gloria is his papa, then I know the answer," Dillon said.

"You're good. Second clue. I have a friend who went through AA twelve years ago. Last name."

"That one is easy."

"Third clue." Rachel closed her eyes and concentrated, but she could not think of a word that started with I. She'd have to improvise. "There's somebody I used to hate a whole lot—more than anybody in the whole world."

"Used to?"

"Right, but . . . not anymore. First letter of the first name. Take the letter before that in the alphabet."

"Fine, I know where you are. Are the concourses labeled with letters?"

Rachel looked at the nearest gate and saw that it was labeled C24. "Yes."

"Then I need one more letter for your concourse. I'll come there and meet you at your gate."

Concourse C. "Okay, what was my favorite ride at the fair? Remember?"

"How could I forget? It had three words."

"Third letter of the third word," Rachel said.

"Can you find somewhere to hide?" Dillon asked. "When I get there, I will call you. Be ready with another authenticator question."

"Bye, Dillon."

"Good-bye, Keryn." Dillon hung up.

Rachel closed the phone, wondering why Dillon had called her Keryn. She walked down the concourse, looking for a bathroom. By the time she found one, three gates away, she had guessed the answer.

Rachel locked herself in a stall, closed the lid on the toilet, and sat down.

And smiled.

D i l l o n

Dillon had excellent luck and needed only ninety-two minutes to buy a ticket and make the flight on Continental direct from

Newark to BWI. He came out on Concourse D and spent ten minutes navigating to Concourse C. He sat down in a quiet corner and pulled out his cell phone. During the short flight, a gnawing fear had been growing in his mind.

Grant had warned him that the authorities could trace the locations of cell phones. Dillon was not sure if this was true, but if so, if somebody was not only listening to their conversations but also vectoring in on their locations, then . . .

He had walked into a trap. He would join Rachel and then they would be taken.

Dillon did not see how they could escape. Whoever was pursuing them seemed to have vast knowledge. They could tap into airline reservation records. They could mobilize FBI men, real or fake. They could probably tap and trace cell phone conversations.

And yet both he and Rachel had somehow evaded them. So far. Was it luck or . . . something else?

Dillon did not know and he did not care. While he had been talking to Rachel on the phone, he had suddenly realized something.

Whenever he heard Rachel's voice, his heart did funny things inside his chest. When she said his name, it was like . . . magic. He had not been able to think of anything but Rachel on the long flight across the country. Rachel's enthusiasm for life. Rachel's brilliant mind. Rachel's dazzling smile.

She was completely different from him. Lacking faith, where he believed in God. An extreme extrovert, where he was a complete introvert. Creative, disorganized, intuitive, where he was methodical and organized and analytical. She had everything he needed, and he had all that she lacked.

And he did not care about any of those things. All that he cared about was that when he looked into her light green eyes, he felt an instant and deep connection with her mind.

There was only one explanation, and it terrified Dillon.

He was in love with Rachel. Had been in love with her since the day he met her. He had not known this or he would have run the other direction as fast as possible. It was a deep mistake to be unequally yoked with an unbeliever. Furthermore, he had also been in love with Keryn. A part of him was still in love with her, even though she was now . . . gone.

He did not understand how this was possible. Rachel and Keryn were as different as two women could possibly be. If he was in love with both of them, then love was a dangerous and illogical thing. And he was not the man he had thought he was. He was no man of logic, of reason.

He was Dillon Richard, double-minded man, unstable in all his ways. All along, there had been two Dillons inside him, each passionate for one woman, interfering with each other and creating turmoil in his soul. Dillon did not like that at all. He could not trust his own heart. Why then should Rachel trust him?

Dillon shook his head. He did not have time to unlock this riddle. He dialed Rachel's number and waited.

"Hello?" Rachel's eager voice, or an excellent imitation.

Dillon did not trust his ears any longer. "What animal is *not* on Papa's farm?"

"Pigs," Rachel said. "What three words should you have told Keryn?"

Dillon froze. It seemed . . . sacrilegious to talk about Keryn now. To talk about her with Rachel. To force the Keryn-Dillon to interfere with the Rachel-Dillon.

"You're not Dillon, are you?" Rachel said.

"I . . ." Dillon's voice caught in his throat. "I . . . love you."

A little sigh. "Okay, you *are* Dillon. Where are you?"

Dillon looked at the gate nearest him. "In your concourse, near Gate 7."

"I'll be right there." Rachel hung up.

Dillon found he could not sit still. He got up and began pacing back and forth, watching for men in dark suits. Five minutes passed and Rachel did not appear. Dillon found the waiting unbearable. An image formed in his mind. Prodigal Papa, up on his roof, wearing running shoes, scanning the road with a telescope, looking for Little Brother.

Dillon's mouth suddenly felt very dry. He found a water fountain and took a long drink. Looked down the concourse.

Looked up the concourse.

Saw movement.

A girl in a huge panda-bear sweatshirt and a blue scarf, holding a fanny pack in her hand.

Dillon began walking toward her.

Recognition lit up her eyes. She quickened her pace.

Dillon hurried forward.

Rachel broke into a run.

Dillon raced toward her, arms spread wide.

Rachel jumped.

Dillon caught her in an enormous hug and staggered backward.

"Oh, Dillon, I missed you."

Dillon squeezed her slender frame. "Thank the Lord I found you again."

"I have something for you," Rachel said. "Look at me."

Dillon looked down into her face.

She lunged up and kissed him.

Dillon felt a great wall of heat sear through his chest. He had never kissed a woman before.

It was excellent.

Rachel

Rachel wanted to stay here in Dillon's arms forever, but she didn't dare. "Dillon, people are staring at us. We'd better go sit somewhere and figure out what to do next."

Dillon released her and they went looking for something to eat. They found a place that sold pizza at outrageous prices. It didn't have pepperoni and pineapple. Dillon got pepperoni. Rachel got pineapple and mushrooms and gave him her pineapples.

"What are we going to do?" Rachel said. "Grant wanted us to come here. He must have had some reason."

"I have a theory," Dillon said. "He did it to make us fight, to separate us. I called Julia during my layover in Denver. She said Grant told her to join him in the Caymans. She sounded very confused."

"What's in the Caymans?"

"Offshore banks," Dillon said. "It is an excellent place for money laundering and tax shelters. There are many wire transfers in and out."

Rachel felt her heart lurch. "If . . . Grant was going to start a life of crime, he could . . . go there and steal a few million."

"He could steal a few billion." Dillon's face was sweating now. "Enough to pay his accomplices any amount of money."

"But I don't get it," Rachel said. "We've got the bio-computer and the software. He's got nothing."

Dillon just looked at her. "How do we know he has nothing?"

"Because he . . ." Rachel didn't want to say, *because he told me so.* That was so stupid it stank.

"Here is a possible scenario," Dillon said. "Grant went into the bio-lab and tried to run the software that night of the break-in. It was no break-in. He had the combination. He knew the combination of the safe too. He compiled the software—"

"Doesn't work." Rachel shook her head and bit into her pizza. "Grant doesn't know Visual C++. There's no way he could have fixed your bugs and got it to compile."

"But Julia could," Dillon said.

"She . . . what?" Rachel dropped her pizza.

"Before he started CypherQuanta, Grant owned a software company. One of his programmers was Julia. She has a degree in Cognitive Science."

"I . . ." Rachel stared at him. "She told me that, but I wasn't even sure what it was. It's a branch of psychology, isn't it?"

"Psychology, computer science, artificial intelligence. Julia was an expert in designing human interfaces. She was very good in C++."

"Oh my . . . gosh!" Rachel felt like she'd just found out her parents weren't her parents.

"There was some sort of scandal," Dillon said. "Grant's wife left him and then he married Julia. She went back to UCSD to study Russian literature and has not written a line of C++ in years, but . . ."

"But it's like riding a bike, right?"

"Good programmers do not forget," Dillon said. "I have heard that Julia was very good."

Rachel felt like she'd been stabbed in the face. "So Grant and Julia went to the lab together, tested the software, and kept the bio-computer, leaving a small amount of it to make it look like an accident. Why?"

"I do not know." Dillon looked utterly lost.

"All right, we'll leave that for now," Rachel said. "Their main goal was to get filthy rich. Which they are now going to do. They have the bio-computer. Grant got the hard drive from the computer after we all got laid off. Which means he engineered the layoffs himself, to get rid of us. It gave him an excuse to leave the country. He took the hard drive and told us it was already gone."

Dillon was looking very unhappy. "So you are telling me he had both the bio-computer and the software? And not satisfied with that, he hired some men to rob us? That does not make sense."

"Okay, so it's got some holes in it. But we agree that Grant's behind all this, right?"

"Something is wrong." Dillon's voice sounded very strained.

"I'm sorry." Rachel was worn out. Exhausted. "If you don't like it, come up with a better theory."

"No, I mean, something is wrong over there." Dillon's eyes pointed over Rachel's left shoulder.

Rachel leaned over to tie her shoe and stole a peek behind her.

A man in a gray suit was talking into a cell phone and staring right at Dillon.

Rachel's heart slammed into overdrive. The pursuit had caught up with them. "Pretend we're fighting and chase me," she whispered. She stood up and slapped Dillon hard in the face, then stalked away.

Dillon's footsteps pursued her.

Rachel began running, hoping that Dillon would have the sense to follow.

At the end of the concourse, she jumped onto the escalators and raced down the steps and past baggage claim. She ran through the doors and out into the humid, sweltering night. A line of taxis waited. Rachel ran up to the head of the line. "Taxi!"

A dark man in a turban flashed a row of crooked white teeth at her. He looked Indian or Pakistani or whatever. "And where is it you are wishing to be going?"

"D.C." She said. "The Grand Hyatt."

He held the back door for her.

Dillon raced up. "Rachel, please!"

Rachel scooted over. "Get in!"

Dillon jumped in and yanked the door shut.

The driver looked at them, astonished. "Ma'am, are you wishing—"

"Drive!" Rachel screamed. "Now!"

The driver hopped around to the front seat and jumped in. "As you are wishing."

The cab lurched away.

Rachel looked out the back window and saw two men in suits race up to the taxi behind them. "Dillon . . ."

"I see them." Dillon's voice sounded like death.

Rachel buried her face in her hands. This was too much. Too crazy. She couldn't spend the rest of her life running away from men in suits.

"Ma'am, are you feeling well?" asked the driver.

"No." Rachel didn't know how she felt. Exhausted. Terrified. Used up. She opened her fanny pack and took out the bio-computer.

"What are you going to do?" Dillon's voice was tight.

Rachel began rolling down the window. "I'm going to throw this out the window. I can't take this anymore."

"Then we are both dead."

"You don't know that."

"They killed Keryn. They will not hesitate to kill us."

"How do we know that was Keryn on the phone?"

Dillon sighed. "Just before the gunshot, do you remember what she said?"

Rachel remembered. "She was . . . crying to Jesus."

"That is her authenticator. Keryn would do that."

Rachel knew he was right. "Dillon, I don't want to die."

"Please roll up the window."

Rachel rolled it up. "We don't have any options."

"Grant now has a working bio-computer," Dillon said. "He has an excellent programmer to help him make it work. He is going to use it, Rachel. We have to alert the authorities."

"They'd never believe us," Rachel said. "Most people think this kind of technology is thirty years away."

Dillon didn't say anything.

Rachel felt sick to her stomach. "You want me to take it to the authorities? Just hand it over to them?"

Dillon took Rachel's hand in his. "Rachel, I will not tell you what to do. It must be your decision. Right now there are two men behind us. I suspect they intend to kill us and take what we have. If we destroy it, they will kill us anyway. We cannot keep running and we cannot hide."

Rachel's heart was beating a ragged rhythm in her chest.

"Rachel, if I die, I will go to be with the Lord. And with . . ." Dillon let out a deep sigh.

With Keryn. Rachel shut her eyes tight. She wasn't sure about this afterlife thing. The whole thing sounded bogus, as Clifton Potter would say. Some oozy, woozy place called heaven, some alternate reality.

Some parallel universe.

Parallel universes were real. Nothing could be realer. Was it possible that one of those universes might be . . . heaven? Or whatever?

She didn't have any proof such a place existed, but she didn't have any proof it didn't either. The bottom line was very simple. If those men caught up with them, Keryn would get Dillon, or else nobody would.

For sure Rachel wouldn't.

Keryn couldn't lose and Rachel couldn't win.

Rachel put the bio-computer back in her fanny pack and pulled out her phone.

"What are you doing?" Dillon asked.

Rachel dialed 4-1-1 and asked for the National Security Agency. The words were bitter on her tongue.

But they were a whole lot better than dying.

CHAPTER
THIRTY-FIVE

Dillon

Late the next afternoon, Dillon finished testing. He and Rachel had been assigned two scientists to validate their claims. Dr. Weinberg was an orthodox Jewish mathematician in his midfifties with a thick untrimmed beard and a habit of talking very fast. Dr. Narain was much younger, probably Dillon's age, a skinny physicist who never seemed to blink and who spoke in a Mississippi accent.

"I am ready." Dillon rubbed his eyes and threw an encouraging smile at Rachel. She seemed very tense. Dillon wondered whether she hoped it would succeed or fail.

Dr. Weinberg handed Dillon a CD. "Okay, here's the drill, my friend, and I'm hoping it works out for you, because this would be extraordinary, just extraordinary, if it's real. On this CD you'll find an ASCII file with six integers, each having a length between 180 and 500 digits. What I want you to do is use your device to factor those integers."

Dillon nodded and started up the software. A text window popped up asking him to type in a number to be factored. Dillon opened the file on the CD and selected the first number. He copied and pasted it into the text window of his program and hit the Enter key.

The computer began logging the various stages in Shor's algorithm as it executed them. Dillon felt sweat sliding down his sides.

Weinberg stood up and began pacing. Narain leaned back and watched the screen.

A hand reached across the table and clutched Dillon's. He took it and held it. A flush of excitement filled his veins. Whatever happened, whether the machine worked or not, he had discovered something of great value.

Dillon picked up his glass of ice water and drank deeply. He was tired, very tired. The people here at the NSA had been very suspicious last night when Rachel called them with her strange and wandering tale about a quantum computer. But it did not take long for one of them to track down Rachel's former professor at Caltech, who told them that Rachel was indeed working on nanoconstruction problems when she had left Caltech. So when the taxi pulled up outside, armed marines surrounded them and spirited them into the building. The two men who had been chasing them in the taxi apparently did not even take the Fort Meade exit. So after spending the night here on site, this morning Dillon and Rachel had—

A hiss of breath.

Dillon turned to look and saw that his program had finished executing and had printed out two integers, each more than filling the width of the text window.

Dr. Weinberg pulled out a slip of paper with the correct answer printed out. He rapidly compared the numbers, muttering digits under his breath as his finger moved across the page. When he reached the end of the second number, he turned and reached out to shake Dillon's hand. "Congratulations."

Dillon backed away and pointed to Rachel. "Please shake her hand, not mine. She did all the hard work."

Rachel stood up and came and shook his hand and Dr. Narain's. Her eyes were glistening.

Weinberg picked up the phone and began dialing, talking all the while. "If you don't mind, I'd like to have one of our colleagues come watch the next one."

"Of course," Dillon said.

"Hello, Michael," Weinberg said. "Yes, the machine factored the first number correctly, a hundred eighty digits, and it chewed them up and spit out the answer. It looks like a winner, so maybe you'll want to come down and watch. I think you'll be very impressed." He put the phone down. "All right, now let's see how you do on the next one. Two hundred twelve digits—that's about thirty-five times harder than the first one, if you were using a conventional algorithm."

Dillon ran the software again and fed it the two-hundred-twelve-digit number, and they waited.

"Who's coming to see this?" Rachel asked.

"My . . . colleague Michael King," Dr. Weinberg said. "Really, this is quite phenomenal, wouldn't you agree, John?" He turned to Dr. Narain.

Narain nodded. "I don't understand the biology, but it seems to work. Explain to me again how you constructed so many qubits in this bio-computer."

Rachel went to the whiteboard and began drawing a complicated schematic of a cell. She drew in a double helix and an arrow labeled *mRNA* to a squiggly line labeled *tRNA*. "I discovered a large class of proteins with slightly different magnetostatic properties, depending on the precise sequence in one stretch of base pairs. I guessed that—"

"It's finished." Weinberg whipped out his paper and rapidly checked the answer. He shook his head and grinned. "You realize that you just broke the record for the largest number ever factored?"

"Who had the record before?" Dillon asked.

Weinberg gave him a quiet smile. "You did. You set it ten minutes ago. The previous record was one hundred seventy-four digits. It took over thirteen thousand MIPS-years of computing power."

The door opened, and a small dark-haired man with a neat goatee stepped in.

Weinberg waved his piece of paper. "Michael, they've just factored a two-hundred-twelve-digit number into two primes. This is really quite amazing. That's about seven hundred bits and—"

"Excellent." Michael came over and shook hands with Rachel. "I'm Dr. Michael King. Dr. Meyers, it's an honor to meet you. And

Dr. Richard." He shook hands with Dillon. "Now I should like to challenge your little computer to something a bit more difficult. Shall we skip straight to the five-hundred-digit problem?"

Dillon ran the program again and pasted in the last number from Weinberg's text file.

The program began churning out lines of text, logging the progress of Shor's algorithm.

They sat in silence now. Weinberg and Narain both seemed rather nervous. Dr. King leaned back in his chair, studying Rachel and Dillon and saying nothing. Dillon poured himself more water. Rachel bit her lip and looked like she might be about to cry.

"We're not monsters, Dr. Meyers," Dr. King said. "We solve problems. Very difficult problems. I have no doubt that you would enjoy—"

"I'm not going to come work for you," Rachel said.

"Of course." Dr. King gave her a soothing smile. "I've gathered you don't particularly admire us. Quite all right. You're well within your rights as a citizen to feel that way. Free speech and all that." He turned to look at Dillon. "And you're quite a programmer, from what I hear, Dr. Richard. Tell me more about yourself."

Rachel looked ready to bolt for the door.

Dillon had no idea what to say. This agency was part of the governing authorities, put here by the Lord to maintain order. Anyone who obeyed the Lord had nothing to fear from the governing authorities. It would be very challenging and interesting to work for the NSA. But Rachel did not feel that way, and therefore Dillon found himself in a quandary. He had realized last night that Rachel helped complete him. They were wildly different, and yet in those differences they had strength. He did not think he would want to work here if Rachel did not.

"Dr. Richard?" Dr. King gave him a reassuring smile. "You're with friends."

Dillon shrugged. "I am an electrical engineer. I know quantum encryption and programming and a few other things."

"Would you ever consider—"

Weinberg's breath caught.

They all turned to look. Two enormous numbers filled several lines of the text window. Weinberg pulled out his paper and compared answers, meticulously running his finger across the lines. Finally, he turned and nodded. "Another record, Michael. Really, this is more than extraordinary. It's a miracle. Give thanks to HaShem."

Michael was smiling now. He lifted the phone and punched in a number. "Monica? Bring me my laptop, if you would."

Dillon wondered what this could be about.

Michael set down the phone and began drumming his fingers on the table.

Two minutes later, a tap at the door. A young woman came in with a laptop and handed it to Michael.

He smiled up at her. "Thanks, Monica." He pulled a small flash drive out of his pocket and stuck it into the USB port. He copied a file onto the flash drive and ejected it. "Dr. Richard, I have a number here which I suspect your machine will not be able to factor."

"How many digits?" Dillon said.

"Nearly eight hundred."

Dillon plugged the flash drive into his computer and started up his software. He copied over the number, which filled up nearly ten lines of text.

The software began working.

"I'm afraid this may take a while," Michael said. "Coffee, anyone? Doughnuts?"

Dillon did not want to go anywhere. "Why do you have an eight-hundred-digit number on your laptop?"

Michael shrugged. "A pet project of mine. Tell me, how are the Padres doing this year?"

Dillon had no idea. He never followed professional sports. But it did not make sense that a man like Michael King would have a pet project of factoring an eight-hundred-digit integer. Until an hour ago, even a hundred-eighty-digit number was outrageously difficult.

Dr. Weinberg paced back and forth, muttering a strange chant under his breath. Dr. Narain did not move at all, but fixed his eyes on Rachel in a way that annoyed Dillon. Michael King sat rocking in his chair, clenching a pen in his hands. His knuckles were so white they reminded Dillon of bones.

The minutes ticked by. Dillon wondered if the device would run out of qubits. In theory it had nearly ten thousand, but—

Dr. King leaned forward and stared at the screen.

Dillon turned to look and saw that the number had been neatly factored into two.

Dr. King did not take a piece of paper out of his pocket. Instead, he transferred the results onto a file on his flash drive and brought it back to his laptop. He opened up the program *Mathematica* and used it to multiply the two numbers. *Mathematica* quickly spit out the answer. Dr. King then subtracted the original number and got zero. He laughed softly and picked up the phone and called Monica to come get the laptop.

Dillon was staring at him. "Did you not already know the answer?"

Dr. King shook his head. "It was ... how shall we say this? It was ... a grand challenge problem. I didn't know the answer, but *Mathematica* verifies that your machine solved it correctly. As you know, multiplication is a trapdoor function. Easy to go through one way, very difficult to come back the other way."

A challenge problem? Dillon could not imagine who would present such a challenge.

Monica came back in and retrieved the laptop, picking it up almost reverently.

Rachel leaned across the table, and her eyes were black with anger. "Whose key was that?"

"I don't think you want to know the answer to that question," Dr. King said.

"What are you talking about?" Dillon said.

Rachel stood up and jabbed a finger at Dr. King. "You just cracked somebody's PGP key, didn't you? You did it with my technology, and you better believe I want to know who you're spying on."

Dr. King shook his head. "I'm terribly sorry, but that information is restricted."

Rachel scowled at him. "Dillon, let's go. I'm not going to let him jerk us around like this."

Dr. King sighed. "Dr. Meyers, you're quite a woman—did anyone ever tell you that?"

"Don't sweet-talk me!" Rachel strode to the NMR machine. "Come on, Dillon, let's just—"

"Dr. Meyers." Dr. King took a pair of reading glasses out of his shirt pocket and polished them on his tie. "I realize you despise what we do here, but we have a job—protecting the security of the United States. As it happens, you may be at risk if you step outside this building."

The words hung in the air.

Rachel pursed her lips and leaned against the whiteboard. "I suppose you're going to offer to make all my problems disappear, right? You'll give me a new name, new face, new . . . everything. Stick me in the Witless Protection Program."

"Something like that," Dr. King said. "In addition, we're prepared to offer you and Dr. Richard a very large sum of money. Fair market value in exchange for a device of extreme importance to the United States and its citizens. And in exchange"—he held his glasses up to the light—"for a certain amount of discretion from you."

"Discretion?" Rachel asked.

"Secrecy," King clarified. "We can guarantee you your personal safety and a very comfortable sum of money. But the value of your machine is sharply dependent on the fact that others do not know of its existence. In particular, there is a certain terrorist—whose PGP key you have just helped us crack—whom we do not wish to know that his communications are now an open book to us."

"Which terrorist?" Rachel said. "Hillary Clinton?"

Dr. King laughed curtly. "Dr. Meyers, for the record, I am a registered Democrat. Furthermore, the National Security Agency's activities are directed against foreign powers and agents of foreign powers. The Fourth Amendment strictly prohibits us or any other government agency from spying on U.S. citizens without a search warrant. The President's Intelligence Oversight Board ensures that we comply with all regulations."

"Which terrorist?"

Dr. King shrugged his shoulders. "We have certain documents you could sign that would make it possible for me to answer that question."

Dillon leaned forward. "Documents?"

"Swearing you to secrecy on pain of prosecution for espionage,"

King said. "I'm sure you've signed nondisclosure agreements in your work."

"Of course," Dillon said.

"Think of these as NDAs with a very long prison sentence attached as the penalty for violating them."

"What if we don't sign?" Rachel said.

Dr. King held up both hands in the air. "You have that option. But we are offering you protection outside these walls as part of the deal. And a sizeable sum of—"

"You can't hold us prisoner here," Rachel said. "If we want to leave, we'll leave."

Dillon sighed. "Rachel, if we leave here without protection, whoever was pursuing us will . . . find us. We cannot escape them."

"Precisely," Dr. King said. "Whereas, we can offer you a rather complete protection package."

Rachel slumped into a chair. "What do you think, Dillon? Are you going to sign?"

Dillon did not see any choice. "Yes."

Rachel's eyes gleamed. Two small drops leaked down her cheeks. She stared at Dr. King for a very long time. Finally, she sighed. "All right, I'll sign. Now who was that terrorist?"

Dr. King told her.

Dillon felt his heart lurch. "Are . . . will you be able to catch him now?"

"Only time will tell. But, of course, there are hundreds of others using PGP. We'll soon be reading their mail and preparing a surprise for each one of them. A very well-deserved surprise, perhaps complete with seventy virgins—or seventy-two, opinions differ." Dr. King picked up the phone and dialed. "Monica? If you could bring those documents down now, I believe our guests are ready to sign." He paused. "Yes, have them wait." He set down the phone. "It'll be just a few minutes. I believe you'll be quite pleased with what we're prepared to do for you."

Rachel

Rachel could not believe she had agreed to sign. "Dr. King? Could I talk to Dillon alone for a minute?"

"Of course." Dr. King stood up and led Dr. Weinberg and Dr. Narain out.

Dillon was looking at her with very wide eyes. "Are you feeling all right, Rachel?"

"I'm just freaking out," Rachel said. She walked over and sat down next to Dillon. "Listen, they're going to offer us a ton of money. Probably new identities. New lives. We'll never be able to see our friends and family again. No phone, no e-mail, no letters."

Dillon appeared to be in physical pain. "I will . . . never be able to see Robert's children. To meet his wife."

"That's right. And what I was thinking . . ." Rachel took Dillon's hand in both of hers. "Listen, it'll be a whole lot easier on both of us if we've got someone along from our old life."

Dillon looked up at her sharply and his mouth hung open.

Rachel laughed. "Don't look at me like that. I know how you feel about me."

Dillon's face colored.

"You called me Keryn on the phone yesterday. And when I kissed you, you kissed back. You're an amateur, but I bet you'd learn quick with a little coaching."

"Rachel." Dillon's voice wavered. "You are an attractive woman. But I think we have some serious religious differences."

"Supposing those could be ironed out?" Rachel said. "I've been doing a lot of thinking lately."

"And. . . ?" Dillon looked into her eyes, and Rachel almost believed she could read hope in his expressionless face.

"I don't hate Jesus anymore."

"I am very glad of that." A smile curled Dillon's lips. "That was part of your clue yesterday. What changed your mind?"

"You'll laugh."

"I promise not to laugh."

"It was that . . . that dumb story Gloria told. I don't know if God exists, but if he does, I guess I'd want him to be like Prodigal Papa. You know, loving his kids no matter what they do, whether they've been wallowing in the pig poop or staying home trying to earn their inheritance. That just busted my heart. It's dumb, but . . ."

"It is not dumb," Dillon said. "It is profound."

Rachel took his hand and clutched it to her cheek. Its strength warmed her. "Did you . . . did you feel anything when she told that story?"

Dillon nodded. "I . . . yes, I did." His Adam's apple bobbed. "I have always thought God was very logical, very rational."

"I guess if he's real, he'd have to be."

"And yet the Bible says he is also a God of love, and that has always disturbed me. Love is not rational or logical."

"Dillon, there's nothing wrong with love." Rachel kissed his fingers.

Dillon's face turned red, but he did not pull his hand away. "If God is rational, then he cannot be completely loving. If God is love, then he cannot be complete rational. I have always thought that God's love must be subordinate to his rationality."

Rachel shook her head. "If I believed in God, I'd want it to be the other way around. I'd want a Prodigal Papa God who loved people so much he wouldn't stop to calculate whether they'd blown their inheritance or wasted their lives trying to earn it. A God willing to create a brand-new universe every time somebody makes a choice. That's what I'd want."

"I think . . ." Dillon sighed deeply. "Remember we talked once about the so-called 'fiery marriage' between relativity and quantum mechanics?"

"I remember." Rachel felt a rush of adrenaline. "You think, maybe . . . God is some sort of 'fiery marriage' between logic and love?"

"I think he would have to be." Dillon looked down at the floor, but not before Rachel read self-loathing in his eyes. "I . . . I do not know the first thing about love. I am a liar and a fraud. A . . . prevaricator." He closed his eyes. Deep pain washed across his face.

Rachel leaned forward and kissed his forehead. "I'd be willing to teach you about love, if you'll teach me about God."

A tap at the door.

Rachel could not imagine a worse time for an interruption. She stalked to the door.

Michael King stood there with a bland smile on his face. "I've got those papers for you to sign."

Rachel wanted to punch his infuriating little lights out. "I told you we wanted some privacy."

"You said nothing of the sort. You said you wished to talk for a minute. It has been several minutes."

Rachel put her hands on her hips and glared at him, wondering if he'd been listening in the whole time. She wouldn't put it past him.

Dillon came up beside her. "I believe we are both ready to sign."

Dr. King nodded. "I hope you'll find that we have several attractive options for you." He held up a thick sheaf of paper. "It will take some minutes to explain the details."

In fact it took over an hour. Dr. King explained in great detail the requirements for secrecy and the penalties for violating them. Rachel nodded vaguely through them all. Basically, she couldn't tell a soul anything—couldn't ever hint that there was a bio-computer or that large integers could be factored. Failure to comply . . . blah, blah, blah . . . would result in prison sentences approximately as long as the age of the universe . . . yada, yada. That was the stick.

The carrot was rather nicer than Rachel had guessed. She was being paid a flat fee of $53.2 million. She had no idea who came up with that number or how it was calculated. Dr. King gave her a very long explanation about the commercial value of "the product" and something called a "mortality factor" that accounted for the fact that her odds of living to commercialize the product on her own were about the same as getting struck by lightning on the way home from winning the lottery.

Dillon was getting a fee of $14.7 million for the software. Apparently, they thought he hadn't worked as hard. Whatever.

In exchange for that, the United States Government and its agents promised to take all reasonable actions to keep them both alive . . . yakity-yak. Rachel had a sick feeling in her stomach. What did *reasonable* mean? But she didn't see any better options. Walking loose from here with an out-of-date driver's license and five dollars in cash wasn't very appealing.

Dillon signed.

Rachel signed and then slapped the pen down on the table, hoping she wouldn't regret this. She leaned over and kissed Dillon on the ear. "Guess we're rich, Little Brother."

Michael King gathered all the papers together and gave them both a polished smile. "Now then, that's taken care of. I believe I have a pleasant little surprise for you. Some visitors."

Rachel narrowed her eyes. "Who?"

King opened the door. "Some parties interested in your achievement. Experts in the field. Please come with me."

Rachel felt a rush of fury in her veins. It was bad enough to sell her soul. Now she was going to have her brains picked clean by the vultures.

Dillon patted Rachel's hand. "Rachel, relax. He said it would be a pleasant surprise."

They followed Dr. King down the hall and around a corner. He stopped at a door and smiled at them both. "A private little suite where I hope you'll be more comfortable."

Rachel doubted that very much. She wanted to turn and run.

King knocked at the door.

The knob rattled and the door swung inward.

Grant and Julia stood there.

Rachel screamed.

CHAPTER
THIRTY - SIX

Grant

G rant hadn't known what to expect, but a scream was low on his list. "Rachel, what's wrong?" He stepped forward.

Rachel slapped him. "You . . . you creep!"

Grant staggered back, clutching his face. "Ouch, Rachel, what's all this about?"

Michael King stepped in. "Oh dear, this won't do, Dr. Meyers. You should be celebrating your newfound wealth together—old friends who've come through a tight spot and are still in one piece."

"Rachel, won't you come in and talk?" Julia said. "We've had quite an upsetting couple of days."

Rachel was staring at them both, looking bewildered.

Dr. King took Rachel's arm and led the way into the room. "Rachel, please be assured that Grant and Julia have done you no harm. Come along, Dillon. I hope you'll be able to contain your enthusiasm a bit better than the good Dr. Meyers."

Grant took Julia's hand and limped back into the suite. He heaved himself into an overstuffed chair. Julia sat protectively on the arm of the chair and draped herself above him. Rachel and Dillon sat in chairs across from Grant, giving him the kind of look usually reserved for dead rats and live congressmen.

"Very good, then!" Dr. King said. "It seems we may have a slight failure to communicate among you friends. Let me invite you all to discuss things as adults." He pointed to the bar. "And may I suggest a round of refreshments? You are all, as of today, quite wealthy." King bowed himself out and shut the door.

"What happened at the airport yesterday?" Dillon said.

Grant shook his head. "I went to my gate and got on my plane. It was America West to Phoenix. Just before takeoff, a couple of men with FBI badges came on the plane and down the aisle with my picture. When they found me, they asked me to come off the plane."

Rachel's mouth fell open in the shape of a tiny O. Dillon looked expressionless, but his eyes bored into Grant.

Grant's heart began racing at the memory. "Guys, I thought I was dogmeat. I knew that FBI impersonators had killed Keryn. I was sure they were going to kill me too, but what could I do? I didn't have any weapons. Nothing. So I went." Grant felt hot all of a sudden. He leaned back and started shaking.

Julia bent down and fanned him. "They escorted him off the plane and took his cell phone. We think they used it to call me. You know, they have some amazing software these days that they can program to sound like anybody's voice. Over a phone, you can't tell the difference from the real thing anymore. Anyway, that's the only way I can think that they left that ridiculous message on my voice mail about going to the Caymans. I didn't know what to do. I've never been to the Caymans, and it just didn't smell right. Then Dillon called me from Denver and I knew something was awfully wrong."

Dillon's face relaxed. "So that was the real you I talked to?"

"That was her," Grant said. "About fifteen minutes after you called her, who showed up at her hotel but a couple of nice men with FBI badges."

"They tracked the phone," Rachel said.

"Apparently." Grant felt very stupid. "I'm sorry, guys. I spent a lot of money in Mexico to get those fake licenses for you. The Visa cards are real. The cell phones—I thought they were secure, or what passes for secure in this crazy world."

"So you both got arrested?" Rachel asked. "Were they real FBI?"

"We don't think so," Julia said. "They brought Grant to join me and kept us locked up in our hotel room for a few hours. Then one of them got a call on his cell phone. They bolted out of there like they were on fire. We were scared to death—didn't know whether to stay or run. Not thirty seconds later, men from the Hostage Rescue Team came charging in with guns. They were the real thing, and after they debriefed us, they kept us under guard overnight and then put us on a plane out here, for our own safety. Dr. King met us and told us you two had come in too."

Rachel had a strange look on her face. "Sorry, but something isn't computing here." She leaned back in her chair and put her feet up on the seat. "How much did you get for signing the NDA, Uncle Grant?"

"A bit over eleven million," Grant said. "Plus, they promised to put heat on the board of CypherQuanta. I'm gonna get my company back and an exclusive contract to make encryption devices for Uncle Sam. They guarantee purchases of a couple of thousand machines right off the bat. In this economy, that gives us a lot of stability. And I can sell to any other customers I can drum up."

Rachel's face had gone a light shade of green. "With certain restrictions, right?"

"Well . . . yes." Grant shrugged. Life was full of compromises. "Anything I sell to a private or foreign entity will have a backdoor in it that lets the Feds take a peek. And I can't say a word to anyone about Rachel's bio-computer. Which means we ain't gonna scare the world into buying billions of our machines, but hey, we're alive. And the world gets privacy from everyone except . . . Big Brother." He gave Rachel an apologetic shrug. "Sorry. It was that or get eaten by the big bad wolf."

Rachel looked like she was going to have a stroke. Grant didn't see what her gripe was. She was getting more money than he was, by a long shot. "Guys, the only explanation I can see is that Clifton sold us down the river. He's been acting real suspicious ever since this thing started. He's been getting phone calls he won't explain. Somehow he must have gotten the combination to the bio-lab. I bet he was the one who stole Rachel's bio-computer. After the lay-offs, he disappeared, and so did that hard drive. We're down to one suspect and Clifton's it, the little weasel."

Julia leaned over and put her hand on Grant's shoulder. "I never did like the way he looked at me."

Dillon looked sick. Rachel had her face buried in her hands as if she were trying to erase the whole world. Grant didn't think he blamed her. Thanks to Clifton, they could all have been killed.

Rachel came and knelt beside Grant. "I'm sorry for slapping you. I . . . we thought you betrayed us."

"Don't mention it," Grant said. "We've all kind of had double vision lately. After a while, you don't know who to trust." He sighed deeply. "I guess it won't take long for the Feds to track Clif down. I hope they throw him in the slammer for life."

A knock at the door.

Nobody moved.

It opened and Michael King stepped in, smiling at them all benignly. "Oh, very good. It appears that peace has broken out again. Excellent." He turned back to the hallway. "Clifton, come along. Don't be shy."

Grant thought he was going to have a heart attack.

Clifton Potter shambled into the room, looking guilty as sin. "Hi, guys," he said in a very small voice.

King stepped to the door, beaming. "Very well, then. I'll just leave you all to smooth over any minor misunderstandings."

C l i f t o n

Clifton took a chair and looked around the circle. All four of them looked pretty chafed. Which was only natural, considering what a wally he'd been. "I'm sorry, guys," he said.

Grant was glowering at him. "I take it you're responsible for all this mess?"

Clifton couldn't look at him. "I . . . guess so. I didn't mean to. It just kind of . . . happened."

"You just kind of accidentally kidnapped Keryn?" Rachel said.

Clifton didn't know what she was talking about. "Whoa, dudes and dudettes. I don't know what you think I did, but kidnapping isn't on the menu."

Julia glowered at him. "Oh. Well, suppose you tell us what you did, then."

Clifton took a deep breath. "I didn't ask for that headhunter to call me. He just called, out of the blue."

"Ted Hunter the headhunter?" Dillon said.

"Dillon Dude, you score!" Clifton said. "He said that was his name, anyway. Had a really spiff interview lined up at Qualcomm and asked was I interested." Clifton didn't want to look at Grant. "Ordinarily, I wouldn't be, ya know. Only wallies go around job-hopping. But the last couple weeks haven't exactly been ordinary, know what I mean?"

Clifton saw from their faces that they knew. "Anyway, so I said maybe. I didn't say yes and I didn't say no. I kind of stalled them. I figured if Dillon Man and Rachelette hit the big pony, then there was no way I'd be interested in the Q. But if they struck out, well, I might as well keep my options open."

Dillon looked like he was getting it now. "So you broke into the bio-lab that Friday night?"

"Bingo!" Clifton jabbed a finger at him. "Dillon Man gets another point. I didn't really break in. That first day we all went over there, I snarfed the keypad combination by just watching Grant push the buttons. Same thing with Rachel's password and the safe combination a couple days later when Rachel was showing me everything. You guys really need to work on beefing up your paranoia. Anyway, Friday night, after Dillon and the Rache Woman went home, I just went over to have a look. Rachel had sworn it was ready to test. All I wanted was to know whether that software was gonna come up winners or losers."

"Did you leak that bio-computer or did you steal it?" Rachel asked.

Clifton felt like an idiot. "It leaked. It was an accident, and I didn't find out till the next day. I loaded it into the NMR machine and compiled the software and fixed a couple glitches in Dillon's code. They were just minor things. I got the code to build and run, but it wouldn't calibrate. I walked through it in debug mode and finally realized I was just wallying around so I decided to bail and come back the next day. But I was afraid you guys would guess I'd been in there and change the lock, so I figured I had to add in my own keypad combination. Then it took me forever to find the manual for the security system. Rachel hid it in the filing cabinet."

"I *cleaned* my desk," Rachel said. "I didn't hide anything."

"Took me two hours to find it," Clifton said. "Then when I left, I forgot to put the bio-computer back in the safe."

"And you had put it in upside down to begin with and probably loosened the top enough so it leaked on the floor," Rachel said.

"A point to Goldilocks!" Clifton said. "I biffed things up bad. I'm sorry, dudes."

Grant cleared his throat. "What else did you do?"

Clifton looked up, mystified. "What else? Wasn't that enough? That got Rachel and Dillon setting fire to each other's shorts, and I just sat there and couldn't say a thing. We lost time and it was my fault."

"And you stole the hard drive?" Grant said.

Clifton's heart thumped in his chest. "Stole it? No way! I rescued it."

"Meaning what?" Dillon said.

"Meaning, after I took the crew over to Karl Strauss, I got to thinking that our prize software was sitting unattended in the bio-lab. Oh yeah, by that time I knew Rachel had a spare copy of the bio-computer. Sorry, guys, but I spied on you. I left a recording gizmo in the lab. So I knew we had to secure that hard drive, even if it was just slightly illegal. I drove over there and grabbed the hard drive and stuck it in my safe deposit box. I did that for you, Grant. I figured you paid for that software, and I was gonna keep it safe for you."

Grant's eyes narrowed. "It would have helped if you'd told me."

"Couldn't get hold of you," Clifton said.

"I was a little out of commission that night," Grant said.

"He was stone drunk." Julia bent over and kissed his bald head. "The wisest thing he could have done under the circumstances."

"Gotcha," Clifton said. "When I got home and told Cindy what happened with the layoffs, she said we ought to go down to Baja and drown our sorrows in some surfing. So we drove down that night and camped out for a few days and caught some waves."

"Who's this Cindy?" Rachel said.

"My lady."

"His girlfriend," Grant said. "Why didn't she come out here?"

Clifton shrugged. "She wasn't invited. We got back to La Jolla last night and found some gentlemen eager to invite me out for some, quote—discussions of mutual interest—unquote. Sounded bogus, but they turned out to not be interested in my opinion of the matter. Meaning, they gave me no choice. So I flew out this morning with one of them babysitting me. Biff dude. Couldn't crack a smile to save his mother."

"So basically, you can't account for about five days." Grant looked as if somebody had stolen his Lexus.

Clifton didn't understand what the problem was. "Hey, I'm just saying—"

"Uncle Grant, it's okay," Rachel said. "I believe him."

"Well, I don't." Grant scowled at Clifton. "There's a hole a mile wide in his story."

"Clif, how much did you get for signing the NDA?" Rachel said.

"Almost as much as Grant," Clifton said. "Just over seven million. Pretty sweet, plus I keep all my stock in CypherQuanta and we're back in business selling widgets to Uncle. Life could be worse."

Grant shook his head. "There's a whole lot that isn't explained yet. There's a carjacking, a kidnapping, a murder, my arrest, and a whole bunch of harassment that somebody's got to take the blame for. If it isn't Clifton, then I'd like to know who it is."

The phone rang.

Rachel picked it up and listened for several seconds, then slammed it down. "That was Michael King. He says he'd like to come by and answer Grant's questions."

Clifton felt violated. "You mean that King dude's been listening in on all this?"

"Surprise, surprise," Rachel muttered.

A knock at the door.

Clifton leaned back in his chair. Grant and Julia didn't move.

Another knock, more insistent.

"Come on, Dillon." Rachel grabbed his hand and tugged him toward the door. "Let's go scratch out Michael King's eyes."

Clifton watched them walk together to the door, holding hands.

It hadn't occurred to him until now that maybe they were an item. *Spiff.*

Before they reached the door, it swung open.

Keryn Wills stood there in a light blue silk dress.

CHAPTER
THIRTY-SEVEN

Dillon

Dillon had been hit in the head once by a baseball bat in grade school. He should have been standing behind the backstop, but he wasn't paying attention to the game, and when Lizzy Robles swung and missed and the bat flew out of her hands, he didn't see it.

But he felt it.

The school nurse gave him an ice pack on his head and shone a light in his eyes and called his mother and she came and took him home. Dillon spent the rest of the day in a haze. His head ached and there was a deep pain in his chest and he got dizzy when he tried to stand.

Seeing Keryn alive again made Dillon feel like that.

He heard Rachel scream.

Saw Keryn step toward him, her eyes shining.

Felt his legs turn to jelly.

There was a great roaring sound in his ears. He could not tell which direction was up.

Keryn threw her arms around him. The smell of her perfume

pierced his heart. She pressed her soft and warm lips to his and kissed him.

Dillon felt like somebody had put a blowtorch to his brain.

From somewhere very far away, Rachel was saying, "Oh my gosh! Oh my gosh!" over and over again.

Behind it all, Michael King was chuckling softly. "I take it we're witnessing the reunion of *friends?*"

Keryn broke off the kiss, and then her cheeks turned bright red. "Oh! Dillon, I'm so sorry. I didn't mean . . ."

Dillon kissed her again.

It was more than excellent.

Keryn

Keryn held Dillon for a very long time, crushing him to herself, bawling her eyes out. She had lost him once. She was never going to lose him again.

Finally, she heard Grant's gravelly voice. "Let me look at her, Dillon."

Dillon's strong arms released their grip.

Rachel clutched Keryn's arm. "Thank God you're alive, Keryn."

"Sweetheart, we thought you were dead," Julia said.

"She looks pretty alive to me," Clifton said. "Somebody explain to me what happened to her."

"I . . ." Keryn suddenly felt very weak. "I think I'd better sit down."

They led her into the suite and everybody sat down. Keryn sat next to Dillon and took his right hand in both of hers. Rachel sat on his left and leaned close to him. For once, Keryn didn't mind. The way Dillon had kissed her told her that any competition from Rachel was over. Way over.

Michael King had discreetly disappeared.

Rachel leaned right up against Dillon. "Keryn, we were so scared! We heard you scream over the phone and then a gunshot and then . . . nothing."

Keryn felt the same rush of terror she'd felt when it happened. "When they opened the trunk, I screamed and one of them shoved a sock in my mouth. Another one fired his gun into the dirt. Then they took out this laptop and played a recording that sounded an awful lot like Clifton saying to shoot me again. They fired into the ground again, and then . . . they put some chemical over my nose and I passed out."

Dillon squeezed her hand. "So Clifton was not there?"

"Of course I wasn't there." Clifton sounded insulted.

Keryn shivered. "There were three men, all in suits."

"Were they FBI?" Rachel asked.

"I . . . don't think so," Keryn said. "When I came to, I was in a hotel room with a doctor and nurse and some military-looking guys. Apparently, somebody had rescued me while I was unconscious. I haven't gotten a straight story from anybody yet on what happened. Early this morning, a federal marshal came and escorted me to the airport and flew out here with me. He was very nice, but he couldn't tell me anything I didn't know. He said we were coming here for my safety."

"Thank the Lord they found you," Dillon said.

She smiled at him shyly. "Dillon, they explained all about what the bio-computer will do for them. They offered me a little over four million to sign some secrecy papers. I'll . . . I'll be able to quit my job and write full-time."

"Hold on, everyone," Rachel said. "Something really smells with this story."

Everybody looked at her. Keryn didn't see what could be wrong with four million dollars.

Rachel took Dillon's hand and held it in hers. "They told me and Dillon we'd have to go into hiding. That we'd have to get plastic surgery and live in Wyoming or somewhere and never talk to our family again."

Keryn gasped. "Never? They . . . nobody told me that. I thought we could just . . . go free."

"Nobody told me that either," Grant said. "I'm going to be running CypherQuanta. Right, Clif?"

Clifton nodded. "If those wallies are jerking us around—"

The door swung open without a knock and Michael King ambled in. "Ah, very good, it seems that all is now righteousness and peace among our merry band."

CHAPTER
THIRTY - EIGHT

Rachel

Rachel had never hated anyone as she hated Michael King. "You . . . you lying piece of filth!"

Dr. King raised his eyebrows. "My dear Rachel, flattery will get you nowhere."

She picked up her can of Coke and threw it at him.

He made no move to dodge. The can hit him in the chest. Coke splashed onto his suit. He flicked off little droplets with his fingers. "Really, perhaps you might want to invest in some anger management classes. I'm told you can well afford the cost."

"You've been spying on us all, haven't you?" Rachel shouted.

"Spying?" A wounded look spread across Dr. King's face. "Dr. Meyers, whatever gave you that idea?"

Rachel wanted to spit on him. "How about if I tell you a little story, shall I?"

King nodded calmly. "Please do. I'm sure we all enjoy a good story, even if it is mere fiction." He threw a benevolent smile toward Keryn. "Not meaning to cast aspersions, of course."

"Once upon a time, there was a certain Big Brother," Rachel said. "And he learned through his web of contacts that Little

Brother was developing technology he might be interested in. So he made sure that Little Brother got into deep financial water. He pulled strings to get a key customer to pull out of a signed contract."

Grant's face had gone pale.

Rachel sat down on the coffee table. "Naturally, Little Brother took desperate measures to bring the technology to completion. Big Brother didn't have a search warrant, so he sent a headhunter to pulse Little Brother." Rachel turned to look at Clifton. "He made an offer nobody in their right mind could refuse. And Little Brother refused it. Big Brother now had reasonable cause to tap Little Brother's phones. Then he watched to see what Little Brother would do."

Dr. King wasn't saying anything. He stood leaning against the wall with a benevolent smile on his face.

Rachel scowled at him. "Quicker than anybody would have imagined, Little Brother got his new technology working. Big Brother pulled more strings, and all of a sudden, Little Brother had a financial collapse. Big Brother sent out his hired guns to steal Little Brother's technology, but he didn't try very hard, because stealing it would be illegal and would raise a stink. So he scared the wits out of Little Brother. He let Little Brother run around making midnight runs, getting phony ID and new cell phones, and all the while Big Brother was watching every move. He was tapping Little Brother's calls, using the GPS in his phone to keep tabs on him, watching him with spy cameras in robotic planes. When the time was right, Big Brother decided to scare Little Brother straight. So he kidnapped Little Brother and faked his murder."

Keryn sat with her mouth open, staring at Rachel. A thin sheen of sweat covered her forehead.

Rachel stood up and jabbed her finger at Dr. King. "Big Brother knew that if things got too hot, Little Brother would break down and offer the technology to Big Brother. But there was a problem. Little Brother had a little sister named Goldilocks who didn't want to sell, and nobody could make her sell. So Goldilocks had to be chased across the country. Big Brother could have caught Goldilocks anytime he wanted, but he didn't. He chased and chased her, just hard enough to scare her to death, until finally she went to Big Brother of her own free will and sold it to him."

Rachel glared at Dr. King. "How does that sound?"

King gave her an innocent smile. "An outlandish story, Dr. Meyers. Completely outlandish."

"It explains all the facts," Rachel said.

"It gives that appearance." Dr. King shrugged. "But it is missing one essential element."

Rachel put her hands on her hips. "Namely, what?"

"Motive," Dr. King said. "If this mythical Big Brother were so powerful, he could steal whatever he wanted with much less trouble. There is no conceivable motive for Big Brother to undertake this"—he flicked his fingers in the air—"preposterous scheme."

"Yes, there is." Dillon stood up.

Rachel stared at him, astonished.

Dillon's face was a mask of fury.

Dillon

Dillon rolled up the nondisclosure agreement he had signed a few hours earlier. He wanted to punch Michael King in the face, but he did not think that would help matters. He stepped up to King and handed him the documents. "I have changed my mind. I do not want to sign these."

King gave him a half smile. "Regrettably, that option is no longer open to you. You have already signed them. I have an official copy in my office."

"Suppose I want my signature back?" Dillon said. "Suppose I am experiencing buyer's remorse?"

"First, let me point out that you are a seller, not a buyer," King said. "Second, there is no cooling-off period in sales of this nature."

"If I walk outside this building and hold a press conference—"

"Then you will be prosecuted to the fullest extent of the law," King said. "The documents you signed prohibit you from making any public disclosure of the nature of the sale."

Dillon felt rage surging through his veins. "That is all? You will not have me kidnapped or killed?"

Dr. King shook his head. "Unfortunately, operations of that nature are prohibited now. I do sometimes wish for the good old days, but . . . no. You would not be killed."

Dillon had never felt so betrayed. Everything Rachel had said was true. They had been manipulated by the governing authorities. Big Brother had . . . prevaricated. Not merely to buy their machine but also their silence in perpetuity. That was unacceptable. Highly unacceptable.

"Please have a seat, Dr. Richard," King said. "There is no reason to—"

Dillon turned on his heel and strode toward the door.

"Excuse me, but where do you think you're going?" Dr. King said.

Dillon yanked open the door. "I am going to tell the truth."

A slow smile spread across King's face.

Dillon could not understand the social context of this smile. Dr. King should be terrified. His entire scam had been designed to force them all into this pact of silence. But the pact was wrong. It was evil. Rachel's deepest fears had proved true. Big Brother would be able to spy on whomever it wished, and nobody would know. Dillon could not accept this. He would have to tell the truth. To do otherwise was to prevaricate.

"That wouldn't be wise, I'm afraid," Dr. King said.

Dillon stared at him. If they sent him to prison, then he would go to prison.

Dr. King turned and pointed toward Rachel and Keryn. "It would be a pity if you spread a malicious tale about your own government and found yourself isolated from such friends as these for the next fifty years."

Dillon's heart felt like it was trapped in a vise.

"Dillon, it's not worth it." Keryn hurried past Dr. King and clutched Dillon's arm. "Please. Don't throw your life away on this. We don't have any proof."

Dillon wavered. Was it possible he was mistaken? It was true that he had no proof that Dr. King had done any of the things Rachel had accused him of. All the facts fit Rachel's story, but . . . those same facts had also seemed to convict both Grant and Clifton.

Rachel staggered toward Dillon. "I . . . I think Keryn's right. We don't have any proof. They've set things up so we'll never have any proof. Let's just go."

"Go where?" Dillon said. "We may be rich on paper, but I do not have any cash."

Rachel turned to Dr. King. "Can you . . . find us a hotel for the night?"

"Of course, of course," Dr. King said. "I meant to tell you when I came in. We've already made arrangements at a place I'm sure will be suitable for you all. I've taken the liberty of sending for a limousine."

"A limousine?" Rachel said. "Isn't that a little . . . excessive?"

"Naturally, the cost will be deducted from your newly gotten wealth," Dr. King said. "But I'm sure you'll agree that it is worth the price. A visit to the Grand Hyatt is best experienced with a bit of flair."

CHAPTER
THIRTY-NINE

Dillon

Dillon found it hard to go to sleep that night. The day had brought many surprises. He had woken up this morning not knowing if the bio-computer would work, not knowing why Keryn was murdered, not knowing who had pursued him and Rachel across the country.

Now he knew the answers to all these questions.

The bio-computer worked perfectly. Keryn was not dead but alive. Rachel and he were no longer pursued.

The entire episode was a grand illusion, designed to drive them all willingly into the arms of the governing authorities. Michael King would deny this, hiding behind his bland smile, but there could be no other explanation.

The proof was very simple. Dr. King had given them no new identity, no special protection. Why? Because he himself had architected the whole vile charade. They were perfectly safe because he was no longer a danger to them. That was the only way he could have assured them of their safety now.

Dillon had yet more proof. Dr. King had even known the very destination Rachel had given the taxi driver when they fled the

BWI airport—this hotel, the Grand Hyatt in Washington, D.C. Coincidence? Maybe. But Dillon was certain that, somehow, Michael King had spied on them even in the taxi.

Dillon felt sick at heart. The governing authorities were supposed to protect the citizens, not prevaricate to them. This was evil, and he had signed a sworn statement to keep it secret. If he violated the confidentiality of his agreement, terrorists would go free, while he himself would be deprived of his freedom and his friends.

All his world was now bent, and how could he unbend it?

The next morning, Dillon woke up early. A terrible confusion clouded his mind. He showered and dressed and went down to the lobby. A large part of the floor of the lobby was cut out so that he could see down to a large shallow pool in the lower level. A grand piano sat on a small island in the pool. The atrium was twelve stories tall, lit by skylights in the roof. Light filled the whole interior. Darkness filled Dillon's soul.

Dillon looked up at the rows of windows of the rooms, all the way up. Behind each window, a hidden room, secrets. People were like that too. They hid secrets that you could never know, however long you studied them from the outside. Clifton had deceived them all after the break-in, saying nothing when he could have ended the controversy at once. Keryn had a secret past that nobody would ever have guessed. Rachel, Grant, Julia—each of them was different on the outside than the inside.

The governing authorities were supposed to be different, but they were not. In order to do good, they had done great evil.

Dillon found that he could not breathe, could not think. He got a map at the desk and went outside the hotel and walked down 10th Street toward the Mall. He passed Ford's Theatre, where President Lincoln was shot. He passed the FBI Building and the Justice Department, both dedicated to a justice Dillon would never have faith in again.

When he reached Constitution Avenue, he turned right and walked toward the Washington Monument. He desperately wanted to see the city from above. To change his perspective. He found his way to a little booth on 15th Street that sold tickets. None were on sale. The tickets were free, but they had all been given out for the day. Dillon checked his watch. Already past 9:00. The booth opened at 8:00.

He wandered aimlessly back down the Mall in the direction of the far-off Capitol. On his right he saw the National Air and Space Museum. Dillon went inside and passed through the security line. He walked underneath the original airplane flown by the Wright brothers. Saw the Spirit of St. Louis, flown by Lindbergh across the Atlantic. Peered inside the window of a couple of the earliest capsules ridden by astronauts into space.

None of it gave him any joy. Machines were wonderful things, the gift of the Lord to make life easier and more interesting. But people were more wonderful. People were more important than things or ideas. Souls were more precious than gold. If he had learned anything in this whole sorry episode, it was that.

He now had more money than he had ever imagined. Yet he felt impoverished. He did not have love in his heart. He did not know the first thing about love. He had thought, for a moment, that he was in love with Keryn. Then he had thought he was in love with Rachel. But something was very wrong, and that thing was himself. He was a double-minded man.

He, Dillon Richard, was bent. How could this have happened? All his life he had pursued the straight way. Even so, he was bent. Only a bent man could be in love with two different women. Only a bent man would have double vision. He was no better than Michael King, who had deceived them all. In fact, he was worse, because he had deceived himself.

Dillon sat in a chair and tried to think how he had gone wrong. He could not blame this on his Asperger's syndrome. That would be a prevarication. An easy way to evade responsibility. He was what he was because of his decisions. Every decision he had ever made had been a turning point in the great maze of the multiverse. He was the sum of a vast welter of decisions. If he was wrong now, it was because he had made wrong decisions. He could undo the wrong in his life by unmaking his wrong decisions.

But which ones?

Dillon's cell phone rang. He took it out and saw that Julia was calling. He flipped open the phone. "Good morning, Julia."

"Dillon, honey, where are you? Grant and I knocked on your door before we came down to brunch, but you didn't answer."

"I am not hungry."

"That's okay, honey. I just wanted to make sure you hadn't been kidnapped or something. Where are you?"

"In the National Air and Space Museum."

Julia laughed. "Why am I not surprised? Listen, why don't you come join us?"

Dillon did not want to deal with a complicated situation right now. "Are you with Rachel and Keryn?"

"No. Rachel's probably still sleeping. Keryn was here earlier, but she's gone up to her room. You need to come back to the hotel, Dillon. We have some things to talk about."

Dillon sighed. If only he had some time to himself, he could straighten out his bent universe.

"Dillon, are you coming? Grant really needs to see you."

Dillon stood up. "I can be there in about fifteen minutes."

"That'll be wonderful, dear. Ta-ta!" Julia hung up.

Dillon put his phone away and began walking. His own problems would have to wait. Grant needed him. If he owed anyone allegiance, it was Grant, who had been like a . . . like a father to him.

Dillon swallowed a great lump in his throat and began walking.

Keryn

Keryn had brunch with Grant and Julia and Clifton in the Grand Café on the lower level of the hotel. She didn't know where Rachel was, and she didn't care. But Dillon was another matter. She really, really wanted to talk to him.

Grant and Clifton were already making plans for the new and vastly better financed CypherQuanta. There were board members to get rid of. Facilities to rent. Production schedules to set up. Keryn was not much interested in all this. She intended to quit her job and write full-time. Julia said little during the meal, but she kept catching Keryn's eye from across the table and winking at her.

After they finished, Clifton went back to his room to get some paper and pens for further brainstorming. Grant sat in a chair near the fountain. Julia caught Keryn's elbow. "That was a lovely dress you were wearing yesterday. I'd love to get some photos of you wearing it. Something to remember this trip by."

Keryn shrugged and went up to her room and changed. When she came down, Julia had her camera ready. "Just have a seat at the piano, dear."

Keryn took off her shoes and stepped across the four-foot gap onto the island. She edged around and sat down on the piano bench. It was an old-fashioned player piano, with an actual paper tape loaded up.

Julia waved. "Just look over here, dear, and I'll shoot a few frames."

Keryn looked over her right shoulder and smiled dutifully.

Julia's camera flashed.

"Oh, that was marvelous." Julia stepped to her right. "Now just look this way."

Several flashes later, Keryn saw Dillon coming down the escalator. He was dressed very nicely in a thick cotton shirt and wool pants and a red tie. Obviously, the NSA people understood his tastes pretty well, but they'd goofed on the tie.

Julia turned. "Oh, there you are, Dillon. You look wonderful. I think I've finished with Keryn, so perhaps you could just step across there and join her."

Keryn's heart speeded up a notch.

Dillon looked at Grant and Julia, then he looked at Keryn and stepped across the gap onto the island.

"Just . . . there on the piano bench. I'd like to get a few of you two together. Keryn, make a little room for him." Julia winked at her.

Keryn scooted to her left.

Dillon came and sat beside her.

"Now just a few shots. Look this way and smile!" Julia moved a bit farther away from them. The lens on her camera zoomed out. "And . . . here we go." A flash. "Just one more." Another flash.

Julia closed her camera. "Very good! Thank you so much. I'll just be on my way. I'm sure you both have a lot to talk about." She slipped onto the escalator and rode up toward the lobby.

Keryn sat there feeling like an idiot. She smiled at Dillon. "I didn't see you at breakfast."

"I . . . went for a walk." Dillon's voice sounded thick.

"Just a walk?"

"I had some thinking to do."

Keryn had been doing a lot of thinking herself. Self-conscious, she looked down at the piano keys. "I'm feeling really hurt that . . . our own government treated us that way. It's like . . . it's like finding out your parents are a couple of stoners."

A long silence. "Yes, that is exactly how it feels."

Keryn looked up at Dillon's face. His eyes were closed and a tear had fully formed in each eye. It must be ten times worse for him. He had always had so much trust in the government.

"Hold still, don't move." Keryn reached up a finger to his left eye and let his tear flow onto her finger. She did the same with his right eye. Then she leaned up and kissed his cheek gently. "Dillon, you've really changed lately, haven't you?"

He nodded, eyes clamped shut.

"I like that. I liked the old Dillon, but I like the new one more. I like that you're still growing and changing. I realized something when those men kidnapped me. Can I tell you about that?"

Dillon opened his eyes. "Yes."

"I thought I was going to die. I thought they were going to kill me and I'd be going to see Jesus."

Dillon bit his lip. "I was very afraid for you."

"I was afraid too," Keryn said. "Not so much afraid of dying. I was . . . afraid of missing out on knowing you." She took Dillon's hand in hers. "Afraid of not having you as my friend. Of never telling you how much I care about you. I hope you don't think I'm very forward, but . . . it broke my heart when I thought I'd never be able to tell you I love you."

Dillon's face reddened and he looked down at his hands.

Keryn was sure she'd blown it. Too fast, way too fast.

Dillon tightened his grip on Keryn's hand. "When I heard the gunshot on the phone, I . . . thought you were gone to be with the Lord." He sighed deeply. "And I wanted to go there too."

Keryn felt a surge of joy in her heart.

Dillon looked like he was going to faint. "I . . . I talked to

Robert, and he helped me understand something." Dillon's Adam's apple rose and fell several times.

"What was that?" Keryn asked.

"That I . . . that I love you, Keryn."

Keryn felt like she had on the day she came to Jesus, the day her whole life changed. "Really?"

"Yes, really." The look on Dillon's face showed some deep emotion that Keryn could not fathom.

"Dillon, did you ever see the movie *Casablanca?*"

He shook his head.

She raised his hand to her lips and kissed it. "You should see that movie sometime. The last line is one of my favorites."

"How does it go?"

" 'I think this is the beginning of a beautiful friendship.' "

"You kissed me yesterday," Dillon said. "Did you . . . mean that?"

"Yes. Did you?"

Dillon's eyes clouded. "Yes, but . . ."

Keryn just looked at him. "But what?"

"Yoo-hoo!"

Keryn spun around to look across the pool.

Rachel Meyers was standing on the other side, wearing a thin T-shirt and short shorts, waving cheerily. "Hi, guys? Mind if I join you?"

Before Keryn could tell her that, yes, she minded very much, Rachel stepped down into the pool and began wading through the knee-deep water toward them.

Rachel

That morning Rachel had slept late and ordered room service for breakfast, then had lain down again on her bed. She felt worn out. The last couple of days had been just too much. Her cell phone rang.

It was Clifton. She ignored it. After four rings, it went to voice mail. A few seconds later, he called again. Rachel groaned and flipped it open. "What *is* it, Clifton?"

"Hey, Rache, where are you?" Clifton's voice was a thin whisper.

"On my bed, *trying* to get some rest."

"Can you see the lobby from your room?"

"What are you whispering for?"

"Just take a look. A word to the wise." Clifton hung up.

Rachel stood up and went to look out of her window. Her room was on the sixth floor, looking down into the lobby. She could see the registration desk. A bellman wheeled a luggage cart across the floor toward the exit. Rachel's eyes followed him. He crossed over the bridge and waved at a man and a woman on the piano bench.

Rachel blinked twice and squinted them into focus. Keryn and Dillon were sitting there, talking. Bad news. Very bad news.

Rachel whirled and strode toward the door. There was no time to be fancy. Keryn was all duded up in that hussy silk dress. A regular vision of loveliness. Great, just great. But Rachel was not going to lie down and play dead.

Dillon wanted a vision of loveliness. Fine, she'd give him a vision. She'd give him double vision. Rachel kicked off her pants and put on a pair of short shorts. The NSA people knew her tastes.

Rachel ran out the door and down to the elevator. The Grand Hyatt had some of the slowest elevators in the world. Rachel waited impatiently. When the elevator finally showed up, she jumped in and punched the button for the lobby. An eternity later, she came out at the lobby level.

She looked down to the lower level and saw Keryn holding Dillon's hand in both of hers. Very lovey-dovey. Rachel saw that if she took the escalator, they would see her coming. That was not the way to make her entrance. Next to the escalator was a set of stairs that went down to one of the restaurant cafés. Rachel took the steps and went to the café. She asked the waiter for a table for one by the pool. He seated her and handed her a menu.

When he disappeared, Rachel stood up and wedged her way past the barrier to the edge of the pool. She waved her arms at Dillon and Keryn. "Yoo-hoo!"

Dillon and Keryn turned to look at her.

"Hi, guys? Mind if I join you?" Rachel stepped down into the pool and began wading across. The water felt wonderfully cool and refreshing. She heard shouts and laughter from the café behind her, but she ignored them. Keryn was shooting her full of laser beams with her eyes. Dillon was staring at her with that unreadable look on his face. Rachel didn't care. She was going to roll the dice and see how it came up. Maybe she'd win and maybe she'd lose, but for sure Keryn was going to win unless Rachel gave her some competition.

Rachel staggered the last few feet and clambered up onto the platform. "Hey, how are you? I saw you two looking lonely over here and just thought I'd join you and liven things up."

Keryn gave her a look that would have frosted a nuclear reactor. "We were discussing . . . us."

Rachel sat down on Dillon's right side. "Good idea. I'd like to discuss us too. What say, Dillon? Shall we discuss us?"

Keryn spluttered. "I don't think—"

"Yes," Dillon said. "Maybe we should."

Rachel dared to breathe again. She hadn't won, but at least she was in the game. It was time to be reckless, to risk it all on one throw. She leaned up against Dillon and planted a kiss on his cheek. "Look, I'll be honest, Dillon. Might as well put my cards on the table. I'll show you mine and you show me yours. Okay?"

Dillon nodded.

"And I'll show mine," Keryn said.

"Fine." Rachel saw that Keryn had hold of Dillon's left hand, so she grabbed his right. "Look, here's the thing. Dillon, you really light my candles. When I'm around you, I feel just . . . really right. I'm hot for you and I think you're hot for me. Am I right?"

Dillon was getting that Bambi-in-the-headlights look in his eyes.

"I kissed you a couple days ago," Rachel said. "And you kissed me back. Was that honest or were you just being polite?"

"It was . . . honest," Dillon said.

"And yet you're sitting there holding hands with Keryn," Rachel said. "Is that honest?"

Keryn's face went rigid. "Rachel, this is really inappropriate."

"Please stop it, both of you," Dillon said.

"Time to stop dithering around, Dillon," Rachel said. "You can't have it both ways. Not anymore. You've been toying with the hearts of the fair young maidens way too long. Time to choose."

Keryn lifted Dillon's hand to her lips. "Choose me, Dillon. We were made for each other. You know it and I know it."

Rachel snickered. "You were made for each other like 'bore' and 'ing.' Face it, Keryn, you're dull. I say Dillon needs an opposite. He's a south pole; I'm a north. Together we make beautiful magnetism."

Keryn's face turned white. "Dillon, there's something in the Bible about being unequally yoked."

"We've discussed that already," Rachel said. "We've got differences. We'll work something out. I was raised in a church. It was an awful, horrible, legalistic one, but maybe I've finally figured out that Jesus isn't the church. Little Brother can come home again, and so can Big Brother. Dillon already promised to help me out with that."

Keryn clutched Dillon's hand to her chest. "Dillon, you're going to have to choose."

Rachel reached up and ran her fingers through his hair. "That's right, Dillon. Time to choose. You've been on the fence way too long."

Dillon's face showed a storm of conflict. He seemed to be trying to say something, but no words came out.

"Perhaps I can be of assistance," said a voice behind Rachel.

CHAPTER
FORTY

Dillon

Dillon turned to look. At the edge of the pool stood Dr. Michael King. He wore a three-piece suit, and he was smiling like a professor who knew all the answers.

Which was good because Dillon did not have any answers. He did not know how he could have allowed this to happen. He was truly in love with Keryn. He was truly in love with Rachel. He was a double-minded man, and however he turned, he would do wrong to one of them. That was a terrible thing to do to a woman. He had not meant to, had not even seen this coming. But now the moment had come and he must choose.

He could not simply try one for a while and then decide. If he rejected that one, the other would no longer be interested. Dillon did not know much about women, but he was certain that no woman would accept being a second choice.

"Your problem is that you want two excellent things and you can have only one," Dr. King said. "In earlier times, this would have been settled by marrying them both." He shook his head sadly. "Alas, that option is no longer permitted to men of good will. How unfortunate. The net effect is that you, Dillon, must choose one of these extraordinary women."

Dillon felt Rachel and Keryn squeeze each of his hands.

"On the one hand," Dr. King pointed to Keryn, "we have the talented and very well-endowed Keryn Wills. A charming woman who shares your faith, or a close approximation to it. She is intelligent—a writer of mystery novels, I believe?"

Dillon nodded. "She is a very good writer."

"Of course. I'm told that her novels pack a surprise all the way to the very last word. A remarkable mind. And"—he began pacing—"a soothing influence on you. When the turbulence of life overtakes you, Dillon Richard, as it will even in your newfound wealth, Keryn will be there to have and to hold, to nurture you, to make it right again. You will rarely argue with her, because she is warm and soft and accommodating. She is a well-trimmed cottage, a white-picket fence, clean sheets and a warm bed. With her, you will find a straight and unbent marriage, but never a boring one."

Dillon felt Keryn's hand squeezing his very tight. It felt soft and warm to his touch.

"Yet, on the other hand . . ." Dr. King pointed to Rachel. "We have the brilliant and fiery Rachel Meyers. She is a woman of genius, as we are too well aware. There might have been a Nobel in her future, had she chosen some more prosaic field of endeavor. She is a dynamic woman, one who will always engage your mind and, if I am one to judge a woman, also your animal passions."

Dillon felt his ears growing hot.

"Ah, nothing to be ashamed of, Dillon Richard!" Dr. King shook his head. "The Bible you are so fond of never minces words nor denies the goodness, indeed the excellence, of love." He paused a moment to straighten his tie. "Rachel will be a most stimulating and exciting companion for you should you choose to accept her. Your fine mind will never lack for interesting discussions on any topic you should care to name, whether it be the nature of God, or predestination, or"—he winked at Dillon—"the ever-intriguing multiverse. You will often argue with Rachel. And worse! You will even fight—nasty, tumultuous, emotional fights. From which you will quickly recover and find, remarkably, that your love has grown deeper and more complex. Rachel is a disorganized house, a wild garden, a roaring fire, and a bearskin rug. With her, you will have a fiery marriage, but never an impossible one."

Rachel's hand gripped Dillon's with heat he had never imagined.

Dr. King gave a sad shrug. "Alas, you must choose one or the other. There is no middle ground. You could refuse them both, but"—Dr. King looked at Keryn and then at Rachel with admiration—"who would be so foolish? Both would make an excellent choice. I know you, Dillon Richard, possibly better than you know yourself. I foresee great joy and great pain with either woman. Joy in having the one. Pain in having lost the other. The joy will outshine the pain in either case. But only if you choose. If you refuse both, or if you dither, then all is as it was before you met them, and that was a dark and cold life."

Dillon shivered. He had not know he was in darkness until he saw the light of Keryn's smile. Nor had he known he was cold until he felt the heat of Rachel's lips.

"Very well, then, the hour has come." Dr. King locked his hands behind his back and smiled serenely at Dillon. "Knowing that you cannot fail to choose well, how, then, do you choose? Will it be the warm and soothing Keryn Wills? Or will it be the fiery and exciting Rachel Meyers?"

Dillon could not imagine how he could possibly choose. Dr. King had said it all perfectly. Dillon saw that he must choose. He wanted so desperately to choose Keryn. He wanted so desperately to choose Rachel.

Dr. King shook his head. "Bad form, Dillon. Very bad form. Indecision may yet spoil your choice. Let me propose a solution that is eminently fair. A means of choosing that both women must admit is completely without bias."

Dillon's throat felt very dry. "What solution?"

Dr. King turned toward the chairs and gestured to Grant, who was still seated near the fountain. "Mr. O'Connell, could I trouble you for the use of one of those demonstration devices you use for your excellent sales presentations?"

Grant stood up and reached into his pocket. He pulled out a quantum coin-flipper.

Dr. King strode over to him and took it. "A marvelous device, this. With odds that are mathematically perfect, it throws the dice

Einstein insisted God 'could never throw. Press this button and the universe will choose for you. Call it God if that hypothesis is your preference. Or call it blind, stupid fate. Call it what you will, but press the button and your choice will be made. Should it land heads, why then, take the divine Ms. Wills for your true love. Should it land tails, without delay take the extreme Dr. Meyers to your heart. And if the multiverse represents the true nature of reality"—King gave them all a broad smile—"then this quantum event will create two universes. In each universe, you will take one of the two. Quite literally, you will have the best of both worlds."

Dr. King stepped onto the island and set the coin-flipper before Dillon. "Are you ladies agreeable? Is this not a solution made in heaven, or the best approximation to it?"

"No," Keryn said.

"Not on your life," Rachel said.

Dillon did not know what to say.

Julia came running down the escalator. For a moment, Dillon was afraid she would make things worse by suggesting her own preposterous idea. But she did not. Instead, she took Grant's hand and pulled him over to the edge of the pool.

Clifton followed them. "Dude, you have like the ultimate spiff deal here. You can't go wrong."

"Clifton, shut up," Julia said. "Grant, maybe you could give Dillon a little fatherly advice."

Grant did not look like he wanted to give any fatherly advice.

In that moment, something clicked into place for Dillon, and he understood what he truly wanted to do.

He stood up and grabbed the quantum coin-flipper.

He threw it in the pool.

Dr. King's eyes bulged. "Dillon, I hardly think that is—"

"Please go away, Dr. King," Dillon said. "From now on, we will make our own decisions, in our own time, without interference from you. Is that clear?"

Dr. King's mouth fell open, and he stared at Dillon for a moment. Then he stepped off the island and walked past Grant and Julia and Clifton. His shiny leather shoes *click-clack*ed all the way across the tiled floor to the escalator. Dillon watched him until he disappeared.

"Dillon, you the man! That was awesome!" Clifton said. "But, dude, you still have to make a choice."

"No, I do not have to make a choice," Dillon said. "Not this minute. That would be foolish. We have all just survived a crisis that has changed our lives. Rachel is rethinking her fundamental notions about God. Keryn has survived a kidnapping and pretended murder. I have just learned that the governing authorities have abused my trust. Each of us needs time to regain our equilibrium."

Julia had a funny expression on her face that Dillon could not parse. "Girls, I think Dillon's right. I mean, let's face it, he hardly knows either one of you, and you barely know him. Maybe you all need to give each other a little space. What do you think?"

Rachel squeezed Dillon's right hand. "Good idea."

"Sounds smart to me," Keryn grabbed his left hand.

"And furthermore, there is one other person I must get to know before I can make any such decision," Dillon said.

Clifton's eyes were bulging. "Someone *else*? Dude, who?"

Dillon looked down at his hands and slowly pulled them away from the two women. "Myself."

PART FIVE

Double Vision

"When you come to a fork in the road,

take it."

YOGI BERRA

CHAPTER
FORTY-ONE

R a c h e l

On the last weekend in July, Rachel sat in her aunt's car, wondering why she had agreed to come. "It looks like a *church*."

"It *is* a church on Sundays. We rent it from the Baptists. Today it's a synagogue." Aunt Esther hopped out of the car. "Davey, tuck in your shirt. Rachel, come on, we'll be late."

Rachel slowly got out and stared up at the building. A church. She had known that Aunt Esther's congregation, Beth Simcha, met in a church. She just hadn't expected it to look like . . . a *church*.

Davey tucked in most of his shirt and clipped a blue yarmulke with white lettering onto his helmet of curly black hair. He ambled off to join a circle of teenage boys in untucked shirts and baggy pants.

Rachel wished she had asked Dillon to come with her. He was such a . . . rock. Somebody she could lean on. She did not want to go inside a church alone, even if it was functioning as a synagogue. It had been a full month since all the craziness in Washington, D.C. After coming back to San Diego, she had spent a lot of time talking with Aunt Esther. Reading some books Dillon recommended. Thinking.

She had finally decided she was never going to get anywhere by just talking and reading and thinking. So here she was. Already it looked like a bad idea.

"*Shabbat shalom!*" said a voice behind her.

Rachel turned to look. A huge bear of a man was coming toward Aunt Esther. He had a thick black beard streaked with gray and wore a satin yarmulke and an enormous smile. Blue and white ritual fringes hung from beneath his suit jacket. Rachel gawked at him.

"*Shabbat shalom*, Rabbi Shaul. This is my niece Rachel." Aunt Esther beckoned to her. "Rachel, come meet the rabbi."

Rachel suddenly felt like an idiot. She was wearing the same tie-dyed shirt she'd worn the day she met Dillon, and she realized that she must look very . . . frivolous.

The rabbi came around the front of the car. "I'm Shaul," he said. "Welcome to Beth Simcha." He appeared to be about Daddy's age, and he had very warm eyes that seemed to look right into Rachel's.

Rachel shook hands with him. His enormous paw swallowed her entire hand. "G-glad to meet you," she said.

"They'll be starting the music soon," Rabbi Shaul said. "Are you a dancer like your cousin Rivka?"

Rachel didn't know what to say to that. She was a very good dancer, but she didn't think her kind of dancing would set very well in a synagogue. "Maybe."

"A firm *maybe*." Rabbi Shaul smiled at her. "We can work with a *maybe*. I have a few *maybes* in my own heart."

"Rachel, come along!" Aunt Esther said.

Rachel went. Inside, she was given a bulletin and hugged by a woman who looked like she was about eight hundred years old. She told Rachel she had been praying for her all week. Rachel didn't know how to respond to that.

A bass guitar began thrumming inside the sanctuary. "Rachel, they're starting!" Aunt Esther tugged at her arm.

Rachel followed her through a pair of double doors and stopped short, gaping.

On the stage was a full band. Drums. A bass. An electric guitar. A saxophone. A couple of singers. Behind a synthesizer stood an enormous young man with piercing black eyes that marked him clearly as Rabbi Shaul's son.

There wasn't a single cross in sight. Behind the band stood an ark. An honest-to-God ark holding a Torah scroll. In front of the stage, a circle of women had gathered.

The drummer tapped out a starting four-count and the band began playing and the women began dancing. The music sounded very Jewish, and the dance looked like a traditional sort of circle dance.

Aunt Rachel led Rachel midway down the left aisle to a seat. Up front there was a computer projection system to display the words of the song. It was a Hebrew song, and Rachel did not know Hebrew. She closed her eyes and let the music wash over her.

It was typical Jewish music, happy and sad, both at the same time. Like the qubit, which could be zero and one, both at the same time. Like these people, Christians and Jews, both at the same time.

Rachel wished she could understand the words. The music seemed to be seeping inside her skin. It was Jewish through and through, and yet . . .

And yet she was sure they did not play music like this in most synagogues. Rachel felt the music caressing her soul. When the song finally ended, Rachel opened her eyes. The dancers returned to their seats. Was that *it*? Disappointment cut through her.

The band switched to a faster rhythm, very Yemenite, very spicy. Rachel's foot began tapping. Some of the dancers went back to the front. Rachel closed her eyes. Again, the words were Hebrew, the melody haunting. An ineffable sadness welled up in her heart. This was her music, her people, her rhythm. Whether or not she believed in God or Jesus or the Bible, this was her universe. Hers.

When the song ended, Rachel felt more alive than she had in a long time. Some of the dancers returned to their seats, smiling. Others stayed in front. The keyboard player began a new song, this one slower, an Eastern-European melody. This time the words on the screen were in English. They looked like they came from the Bible, more or less.

> The Lord is my Rock,
> The Lord is my Rock,
> The Lord is my Rock,
> In Him will I trust.
> The Lord is my Strength,

The Lord is my Strength,
The Lord is my Strength,
In Him will I trust.

Rachel felt all the breath go out of her body. She *needed* a rock in her life. Needed a fixed point. Like Dillon.

But Dillon was not enough. No guy could be enough. Because, basically, everybody was in the same boat. Everybody was part of the multiverse, making decisions, drifting this way and that, splitting and resplitting in a billion different directions. Everybody was fragmented, partly yes and partly no. Everybody was maybe.

Everybody except God. That was the theory, anyway. God was supposed to be the Ultimate Ground of Being, the Ancient of Days, the One.

Could she buy into that?

Rachel sank down onto her pew and closed her eyes. She honestly didn't know.

Maybe yes.

Maybe no.

Maybe maybe.

Dillon

"You're sure you want to do this?" Robert looked very concerned. "I can do it myself, if you're not—"

"I am sure." Dillon hopped into the passenger seat of Robert's rented minivan. "Anyway, I am looking forward to seeing your brother."

Robert jumped into the driver's side. "Hey, thanks for buying his airline ticket. That was really . . . generous."

"Trust me, it was nothing."

Robert started the engine. "So . . . are you looking for a new job yet?"

"No."

They drove in silence until they reached the freeway. Robert merged in with traffic, heading north toward John Wayne Airport. "You really can't tell me anything about what happened back east last month?"

"I am very sorry."

Robert turned on the radio. "How's Keryn doing? I'd love to have her come to the wedding this weekend, if she can make it."

"I have not talked to her lately. She has a book due two weeks from today, and she is working very hard."

Dillon wanted very much to talk to Keryn. And Rachel also. He had not seen either of them since they'd arrived home a month ago, though he'd talked to both of them on the phone once or twice per week. He was glad he had taken time to sort out his life, and he felt very sure they were also glad. He did not think a relationship was something that would be harmed by a little distance and a little time.

He had quit his job at CypherQuanta. It felt strange to not go to work every day, but he had spent a very pleasant month doing nothing and getting to know himself better. And this week he had kept busy helping Robert. The wedding was only three days away, and there were very many things to do.

Robert said nothing more until they reached the airport. Dillon's pulse was racing. Fear clogged his throat. He should not have come. Robert could have come alone. Now it was too late to back out.

Robert parked in the lot nearest the terminal, and they got out. Dillon wiped his sweating hands on his blue jeans. The cloth felt very coarse. He did not like blue jeans, but he thought they would help. He was also wearing a short-sleeved knit shirt and no tie. And running shoes. Robert had helped him buy the clothes.

"We're a little late," Robert said. "Are you *sure* you want to do this?"

Dillon started walking toward Terminal A. "We should hurry."

When they reached the terminal, the automatic doors *whoosh*ed open. There was a large baggage claim area directly in front of them. Dillon checked the Arrivals screen and saw that the flight from Chicago had gotten in a few minutes late.

"The escalator is that way." Robert began walking toward it.

Dillon followed him.

"There's Patrick!" Robert pointed toward a tall man near the top of the escalator.

Dillon spotted him an instant later. Patrick had a very wide smile, and he was wearing a Cubs cap and holding tightly to a large

G.I. Joe action figure. The toy was more than thirty years old. Dillon could remember playing with it when they were six years old. Patrick still took it everywhere with him. That embarrassed his parents very much, but Patrick did not know that.

Behind Patrick on the escalator was an older couple in their mid-sixties. It had been a very long time since Dillon had seen them, and he almost did not recognize them. The woman had a hand on Patrick's shoulder. The man was leaning down, speaking into the woman's ear.

The escalator was very crowded. Dillon and Robert stood near the rest rooms, waiting. Patrick staggered when he reached the bottom of the escalator.

"Patrick!" Robert shouted and ran forward.

"Bobby!" Patrick found his footing and raced toward Robert. They collided violently. The G.I. Joe flew out of Patrick's hands and skittered across the floor toward Dillon.

Dillon picked it up and walked toward them.

The man and woman caught up to Patrick. The man shook hands with Robert. The woman's eyes fell on Dillon. She gave a little shriek and tugged at the man's arm, pointing.

Dillon kept walking.

The man looked at Dillon. Astonishment filled his eyes.

Dillon reached the group. His hands suddenly felt very weak. The G.I. Joe fell on the floor.

"Dillon!" Patrick shouted.

The woman screamed.

Dillon threw his arms around the man.

The man's body spasmed.

"I . . . I love you, Dad," Dillon said.

His father let out a sound like a sob. "My boy's come home! My boy's come home at last!"

Dillon wept.

Keryn

Keryn woke up to the sound of the phone ringing. She did not want to face the phone. Yesterday, she had slammed out forty-five pages, more than eleven thousand words, to finish her novel by her deadline. She had not even spell-checked it. At 3:00 A.M. she had e-mailed the thing in to her editor and collapsed into bed. It was probably horrible, but it didn't matter. She had made her deadline.

The answering machine in her office picked up and played her recording. After the beep, Sunflower's voice broke in. "Sweetheart, it's me. You haven't called in ages and you're not answering your phone and I'm just *frantic*. I know you're listening. Either that or you're dead. If you don't pick up that phone right now, I'm going to call the cops to come find your body."

Keryn smiled. Sunflower was such a sweetie. She meant well. Really. But she wasn't going to set the terms for their relationship anymore. If that meant the cops came busting in on Keryn, well, that's just the way it would be. She'd call when she was rested. The last six weeks had been a horrible rush, but she had finished on time without the humiliation of asking for an extension.

"All right, then, I'm really calling the cops right . . . now. Really." Sunflower's voice sounded deflated. "Bye, honey."

The machine clicked off.

Keryn rolled over and tried to go back to sleep. The next thing she knew, the phone rang again. This time it was her editor.

"Keryn, this is Janey. I read through it just now, and I *love* it! Wow! Excellent, really excellent. There are just a *couple* of little problems I want to discuss with you. Call me when you get a—"

Keryn grabbed her bedside phone. "Hi, Janey, sorry! I was up so late last night, it was early when I went to bed. Do you really like it?"

"It's . . . *wow*. Very different from your usual style, though. This isn't the story line you put in the proposal."

"No, but . . . sometimes things change."

"Keryn, this is *way* different. Kind of farfetched too. Not your usual reality fiction. Don't get me wrong, I *like* it. But listen, it's stepping quite a bit outside your brand. Would you mind very much if we published it under a pseudonym?"

Keryn hadn't thought about that. "I guess I'm okay with that."

"A *male* pseudonym? Marketing thinks it would fly a lot better that way. Women writers don't usually do a science kind of back-drop."

"Whatever makes it fly." Right now Keryn was too tired to care.

"One other thing," Janey said. "The ending's a little ambiguous. We like to see a bit more . . . resolution."

Keryn closed her eyes and reminded herself to be firm. "The ending *has* to be ambiguous. The book is *about* ambiguity. I'm not sure I can do better than that."

"Try. Okay?"

Keryn pursed her lips. "Listen, I'm really tired right now. I'll *think* about it, but I think it works the way it is, and I'm going to leave it like that unless some serious inspiration falls out of the sky."

"Great, I knew you'd see things our way. Okay, I know you need your beauty sleep, so I'll let you go. Talk to you later. I am *really* excited about this. It could be your breakout book."

"Bye, Janey." Keryn hung up and went out to the kitchen to get a drink of water.

The phone rang again as she was heading back to her bedroom. That had to be Janey with one last tidbit. Keryn went into her office and scooped it up on the third ring. Then she saw the caller ID and her insides twisted into a knot. "Oh . . . hello, Dr. King."

"Keryn, I'll get right to the point. You are not going to publish that novel. Do I make myself clear?"

Keryn sat down in her chair and pressed the Record button on her fancy new phone. "This is Keryn Wills, and I'm speaking with Dr. Michael King of the National Security Agency. Dr. King, I don't speak with anyone unless they consent to be recorded. Do you consent to be recorded?"

A very long silence. "Keryn, it is a felony if you publicly identify me or my employer."

Keryn rocked back and forth a couple times to calm her heart. "Fine, I realize that. But you listen up, all right? Dillon did a little checking, and we know for a fact that, one, your name is not Michael King and, two, you do not really work for the NSA."

A quiet laugh. "Ah, very good, very good. I'm glad we've got that little prevarication out in the open."

"I'm assuming you work for one of those secret government agencies that officially don't exist?"

"Keryn, you know I can't answer that question. If it's any comfort, Dr. Weinberg and Dr. Narain are really with the NSA, and—"

"We know that. Do you consent to be recorded?"

"Yes, since I apparently don't exist, fine," Dr. King said. "But getting back to my main point, you are not going to publish that novel."

"I know the rules," Keryn said. "I didn't give any description of anything inside the NSA. From what I wrote, you'd never know I'd even been inside the building."

"Yes, you managed that rather well," King said. "But that's not the problem. You've violated your NDA."

Keryn pulled up the last page of her manuscript. "Excuse me, but did you bother to read the author's note at the end of the book?"

A short silence. "Hold on, I'm looking now."

"I'll save you the trouble," Keryn said. "It reads, 'This is a work of fiction and is not meant to represent actual events or characters.' Which means that I assert that none of it really happened. How does that violate my NDA?"

"It is painfully close to the actual events. You've managed to change a few details, but—"

"Tell you what," Keryn said. "I just talked to my editor and she loves it. Well, except for the ending. Now you want me to call her up and say that a man who isn't named Michael King and who doesn't work for the National Security Agency doesn't want her to print that story?"

"Yes, that's exactly what I want you to do."

"And Janey's going to ask why, and I'll just tell her Mr. No-Name from the No-Such-Agency has decided that the story line is, quote—painfully close to the actual events—unquote. Am I understanding you correctly?"

Long silence. "Keryn, we do not want people to believe that conventional encryption techniques might be insecure. There are too many people who don't trust us already, and—"

"I wonder why that might be," Keryn said.

Dr. King cleared his throat. "The bottom line is—"

"No, excuse me, but I'll decide what the bottom line is." Keryn leaned forward. "I am going to print that story just as it stands. Even my editor thinks it's farfetched. And it is. Nobody is going to believe that story has anything remotely to do with reality. Oddly enough, it's too close to the facts to be believable. That's just one of life's little ironies, isn't it?"

"Keryn—"

"If you have a problem with that, take me to court," Keryn said. "You'll look like an idiot and I'll get a ton of free publicity." She slammed down the phone and turned off the recording.

Oh, Lord, I hope I handled that right.

The phone rang again. Keryn saw from the Caller ID that it was Michael again. She sat down in her chair and crossed her arms. Let him try to mess with her.

The machine picked up and her recording played. Michael's voice came on. "Keryn, I apologize if I was a little brusque. Please excuse me. I'll send you some flowers as a small token of my—"

The doorbell rang. Keryn gasped. That had to be the cops. Sunflower had actually called the cops. Keryn raced to her bedroom and threw a bathrobe on over her nightgown. Her hair was a wretched, horrible mess, but there wasn't time.

The doorbell rang again.

Keryn dashed out to the living room and flung open the front door. "I'm okay. I'm—"

A flower delivery man stood there holding a bouquet of roses and a clipboard. "Delivery for Keryn Wills. Can you sign for this?"

Keryn covered her mouth with her hands. Thank God it wasn't the cops, but this was almost as bad. Michael King was playing with her head. He was manipulating her again, the little slimeball. Nobody could be that fast. Nobody.

"Sorry," Keryn said. "I can't accept it."

The delivery man gaped at her. "There's a card with the flowers." He handed it to her.

Keryn slipped the card out of the envelope and studied it suspiciously. It had a gorgeous picture of a bluish-colored galaxy. She flipped the card open. It was handwritten in block letters.

ROSES ARE RED,
THE MULTIVERSE IS BLUE.
IN ONE WORLD I CHOSE RACHEL,
BUT IN THIS ONE . . . I CHOOSE YOU.

Love, Dillon

AUTHOR'S NOTE

This is a work of fiction and is not meant to represent actual events or characters.

The physics ideas in this book are real. Single-qubit quantum encryption devices are commercially viable now and provide unbreakable encryption. Multi-qubit quantum computers also exist but are not as advanced as I have portrayed. Shor's algorithm was published in 1994 by Peter Shor of AT&T. It was demonstrated in 2001 on a seven-qubit quantum computer by Isaac Chuang of IBM. The technology used was essentially the same as the NMR qubit portrayed in this book. If Rachel's bio-computer could be constructed, then it would really be possible to factor large numbers and the standard public-key encryption schemes now in use would be insecure. There is no reason to believe that such a bio-computer exists. There is no way to prove it does not.

The largest integer factored by a general method using conventional computers at the time of this writing is a 174-digit number (RSA-576) reported on December 3, 2003.

The National Security Agency has a budget that is classified, but the agency is believed to be the largest single employer of mathematicians in the world. The NSA is no doubt a very decent group of people, but many cypherpunks distrust them deeply, for no better reason than that the agency is part of the government. You may decide for yourself whether this distrust is warranted.

I wrote this book while working at a startup high-technology company in San Diego. I have been threatening my co-workers for the last three years that they had better treat me nicely or I'd put them in this book. To all my friends at Q3DM, Inc. . . . I was bluffing. Bwaa ha ha!

If you would like to know more about Dillon's friend Bob Kaganovski, you may enjoy the Mars novels I co-authored with John Olson: *Oxygen* and *The Fifth Man*. If you are interested in Rachel's cousin Rivka, then you might like to read my time-travel novels *Transgression*, *Premonition*, and *Retribution*.

For more information about all my books, I invite you to visit my Web site at *www.rsingermanson.com*. You can e-mail me directly at doublevision@rsingermanson.com.